Praise for the Inspector Bordelli novels:

'Vichi's prose transports readers to the deserted, sweltering streets of down-and-out Florence, thanks to a translation by Stephen Sartarelli that conveys the dialogue with a lyricism and tongue-in-cheek wit one instinctively senses were present in the original. Straight from the city that brought us da Vinci and Dante, Vichi is on a par with writers like Henning Mankell and Elizabeth George who have elevated the police procedural to a work of art.' *www.shelf-awareness.com* on *Death in August*

'Vichi's crime novels are enjoyable, mystifying and well worth reading.' *Literary Review*

'Vichi's stellar first in a new mystery series introduces endearingly melancholic Inspector Bordelli ... [and] delivers a plausible solution worthy of a golden age crime novel. Readers will look forward to seeing more of this flawed hero.' *Publishers Weekly* starred review on *Death in August*

'Over the course of his police procedurals, Vichi shows us ever more secret and dark sides to an otherwise sunny and open city. But his happiest creation, in my opinion, remains the character of Inspector Bordelli, a disillusioned anti-hero who is not easy to forget.' Andrea Camilleri

'Fuses social commentary with fine cuisine and serves it up on a charming bed of criminality, and is a creditable advert for Italian crime fiction ... definitely one to savour.' *www.bookgeeks.co.uk* on *Death in August*

'Filled with interesting character sketches and the dirt of Italian street life *Death and the Olive Grove* is a haunting and troubling crime story.' Barry Forshaw. *www.crimetime.co.uk*

Also by Marco Vichi

Death in August
Death and the Olive Grove
Death in Florence

About the author

Marco Vichi was born in Florence in 1957. The author of twelve novels and two collections of short stories, he has also edited crime anthologies, written screenplays, music lyrics and for radio, written for Italian newspapers and magazines, and collaborated on and directed various projects for humanitarian causes.

There are five novels and two short stories featuring Inspector Bordelli. The fourth novel, *Death in Florence* (*Morte a Firenze*), won the Scerbanenco, Rieti, Camaiore and Azzeccagarbugli prizes in Italy. Marco Vichi lives in the Chianti region of Tuscany.

You can find out more at www.marcovichi.it.

About the translator

Stephen Sartarelli is an award-winning translator. He is also the author of three books of poetry. He lives in France.

MARCO VICHI

DEATH in SARDINIA

AN
INSPECTOR BORDELLI
MYSTERY

Originally published in Italian as *Il Nuovo Venuto*
Translated by Stephen Sartarelli

HODDER

First published in Great Britain in 2012 by Hodder & Stoughton
An Hachette UK company

This paperback edition published 2012

5

A CIP catalogue record for this title is
available from the British Library

Paperback ISBN 978 1 444 71227 8

Typeset in Plantin Light by Palimpsest Book Production Limited,
Falkirk, Stirlingshire
Printed and bound by Clays Ltd, St Ives plc

Hodder & Stoughton policy is to use papers that are natural, renewable
and recyclable products and made from wood grown in sustainable
forests. The logging and manufacturing processes are expected to
conform to the environmental regulations of the country of origin.

Hodder & Stoughton Ltd
338 Euston Road
London NW1 3BH

www.hodder.co.uk

To Vittoria

God, too, is starting not to listen

Anonymous, twenty-first century

For your good luck
may the moon shine bright your every night,
may you never know sorrow,
may the sun light up your every day,
such is my good wish,
from now until God wills.

Grazia Deledda

Florence, 12 December 1965

Sergeant Baragli lay in the bed nearest the window, a small tube stuck in his arm. He was looking outside. Behind the hospital buildings he could just glimpse the tree-covered hills of Careggi. The small white clouds dotting the sky looked like a flock of sheep. According to the old wives' tales, it would be raining cats and dogs in a couple of hours.

Baragli's face was covered in sweat and very pale. He'd lost a good ten pounds in just a few days. He hadn't yet noticed that he had a visitor. Bordelli brought a chair close to the bed and unbuttoned his jacket. It was very hot in the room.

'How's it going, Oreste?' he asked.

'Inspector! I didn't see you come in. My wife left just a few minutes ago.'

'I saw her downstairs. When are they going to send you home?' Bordelli asked, pretending not to know that the doctors considered him a lost cause.

'I don't know anything yet,' the sergeant said. He was short of breath and spoke with difficulty. Just over sixty years old, he'd spent his whole life on the police force and had had a rough time of it during the twenty-year reign of Fascism, given his lack of sympathy for the Mussolini regime. He'd retired three years before and fallen sick the following month. He'd had several operations on his stomach, the last only a few days before.

'How's your son?' Bordelli asked.

'He's still in Germany, Inspector. He might come for Christmas.'

There were five beds in the room, all taken. Some of the other patients had visitors. One looked rather young. His face was yellow and gaunt, but he tried to smile. His wife had brought him some newspapers.

'You need anything, Oreste?' Bordelli asked.

'I'd like a book, a good book I could get excited about.'

'I'll bring you one next time.'

'Thanks, Inspector. Everything all right with you?'

'I wouldn't go that far . . .'

'You know what? If I were reborn, I would become a cop all over again,' Baragli said, looking resigned. The inspector smiled. He felt sorry for the old policeman wasting away with illness. Baragli had always been nice to everyone, even those he arrested. The prostitutes were fond of him and called him *nonno*. But there were certain categories of criminals Oreste had never been able to stomach, especially pimps. Whenever he had one within reach he'd slap him around, and nobody had ever bothered to stop him. They were good, healthy slaps, the kind a parent deals out to a child.

'Any murders lately, Inspector?' Baragli asked.

'Nah, nothing new.' The inspector started telling him a few anecdotes about things that had happened at headquarters. He knew Baragli enjoyed hearing talk of his colleagues. Every so often the old sergeant cast a glance out the window. His lips were shrivelled and his sparse hair had turned completely white. He had aged a great deal in the past six months. Trying to sit up in bed, he groaned in pain and brought a hand to his stomach, grimacing.

'What's wrong, Oreste?' asked Bordelli, standing up.

'It's nothing, just the stitches pulling,' said Baragli, falling back on to the pillows.

'Were you looking for something?'

'My wife brought me some playing cards, they're in the drawer there.'

The inspector grabbed the new deck of Modiano cards and they started playing *briscola*[1] while making small talk. The sergeant played with the tube in his arm, moving his hands slowly.

Bordelli lost the game and shuffled the cards before dealing again. Baragli wiped his face with the handkerchief he always kept within reach.

'The minute I get out of here I'm going to go fishing for a year,' he said.

'We'll go together – at least once,' Bordelli lied. They played for a while longer, as Baragli grew weaker and weaker. His hands shook and he had trouble breathing.

'I hope to be home by Christmas at least,' he said as the inspector reshuffled the deck. Bordelli had lost again. He couldn't quite get into the game.

A fine rain began to fall outside. The drops left bright streaks on the dirty windowpanes.

'My wife said Rita Pavone was on the telly yesterday. Did you see her?' the sergeant asked.

'I got home too late.'

'I really like that girl . . . Your turn, Inspector.'

By nine o'clock the visitors had all left. One of the older patients had fallen asleep and was snoring lightly, eyes half open. He was in the bed directly opposite Baragli's, and the skin on his face seemed stretched right over the bone. At last the inspector won a game. He looked at his watch.

'I have to be going,' he said. He put the cards back in the drawer and stood up, resting a hand on one of Baragli's, which was thin and covered with veins.

''Bye, Oreste.'

'Thanks, Inspector. Give everyone my best.'

'I'll be back soon,' said Bordelli, squeezing the man's fingers. When he made to leave, Baragli held him back.

'How's the *Sardegnolo*?'

'If Piras could hear you . . .'[2]

'He must be used to it by now. Can he walk yet?'

'Only on crutches at the moment, but he says he's making progress.'

'Tough as nails, those Sardinians.'

'He'd like to return to work in January, but I don't think he'll manage it before March . . .'

'I like that kid,' said Baragli.

'Me too.'

'Give him my regards.'

'Next time I'll bring you a book,' Bordelli said, half smiling. He headed towards the exit, feeling terribly sad. He turned round in the doorway to wave goodbye, but the sergeant had turned towards the window and didn't see him.

Piras was in Bonarcado, Sardinia, at the home of his father Gavino, a companion-in-arms of Bordelli's during the war of liberation.

Three months earlier, during a routine check on the Via Faentina, Piras's squad had stopped an Alfa Romeo Giulietta with Bologna licence plates, but instead of taking out their papers, the four men in the car had pulled out machine guns and pistols and started firing madly. Turning the car promptly around, they escaped the same way they had come, leaving three policemen and a great deal of blood on the road behind them. Officer Cassano died on the spot, struck in the head by a burst of machine-gun fire; Sbigoli came away with just an arm broken in two places; and Piras was rushed to hospital with his face covered in blood. He seemed to be at death's door, but the blood pouring over his face and chest came from a superficial wound on his forehead. Another bullet had struck him in the right shoulder and come out the other side without causing any serious damage. He'd been more seriously wounded in the legs, however: three bullets had entered his right thigh, shattering the femur, and two had lodged in his left leg, one very close to the knee. All in all, he'd been quite lucky, as the men in the Giulietta had aimed for the head and chest. The first shots had hit Piras in the shoulder, knocking him down, and the only reason the subsequent bursts of fire hadn't reached their target was because it is much more difficult to hit a man lying down than one on his feet.

The Giulietta was later found abandoned at the side of the road only a few miles from the shoot-out, having obviously been stolen. Bordelli had personally led the manhunt, which ended a few days later in the countryside near Bivigliano with two arrests and two dead bodies. The two deaths could probably have been avoided, but the policemen who had flushed out the fugitives didn't feel much like holding their fire.

The four men in the Giulietta were all ex-convicts from Milan, three of whom had escaped just a month earlier from San Vittore prison. They were well armed and had planned to carry out robberies in Emilia Romagna and Tuscany before returning to their base in the Apennine mountains near Sasso Marconi.

The day of the shoot-out Bordelli phoned Piras's girlfriend, Sonia Zarcone, a beautiful blonde from Palermo with whom the young Sardinian had fallen head over heels in love. The girl didn't even cry upon hearing the news, but merely busied herself doing everything she could to make life easier for her boyfriend during those first difficult weeks in hospital.

Piras had undergone several operations at Santa Maria Nuova hospital, and each time it seemed it would be the last. In the end the surgeons decided that there was no more they could do, and they 'set him free', as Piras himself put it. The doctors forced him to take a long holiday to recover, and he'd decided to go to Sardinia to stay with his parents, who before his arrival hadn't known a thing about what had happened to him. Sonia had stayed in Florence to sit two important exams. After a number of domestic battles, a phone was finally installed in the Piras home, and now the two lovers could stay in constant contact. Otherwise young Piras would have had no choice but to use one of the few telephone lines in town, the priest's. And a sacristy really wasn't the right sort of place to say certain things, Piras later related, chuckling. Apparently the beautiful Sonia liked to express herself rather explicitly, all the clichés about Sicilians be damned. Her free and easy manner came from her rather unusual family; her father was half Sicilian and half Spanish and a professor of economics at the University of Palermo, while her mother was from a very old Sicilian family.

But the installation of a telephone in the Piras home had another consequence as well. Bordelli had at last been able to talk directly with Gavino. They'd immediately started reminiscing about friends they'd lost during the war and remembering the most dangerous moments. Speaking with someone who'd lived through the same things made everything more vivid and painful. Gavino cursed the mine that had robbed him of one of his arms, and his rage against the Germans was still as keen as twenty years before. Then they cut short the war talk and started briefly recounting what they had done since the damned war. They promised to get together soon, but with the sea between them and all the work that neither could take a break from, it wasn't going to be easy for either one to keep his promise.

From time to time Piras the younger would phone Bordelli to say hello and also to learn whether he was missing out on any interesting cases. Their last communication dated from a few weeks before.

'I'm feeling better and better, Inspector. I still limp a little, but it's not a problem. I'll be back at work by January.'

'No need to rush things. You'll return when the doctors say.'

'Any murders?'

'Fortunately not . . . How's Sonia?'

'Fine . . . But I'm beginning to think Sicilians are even more stubborn than Sardinians.'

'Don't complain, Piras, you're a lucky man.'

'I know, Inspector, I know . . . How's Baragli doing?'

'Worse and worse.'

'Damn . . .'

'It's a bloody mess.'

'Poor bloke . . . Give him my best.'

'How's Gavino?'

'The guy's going to outlive us all! He's made out of the same stones as the nuraghi.[3] He's always in his field, hoeing and sowing, and now he says he wants to buy himself a rototiller in the spring.'

'Won't that be a problem for someone with only one arm?'

'He tried using a friend's machine and says it's fine.'

'Give him a big hug for me.'

'Thanks, Inspector . . .'

'And give Sonia a kiss for me.'

'Sonia only gets kisses from me.'

'You're starting to sound like a Sicilian.'

'I'll be on that ferry before the first of January, Inspector, you have my word.'

'Ciao, Pietrino, let's talk again soon.'

15 December

They found him on Wednesday with a pair of scissors stuck deep in his neck, at the base of the nape. Office scissors, the kind with pointed tips. When the stretcher-bearers of La Misericordia took away the body, all the building's tenants stood in their respective doorways to watch. Seeing them pass, a woman on the second floor said: 'That'll teach him, the pig!' Then she quickly crossed herself so that she might be forgiven for saying something so wicked.

The murder victim, Totuccio Badalamenti, was a loan shark. He lived only a few blocks away from Bordelli, in Piazza del Carmine, on the top floor of a fine old stone building. He was from southern Italy, like many outsiders in the city at the time. He'd been in town for a little over a year and worked as an estate agent as cover. In the neighbourhood they called him 'the newcomer' and probably would have kept on calling him that for ever had he not been killed. The whole San Frediano quarter knew exactly what he did, even though Badalamenti was careful not to 'do business' with anyone who lived near by. Every so often the inspector used to see him driving down those impoverished streets in his new red Porsche. He wore very fine gold-rimmed glasses and had a square-shaped head and frizzy hair you could scour a frying pan with.

Badalamenti lent out money, even very small sums, but always demanded outrageous rates of interest. Anyone who was late with payments faced the sort of penalties people commit suicide over. He was a violent man. Rumour had it that he beat the prostitutes he brought home with him, even though he usually made amends afterwards by paying them double. He was very rich and was always investing his money profitably in every imaginable sort of traffic. His wealth was legendary. One story had it that he'd bought a whole island down south just so he could swim undisturbed. He would buy houses and land at auction and then resell them, and often they'd belonged to the very people he had ruined. At other times he would rent squalid apartments cheaply, then fix them up at low cost and sublet them out for three times the amount to people in financial straits, petty criminals, prostitutes and the like. He kept copies of all the keys to his flats, and if a tenant went away for more than two weeks, he would manage to rent the place out to some other wretch, who would pay dearly for it. Some even said that he had a circuit of whores working for him in the south, and that he had dealings with the Cosa Nostra. There certainly was no lack of gossip about Badalamenti, some real, some invented, but nailing him wasn't easy. He was very clever at using his work as an estate agent to camouflage his real occupation.

Bordelli dealt in murder, but having that loan shark so close to home really bothered him, like a pebble in his shoe. And so a few months earlier he had started concerning himself personally with the problem. As far back as the previous February he had spoken to Commissioner Inzipone about it, explaining who the man was and how difficult it was to find evidence to warrant arresting him.

'We need someone who will press charges,' Inzipone said, thoughtfully pinching his chin between thumb and forefinger. He didn't seem terribly interested in the matter.

'You know perfectly well that nobody will ever do anything of the sort, because they might well end up dead,' Bordelli replied, annoyed.

'Well then, stop wasting my time and tell me what you have in mind.'

'I want a search warrant.'

'Oh, do you? On what grounds?'

'Whatever you can think up . . . By now even the cobble-stones know who the man is and what he does.'

'I'll have you know that until proven otherwise, it might just all be malicious gossip, Inspector . . . And, anyway, you're supposed to investigate murders, or am I mistaken?'

'All right, but if you won't get me the warrant, I'll handle it my own way,' the inspector said, standing up.

'And what will you do, Inspector? Break into the man's home illegally . . . as you've done on other occasions?'

'I'm a policeman, and I try to do my job to the best of my abilities.'

'A chief inspector who picks locks . . . Is that any way to do things? Can you imagine what would happen if—'

'Just tell me one thing, sir: will you help me get that warrant or won't you?' Bordelli retorted, standing in front of Inzipone's desk. The commissioner sighed deeply, chewing his lips.

'I'll see what I can do,' he said.

'Well, be quick about it. That man must be stopped.'

'And what if your search yields nothing of interest?'

'I'll turn his flat upside down, take it apart piece by piece . . . I'm convinced something will turn up.'

'You're really so sure, are you?'

'Let's say I'm certain it's worth the trouble of trying,' Bordelli concluded, and with a nod, he headed for the door. Inzipone stood up.

'Bordelli, have I ever told you I don't like your methods?'

'I think you have.'

'Well, then let me repeat it. I don't like your methods one bit.'

'I'm truly sorry about that.'

Closing the door behind him, Bordelli heard the commissioner sputtering curses between clenched teeth.

In the days that followed, he learned that the judge had thrown a tantrum. Without a formal denunciation or concrete evidence, the possibility of a search warrant was less than a mirage. Seeing red, Bordelli had decided to go and talk directly with Judge Ginzillo, the man with the smallest head he'd ever seen. He'd had to deal with him a number of times in the past, and it had never been pleasant.

'Dr Ginzillo, please don't always throw spanners in my works, if you can help it,' Bordelli said politely the moment he was allowed into the judge's office.

'Please sit down, Inspector, and excuse me for a moment,' Ginzillo said without looking at him. He was busy reading something and seemed engrossed. Bordelli sat down calmly, repressing his desire to grab him by the ears and lift him off the ground. He even resisted the desire to light a cigarette, but not for Ginzillo's sake. He'd decided to stop smoking and was always trying to put off the next cigarette for as long as possible.

The judge glanced at his watch, took a sip of water, and drummed his fingers on the desk, all the while hypnotised by that bloody, stamp-covered piece of paper.

'All right, let's hear it, Inspector, but make it brief,' he said suddenly, without looking up. Before the inspector could open his mouth, a forty-something secretary dressed like an old maid walked in carrying a number of documents that urgently needed signing. The judge adjusted the glasses on his nose, and with a solemn mien sought the proper pen on his desk, found it, then started skimming the documents, murmuring the words as he read them. When he got to the end of each document, he gave a nod of approval, appended his signature, tightening his lips, then pushed the paper aside and went on to the next.

'Go ahead, Inspector, I'm listening,' he muttered, still reading. Bordelli didn't reply, for fear he would utter an obscenity. When the secretary finally left, Ginzillo removed his spectacles with a weary gesture, cleaned them with a handkerchief, and put them back on. Then he resumed reading, fiddling with a very sharp pencil with a rubber at the end. He was holding it between two fingers and making it bounce off the wooden desktop.

'So, you were saying, Inspector?' he said, still hunched over the sheet of paper.

'I haven't breathed a word.'

'Then please do. What are you waiting for?'

'When I speak to someone I like to be able to look them in the eye, sir. It's a fixation of mine.'

Ginzillo raised his head and, sighing, set the pencil down on the stack of papers. It seemed to cost him a lot of effort.

'Go ahead,' he muttered, looking at Bordelli with what seemed like great forbearance.

'I need that search warrant, Dr Ginzillo.'

'What search warrant?'

'Badalamenti,' the inspector said, staring at him.

'We needn't be so hasty.'

'Hasty? Tell that to the people who've left their bollocks on the loan shark's table.'

'Please don't be so vulgar, this is no place for that kind of talk.'

'Why don't you go some time and have a look for yourself at all the misery the man has caused? It's not catching, you needn't worry.'

'Please, Bordelli . . .'

'I said *misery*, sir, and while it may indeed be an obscenity, it's not a bad word.'

The judge was getting upset. He put the pencil back in the cup and wrinkled his nose as if noticing an unpleasant smell.

'Please sit down, Inspector, I want to have a little talk with you.'

Bordelli was already seated. Indeed, it felt to him as if he'd been sitting there for ever, and now he wanted to leave.

'I don't need to have a little talk with you, sir. What I need is that search warrant . . .'

The judge raised his eyebrows, looking irritated.

'Just bear with me for a moment, Inspector,' he said, sighing, putting his open hands forward as if to defend himself from the muzzle of a drooling, excessively friendly dog. Having caught his breath, he then stressed every syllable as if he were hammering nails.

'If you really want to know, Inspector, Mr Badalamenti has a number of friends in our city government and socialises with some important families . . . Do you get the picture? Or can you think of nothing but your precious warrant? If I did as you ask and you found nothing . . . What would we do then? Can you imagine what the newspapers would say? Or have you already forgotten what happened with the Colombian jeweller?'

His voice came out through his nose with a metallic sound.

'That wasn't my case,' Bordelli said, glancing compassionately at the timorous judge. Ginzillo raised his forefinger and his voice came out in a falsetto.

'That's exactly my point! If you're wrong, it will be the first time for you, Inspector . . . but the second time in six months for the police force. Do you understand what I'm saying? The *second time*! And if you think I'm going to . . .'

'Goodbye, Dr Ginzillo,' Bordelli said unceremoniously, getting up and leaving the room.

As he had given Commissioner Inzipone to understand, the inspector had decided, after his fruitless meeting with Ginzillo, to enter the usurer's flat illegally and search high and low for any evidence that might help to nail him. He was convinced he would find something but, truth be told, he was also hoping for a little luck.

That same night, at about three in the morning, he'd gone to inspect the site, to determine how difficult a job it would be. The small *palazzina* in which Badalamenti lived was quiet and dark. It was February and very cold outside. In the glow of the street lamps he could see a fine rain falling and turning to sleet.

Some years before, the inspector had taken lockpicking lessons from his friend Ennio Bottarini, known to intimates as Botta, a master of the art of burglary, and he was now able to pick some two-thirds of all the locks on the market with a mere piece of wire. His intention was to ask one of his friends from the San Frediano quarter to keep watch while he broke into Badalamenti's flat right after the loan shark went out.

He managed to open the front door to the building in just

a few seconds. Then, after tiptoeing up the stairs to the top floor, he met with disappointment. One look at Badalamenti's door and he knew he was faced with a lock that his teacher classified as 'curseworthy'. Bordelli was incapable of opening that kind. Only Botta could.

The following day the inspector had gone looking for him at home, only to learn that he'd been in jail for several weeks. He'd been arrested near Montecatini, at Pavesi di Serravalle, trying to shift a television set stolen from the office of a service station. Botta was an artist of burglary, and a very good cook, but he was terrible at disposing of stolen goods. The inspector was shocked to learn he'd started doing these small jobs again. The last time he'd seen him, Botta was still coasting on the money he'd made on a successful scam in Greece.

The following Sunday morning Bordelli had gone to see him at the Murate prison. A guard accompanied him down the long corridors, opening and closing gates along the way. Water dripped from the ceilings, and the floor was scattered with dirty little piles of sawdust. The doors of the some of the cells were open, and the inmates walked about the corridors in groups, dragging their feet. Under the general murmur of voices the inspector heard the distant sound of an ocarina.

After the umpteenth barred door, the guard pointed to a man scrubbing the floor at the end of a long, deserted corridor. It was Ennio. The inspector went up to him and tapped him on the shoulder.

'Ciao, Botta, how's it going?'

'Inspector! What are you doing here?' Ennio asked, feeling somewhat embarrassed.

'How much time did they give you?'

'Fourteen months, Inspector. I'm supposed to come out in March of next year, but by now I know how these things go. If I'm good, they'll let me out for Christmas.'

'And the money from Greece?'

'The horses, Inspector. It's the last time, I swear.'

'I certainly hope so, for your sake.'

'Fourteen months for a television set . . . Though I must say it was a Voxon, one of the best.' Botta sighed histrionically.

'Why don't you ever call me when you have a problem, Ennio? You know I'll help you if I can.'

'But you already own a television set, Inspector! A beautiful Majestic . . .'

'That's not what I meant.'

'And I hadn't even stolen it myself! I was just lending a friend a hand . . . You know who gave it to me?'

'I don't want to know. Listen, I'm here to ask you a favour.'

'A nice Greek dinner at your place?'

'That too . . . but there's something else.'

'What is it, Inspector?'

'I want you to pick a lock for me,' Bordelli said, lowering his voice.

'Did you lose the keys?' Botta asked, laughing.

'I want to get inside the flat of someone who should be in here instead of you.'

'And what about all those things I taught you?'

'It's the kind of lock that calls for Botta.'

Ennio puffed up with pride.

'No problem, Inspector, as soon as I get out of here I'll open it for you.'

'Just so it's clear, what we're going to do is illegal. If they catch us, they'll bugger us both.'

'No problem all the same, Inspector. If you're there it's fine with me.'

'Thanks.'

'At any rate I assure you, Inspector, you've got a real knack for it. I mean it.'

'What are you talking about?'

'You'd make a pretty decent burglar yourself.'

'Well, coming from you, that's a compliment.'

'I'm not kidding, Inspector, it's the truth.'

'You're too kind, Ennio,' Bordelli said, and as he shook Botta's hand before leaving, he slipped two thousand-lira notes in his friend's shirt pocket.

'This may come in handy.'

'I owe you one, Inspector,' Ennio said, winking.

'Don't forget to give me a ring as soon as you get out.'

'You'll have to be patient, Inspector, I've still got thirteen months to go. And even if I get out at Christmas, that still leaves ten.'

'We can wait. Break a leg, Ennio.'

'Thanks.'

For some time thereafter the inspector had carried on his personal investigation of Badalamenti, without results. He had discreetly tried to initiate a review of the city's banks, in order to comb through the usurer's accounts, but without a court order it would have been like trying to empty the ocean with a spoon. He had even thought of having Badalamenti's phone tapped, but it was too risky and, most importantly, would have involved other people. He didn't feel like taking anyone else into his unsteady boat. And it was anyone's guess whether it really would have helped. Badalamenti was very shrewd and seemed to feel quite protected by his acquaintances. As Ginzillo had said, the man had an entrée into the homes of rich businessmen and ambitious young politicians. It led one to the disturbing conclusion that everyone present at those dinner parties had something in common. This was one of the more unpleasant faces of the new, changing Italy, Bordelli said to himself, thinking of all those who had died in the hopes of leaving a better world to their children . . .

In short, stopping Badalamenti had proved to be a far more difficult matter than expected. But the inspector was determined to see things through. He would have to wait for Botta and hope for a bit of luck.

The months went by.

The second channel of the RAI, the national television network, inaugurated by Mina[4] three months earlier, expanded its programming, and to some it seemed as if the world had doubled in size. The television news programmes vomited out information from all over the world. From Algeria came troubling reports: after a century of colonialism and a million deaths, the country was in chaos. The French were leaving en masse, including legionnaires and *pieds noirs*, heeding the advice of the FLN, whose slogan was: 'The boat or the coffin'. In June Ben Bella was swept away by Colonel Boumedienne, while, back in France, De Gaulle was preparing for the presidential election against the socialist Mitterrand.

From the US and the UK came new music, new faces, new fashions. Girls' skirts became impossibly short, men's hair grew longer and longer. It was anybody's guess what it all meant. Everywhere one heard the songs of Adriano Celentano, Bobby Solo, Nicola di Bari and Gigliola Cinquetti. Bordelli often found himself humming a tune of Petula Clark's, but could never remember the words.

Italy was advancing at a gallop, even though there weren't enough horses for everybody. The number of Motoms and Vespas on the roads steadily increased, and there were more and more cars, especially Fiat 600s and 1100s. But there was no lack of Lancias and Alfa Romeos, either, and there were even a few Jaguars here and there. The traffic was already worse than the year before; at certain hours of the day one had to queue up at junctions. Billboards were getting bigger and bigger, and the laundry was now done by a machine. Everything seemed to be going right. Money seemed to reproduce like loaves and fishes, the dream of wealth spread like a disease. But one had to be on the right side, or there was trouble. Trains kept coming up from the south, full of men without return tickets heading north to sell their flesh and muscles, dragging their poverty behind them. They kept the whole sideshow moving, but couldn't climb aboard . . .

More than anything else, one felt the young people's yearning to change the world, which to them seemed to have grown old and decrepit. Bordelli thought that it wasn't only, as some believed, a desire to have fun. Nor was it only that they wanted to be rid once and for all of the dark past the old people were always telling them about with reproach and admonishment in their voices. At least from a distance, these kids almost looked as if they were of another race. They didn't give a damn about the war that had ended not long before and which their parents claimed to have won.

For the first time, Bordelli felt all the violence of a real transformation in the air, even though it was hard to say exactly what it consisted of. The forces heating up across the country were diverse and numerous. In a sense, everything was being renewed. New wealth, new poverty. The word 'freedom' was being used in new ways, and the prisons to be destroyed had names never heard before . . .

More and more people were abandoning the countryside without regret. The old peasant houses and villas outside the cities were being sold at cut rates behind closed doors, furnishings and all. More than once during those months, Bordelli had wandered about with the idea of buying a ruin with a bit of land and growing old there, but he continually postponed acting on his desire. Before taking such a step, he had to think it over very carefully.

And so the months went by.

December had arrived. Christmas was approaching with its coloured lights and stacks of fir trees on street corners. All that was missing, as usual, was snow.

Ennio might call at any moment, and Bordelli was ready to do what he'd been planning for months. But fate had decided otherwise. Someone had killed Badalamenti.

The body was discovered that Wednesday, but the murder had occurred a few days earlier. The building's other tenants had been smelling a sickly-sweet odour in the stairwell for some time and, sniffing around one morning, traced it to Badalamenti's flat. Only then did they realise they hadn't seen him for several days, and that his red Porsche hadn't moved from the square for a while. They all agreed they should call the police. The report was passed on to Bordelli, who immediately got down to work.

The firemen were summoned, and they broke down Badalamenti's door with the solemn imprimatur of the law. The stench of death immediately assailed with full force the nostrils of everyone present. Bordelli had smelled that sweetish odour many times, too many, perhaps, and had never got used to it. He went in first, handkerchief pressed firmly against his mouth and nose, and opened all the windows.

Badalamenti's body lay face down on the floor of a small room done up as an office, halfway down the central hallway. His hands were curled, and he had one eye wide open, the other at half-mast. His half-open mouth rested against the tiled floor, and there were two dark spots of dried blood beside it. His eyeballs were already in bad shape. The scissors were stuck deep inside the flesh beneath the neck.

Bordelli immediately sent for the assistant public prosecutor. A police officer took a number of snapshots of the corpse from a variety of angles. The chief of forensics, De Marchi, and his assistants pulled out their tools and started searching the flat for fingerprints, cigarette ash, and anything else that might be of use, taking care not to move anything. De Marchi was just over thirty years old and had the face of a nerdy schoolboy, but was a real bulldog when it came to his work. Bordelli had a great deal of confidence in him. Even though he knew him only on a professional basis, he addressed him in the familiar form, since the forensic expert was young enough to be his son.

The apartment had been visibly and thoroughly ransacked without compunction. It had a number of rooms, all furnished in more or less the same fashion – that is, with a lot of money and little taste. Faux-antique dressers and wardrobes next to green Formica tables, huge mirrors with modern gold-plated frames, ugly but flashy paintings, and imposing beds intended for much larger rooms.

Half an hour later the young assistant prosecutor, Cangiani, arrived. Standing in front of the corpse, he visibly gagged several times, then called Bordelli aside.

'I've already seen what there is to see. Once the forensic team and the pathologist are done, you can go ahead and take the body away,' he said, and then rushed out of the apartment.

Bordelli wanted to inspect the flat in his own good time, and alone, after everyone else had left. Possibly even the next day. He was in no hurry. Phoning the station, he asked for Rinaldi.

'I want you to come here with six or seven men and interrogate everyone in the building, and all the tenants in the buildings on Piazza del Carmine,' he said.

'Very well, Inspector.'

'And try to find out if Badalamenti had a cleaning lady. I want a detailed report of everything.'

'That's a lot of work, sir, but I think we can manage,' said Rinaldi.

Dr Diotivede, the police pathologist, arrived shortly thereafter, black leather bag in hand, wearing his seventy-two years like an ornament. He still had the face of a child not yet fully formed, and not even the bifocal lenses of his spectacles managed to make him look old. As he came in, he greeted everyone with an icy smile.

'Who's the victim?' he asked, looking at Bordelli.

'His name was Badalamenti. A loan shark . . .'

'Ah, I see.'

Diotivede loved his work. Whenever a dead body turned up, he wanted to be informed at once, because he always insisted on seeing the victim at the scene of the crime.

As the others covered their noses with handkerchiefs or ran off to vomit, the doctor knelt down beside the corpse without so much as a grimace, and brought his face, and therefore his nose, close to the wound, which was already ringed with maggots, squinting with the same expression as a collector examining the fine toothing around the edges of an antique stamp. The only thing that flustered him was a murdered child, and he'd had to look at several of them the previous spring, when a madman strangled four little girls . . .

Cold gusts blew in from the open windows, and in the end they decided unanimously to close them all except for the one in the study, where the body lay.

Diotivede spent a whole minute studying the scissors planted in Badalamenti's neck. Then he pulled his little black notebook out of his pocket and started making his first notes. Every so often he would stop, looking thoughtful, and run a hand through his snow-white hair. He bent down again. He touched the dead man's face with a finger, prodded his shoulder, then resumed writing. Nobody dared disturb him. When he had finished he stood back up and put the notebook away, looking satisfied.

'What can you tell me?' Bordelli asked, going up to him.

'He must have died at least five days ago, maybe six. I'll try to be more precise after the post-mortem, but don't bother asking me the exact time of day . . . Too much time has passed.'

'Anything else?'

'I didn't see any signs of a struggle. No bruises or scratches, no torn clothing.'

'Caught by surprise from behind?'

'Most likely. If the adrenalin tests confirm it, I'd say he had no idea, until the very last second, that he was about to be stabbed in the neck.'

'What would you prefer, Doctor? Would you rather know or not know you were about to die?'

'I think being stabbed with scissors like that must be a pretty nasty way to die,' the doctor said with a chilly smile.

Bordelli grimaced, unable to stand the stench any longer. 'Can we take the body away?' he asked as two cowled stretcher-bearers from the Misericordia came in.

'I'm all done,' said Diotivede, raising his hands.

'When are you going to work on him?'

'Are you in such a hurry?'

'Less than usual.'

'I have to finish up an elderly lady, then I'll do this one for you,' said the doctor, looking down at the corpse at his feet. Bordelli gestured to the two men in black frocks.

'You can go ahead,' he said.

The two cowled figures approached and without a word lifted Badalamenti on to a stretcher and carried him away.

The lads from forensics were also done. De Marchi whispered to the inspector that they'd combed the place very carefully and taken a few specimens. But they hadn't found much, he said, shaking his head. At any rate, he would send over the results as soon as possible.

'No fingerprints on the scissors. They were either wiped clean with a handkerchief or the killer was wearing gloves,' he said, throwing up his hands. And he added that everything would be analysed and catalogued using the new techniques and procedures developed in the US and the UK, and that—

'Fine, fine,' Bordelli interrupted him, convinced that nothing would come of these analyses.

'When should I drop by?' he asked Diotivede, calmly walking him to the door.

'Whenever you like.'

'Maybe I'll even give you a hand. I've always been fascinated by the idea of opening up dead bodies and pulling out their guts.'

The pathologist heaved a sigh of irritation at that thousandth idiotic quip about his perfectly normal profession. Bordelli knew such comments irked him, but that was precisely why he enjoyed making them. It was fun to see Diotivede tense up for a second like an offended child.

'I guess you're right, Inspector. It's much more fun to be a policeman. You have the pleasure of tracking a man down, slapping handcuffs on him . . . or maybe even shooting him in the back.'

'Need a lift home?'

'I'm happy to get some exercise.'

'Forget I asked.'

They calmly descended the stairs, side by side, without

another word. Outside the front door was a throng of journalists, who immediately tried to get inside. Bordelli raised a hand and said nobody could go upstairs. Anybody wanting any information had to go to police headquarters and wait. The newsmen protested as usual, but in the end they left. Bordelli shook his head.

'How the hell do they always find out so fast?' he asked.

'Maybe it helps that they're not policemen,' Diotivede quipped, then waved goodbye and went off towards Santo Spirito.

'Thanks,' Bordelli muttered, watching him walk away.

A little boy on a woman's bicycle bigger than he was came out from Borgo San Frediano, standing on the pedals. He'd attached a folded-up postcard to the frame so that it rattled the rear spokes and sounded like a motorbike. Passing by the front door of Badalamenti's building, the child shot a glance at the inspector and started pedalling harder. Bordelli followed him with his eyes and watched him disappear beyond Piazza Piattellina. A thousand years ago he too used to put a postcard in his bicycle's spokes, and hearing the sound now only made him feel old. He ran a hand over his face and pressed his eyeballs with his fingertips. He wasn't that old, really, but he was certainly too tired to start searching the dead man's home right now. He realised he wished he had Piras at his side for the investigation. Sticking a cigarette between his lips, he decided at last to put the whole thing off till tomorrow. It wasn't the kind of murder that made one feel anxious to get things moving, he thought, blowing the smoke towards the sky.

He woke up in the middle of the night after a bad dream and instinctively turned on the light. He looked around the room to reassure himself. Everything was the same as it always was, but the dream left him with a feeling of precariousness that seemed to presage death. It was almost three o'clock. He'd only been asleep for about an hour. His heart was beating wildly. He turned the light off and lay back down. He'd retained no precise image of what he'd just dreamt, and remembered only that he was struggling terribly to free himself from a sort of spider's web in which he'd got caught. He was hoping to fall back asleep immediately. But, try as he might to keep his eyes shut and not move, his tired brain was still busy thinking about unpleasant and dangerous things.

He was imagining his heart imprisoned between the lungs, contracting and expanding, and it looked to him like a repugnant muscle that after years of spasms wanted only to burst or simply stop. His heart had broken many times, always because of women. The muscle had functioned quietly and well during the war, never asking him for anything. The years had gone by, and he'd suddenly found himself, at fifty-five years of age, feeling as if he'd never actually lived.

Deep inside he never really stopped thinking about death. It was always on his mind, every minute of the day, and had become a sort of habit. At moments he found himself imagining his own death in a variety of different ways. There was no good reason for it; that was just the way he thought. Even at the best of times. Now and then he would become fixated on heart failure, especially when he felt tired, as now. The idea of dying suddenly, without having the time to understand what was happening to you, frightened him even more than death itself. He was hoping to be conscious at the exact moment at which he went over to the other side. From time to time he would wonder whether his comrades who'd been blown sky high by German mines had had the time to realise anything.

He'd made it back from the war alive, but there had been many occasions when he could easily have died. He'd been lucky. It was almost though he was protected by a star in the heavens. In 1941, shrapnel from a British torpedo had breached the wall of the submarine he was in. He'd heard it hiss a centimetre away from his temple and lodge itself in the side of the ladder. He'd gone and dug it out. Inside one of the metal curls a greenish strand of seaweed had got stuck. Wrapping the splinter in a handkerchief, he'd put it in his pocket. He must still have it somewhere.

To take his mind off his beating heart he started thinking about the war, and he remembered the time he was trapped with five of his men in a field of maize under the sudden fire of the German artillery.

They spread out and hit the ground. The earth was shaking violently. They had to prop themselves up on their elbows with bellies raised, tongues pressed hard against palates to keep from biting them, hands over the ears to protect their eardrums from the explosions. The clods of dirt thrown into the air by the mortar shells kept raining down on them without cease. Staccioli and Bordelli were lying next to each other. With each blast they pressed their faces into the ground, and between explosions they exchanged glances and cursed the Nazis. Before exploding, the mortar shells whistled through the air. There was a moment of hell, with grenades falling around them one after another, the earth flying up into the air as if catapulted. Bordelli closed his eyes and kept his face pressed to the ground until silence returned. All of a sudden he heard a dull thud, like a boulder hitting the ground. He turned towards Staccioli.

'Did you hear that?' he asked, but Stacciolo couldn't hear anything any more. An unexploded shell had fallen on his neck, and his face was buried in the ground. Bordelli just looked at him for a few seconds, suppressing the absurd desire to talk to him. Then he yanked off his friend's dog tags, not bothering to pull the chain over his head. If the shell had done what it was supposed to do, there wouldn't have been a shred of either of them remaining.

Very few were as lucky as he.

Capo Spiazzi died in the Veneto three weeks before the end of the war because of a moment's inattention. It was a dark night and, lost in thought, he'd lit a cigarette while standing in front of a window. The German sniper aimed a couple of inches above the flame and hit him square in the forehead. Bordelli heard the glass shatter and ran to see what had happened, and found Capo Spiazzi sprawled across the floor, face up and eyes open. The cigarette had remained between his lips, still lit.

Giannino had died, too. Of gangrene. Bordelli had tried to stop the infection with the tools he had available. He poured two big glassfuls of cordial down his throat, tied a tourniquet of string very tightly just under the knee, then put a plank under his leg and amputated his foot with a hatchet. It took two consecutive, decisive chops. As a disinfectant he used some twenty tablets of sulphamide ground to a fine powder. But it was no use. Giannino lived only three more days. As he was dying he kept saying his right foot hurt, the one that had been amputated.

The inspector felt his heart start to grow calmer. He lay down on his back and, looking into the darkness with eyes open, continued to wander randomly through his memories. He remembered Cayman's broad smile. They called him that because of some silly resemblance he supposedly had with the animal. The war had reached Cayman during his third year of studying philosophy at university. He shamed everyone with his vast culture, but one was always sure to be amused in his company. He said Jesus Christ was just a poor fanatic who had read too much Plato, and that was exactly why he liked him. But to believe he was the son of God was a bit much. Despite the sophistication of his arguments, Cayman cursed like a docker, and when he wasn't talking he looked like the coarsest of them all. He had survived five years of mines and bombs only to die at the hands of a drunken Pole after the war had ended. Stabbed twice in the back for an empty wallet. Bordelli saw again the train that had taken Cayman back home: a train full of corpses crossing half of Italy, dropping off more dead at each stop. A dirty train driven by dirty men. But there was also something cheerful about it, because it travelled through a country free at last of Nazis and home-grown Fascists, a destroyed, shattered country that nevertheless hoped for something better than having to deal with pricks like Badalamenti.

16 December

When he opened his eyes that morning, the first thing he thought of was his beating heart. Putting his hand on his chest, he had the impression it was more sluggish than usual. But it was only an impression, he told himself. It was already nine o'clock. Getting up out of bed, he immediately felt dizzy, but for only a second or two. No need to worry, Inspector, you're just a little tired. You really ought to take some time off every now and then. A proper holiday. It's probably been ten years since you last lay down on the sand by the sea, thinking of nothing . . .

He went into the kitchen in his underpants to make some coffee, then drank it slowly, looking out the window. The sky was clean. He felt strange and ached a bit all over, but perhaps he'd only slept badly. He slowly got dressed and went into the bathroom to shave. Grabbing the shaving brush, he moistened it, slapped it across the soap a few times, and before lathering up his face, stood there with his hand in the air . . . He'd often heard such things as: *He lathered up his face, started shaving, when suddenly, pow! He collapsed on the floor.* No, he wouldn't like that. He rinsed the brush and put it back in its cup. No shave today, he thought, looking at himself in the mirror . . . No shave, no heart attack. Not that he really believed it, but that morning he simply preferred not to shave, nothing more.

He went out into the street and pulled his trench coat tightly around him. The sun was shining brightly, but it was cold. He bought a newspaper in Piazza Tasso and started walking towards Badalamenti's building. On the front page blared the headline: THE MOST AMAZING FEAT IN AERONAUTICS HISTORY: RENDEZVOUS

27

IN SPACE. Gemini 6 and Gemini 7 had met up in weightless space, and the astronauts had waved 'hello' through their portholes. Everything had gone quite smoothly, and the Americans had reconfirmed their supremacy in matters of space travel.

Bordelli folded up the newspaper and stuck it under his arm. Before long they would be travelling to the moon, while back on earth, loan sharks still preyed on honest people.

There was only one week left before Christmas, and the shop windows were full of blinking lights and colourful festoons to enchant children of all ages. He absolutely had to remember to get a present for his friend Rosa, a former prostitute. He knew how much it meant to her. Even at her age, Rosa was as innocent as a child, and she loved getting presents. But Bordelli lacked imagination when it came to such things, and he feared that on the evening of the 24th he would still be wandering about the centre of town without any idea of what to get her.

When he got to Badalamenti's building, he opened the front door with a key and climbed the stairs to the top floor, feeling winded. Bloody cigarettes. He removed the seals and pushed the door open. The sickly-sweet smell of death was still strong and seemed to stick to his skin.

He started wandering lazily about the flat. The rooms were rather large and had high ceilings. There were two bedrooms, a sort of sitting room, the study in which the body had been found, a big kitchen and a spacious bathroom with a tub. The killer had had the sangfroid to remain a good while in the apartment and ransack every room, including the bathroom. To judge from the state the flat was in, it had been an angry and summary search. Drawers upended on to the bed, clothes scattered across the floor, papers everywhere. Who knew whether the killer had found what he was looking for? Maybe not. Otherwise, instead of continuing to turn the flat upside down, he would have stopped at some point.

Bordelli postponed his first cigarette of the day until later and phoned police headquarters from the study. The previous

day Rinaldi and company had continued to question the neighbourhood residents until late in the evening. He had faith in
Rinaldi, who was young and efficient.

'Anything of interest?'

'Not much, Inspector. There was only one witness, an elderly
lady called Italia Andreini, who lives in one of the buildings
opposite Badalamenti's . . .'

'What did she say?'

'She said that one night about ten days ago she couldn't
sleep, and so she bundled herself up, opened the window and
started looking outside. It was raining hard. It was about two
o'clock in the morning, and the piazza was empty. After a
while, she noticed someone coming out of Badalamenti's
building. Average height, slender build. From the way he moved,
she thought he was young. But that was all she could say,
because the square was dark and the guy's head was covered
with a hood because of the rain. The lady is certain he didn't
see her, because she had the lights off. The guy walked fast
and went towards Piazza Piattellina. But that's all, Inspector.'

'No cleaning lady?'

'Nobody knows anything.'

'Very well, then, go and get some rest,' said Bordelli,
hanging up.

They were getting nowhere fast. He went back into the
hallway, hung his trench coat on a peg and got down to work.
He started searching the rooms calmly one by one. He rifled
through armoires already ransacked by the killer, pulled them
away from the wall to look behind them, searched under and
on top of every piece of furniture, under the beds, pulled out
the few drawers left in place and emptied these out on the
carpets, climbed on to chairs and tables to search the ceiling
lamps. In the kitchen he even looked inside the coffee can and
the sugar bowl. In the study where the body had been found
there was a brown jacket hanging from the back of the chair.
Searching its pockets, he found a golden key chain with the
keys to the Porsche and put it in his own pocket.

The more he got to know the flat, the more depressing and cold it seemed to him. It was a far cry from the sort of cosy nest most people like to withdraw to. He realised that his own place was a lot nicer . . . with its grit-tile floors, its bathroom with fine, yellowed porcelain, its worm-eaten furniture inherited from some old aunts of his father's whom he'd seen only in photographs.

He stuck a cigarette between his lips and, without lighting it, continued searching the flat. He did it calmly, convinced that sooner or later something would turn up. He had all the time in the world. If he'd searched his own place the same way, he would surely have found countless things he didn't even remember he had.

By late morning there were only two rooms left to scour, and he still hadn't found a thing. On the other hand, he had managed not to smoke, and this gave him a certain satisfaction. If he'd prevailed over the Nazis, he could prevail over that stupid vice.

He decided to search Badalamenti's bedroom first. He went in and turned on the light. Ugly room. A light fixture of glass fruit, small metal lamps painted with green enamel, light brown furnishings reminiscent of a post office. A large rectangular mirror with a light blue frame hung from a wall. But the *pièce de résistance* was the gold-plated wooden bed, with a headboard inlaid with fanciful squiggles. On top of it was a great pile of clothes removed from the drawers. Bordelli rummaged through them. Underpants, vests, socks, all fine brand-name stuff. Beside the window was a small writing table with a black marble top and a rather fancy Leica camera on it. It was clear the killer hadn't committed the murder during a robbery.

The two drawers of the desk had already been rifled through, like everything else. Papers large and small lay scattered across the floor: old bills, money orders to be filled out, empty envelopes, stamps. Nothing of importance.

He cast a 360-degree glance around the room. Hanging on the wall above the headboard of the bed was a print of a

Quattrocento Christ inside a thick frame of black wood. Bordelli lifted it off of its hook to look behind it, and something fell on to the pillow. Setting the picture down, he picked up a small stack of black-and-white photographs held together by a broad rubber band. There was even a small envelope with the negatives. The first photo was of a beautiful girl in a bikini, very young, with long black hair. She was standing, leaning back against a door jamb and smiling innocently. On the whole, a rather provocative picture. She had a very beautiful body, if a little immature. But she wasn't far from her full flowering. Bordelli brought the photos into the light and removed the rubber band. There were twelve in all. The dark young girl was as beautiful as the sun. Three of the shots showed her in a bikini; in a few others she was wearing a very short dress revealing two magnificent legs; and in a couple of others her breasts could be seen behind her folded arms. In the background, a few corners of Badalamenti's flat were recognisable. Written on the back of each snapshot was a name: *Marisa*. He wondered why Badalamenti kept them hidden. Putting the rubber band back around them, he put the photos in his pocket and resumed sifting carefully through everything, with no results. At last he gave up and went into the sitting room, the last to be searched. It was a rather spacious room, with large red terracotta tiles and floral curtains that dragged along the floor. Between the sofa and the black leather armchairs was a low glass table that Badalamenti must not have cleaned very often. The only other piece of furniture was an unsightly modern glass-fronted cabinet full of glasses and bottles. The inspector opened both doors to have a better look. Cognac, whisky, Spanish brandies, all expensive stuff. Below, next to the glasses, was a tin can of the sort used for varnish. He grabbed it and pried off the lid with his house keys. It had grey putty inside. What the hell was a can of grey putty doing with the drinking glasses? He put the can back in its place and glanced at his watch. It was almost one o'clock, and he was starting to feel hungry. He would resume his search calmly after lunch.

He went down into the street with the intention of walking over to the Osteria di Santo Spirito for a panino and a glass of red. Then he changed his mind. He got in his Beetle, drove through the centre of town and parked the car in the inner courtyard of police headquarters. The sky had clouded over, and it felt a little less cold outside. After spending all morning holed up in that ghastly apartment, he felt like walking for a while in the open air.

Crossing Viale Lavagnini, he slipped into the Trattoria da Cesare, where for many years he'd been eating almost daily. As he entered he greeted the owner and waiters with a nod and exchanged a few quips with them. It was almost like being among family.

The inspector never sat at a table. His place was in the kitchen with the Apulian cook, Totò, where he had his very own stool. He considered it a privilege, and probably would have made a stink if anyone else were ever granted permission to enter that paradise of splashing sauces and drums full of offal.

'Have you ever thought of getting married, Totò?'

The cook was enveloped in a cloud of infernal smoke, with six pans on the cooker at once. Bordelli watched in amusement as the material was transformed. A chunk of butter, a bit of meat, and some other insignificant thing turned into a pleasure for the tongue and palate. Totò was a shrimp, but had the touch of a bullfighter. Any animal had to feel honoured to be mistreated by him. He could handle many pots at a time, and he bragged about it like a little boy. He kept the whole kitchen going all by himself.

Finishing up his *spaghetti alla carbonara*, Bordelli thought with pleasure of the cigarette he would smoke once he'd finished his lunch. Totò emerged from his inferno and came up to him.

'I'll serve you in a second, Inspector. Wait till you taste the osso buco.'

'I can't wait.'

'Did you like the pasta?'

'Love at first sight.'

'Don't you think there was a little too much pancetta? Sometimes even I get it wrong.'

'Cut the false modesty, Totò, you're not convincing anyone.'

'Nobody's perfect, Inspector,' the cook said, grinning like a braggart, before returning to the hob to see to the customers' orders. Bordelli refilled his glass.

'Totò, did you hear my question earlier?' he asked.

'What question, Inspector?'

'Never mind,' said Bordelli.

The cook drew near with a frying pan in his hand.

'You like it hot, right?' he asked.

'I can't live without it.'

'Then have a taste and see if you like this osso.'

The meat was practically submerged in rather dense red sauce.

'Your own invention?'

'Almost . . . It's sort of done in the Algerian style.'

'You're becoming as cosmopolitan as my friend Bottarini,' Bordelli said to provoke him. The previous year Botta had replaced Totò in that kitchen for a few days, keeping the restaurant going without much trouble, and when Totò had returned from his trip to the south he'd heard tell that his stand-in knew how to cook *foreign stuff*, not knowing that Botta had learned all those dishes by spending time in the prisons of half the countries in Europe and even a few in North Africa.

'Give me a break with this Botta, Inspector! I've always known how to cook those dishes! It's just that nobody ever asked to me to make them before,' said Totò, lower lip jutting in disgust, waving his greasy hands in front of his face.

'There's certainly nothing wrong with learning new things, Totò,' Bordelli persisted with feigned innocence. Totò shook his head dramatically and sighed.

'Keep that wine close to you, Inspector, this stuff is pure fire,' he said, then turned back towards the cooker with his arms dangling. Never tell a cook he could learn something from anyone, Bordelli thought, studying the osso buco. It looked magnificent but dangerous.

Totò was endlessly filling dishes and bowls and passing them to the waiters through the semicircular hatch that gave on to the dining room. Bordelli put the first bite of meat in his mouth and felt his gums burst into flame. He took a long sip of wine.

'Very good,' he said with tears in his eyes.

'I'm glad you like it,' Totò said slyly.

'What are you doing for Christmas, Totò? Going down to see your folks?' the inspector asked, to change the subject. The cook paused for a moment, then approached, wiping his hands on his apron.

'This year they're coming up here. Cesare has decided to keep the restaurant open over the holidays. And what are you doing?'

'I don't know yet.'

'Why don't you come and spend Christmas with us, Inspector? There's more than fifty of us, and we make enough noise to wake the dead. And you really ought to see some of my lovely cousins . . .' he said suggestively, drawing the shape of a woman's curves in the air with his hands.

'Thanks, Totò, I'll keep it in mind,' said Bordelli, cautiously continuing his journey through the Algerian fire. He didn't really feel like thinking about women at the moment. His last affair, which had ended badly, still weighed heavy on his mind. Milena, a twenty-five-year-old Jewish girl, had left a wound inside him that hadn't yet healed. To chase the thought from his head, he put another piece of that devilish osso buco in his mouth.

Pietrino Piras came home from a difficult walk on crutches. The doctor had told him that the more he moved, the more quickly he would heal, and he couldn't wait to get back to Florence. He didn't like sitting around twiddling his thumbs. And Florence meant being with Sonia. He was dying to see her. At the moment she was in Palermo with her family and would spend the entire holiday with them. They talked over the telephone three or four times a week, and his mother kept trying to find out who this girl was who called so often asking for her Nino. He pretended it was nothing and wouldn't even tell her the girl's name. He was always jealously guarded about his things, and especially about Sonia.

It was lunchtime. In one corner of the kitchen stood a small Christmas tree adorned with the same baubles of coloured glass he'd known since childhood. His mother had decorated it that morning, much later than in years gone by. A fire had been burning in the hearth since the morning. Pietrino sat down at the table with his father, and Mamma arrived with a serving bowl of spaghetti in tomato sauce.

'Zia Bona dropped by,' she said, filling their plates. 'She's going to get the spumante for Christmas dinner.'

'Mamma, this is enough pasta for four . . .'

'Eat, Nino, the doctor said you must eat.'

'It's too much.'

'It's not, you'll see.'

'If you force him he won't eat any meat afterwards,' Gavino said to his wife.

His parents coddled him like a child. They were happy to have him at home, even if it was because of that frightful incident. Piras's mother, Maria, was a small woman but full of energy. She worked like a slave and never let up. She spoke in Sardinian dialect, but had gone to school up to the third grade and knew Italian fairly well. She always wore a headscarf tied under her chin and had dramatic eyes. She took care of the animals. She and Gavino had a few chickens, a lot of rabbits and two pigs.

'Gigi and Pino won't be coming this Christmas, either,' said Maria. They were the two other sons, both older than Pietrino. They were married and had been living in France for many years.

'We've known that since October. Why repeat it?' Gavino said.

'Well, they could have come,' Maria said.

'They'll come next year,' said Gavino, pretending it didn't bother him.

'I understand them, Mamma, it's too expensive.'

'Not even for Christmas . . .' said Maria, staring at her plate. They carried on eating in silence. There was only the sound of fire consuming wood.

Gavino kept himself busy working his small plot of land. He'd lost an arm in combat in '45, while fighting at Bordelli's side. But he worked as if he had three arms instead of one. He dug holes, pruned trees, harvested tomatoes. He was very proud of his plot of land and wanted to do all the work himself for as long as he could. Every morning at dawn a friend would come by in a little Fiat 600 van, buy a bit of everything, and sell it at the market in Oristano.

Pietrino realised he was hungrier than he thought and finished all the spaghetti on his plate. His mother smiled with satisfaction when she took the empty dish away. Mothers are always right. The wine was tart and light and still smelled of grapes. Gavino made it himself, repeating each year everything he'd seen his grandfather and father do.

Maria brought two frying pans to the table. Polenta with *cavolo nero*[5] and *pezz'imbinata*, little strips of pork marinated in red wine and then grilled. Pietrino knew those flavours well. They were as much a part of his life as the walls of the house or the small picture of Santa Bonacatu hanging over the fireplace.

'I made this cabbage with my own hands,' Gavino said, dipping his spoon into the polenta.

'You have only one hand, Gavino, and only God can make living things,' said Maria, ribbing him. Her husband ignored her and looked at his son.

'Eat. Taste that? It's good because there's hard work in it,' he said, squeezing Pietrino's arm.

'You say that every day, Dad,' said Nino, smiling.

'And you eat every day,' said Gavino, entirely serious.

Pietrino continued eating in silence. After lunch he went and rested in the armchair next to the fireplace and in front of the television, a fine twenty-one-inch Sylvania on the plastic stand he'd given to his parents for their last anniversary. Maria didn't like having the antenna on the rooftop. That metal contraption would attract lightning, she said. The Piras family owned one of the few television sets in town, and often friends and relatives would come by to watch a programme or two, especially on Saturday nights and Sundays.

As his mother was washing the dishes, Pietrino distractedly watched the end of a programme on natural science, and then the test card came up. He leaned forward and, without getting up, extended a crutch and turned the set off with the tip. He tried to read a few lines of Simenon, but his full stomach and the warmth of the fire put him to sleep.

He woke up around three o'clock and sat there in a daze, staring at the lifeless television. He yawned, feeling tired from so much leisure.

Gavino was doubtless already out in the field, while his mother had gone to see to her bees. Sometimes Piras would go with her, but he never got close to the hives. He was always amazed to see hundreds of bees land on his mother's arms and face without ever stinging her.

Reaching down, he picked up the Simenon novel again. He'd brought a whole suitcase full of books with him from Florence, lent to him by Simone, a close friend of Sonia's who he was a little jealous of at first. Partly because he lived right across the landing from her, but mostly because he was very good looking.

Piras was only a few pages from the end of the novel. He read them in a few minutes, then closed the book and tapped it with his hand. He always did that when finishing a novel he liked.

Feeling a little groggy, he stretched and some of his joints cracked. To avoid falling back to sleep, he stood up, leaned on his crutches, and went out into the street. Staying indoors too long made him restless. There was never anything for him to do besides reading, and in his present condition he couldn't even give his parents a hand in the field or in the stables. He would have been glad to do so, if only to help the time go by faster.

The inspector left Totò's kitchen feeling as if he wanted to sleep. When all was said and done, he realised he had drunk nearly a whole bottle of wine by himself. The avenue was full of Christmas traffic. He headed towards Via Zara, repressing the urge to light another cigarette. It wasn't raining, but the sky had turned into a slab of lead, and he could feel the humidity in his bones. He preferred snow, but it hardly ever snowed in Florence. He'd once slept in snow, on a night in Umbria in 1944, and it was one of the few times sleeping out in the open when he hadn't felt cold. *Sotto la neve c'è il pane, sotta la pioggia c'è la fame*, the peasant saying went. *Under the snow there's bread, under the rain there's hunger*. He and his comrades had spent the night in their sleeping bags and woken up the following morning covered in sweat, under a ten-inch layer of snow . . .

There was no getting around it. No matter what he thought of, it always brought back memories of the bloody war.

As he entered the courtyard of police headquarters, he greeted Mugnai with a nod and went to look for Rinaldi and Tapinassi. He wanted to give them the photographs of the girl that he'd found in the loan shark's house, and tell them to track her down fast. The photos had been taken by Badalamenti with his fancy Leica, and Bordelli thought rather optimistically that it was a fair bet the girl lived in town. If they couldn't find her, then they would have to start looking for her in the outlying province, and then in all of Italy. At any rate, it was a lead that deserved to be followed to the very end. He found the two officers standing in front of the Flying Squad office.

'I want you to find this girl for me,' Bordelli said, handing Tapinassi two of the photos of Marisa which he'd cut below the chin. The rest he kept under lock and key. Tapinassi looked at the photos and blushed so thoroughly his ears turned red.

'Let me see,' said Rinaldi, taking them out of his hand. When he saw the girl his eyes opened wide.

'Blimey,' he said. They looked like a couple of idiots. It was a good thing they were seeing only the censored photos, thought Bordelli, shaking his head. Standing shoulder to shoulder, the two policemen couldn't take their eyes off them.

'You'll have all the time in the world to admire her. Take one photo each and don't make any copies. I want only you two to look into this; you mustn't tell anyone else. Understand?'

'We'll do our best, sir,' said Rinaldi.

'Try the schools, too, but nobody must know why we're looking for her. Invent some excuse, if you have to.'

'Why *are* we looking for her, Inspector?' Tapinassi asked.

'You don't need to know, for now. When you find her, don't approach her, don't do anything at all . . . Just report to me at once.'

'Very well, sir,' said Tapinassi, eyeing the photos in his colleague's hand. Bordelli slapped him on the back.

'But don't take a week. We're not in New York, after all,' he said.

'We'll manage, sir,' said Rinaldi, standing to attention.

'Maximum discretion,' the inspector reiterated, heading for the door. Before leaving he dropped into his office, for no real reason. Maybe just to have a look at the room. Every time he went in there he felt at home, and this worried him. It was very hot. He touched the radiators; they were boiling, at public expense. He put an unlit cigarette between his lips and left the matches on the desk. Leaving the room, he headed for the stairs, determined to smoke only if he ran into someone with a light.

He crossed the courtyard, pulling his trench coat tightly round his body. Passing Mugnai's booth, he waved a greeting. Mugnai bolted out and came up to him.

'Need a light, Inspector?'

Bordelli sighed and lit the cigarette on Mugnai's match. His

39

strategy hadn't worked, but in truth this was what he'd wanted. Otherwise he wouldn't have gone around the station with an unlit cigarette in his mouth.

'Thanks,' he said, blowing the smoke far away.

'You can keep 'em,' Mugnai said, slipping the box of matches into the inspector's coat pocket.

It was hopeless. If he wanted to quit smoking, he had to rely on himself.

'I'll buy you another box,' Bordelli said.

'No need, Inspector. I don't smoke.'

'How did you manage to quit?'

'I never started.'

'I think you and Piras would get on well together,' Bordelli said.

'How's he doing, now that you mention him?' Mugnai asked.

'He can't wait to get back to hunting down killers.'

'Give him my best.'

'Will do.'

Bordelli got into his Beetle and drove away, imagining Piras with his crutches and his father Gavino with only one arm.

He glanced at his watch. Just three o'clock. Before returning to Badalamenti's apartment he wanted to drop in on Diotivede. He turned on to the Viali and tried to smoke the cigarette as slowly as possible, to make it last. Driving past the Fortezza da Basso he saw a man in the distance talking to a little girl near the pond in the garden. At first he paid no heed. But when he approached the intersection with Viale Milton, he stopped the car and threw it into reverse, ignoring the horns blasting in protest. He parked the Beetle between two trees and got out. He thought he'd recognised Lapo, the thirty-year-old son of a couple of businesspeople in the centre of town. Lapo had been convicted several times of sexual harassment of minors. His parents were wealthy and always managed to save him by hiring expensive laywers who tried to pass him off as insane. But Bordelli was not a judge. Crossing the busy avenue in a hurry, he walked towards the pond. The young man had his back to him and was on his knees, talking to the little girl.

'Is there a problem here?' Bordelli asked gruffly. The young man snapped his head around, saw the inspector, and stood up.

'You scared me, Inspector.'

It was indeed Lapo, with his coat-hanger shoulders and hips as wide as a woman's. He was trembling lightly from the fright.

'It's you who scare me, Lapo,' the inspector retorted. The girl looked about ten years old. Long blonde hair and carrying a red satchel.

'Are you the man with the toys?' she asked Bordelli, looking him seriously in the eye.

'Of course I am . . . Aren't you going to introduce me to your daughter?' the inspector said to Lapo.

'He's not my daddy,' the little girl said.

'She's not my daughter,' the young man stammered. He had a gaunt face, eyes too big, and his skin was always shiny. Bordelli approached the girl, smiling.

'What's your name?'

'Beatrice. And you?'

'Franco. What are you doing outside all alone at this hour?'

'I was playing with my friend . . . she lives over there,' she said, pointing a tiny finger in the direction of Via dello Statuto.

'And where do you live?'

'In that building there,' said the little girl, pointing to a door across the avenue.

'Come, I'll walk you home,' said Bordelli offering her his hand.

'And what about the toys you promised me?' she asked. The inspector shot a glance at Lapo, who looked away.

'I forgot them at home.'

'Ohh! And when will you bring me them?'

'We'll talk it over with your mamma,' Bordelli said, to wriggle out of the bind. Then he went up to Lapo.

'I'm going to take her home and come back. If you move even an inch, you're in big trouble,' he whispered.

'I'll wait right here, I promise,' said Lapo, averting his eyes.

Bordelli took the child by the hand and escorted her to the front door of her building. Ringing the buzzer, he told the girl he wanted to talk to her mother about the toys. The mother came downstairs to meet them. The woman listened to him attentively and thanked him, then started saying a few words to her daughter, who looked at her in astonishment. Bordelli waved goodbye, and as the big door closed behind him, he could hear the little girl complaining that the toy man had tricked her.

He walked calmly back to the park. Lapo was huddled up on a bench, green greatcoat pulled tightly around him, smoking a cigarette. The inspector sat down beside him. He remained silent for a moment, gazing at the dark silhouettes of the oaks in the park and the naked branches of the plane trees lining the avenue. Cars drove by fast, as the volume of traffic increased. He turned towards the young man and extended his arm over the back of the bench.

'I was going to give you a little lecture.'

'Of course, Inspector,' Lapo said, still looking down. He stank of sweat and eau de cologne. Bordelli sighed with irritation.

'I want you to listen very closely, because I don't like to say things twice.'

'Of course, Inspector,' Lapo repeated. Bordelli turned round to face the avenue.

'From now on I'm going to have my men follow you, day and night. If I find out that you've come within ten yards of any little girl, I'm going to come and get you personally and take you straight to the Murate and charge you with rape. I'll have forty-eight hours to investigate and establish the facts. But rumours travel fast in jail, and you know what the other prisoners do to people like you? They cut their balls off. So do me a favour now and repeat what I just said . . . word for word.'

Bordelli had seen something similar in a Western whose title he couldn't remember. He had to admit that it had made an impression. Lapo took a deep breath and started speaking.

'From now on I'm going to have you followed . . . and if I hear that you've approached a . . . a little girl . . .'

'Well done. Now finish the sentence.'

'. . . I'm going to come and get you and . . . take you to the Murate . . .'

'Go on.'

'. . . and in jail . . . they'll . . . cut off . . .'

'What'll they cut off? Come on, it's easy.'

'. . . m . . . my balls . . .'

'Good, now I know you understand. And do you know what happens when someone cuts off your balls?'

'No,' said Lapo, pale as a corpse.

'Well, if you want to find out, just try to bother another little girl and it'll all be clear to you. Think you need any more explanations?'

'No,' said Lapo, and a second later he covered his face with his hands and burst into tears like a child. His shoulders shook as if they had an electrical current running through them.

'Have you got a cigarette?' Bordelli asked. The young man passed him a packet of HB without raising his head. He continued whimpering and sniffling. The inspector took a cigarette and put the packet back in the man's pocket. Then he stood up and headed for the Beetle. Had he remained a second longer he might not have been able to refrain himself from boxing the ears of that rich, sick kid. But he'd never liked beating people up, and so he'd left. Getting into the car, he imagined Lapo with his hands on a little girl and lit the cigarette with Mugnai's providential matches.

He took the last drag at the bottom of Via Alderotti, and after flicking the butt out the window, he left it open to get rid of the smoke. It was bloody cold outside. He hadn't noticed when sitting in the park with Lapo.

Before it got dark, Piras wanted to go another couple of kilometres towards Santu Lussurgiu. It was a beautiful route, and there was still an hour of daylight left. His house was at the edge of town, almost directly in front of the crossroads for Seneghe, and to go to Santu Lussurgiu, one first had to cross all of Bonarcado. There was a bit of wind, but it wasn't too bad. The sun was warmer than in Florence.

Walking with crutches was hard, but he could feel himself getting closer to recovery and managed to enjoy the effort. Every day that went by he felt a little steadier on his feet. He wanted to be the way he was before, and soon . . . Hunting for killers and making love with Sonia.

A donkey brayed as though suffering. It must have been one of the Perra family's animals. Through the windows of the houses, Piras could see Christmas trees with coloured baubles. There were children playing football in the middle of the street with a deflated ball. They ran about like mice and raised smoke from the ball every time they kicked it. He himself had once played in these same streets, not too many years before.

He walked past the church of Santa Maria, which was large and massive, almost too big for such a little town. It was made of dark stone, and the bell tower made a fine impression. The façade was on the other side, looking on to the woods covering the hill. The church looked as if it was turning its back to the town. When he was a little boy his parents used to bring him to hear mass every Sunday. He still remembered how bored he felt during those moments, with the village elders singing, the priest speaking a strange language, his mother always telling him to go to confession, the gnarly candles dripping on to the terracotta floor, the smell of dead flowers, the round eyes of the Christ looking at him from behind the altar . . . Whenever he left that place he felt reborn, and he wondered why everyone in town went and did something so sad every Sunday. At age fifteen he finally rebelled, and in the end his parents stopped taking him there.

The only time he ever went back inside the church was for funerals. The last time was three years before moving to Florence, when his grandmother, Maria Serena, passed away. Back then the priest was Don Beniamino, a fat tub of lard who always smelled of grilled pork and wine. His homilies were unending, and his funeral orations even longer. He had a shrill voice and always said things that made one feel anxious. Then one day Don Beniamino did something he shouldn't have done: he started secretly selling the land traditionally attached to the church of Bonarcado. When somebody found out, the rumour spread in barely half an hour. Everyone in town took to the streets, even women and children. That land belonged to Bonarcado, and must never be touched. They all went to the church to get the priest, and then tied him to his donkey with a sign around his neck, *l'ainu asub 'e sa bestia*: 'the ass riding his beast'. Then they whipped the poor animal and sent the priest down the road to Paulilatino, following behind and shouting at him never to come back. And that was the last they ever saw of Don Beniamino.

Piras was forcing himself to keep up an almost normal pace, but the road to Santu Lussurgiu was all uphill and the effort was tiring him out. Every so often he would stop to catch his breath. It was shortly before sunset. He wanted to get as far as Morgiu's stable, and so he sped up. Many years before he was born, something had happened along this road. One morning at dawn, in early summer, a stranger was found sprawled out in the dirt like a wretch, eyes open to the heavens, killed by a blast from a sawn-off shotgun that had ripped through his neck. He must have been over seventy years old and had almost no teeth. When they lifted him off the ground his head came detached from his body and rolled down the road. Nobody ever found out who he was or who had killed him. The priest held a mass for him, and then he was buried. A blank tombstone was laid over his grave. People talked about the affair for a long time afterwards, and a few years later the legend of a headless man, combing the countryside in search of his killer, began to spread. Mothers often used that story to make their children behave. 'If you don't go to bed at once, the headless man will come and take you away.' Piras's own mother had said that to him many times, and little by little the story had worked its way into his brain, rather like the sharp point of a nail. For years he had gone to sleep every night thinking that one day he would become a policeman and solve the mystery of that old man's murder. By now, of course, he understood that the headless ghost who roamed the countryside would never find rest.

Bordelli parked under the plane trees on Viale Pieraccini and slowly began to climb the stairs that led to the forensic medicine laboratory. When he got to the top, he stopped for a moment to look at the sky. He wished it were white and full of snow. He wanted his skin to feel the dry cold of certain winters he'd experienced as a child. But these clouds were dark and promised only rain.

He went into the building. Even in the corridor one smelled the sickly-sweet, acrid odour typical of such places. Pushing open the door to the lab, he saw his friend, the pathologist, standing in the middle of the room staring at the wall. In his hand he had a test tube half filled with dark liquid, but wasn't paying any attention to it.

'Diotivede, what's wrong?'

The doctor shook his head and went and set the test tube down near the microscope.

'I'm retiring in three years. I just found out today,' he said drily.

'You can't do this to me.'

'One life is not enough. You barely manage to understand two scraps of rubbish and it's already time to feed the pigeons.'

'If you go on I'm going to start crying,' said the inspector.

Diotivede walked over to a gurney. With the ease of habit he pulled back the sheet covering a corpse, then folded it up like a housewife and put it away on a shelf. Bordelli immediately recognised Badalamenti's face, which was disagreeable even in death. The corpse's abdomen had already been opened. Diotivede calmly put on his gloves and then got down to work with the forceps. The inspector approached the gurney. The loan shark's eyes were clamped shut with two pins. Diotivede didn't like to work on a corpse whose eyes were open.

Bordelli studied the stocky, hirsute body of Totuccio Badalamenti. He had short, almost dwarf-like thighs. It looked as if he had grown only from the waist up. The tip of each finger was stained black with ink. De Marchi had already come and taken the corpse's fingerprints.

'Any news?' Bordelli asked, gesturing towards the body. The doctor didn't answer.

'Diotivede, can you hear me?'

'Eh?'

'Have you got any news about Badalamenti?'

'I just opened him up a short while ago. I was very behind in my work.'

'Such delicacy . . .' said the inspector.

He stuck a cigarette between his lips but didn't light it. In the fiefdom of forensic medicine, smoking was forbidden.

'Diotivede, have you ever done this stuff on a friend? Must be strange, no?'

The doctor said nothing. He seemed quite engrossed. He had both hands inside the corpse and was talking to himself.

'Damn it all . . .' he muttered. He was clearly in a bad mood and even looked slightly dishevelled, though this was only an impression. The hair that stood straight up on his head could never be dishevelled. Bordelli sighed.

'Three years is a long time, and anyway, you can always keep working in one way or another afterwards, don't you think?' he said, twirling the unlit cigarette between his fingers.

'You're right. I could start dissecting dogs and chickens to find out how they died.'

'Why not? You could set up your own private morgue.'

Diotivede gave a slight, cold hint of a smile, then stuck his forceps farther into Badalamenti's belly. The physical effort made it look as if he was repairing a bathroom sink.

'Anyway, retirement's not such a bad thing,' the inspector continued.

47

'I found out today . . . I don't know, it's had an unpleasant effect on me . . . But where the hell did that thing go . . .?'

'Looking for the heart? Don't bother; this model hasn't got one.'

Diotivede wasn't paying much attention to Bordelli. He carried on searching the usurer's intestines and at last found what he was looking for.

'So I wasn't mistaken after all,' he said in satisfaction, holding the forceps up in the air. Between their pointed tips was a small metal ring covered by a dark patina. The inspector drew near, curious to know what it was.

'What the hell is that?' he asked.

Diotivede didn't answer. Holding the forceps before his eyes, he went over to the sink with the inspector following behind, turned on the water and let it run over the mysterious object. The patina faded and the mystery was revealed: it was a gold ring.

'Excuse me a minute,' Bordelli said, taking the forceps out of Diotivede's hand and bringing them close to a lamp. It was not a wedding band. On one side the ring narrowed to where it was barely thicker than a thread, and on the broader side a tiny little diamond was set. Inscribed inside the band was a name: *Ciro*.

'Can you tell me how long it was before he died that he swallowed it?' Bordelli asked.

'Not long before – not more than half an hour.'

'Are you sure?' the inspector asked distractedly. Diotivede stopped dead in his tracks and looked him hard in the eyes.

'I always speak only when I am sure of something; otherwise I keep quiet,' he said curtly.

'No need to get upset.'

'I should think you would have learned that by now.'

'It was just an offhand question.'

Bordelli kept studying the ring as if the killer's name were somehow written on it. The doctor removed his gloves and went to wash his hands. Three times, as usual. He already seemed to have calmed down.

'I'll be done with this one fairly soon,' he said, drying his hands carefully. 'But don't expect any big surprises. The cause and time of death are already pretty well established.'

The inspector put the forceps down.

'Stabbed to death with a pair of scissors in the neck,' he said, stating the obvious.

'That's right,' said the doctor, half closing his eyes like a schoolmaster pleased with his pupil.

'When did he die?'

'Almost certainly last Friday, but as I said, it's impossible to say at what time of day.'

'Too bad,' said Bordelli, thinking that this made the whole thing more difficult.

'I'm almost positive the killer is left-handed, but I still need to check a few things.'

'*Almost positive* doesn't sound like you,' said Bordelli.

'Actually I wasn't even going to tell you,' said Diotivede, taking his glasses off to clean the lenses. He did this dozens of times a day. It was a long process that he executed very methodically. It was through those lenses that he saw the world, and he wanted them always immaculate. Bordelli brought the ring into the light again and examined it for a few seconds more. Then he walked towards Diotivede, holding the forceps in the air.

'I'm going to keep this,' he said.

'As you wish.'

'Will you wrap it up for me?'

'There are some small envelopes in that drawer.'

The inspector put the ring in an envelope, which he then put in his pocket.

'And please don't ask me to go to the pointless trouble of reporting this. Since, at any rate, only you and I know about it,' he said.

'I trust you . . . but if you sell it, we go fifty-fifty.'

'Absolutely. Then we can open a Swiss bank account.'

'I think I'd rather stuff the money into my mattress than give it to those milksops,' said Diotivede with a sneer.

'You doing anything for Christmas?' Bordelli asked.

'I think I'll go to bed early,' the doctor said, still wiping his lenses with a piece of cloth. When he took his glasses off, his face changed; it looked empty, almost funny.

'Aren't you going to see your relatives?' Bordelli asked

'I'm invited for lunch on the twenty-fifth, as always.'

'If you like, we can have dinner at my place on the evening of the twenty-fourth. We've known each other for so long and we've still never spent Christmas together.'

The doctor put his glasses back on.

'I'll think about it,' he said.

'But don't expect any presents.'

'You could have let me get my hopes up,' said Diotivede.

'We'll have a nice big dinner, like two years ago. We'll drink a little wine and talk about women . . . What do you say?'

'I'll think about it.'

'Well, let me know soon. Christmas is just around the corner.'

'I'll think about it,' the doctor said for the third time.

'All right, then. If you have any news about our friend Badalamenti, ring me immediately.'

'There won't be any news.'

'You could have let me get my hopes up,' said the inspector.

'I'll give you a ring when I've finished with him.'

Diotivede nodded goodbye, and as Bordelli was heading for the door, the doctor started putting the instruments he'd used in a tub of disinfectant.

Around half past four, the inspector parked his car in Piazza del Carmine, right in front of Badalamenti's building. The sun was setting and the street lamps were already lit. The dark sky had been threatening rain for hours, but nothing had happened yet.

Entering the usurer's building, he climbed the stairs without haste. He was determined not to leave the flat until he found what he was looking for. If necessary, he would comb the place inch by inch. There had to be something there. If not, he would feel defeated and would have to admit that Judge Ginzillo had been right. That would be a hard pill to swallow. Rat-face Ginzillo couldn't possibly be right.

Bordelli stopped to catch his breath on the landing of the last floor but one. He'd eaten and drunk too much, and he wasn't a kid any longer. He would have to start going to the gym now and then, maybe to see his friend Mazzinghi and do a little sparring, as in the old days.

Having climbed the last flight of stairs, he went into Badalamenti's flat. Aside from the smell of death, there was also an unpleasant feeling that came over him as it had every other time he'd entered the place. He went straight into the sitting room, opened the glass-fronted cabinet and poured himself a cognac. He took a sip. It was very good, but not in the same league as De Maricourt.

He picked up the can of grey putty he'd seen before lunch and sat down in an armchair. For the moment it was the only odd thing he'd found in the flat. Sipping the cognac, he tried to fathom why Badalamenti kept that putty in the living room, among the glasses in the liquor cabinet. There was no real point in knowing the reason, but he was used to paying close attention to little details, even those that appeared insignificant. He set the can down on the low glass table and began to study it. In reality he was amusing himself, rather as he used to do as a child, during treasure hunts at the home of his cousin Rodrigo. What had become of Rodrigo, anyway? He hadn't seen him for a good while, and hadn't even had the honour of meeting his new girlfriend, the woman who had succeeded in changing the curmudgeonly Rodrigo's life . . . Assuming, of course, that they were still together. He had to remember at least to give him a ring to wish him a happy Christmas.

Drinking his cognac in little sips, he continued to contemplate the can of grey putty. He began with the most elementary things. He looked around. There was no other furniture in the room that Badalamenti could have put it in, if for some reason he wanted to keep it in the living room. But why do that?

Drinking the last sip, he felt like smoking a cigarette but tried to resist. Perhaps Badalamenti often had need of the putty in that room and didn't feel like always going and fetching it from another room. But why would he have needed it so often in the living room? Normally you spread it out and leave it for a while. This was getting interesting. Bordelli got up and looked at the windowpanes. There was no trace of fresh putty round the edges. He poured himself another cognac and collapsed into the armchair again. Putting his feet up on the glass table, he leaned his head back in the chair. Putty . . . He was almost there, he could feel it. He closed his eyes and remained that way for a few minutes, in danger of falling asleep.

All at once he sat up, a smile on his face. He'd figured it out, maybe. He finished his cognac in one gulp and stood up. He went into the kitchen and started opening the cupboards and drawers until he found a little box of toothpicks. Taking two, he went back into the sitting room, got down on all fours, and started scratching the grout between the tiles, one after another. The floor was made up of old terracotta tiles, about ten inches square. He carried on like this crawling like a child at play, not minding the dust. He couldn't stop smiling.

At last, in a corner by the window, he found what he was looking for: the grout around one tile was still soft. He scraped it all away with the toothpick and tried to lift the tile with his fingers, but couldn't. He went back to the kitchen to get a knife and, using the tip as a lever, was able to raise the tile without effort. He found before him a cement cavity about the size of a shoebox. There were a number of different things inside. A small black accordion purse, a large, bulging yellowish envelope, a small round box covered in blue velvet, and a bundle of white cloth. Taking it all out of the hole, he noticed that the bundle was heavy and opened it. Inside he found a Glisenti 7.65 Parabellum with the serial number sanded off. Pretty clever, our little Totuccio, thought Bordelli. He wrapped the pistol back up in the cloth and opened the blue velvet box. It had a number of gold rings inside, mostly wedding bands. Almost all of them had the spouses' names and wedding dates inscribed inside: *Argia Ferdinando, 2 October 1902*; *Nora Goffredo, 14 August 1897*, and so on.

Badalamenti was very meticulous, even fastidious. To each wedding band he had tied a tiny label with a piece of thread, and on each label he had written the debtor's name and surname in red pen. The name on the label always corresponded to one of the two inscribed inside the ring, except in one case. No doubt it had been a son or grandchild who had pawned that ring . . .

But what was he doing in such an uncomfortable position?

He brought all the stuff he had found over to the glass table and went and poured himself another serving of cognac. Then he sat down in the armchair, put the accordion bag in his lap and opened it. Hundreds of promissory notes, arranged by date. Each compartment in the bag contained one month's dues. In the last section were three sheets of paper folded in four. This was Badalamenti's 'ledger', the complete list of his debtors. Dozens of names and dates written in such tiny handwriting that one almost needed a magnifying glass to read it. Bordelli lit a cigarette and with some effort started scanning that list of poor devils. They were quite an army. He let himself fall back again in the chair. His head was spinning a little, but it was a pleasant enough sensation. The cognac was actually quite good. He put the list away and pulled out some promissory notes. One month's payments together amounted to a tidy sum: about the same as what a chief inspector earned in a year. One had to keep busy to maintain a Porsche.

He put the IOUs back and opened the yellow envelope. Out came a great assortment of papers, and he set these down in his lap. More promissory notes, provisional sales agreements, contracts of different kinds. He picked one up at random: an old woman with no heirs had made over to Badalamenti the residuary right of ownership of her villa in Settignano for two million lire. Bordelli couldn't help but smile. Now that Badalamenti was dead, the residuary ownership reverted automatically back to her. That was one matter, at least, that had been settled all by itself. There were a number of contracts transferring owner-ship and some deeds of sale, always for amounts far below market value. One needn't have been an estate agent to realise this. There were also some chequebooks for banks in the south, almost unused. Bordelli opened an envelope held shut by a rubber band. Inside was a thick little bundle of promissory notes for fifty thousand lire, with the photograph of a house pinned to the top note. It was a small, modern house with a garden and a hedge of bay laurel inside an iron grille, and two terracotta pine cones crowning the gateposts.

'Shit . . .' said Bordelli, not believing his eyes. He flipped the photograph over. On the back, written in the usual red pen, were a name and address, the same as on the promissory notes: *Mario Fabiani, Via di Barbacane 65.* Underneath, Badalamenti had added: *Interesting.*

Bordelli shook his head. He'd known Dr Fabiani for years and sometimes even invited him to dinner. He was a psycho-analyst, aged seventy, more or less retired, an innocent soul with a passion for plants. He'd never said a word to the inspector about his financial difficulties. Bordelli felt embarrassed by the very idea of going to see him, even if it was only to give him the good news that Badalamenti was dead. He sighed and put that thought away for later.

Still rummaging through the papers, he found a crumpled letter addressed to the 'Distinguished Totuccio Badalamenti, Esq'. Appended to the envelope with a paper clip were a number of promissory notes for fifty thousand lire and a smaller enve-lope with photographs inside. There were five of them, all black and white, taken in a place that looked in every way like a sort of bordello for American soldiers. A half-naked blonde girl in spiked heels and garter belt was standing in the middle of a group of smiling GIs who were vying with one another to get their hands on her. In one of the photos a black man about six foot six, hand miming a pistol, was sticking his enormous index finger into the blonde's mouth. She had her hands raised and eyes wide open, and everyone else was laughing. A photo souvenir of a lost war.

Bordelli opened the letter and started reading it. The handwriting was neat and round. It was a woman's. She begged the 'good' Mr Badalamenti not to ask her for any more money, because she didn't have any left. It ended as follows:

I beseech you, whatever may happen, never to tell my son what you found out about me. I don't want Odoardo to grow up burdened by his mother's guilt. I put my trust in your goodness and ask the Blessed Virgin to forgive you and myself.

May God bless you.

Yours sincerely,
Rosaria Beltempo

She'd written it in October 1964, and on the back of the envelope was the sender's address. Underneath, Badalamenti had written in red ink: *House not worth much, olive grove 2 hectares.*

The whole thing looked very much like blackmail, paid off in instalments and guaranteed with IOUs. A rather brilliant invention. Bravo, Totuccio. The inspector sighed deeply and smiled . . . He'd suddenly thought of Judge Ginzillo. Perhaps now the rat-face would listen to him; maybe now he would understand just who Badalamenti was. But, knowing Ginzillo, he knew he would rather pee his pants than admit his own idiocy. Bordelli couldn't wait to go and see the genius.

He heard some dripping and went over to the window. It had started raining outside. Going back into the kitchen, he found a plastic shopping bag under the sink. He put everything he'd found inside it, and slowly checked each room one last time before leaving. He tried to imagine the extortionist pacing about his flat with satisfaction, counting in his head the money he'd earned that day. But he wouldn't be making trouble for anyone any longer. Someone had taken a pair of scissors in hand and said: enough. Bordelli went into the bathroom and looked at himself in the same mirror in which Badalamenti had seen his own reflection a few days before.

Very well. There wasn't anything left to do in this place. He could go now. He locked the door behind him and descended the stairs slowly, plastic bag swinging at his side. Despite the satisfaction, he felt a little melancholy.

Only a week remained until Christmas. At midnight it was still drizzling outside, tiny cold drops that refused to turn into snow. In one corner of Rosa's small living room stood a fir tree about five feet tall laden with coloured baubles and little blinking lights. The big dining table was covered with presents, some wrapped and others yet to be wrapped. Gideon, Rosa's big white tomcat, was lying on his back, asleep, feet in the air, atop a sideboard. He was the very symbol of deep sleep.

'I wrap everything myself . . . Aren't they pretty?' said Rosa.

'Absolutely beautiful,' said Bordelli, half lying on the couch and holding an almost empty goblet of red wine between two fingers. He was looking at Rosa and smiling inside. Despite the life she had led and the riffraff she'd had no choice but to frequent, Rosa was as pure as the driven snow. That evening she was wearing a decolletée dress with a blue floral print and violet high heels.

The inspector sat up and refilled his glass. Rosa's living room had a big, glorious window which, behind the flimsy curtains, gave on to a long perspective of rooftops and, in the distance, Arnolfo's tower. It had taken Rosa a long time to find the right place for her. All her life she'd worked in brothels, winter and summer. Then MP Lina Merlin had come along and said, *That's enough, ladies,* and Rosa simply couldn't see herself pounding the pavement . . .[6] It seemed so sad, so vulgar . . . As she'd always been thrifty, she'd managed to set aside a decent nest egg. She deserved a hard-earned rest in a flat looking out over the rooftops. The light in her place was always warm and welcoming, and always shone from the corners of the room.

'Are they only for this Christmas, or do they include next year's presents as well?' asked Bordelli, seeing the dozens of gifts covering the table. Rosa was tying a bow and started singing.

'*Non essere geloso se con gli altri ballo il rock . . .*'

'Are you talking to me?'

'*Non essere geloso se con gli altri ballo il twist . . .* There's a present for you too, you big ugly monkey.'

'You shouldn't have, Rosa.'

'Liar. You always love my presents.'

'That's not what I meant.'

'Why don't you ever say what you mean?'

'That's not what I . . .' Bordelli began, but he stopped before he repeated himself. Rosa kept on singing.

'*Con te, con te, con te che sei la mia passione / io ballo il ballo del mattone . . .*'[7]

Bordelli swallowed a sip of wine and lit his cigarette. It was past midnight, and it was already an achievement to have smoked only six all day.

'So you're not going to tell me who all those presents are for?' he asked.

'Don't you know I have a lot of girlfriends?'

'Colleagues?'

'They're not all whores, you know. D'you think that's all I ever did in life?' Rosa's lips were enlarged by her lipstick, and when she wasn't speaking, her mouth looked like a heart.

'Just curious,' said the inspector. She kept on wrapping presents, using a nice sharp pair of scissors to curl the ribbons.

'You know, Rosa, that guy who was murdered not far from my house was killed with a pair of scissors rather similar to those.'

'How nice of you to tell me,' she said.

'Sorry, but I can't stop thinking about it.'

'If you ask me, you'll never catch him.'

'Thanks, Rosa,' said Bordelli, still ruminating. That afternoon he'd passed the list of the usurer's debtors to Porcinai, the police archivist, asking him to find all their addresses and telephone numbers as soon as possible. It was merely a first attempt to get the ball rolling. The only name he'd struck off the list was that of his friend Fabiani, whose address he already knew. He also knew Rosaria Beltempo's, which was written on the envelope of that painful letter addressed to the 'Distinguished Totuccio Badalamenti, Esq'.

Rosa finished wrapping a tiny little box, which she then held in the palm of her hand, arm extended, to have a long look at it.

'This is for Tiziana,' she said. 'It's a lipstick you can only find in Paris.'

'So how'd you get your hands on it?'

'Somebody sent it to me from Paris for my birthday, and since it doesn't look good on my own lips, I thought . . .'

'Rosa, it's not nice to recycle presents from other people.'

'So you think I should have just thrown it away? I redid the tip, and now it looks as good as new . . . And this way, someone else can get some use out of it.'

'Well, when you put it that way, it sounds like a fabulous gift.'

'You've got too many outdated ideas in that ageing head of yours,' said Rosa, wrinkling her nose. Putting the little box aside, she turned her attention to another. Bordelli blew smoke at the ceiling. He saw again the scissors planted deep in Badalamenti's neck, and the thought of the killer elicited some very ambiguous feelings in him.

'Hey, what's with the long face tonight? . . . Are you hungry? Shall I make you another tartine?' she said, getting up and coming over to him.

'Thanks, Rosa, I'm fine.'

'Well, that's enough red wine. Now we're going to drink some Monbazillac,' she said, taking the glass out of his hand.

'Another gift from Paris?'

'*I love Paris in the springtiiiime . . .*' Rosa blared, fluttering all the way to the kitchen in her purple pumps. A hammer would have made less noise.

'Aren't the people downstairs going to complain?' Bordelli asked loudly.

'No, there's only an old witch who's deaf,' Rosa yelled from the kitchen. You couldn't really say she didn't have a knack for concision.

It was still drizzling outside. Every so often a drop left a long, thin trail on the windows that gave on to the terrace. Gideon hadn't moved. He looked like a rag. Bordelli stubbed out the cigarette and lay down. With eyes closed he started listening to the hiss of the rain on the rooftops. From the kitchen came the hammer-blows of Rosa's high heels. She returned to the living room, carrying a transparent plastic tray with a bottle and two wine glasses.

'Ta-da! Ta-da!' she said, advancing in dance steps. Bordelli, who was nearly asleep, gave a start. 'Inspector . . . You wouldn't be turning into an old fogey on me, now, would you?' Rosa asked, setting the tray down on the coffee table in front of the sofa.

'Maybe I am,' he said, yawning. Rosa popped the cork out of the bottle. Bordelli sat up and yawned again. The just-opened Monbazillac gave off a sweet odour of nobly mildewed grapes, and Bordelli felt at peace with the world.

'Uncouth as you are, you'll probably think it tastes like Lambrusco,' she said, filling the goblets. Bordelli picked his up, but as he brought it to his lips, Rosa grabbed his arm.

'Wait, you big monkey! We need to make a toast!' she said, all excited. One could never open a bottle at her place without toasting. She'd picked up the habit in France – that is, in Paris, which she seemed to think counted for all of France.

'To your marriage,' Bordelli proposed, trying to clink his glass with Rosa's, but she pulled hers away suddenly, almost spilling the wine.

'I've manage to avoid it for this long . . . You little shit!' she said.

'Then you decide.'

'Let's toast the person who bumped off the loan shark . . . May he live long and never be caught by you. What do you say?' she asked, raising her glass.

'We can certainly toast him, though you know of course he'll never escape me.'

They were about to clink glasses when Rosa pulled hers away again.

'*Dahnlezyé* . . .'[8] she said. 'Don't cheat, monkey, look me in the eyes or it doesn't count.' Another Parisian custom, according to her.

'How's this?' Bordelli asked, looking her straight in the eye with his own wide open. The glasses touched and made a fine crystal sound. They drank a sip. Words could not describe the fragrances rising into their noses. Gideon stretched, opened his eyes, cast a bleary glance at them and went back to sleep.

'You can't send him to jail,' said Rosa, a gleam of triumph in her eye, 'he's done humanity a favour.'

'I certainly can, just you watch.'

'No, no, no,' she said, smiling, taking a generous sip of wine. Bordelli did the same, emptying his glass.

'This yellow nectar's not bad,' he said. She refilled the glasses, trying to impart great refinement to her gestures. As she grabbed the bottle by the neck, her little finger immediately shot up. Bordelli had once tried to tell her that if she moved more naturally she would be even more beautiful, and she had replied with something like: 'Do you mean to say that an old whore who never got past the first grade can only spit on the floor, curse, and scratch herself between the legs?' But this was another reason Bordelli was so fond of her: she never minced words. Rosa slapped him lightly on the knee.

'Hm?' he replied groggily, again lost in thoughts about Badalamenti.

'What's wrong with you? Have you fallen in love again?' asked Rosa, worried.

'I'm just a little tired.'

She seemed satisfied with his answer.

'Another toast, Inspector?'

'To your beauty.'

'Oh, go on!' she said, giggling, and held up her glass.

17 December

'A loan shark?' Baragli asked, opening his eyes slightly wider. Although it was early morning, he was very weak.

'He lived near me,' Bordelli said.

'Inspector, those who sow the wind . . .' said Baragli, lifting his shoulders just enough to make his point. The inspector approved with a nod.

'Here, I brought you this,' he said, taking a book out of his coat pocket.

'Thanks, Inspector.' Baragli took the book in his trembling hands and looked at the cover: *Edgar Allan Poe – Stories*.

'They're tales of the mysterious,' said Bordelli.

'Just what I needed . . . Could you put it over there, please?'

The inspector laid the book down on the bedside table. Baragli had lost more weight, and one could see the shape of his skull through the skin on his face. A nurse came in and put some pills in his hand. She had dark hair, looked about thirty, quite pretty and full of life.

'How are we doing today, Oreste?' she said, handing him a glass of water.

'Whenever I see you I feel a lot better,' he said, smiling.

'Then tonight I'll come and sleep in your bed.'

'Do you want me to choke on my medicine?' the sergeant said with the pills already in his mouth. The nurse laughed and exchanged glances with Bordelli. Then she left, humming.

'Cute,' said Bordelli.

'All nurses should be like her.'

'I agree.'

'So, with a pair of scissors, you were saying?' Baragli resumed.

'Yeah, right here, in the neck,' said Bordelli, touching the base of his nape with a finger. Then he started telling the sergeant how he'd discovered Badalamenti's hidey-hole, the IOUs and rigged contracts, and the woman who'd been blackmailed. The sergeant listened to Bordelli with great interest. The nostalgia for his former job shone in his eyes.

'It was probably one of his debtors that did it,' Baragli muttered with a wheezy voice.

'That's exactly where I'll begin.'

'You've got your work cut out for you, if there are as many as you say.'

'I'll try to be patient.'

'What does Dr Diotivede think about all this?' Baragli asked.

'He hasn't finished with the body yet, but according to him, he's already told me all there is to say.'

'You never know . . .'

'I also found some photographs of a very young girl hidden behind a picture frame on the wall. I've got some men looking for her,' said Bordelli, to let him feel part of the investigation. And indeed the sergeant seemed pleased.

'Pretty?' he asked.

'Very,' said Bordelli.

Baragli turned slowly towards the window and remained silent for a while, looking outside. The weather was still nasty. Now and then a couple of drops fell, but it wasn't really raining yet. Bordelli looked at the sergeant and thought about all the years they'd spent together in Via Zara . . . it seemed like yesterday . . .

'A game of cards, Inspector?' asked Baragli, trying to sit up in bed.

'Why not?'

Bordelli took the cards out of the drawer and they began to play. Baragli was very weak. He took a long time choosing his card, then simply dropped it on the sheet. Every minute or so he grimaced and touched his stomach. A few minutes later the surgeon came in, followed by two very young assistants.

'How are you feeling, Sergeant?' the doctor asked, reading the hospital chart at the foot of the bed. He was short and looked like a wicked pistolero in a Western.

'I can't breathe, Doctor, and I'm having terrible shooting pains here,' said Baragli, touching his upper abdomen.

'That's normal after an operation like yours.'

'It gets worse every day . . .'

'It'll get better soon,' said the surgeon. The two assistants exchanged a glance. Baragli noticed but said nothing. Bordelli saw everything and felt a pang in his heart. The doctor wrote something on the chart, said goodbye, and went to talk to the other patients, still followed by his assistants.

'He didn't tell me the truth,' the sergeant said in a soft voice, sighing.

'Whose turn was it?' Bordelli asked.

They resumed playing, but the inspector kept an eye on the surgeon. As soon as he saw him leave the room, he told Baragli he needed to go to the bathroom. He followed the surgeon and caught up with him at the end of the corridor.

'Excuse me, Doctor, I'm Inspector Bordelli, a colleague of the sergeant's.'

The doctor shook his hand.

'Pleasure. Cataliotti.'

'How is Baragli, Doctor? Tell me sincerely.'

The doctor shook his head and lowered his voice.

'Unfortunately he hasn't got much time left,' he said.

'Are you sure?'

'I'm afraid so.'

'How long?'

'It's hard to say. Could be a few weeks, maybe less. Nobody can really know for certain,' he said, throwing his hands up.

Bordelli sighed and ran a hand through his hair. 'Thank you, Doctor,' he said.

'Not at all.'

They shook hands again and the surgeon walked away. The inspector stayed in the corridor to smoke a cigarette in front of a large window. It was starting to drizzle, and a light wind was moving the treetops. A few open umbrellas could be seen along the hospital's footpaths outside.

He stubbed out the butt in a large ashtray on a tripod, then returned to Baragli's bedside. He found him asleep and felt pleased. If he'd been awake he might have been able to read in the inspector's face what he'd just learned from the doctor.

Bordelli put the cards away, adjusted the pillow behind Baragli's head, and turned off the light on the bedside table. Glancing at the chart at the foot of the bed, he read what the surgeon had written: *morphine*. As he left he crossed paths with the pretty dark-haired nurse, and they exchanged a smile.

'Tell me, Inspector Bordelli, what else can I do for you?' Judge Ginzillo said, sighing.

'*What else*', *my arse*, Bordelli thought, but said nothing. Ginzillo flashed a cold smile and seemed a little tense. His hands were resting on the desk, entwined like creeping vines, and his rat-face was staring at the inspector. Bordelli had sat down in front of him without removing his trench coat and was sweating a little. It was always too hot in that office, even hotter than at police headquarters.

'Nothing special, sir. It's just that this morning I woke with a keen desire to come here and thank you,' said Bordelli.

The judge got a whiff of the irony and pinched his nostrils. 'For what?' he said, pretending not to know.

'Do you remember the search warrant I asked you for, way back in February of this year?'

'What was that in connection with?'

Bordelli refrained from telling him to his face that he was a spineless hypocrite.

'Don't you remember?' he said simply, smiling.

'I can hardly remember everything, now, can I?' said Ginzillo, pushing his spectacles up the bridge of his nose.

'I'm sorry, you're right. May I refresh your memory?'

'Please.'

'I came here and asked you for a search warrant for the home of a certain Totuccio Badalamenti, a loan-sharking son of a bitch and extortionist,' he said in a serene tone of voice.

Ginzillo threw up his hands. 'Why must you always be so vulgar, Inspector?'

'Was I being vulgar? I'm sorry, I wasn't aware of it.'

'Go on,' said Ginzillo, wiping away a drop of sweat from his chin.

'I wanted to point out to you that now Badalamenti's dead, I don't need the search warrant any more . . .' said Bordelli. 'And this is a great boon for the bureaucracy, don't you think?'

The judge nodded almost imperceptibly, a smile of suspicion on his face. He couldn't make out what the oddball inspector was getting at.

'A nasty murder. You're handling the case, are you not?' he said.

'Yes, I'm handling it.'

'Have you already discovered something?'

'Do you really care?' asked the inspector, pretending to be greatly surprised.

Ginzillo was getting nervous. 'Why all this bitterness, Bordelli?'

'No bitterness at all, sir, on the contrary. As I said, I've come here to thank you. I would much rather have someone like Badalamenti dead than in jail. And if you want to know how I really feel, I think whoever killed him should be given some sort of medal of honour by the state.'

'Be careful what you say, Inspector. Don't forget you're talking to a judge.'

'In the end it was you, sir, who decided Badalamenti's fate. One could almost say that it was you who killed him.'

The judge screwed up his mouth, looking hysterical.

'What the hell are you saying?' he said, squirming in his chair.

'I'm saying that if you'd locked the prick up in jail—'

'Lower your voice.'

'Let me finish . . . If you'd locked that giant prick up, he would still be alive today. Maybe forced by his cellmates to eat his own balls for breakfast, but alive, at no small daily cost to honest, taxpaying citizens. So, in short, with this murder, everybody wins, even the state. And it's all thanks to you,' Bordelli concluded. He was really starting to have fun. This was why he'd gone to see the rat in the first place, to lure him into the trap, step by little step.

The judge adjusted his glasses with his forefinger, with the expression of someone making a great effort to tolerate another's unacceptable behaviour.

'I must confess that I really don't like policemen of your ilk one bit, Inspector Bordelli,' he said, staring at him.

'Coming from you, that makes me very happy,' said the inspector, relaxed.

Ginzillo pretended not to understand the subject of the discussion. He was far more interested in what he still hadn't grasped. He felt uneasy and tried to assume an air of authority.

'My dear Inspector, it seems to me you're in need of a little lesson.'

'I'm all ears, sir.'

'Until you show me some evidence to the contrary, Signor Badalamenti, whether dead or alive, is an honest citizen like everyone else, is that clear? Perhaps you should review the police manual,' said Ginzillo, satisfied with his own irony.

Bordelli could barely suppress a smile. Since first entering that office he'd been waiting for just such a statement, and he wanted to enjoy the scene while it lasted. Allowing a dramatic pause, but not too long, he finally beamed, one of those smiles that Ginzillo didn't like at all.

'Actually I came just to tell you that yesterday I went to Badalamenti's apartment and found what I was looking for.'

'Namely?' asked the judge, a little anxious.

'Namely . . . Under a tile in the living room, I found his secret cache.'

'His secret cache?' asked the judge, exposing his gums.

The inspector pulled from his pocket the pistol he'd found at Badalamenti's and set it down on the desk. Ginzillo looked at it as though someone had laid a dog turd down in front of him.

'The gun is unregistered. That alone would be enough to send him to jail,' said Bordelli. Then he pulled out an envelope, extracted a little stack of promissory notes, and slid these under the judge's nose. Ginzillo withdrew his hands and looked at them without touching them. Bordelli smiled.

'It's not shit, sir. They're promissory notes,' he said.

The judge's mouth tightened as he swallowed yet another obscenity by the arrogant inspector.

'I can see for myself that they're promissory notes. So what?' he said, his voice quavering a little. Bordelli pulled out a cigarette but didn't light it.

'There's also a complete list of the names and amounts lent out, with the interest and due dates. It doesn't take much to realise that with that sort of arrangement you could ruin even Fiat.'

'Jesus . . .'

'And that's not all. I also found a number of wedding rings that had been pawned, highly incriminating sales agreements and other interesting tidbits, such as, for example—'

'Have you got it all here with you?' Ginzillo interrupted him, stiff in his chair.

'Let me finish. Signor Totuccio Badalamenti was also blackmailing a woman with some compromising photographs and was about to steal her house . . .'

Ginzillo sat up straight and let his gaze wander about the room for a moment, like a man about to make a big decision.

'I'll talk to Cangiani straight away and order the immediate sequestration of all of Badalamenti's possessions,' he said with a certain severity. He was an inflexible judge.

'Before or after Epiphany?' Bordelli asked.[9]

'What? I'll do it this very day.'

'Don't forget the Porsche, which is parked in Piazza del Carmine,' said the inspector, dropping the golden key chain in front of him.

'Well, Inspector, you've done an excellent job. Go immediately upstairs to Barzi's office and turn everything over to him for cataloguing,' said the judge, in the tone of someone very anxious to get the wheels of justice turning.

Bordelli shook his head. 'You can take the pistol, but I'm keeping the rest myself,' he said.

'That's not legal,' said Ginzillo.

'I know.'

'All these things need to be registered, you know that, Inspector.'

Bordelli gathered up the promissory notes, put them back in their envelope, and slipped it in his jacket pocket. He felt quite untroubled.

'Since I want to go and talk to them anyway, I'll return the IOUs personally to the people that signed them. We can call it my Christmas present to them,' he said.

The judge looked at him with as much severity as his rat-face could muster. 'If these notes aren't deposited, they're as good as waste paper, Mr Bordelli, and the courts are certainly not going to demand that the sums in question be paid to a dead usurer. Surely you can see that your Zorroesque gesture is absurd and pointless.'

'You're thinking only in terms of the law and forgetting the *spiritual* side of this.'

'The *spiritual* side?' said Ginzillo, wrinkling his nose.

'Whoever signs such notes to a usurer usually has a great many ball-aches, sir . . . So I've decided to do a charitable deed.'

'How noble of you,' said the judge.

'I've become a boy scout and must do at least one good deed a day.'

'How very kind of you . . . Unfortunately normal legal procedure dictates that in cases such as this—'

'I've already decided,' Bordelli interrupted him, politely but decisively.

Ginzillo heaved a long sigh, like a highly irritated man of power. Then he pointed at the inspector and said: 'All right, then, I'll discuss it with Dr Cangiani, and, you'll see—'

'Don't keep putting spanners in my works, sir. I wouldn't want the assistant prosecutor or the press to know about that famous warrant you refused to give me last February. Know what I mean?'

The judge leaned forward and thrust a pen brusquely back in its holder, a sort of pewter sugar bowl.

'What's that got to do with anything?'

'I'll explain. I could have arrested Badalamenti almost a year ago, but you defended him, saying he had friends among the city's politicians and important families . . . Maybe it's better if Prosecutor Cangiani doesn't know this. You know how wicked journalists can be. And if I say I'm going to give these promissory notes back to those who signed them, I assure you I will do it.'

The judge listened to him with one hand hooked behind his neck. There was contempt in his eyes.

'Just this one time, Bordelli . . . because it's you,' he said. And he even managed a sort of smile, but only with his mouth.

The inspector stood up. 'Have these accounts frozen as quickly as possible,' he said, leaving Badalamenti's chequebooks on his desk.

'Obviously,' said Ginzillo.

'I'll leave you to your work, sir,' the inspector said, standing up, but the judge still wanted to talk.

'Don't forget that we are both in the same boat, Inspector, and we pursue the same goals.'

'That might be worth clarifying.'

They looked each other hard in the eye for a few seconds, with neither of them managing to say what he had on the tip of his tongue.

'What do you intend to do about the murder?' the judge asked, to change the subject.

'Find the killer, naturally.'

'So then it's already in the bag, I trust,' said Ginzillo, who at this point only wanted the case to be concluded quickly, no matter how, shut up inside a folder and buried in the dust of an archive.

Exiting the Palazzo di Giustizia, the inspector crossed Piazza San Firenze and took the Via del Proconsolo to return to police headquarters. He'd left his Beetle in the courtyard and gone out on foot. The rain had stopped during the night. It was rather cold outside, but the air had turned drier. There was still a chance it might snow.

Although it was barely ten o'clock, the streets were already thronged with people and cars had trouble moving. Tourist carriages had also entered the mix, and every so often one got a good whiff of fresh horse manure. The same festoons and lights as last year hung between the buildings. Shop windows were full of cotton tufts and flashing little lights of all colours. The shopkeepers were making a fortune.

He turned down Via Cavour. In the distance he heard the plaintive drone of a *zampogna* bagpipe, one of the saddest sounds in the world. He remembered what Christmas was like when he was a child: no cars, no flashing lights, no noise . . . other than the sound of the horses' hooves and the lament of the *zampogne* that seemed to rise up from the bowels of the earth. An atmosphere of magic seemed to fill the air at home and follow him all the way under the covers.

He chucked his cigarette and tried to think of a present for Rosa. He slowed his pace so he could look in some shop windows, sometimes stopping, then deciding against whatever it was. He couldn't make up his mind.

When he reached the end of Via degli Arazzieri, he turned down Via San Gallo and went into the courtyard of the police station. He nodded to Taddei, who was on duty in the guard's booth at the entrance, and the policeman returned his greeting with a vaguely military salute, bringing a fat hand to his bullish head.

Entering his office, he scanned his desk for Diotivede's report on Badalamenti, but it wasn't there. He rang him at the lab, and the doctor said he'd had to interrupt his work for an urgent post-mortem and hadn't finished.

'Could you give me a ring when you're done?' Bordelli asked.

'I'll send the report to your office.'

'I'd rather come there.'

'I'll be working this Sunday. Try coming by in the afternoon, if you feel like it.'

'I'll think about it . . . Have you decided about Christmas dinner?' Bordelli asked.

'We'll talk about it when you come.'

'All right.'

They said goodbye and the inspector went and opened the window, to let in a little air. A cold gust of wind blew in, smelling of snow. The sky was a uniform slab of a colour between white and grey, but normally it only snowed in the hills around the city.

A second later Mugnai knocked on the door and told Bordelli that the commissioner was looking for him and had asked for him to come to his office as soon as possible. The inspector smiled. He had expected this, after his conversation with Judge Ginzillo, but not quite so soon.

'Mugnai, do you know whether anyone has managed to talk to Badalamenti's next of kin?'

'I did myself, Inspector,' said Mugnai, seeming proud of the fact.

'Who'd you talk to?'

'His mother. She started crying and screaming like a madwoman and saying that her son was a saint. It was a pretty painful scene, sir.'

'Did you tell her we can't release the body just yet?'

'I did, but she kept on yelling and I don't know if she heard me.'

'Send a telegram to the local police.'

'Of course, Inspector . . . How's Piras doing?'

'Much better. You'll see, he'll be back at work in a few weeks.'

'Please give him my best.'

Mugnai look his leave and left the room with his typical duck waddle. To get it over with, Bordelli immediately went upstairs to see the commissioner. He knocked and went in. Inzipone seemed fairly upset.

'At last! Do you know who called me, Bordelli? Judge Ginzillo,' said the commissioner, standing up.

'To wish you a happy Christmas?'

'Spare me the wit, Bordelli . . . Don't you ever realise that you take things too far?'

'Not this time – at least, I didn't think so.'

Inzipone shook his head.

'Threatening a judge . . . Have you gone mad?'

'Ginzillo is too touchy.'

'You make life difficult for me, Bordelli, and I really don't need that right now. And what's this business about the promissory notes?'

'I'm going to give them back to their rightful owners. It'll be a sort of Christmas present to them.'

Inzipone sighed, seeming already resigned.

'You are well aware, Bordelli, that the law calls for different procedures,' he said without conviction.

'Yes, I know, but I think what I've decided to do is better.'

The commissioner sighed and ran a hand over his face. He seemed tired.

'I'll look the other way this time, but it will be the last,' he said. Deep down he seemed happy with the decision. But, just so as not to give Bordelli too much satisfaction, he stared long and hard at him, purposely donning the expression of the man of authority struggling to tolerate yet another breach of discipline.

'That's all I have to say, Inspector,' he said at last, sitting back down. Bordelli had already opened the door when Inzipone called to him again.

'How's our boy Piras doing?' he asked.

'He's recovering.'

'Next time you hear from him, give him my regards and best wishes for the holidays.'

'I certainly shall.'

The inspector closed the door behind him and walked slowly back to his office. Sitting down at his desk, he started turning his swivel chair round on its base: right . . . left . . . right . . . left . . . He was worried . . . If something didn't turn up soon, this murder was likely to end up on the stack of unsolved cases begun by that of poor Wilma Montesi ten years ago. He had to admit that he would rather find out who killed Montesi than catch a loan shark's killer, even if unsolved murders were detrimental to the social order on the whole. They set a bad example and only served to encourage those who hoped, literally, to get away with murder.

Around two o'clock he realised he wasn't very hungry and went out to eat a panino at the bar in Via San Gallo. He never ate at the station's cafeteria. If he didn't at least go out to eat he would feel like a prisoner.

After taking coffee he returned to the office. Lighting his second cigarette, he continued thinking distractedly about Badalamenti. Whoever killed him had to have had a great deal of rage in him to attack him in that fashion. The scissor blades had penetrated deep into the stocky usurer's thick neck, as if they'd been pounded in with a hammer. And Diotivede was almost certain the killer was left-handed. For the moment, that was all they had to go on.

He calmly stubbed out his cigarette in the ashtray and then rang De Marchi, chief of the forensics lab, to find out the results of their search of Badalamenti's flat. De Marchi was precise as usual. He promised straight off that he would send the written report by the end of the day. Bordelli thanked him and asked him to tell him the results straight away. De Marchi said he'd analysed the ashes and butts of a few cigarettes. They were all of the brand 'Muratti Ambassador' with filter, just like the packets that were found scattered about the flat. To all appearances they were the brand the victim smoked. But in the same ashtray, and also on the floor in the study, they had found some ash residue of an Alfa brand cigarette, though they were unable to recover the butts. Perhaps the cigarette had been smoked down to the end, since that brand had no filter. But as far as that went, De Marchi continued, Alfas were a common cigarette. As for the rest, they did find some hair besides the victim's, almost all bleached blond, but not all belonging to the same person. And the three strands of dark hair they found belonged to two different people.

'Obviously they could belong to anyone who set foot in that flat over the last few months,' De Marchi said.

'Fingerprints?'

'Aside from Badalamenti's, we found fingerprints belonging to sixteen different people, with a particularly high concentration in the study. I don't know how useful they'll be. They could have been made by just about anyone, on any day, but I'll have them checked to see if any belong to any previous offenders. As for the scissors, as I've already said, they were cleaned with a handkerchief or cloth . . . Or else the killer was wearing gloves.'

'The result is the same,' said the inspector.

'With all the movies they make these days, even children know you have to wear gloves when you kill someone,' De Marchi said, sighing.

'Anything else?'

'Not much. We picked up some other stuff from Badalamenti's clothes and around the body, but nothing important: a few little bits of tomato, breadcrumbs . . . that sort of thing.'

'And that's all?'

'And that's all, Inspector.'

'Thanks. Please send me the written report as soon as you can.'

'Of course, sir.'

Bordelli hung up and leaned back on the springs of his chair, making it squeak. De Marchi was right to be pessimistic. All those fingerprints were practically useless. Clearly the killer had taken care not to leave any traces about the flat, just as he had been careful with the scissors as well. The other fingerprints could belong to just about anybody. Everyone on the list of debtors had a plausible reason for entering the apartment, and for the moment they were the only hypothetical suspects.

He shook his head. Given the nature of the case, the findings of the forensics lab seemed to lead nowhere. The only element unlike the rest was Marisa, the beautiful girl in the photographs.

It was almost midnight. Piras was playing poker with two friends, and between the three of them they'd already drunk half a bottle of *filu e ferru*.[10] They were at the home of Angelo Nireddu, in front of a warm fire. Angelo lived on a small, steep street near the church and worked as a surveyor for the town of Oristano. The other friend was Ettore Cannas, a muscular, nervous lad who worked as a farmhand. He lived nearby with his parents and a much younger sister, but he also had three older brothers who had gone to live in Italy proper, whom he often spoke of as heroes to emulate.

All three card players had been to Piras's house, along with a few other neighbours, to watch Giorgio Gaber on the telly. When the half-naked dancing girls appeared, Maria looked out of the corner of her eye at Gavino and shook her head while she continued cleaning the vegetables.

After the final evening news report, Pietrino and his two friends had walked to the Nireddus' house. The kitchen was the warmest room. A log of olive wood was burning its last between two rough-hewn stones that served as firedogs. After adding more wood, they'd pulled out the playing cards and a bottle and sat down at the table. Angelo's parents and younger brothers had gone to bed some time before, but they all slept in the other part of the house behind closed doors, so there was no need to whisper.

As they were playing, Angelo started telling an old story his grandfather Pietro had told him a year before he died. It related to events that had taken place in Bauladu just after the war. To play one of their many pranks on the sexton, some lads from town had brought a coffin to the cemetery with someone alive inside. A little while later the sexton had heard some knocking and opened the coffin to see what it was, only to find a living person inside. Without wasting a second, he bashed the man in the head with his shovel a good dozen times, until he seemed truly dead. Then he went to the mayor and said to him: 'Listen, when you bring me a dead person, he'd better be dead, because today you brought me a live one and I had to kill him.' Since that day nobody had ever played any more tricks on the sexton.

They carried on chatting of this and that, from women and old tales of revenge to town gossip and bizarre stories like the one about the sexton. And they ended up talking about the bandits of Orgosolo. Ettore immediately got worked up. He was a bit thick-tongued and had a square head that hardly moved when he spoke.

'Mesina's right.[11] And anyway, he never kills anyone. Those pricks in Rome made us a thousand promises and then forgot about us. In Italy there's money for everyone, and here we're all broke . . .'

'Play,' said Angelo.

'There's poverty everywhere, Ettore, even if they don't show it to you on the telly,' said Piras.

'But Mesina's right, bloody hell!' Ettore retorted. Piras didn't feel up to contradicting him.

'Play,' said Angelo.

'How's Cadeddu doing?' Piras asked, to change the subject.

'He's found himself a wife up in Milan,' said Angelo.

'Have you seen her?'

'Only in a photo. Pretty girl, but she's blonde,' said Ettore, screwing up his mouth.

'You got something against blondes?' asked Piras, whose girlfriend Sonia was a blonde Sicilian.

'When you look at 'em close up it's like they got no blood,' said Ettore.

'You won't find their blood in their hair . . .'

'Bravo, Pietrino, now we know your girlfriend's blonde too,' said Angelo, sniggering, then throwing two aces down on the table.

'That beats me,' said Ettore, putting his cards back in the deck.

'Three eights,' said Piras, laying his cards down and picking up the kitty.

'So she's a blonde . . .' Ettore persisted, not caring that he'd lost the hand. He was the oldest of the three and had arms as big as tree trunks.

'And what makes you think I have a girlfriend?' asked Piras, feigning indifference.

'We could tell by your face,' said Ettore.

'Well, I haven't got one,' Piras quipped, shuffling the cards.

'Oh, go on, everybody in town knows you do,' said Angelo.

'Everybody but me,' said Piras.

'Is she Florentine?' asked Ettore.

'Hey, what's with you guys? Are you working for my mother or something?' said Piras, and as he was dealing the cards he couldn't suppress a smile.

'Beware of those city girls, they'll cut you open like a sheep and eat your heart out,' said Ettore, staring at him. His eyes were as black as wet stones.

'Just cut the crap and play,' said Piras, looking at the cards in his hand. Three kings, an ace and a nine. The cards were treating him well that evening, but remembering the famous dictum about luck at cards, he wasn't terribly pleased. Who knew what Sonia was doing at that moment, down in Palermo.

Ettore and Angelo kept needling him about his mysterious girlfriend but were unable to extract any information. They played another two or three hands, and the luck remained with

Piras, who threw his cards down in the end and stretched in his chair. He'd won about eighteen hundred lire.

'I'm going to bed,' he said.

'The last drop,' said Ettore, already filling their glasses. He was the one who had to get up at the crack of dawn, but it had never bothered him much to go without sleep.

'What do you say we all go to Sassari on the twenty-sixth?' said Angelo.

'What for?' asked Ettore.

'To look for girls.'

'I've already got a girlfriend,' said Ettore, shrugging. She was a twenty-year-old from Santu Lussurgiu whom he saw on Saturdays and Sundays.

'Well, then Pietrino and I'll go,' said Angelo, looking at Piras.

'I don't go looking for girls while I'm hobbling on crutches,' said Piras.

'Why not? Maybe they'll feel sorry for you.'

'Exactly,' said Piras. He downed his glass and stood up, leaning on his crutches.

'Want some company?' asked Ettore, who lived right next door and had only to cross the courtyard to go home. Piras, on the other hand, lived practically on the other side of town.

'Only if you carry me piggy-back,' said Piras, moving his tired upper body. He'd sat for too long and his back hurt.

'If you want I could drive you home,' said Ettore, standing up. He'd just bought a new Fiat 500, the kind whose doors opened the right way. Coral red, almost like a Ferrari. He kept it in a stable his father no longer used.

'Thanks, Tore, but I think I'll hoof it,' said Piras, heading for the door. After all, he lived only about half a mile away, and every opportunity to use his legs was beneficial.

The three went out into the street. After all the grappa, it was nice to feel the cold air on their faces. The sky was clear, the moon on the horizon. Piras heaved a big sigh.

'Noschese's going to be on TV tomorrow,' he said.

His friends gestured as if to say they'd be there.

'*A si bìere,*'[12] said Piras, starting on his way down the sloping street.

'*A si bìere,*' replied Ettore and Angelo, almost in chorus.

Taking care not to slip on the damp cobblestones, Piras arrived at Corso Italia, the village's high street. There were few street lamps in town, and some were extinguished. Beyond the cones of light lay the darkness of night. When it got dark there, it got really dark, not like in Florence. The sky was clear, and the moon in its first quarter was rising right in front of him. After a few minutes' walking, he saw the silhouette of his house loom ahead, low and broad. Attached to one side of it was the Urtises' house, whose façade was entirely covered with seashells large and small, the work of their great-grandfather Efisio at the time of the unification of Italy.

He heard some dogs barking in their kennels behind the stables. He could recognise each by the way it bayed. Zia Bona's German shepherd let out a long howl at the moon that sounded like an amorous lament. Piras stopped to listen, feeling chills at the back of his neck as when he was a child. The moment the dog stopped, a chorus of even more sorrowful wails started up, and it seemed it would never end. These were the feral dogs of Montiferru, which every so often came down to the plain.

Bordelli crushed his last cigarette butt in the ashtray, switched off the light and turned on to his side. He wanted to sleep but couldn't stop thinking. He'd noticed that during the day he'd paid more attention to the women on the street than usual, feeling a mild but persistent desire for all of them, which was like saying for none. Perhaps he was finally breaking free of the beautiful Milena's spell. That afternoon, in Via San Gallo, he'd seen a very fine woman with black hair in an off-white overcoat that she wore wrapped around her like a mummy's shroud, and as if in jest, he fantasised about her a little. It was a game he knew well and had played since early adolescence, but for some time now he'd found it boring. By this point in life, he felt as if he knew certain things too well and could no longer take dreams seriously. It was all much more thrilling before, when he was young and still hoped that something might change his life from one day to the next. Now he no longer believed it, and that was perhaps another reason why he lately felt the full weight of his fifty-five years. At times he imagined himself facing death alone, and at moments he even liked the idea. There was, of course, a bit of self-pity in this, and he was well aware of it. On the other hand, at the end of Westerns the hero always went away alone, without ever turning back, and that always made one hell of an impression. Usually there was a woman there crying for him, who would remember him for the rest of her life . . . But the cowboy always left anyway, into the unknown, on his white horse, gaze impassive . . .

He buried his face in the pillow, trying to sleep, but his brain really had no intention of turning itself off that night. Perhaps it was because of the change of season or the moon. Sleep seemed like a mirage.

In his somnolence his thoughts slowly drifted into remote images from when his mother and father were still young . . . He saw himself as a little boy again, with a great big head, dirty knees and scrapes on his toes. It seemed like a century ago. He didn't like the thought of growing old. For some time now he had been constantly checking the wrinkles on his face in the mirror. His brain still functioned well, for the time being; it was his skin that was deserting him. Turning on to his other side, he kept still in the hope of falling asleep, but as soon as he started to drift off, he would suddenly wake up as if someone had knocked at the door. In the end he turned the light back on and tried to read, but he only kept reading the same sentence over and over without understanding a thing. He threw the newspaper on to the carpet and got up. He'd brought a bottle of Badalamenti's cognac home with him, and he went into the kitchen to get it. He poured himself a glass, lit his very last cigarette of the day and smoked it while pacing back and forth.

The alarm clock beside his bed read 4 a.m. He looked distractedly at the spines of his books, the shirts hanging one on top of the other on a clothes hanger, a stack of old newspapers on the chair. He stopped in front of the two framed French prints that for years had hung in the entrance of the house in Via Volta, where he was born. They were hunting scenes of faithful dogs and dead pheasants. Not great art, but Bordelli was fond of them. All he sought in them was a taste of the past.

He put out the cigarette butt and went back to bed. He left the light on and, instead of lying down, sat leaning back against the headboard. He started staring at the wall in front of him, then slapped himself on the head. It was a method he'd learned during the war from Poti on a very silent night. 'When you can't sleep, sit up in bed with the light on, as if you wanted to stay awake, and you'll see, in a little while your eyes will shut all by themselves.' It usually worked, but this time, what came to him was not sleep but memories . . . Of the war, same as always . . . It had left a deep furrow in his brain, a sort of boundary between before and after . . . One morning in '44 he'd broken away from a patrol in the Umbrian countryside with three of his men, all jailbirds. Day was breaking. Marshal Badoglio's San Marco regiment was advancing ahead of the main body of the Allied forces, demining the roads and fields and signalling the positions of the German divisions to the rear lines. That morning Bordelli and his men were walking with their heads down through a densely wooded area. They knew the Germans were very close, but they had no idea how close. After crossing a stream they started climbing a slope, eyes wide open and breathing softly. When they reached the top, the terrain evened out, and there before them, enveloped in a light fog, was a German camp. Dragging themselves along the ground with their elbows, they approached the first tent. There was a rent in the fabric. Looking inside, they saw at least fifteen bare-chested German soldiers shaving. They were laughing heartily, splashing one another and trading insults. There was a very young soldier with blue eyes and a delicate face whose braces were unhooked so that his trousers were sliding down his hips. The others were whistling at him and slapping his bottom, calling him 'Fräulein' and laughing. Bordelli released the safety catch on his machine gun, and the other three did the same. Then they stuck the barrels through the rent in the tent, ready to open fire. They stayed that way for at least a minute. Bordelli looked at the uniforms hanging from hooks and pondered. The other three were only waiting for their commander to decide to begin the festivities. They could have slaughtered them all in a few seconds and raced back down the slope, protected by the woods. No one would even have seen them. But suddenly Bordelli put the safety back on and signalled to the others to do the same. As they went back down the slope, all four of them realised they were drenched in sweat and exhausted from the tension. They walked briskly, in silence. When they were far enough away, Sgatti pulled up alongside Bordelli and tapped him on the elbow.

'What do you think, Commander, were we right not to open fire?' he asked.

Bordelli didn't answer but just kept on walking. His head was fuming. The next day those same Nazis might be lining civilians up against the wall and shooting newborns and raping every woman under fifty. And maybe the blue-eyed lad was the worst of the lot. Bordelli was worried that sooner or later he might regret not having shot them all, but at that moment he was satisfied with his decision. He hadn't felt like killing men with lathered-up faces, even if they were Nazis. He knew well that the SS, in their place, would have committed a massacre without thinking twice, but wasn't this very difference the reason they were fighting them to the death?

Maybe some of those Nazis were still alive today and married with children. They would never know how close they had been to dying at the hands of the San Marco regiment.

He emptied his glass, put out the light, lay down and turned on to his side. A few minutes later he was snoring.

18 December

It was Saturday and the sun was shining. Italy was mourning for Tito Schipa,[13] who had died during the night. Giorgio La Pira was continuing his pointless attempts to 'mediate' a solution to the war in Vietnam, as the United States continued to triumph in outer space with its Gemini missions.

Among the many fingerprints taken from the usurer's apartment, De Marchi had found those of two persons with prior convictions for larceny, one now seventy-seven years old, the other eighty-two. Going by what Diotivede had said, this was useless information; they were both too old to kill anyone in that fashion.

Young Marisa still hadn't been located, and by late morning Bordelli was getting impatient to talk to her. Rinaldi and Tapinassi were still carrying on the search. Rinaldi was combing the Identity Cards Office at police headquarters, looking for all girls of about that age who were called Marisa and lived either in Florence or the surrounding province, and checking the photos on the index cards. It was going to take time. Tapinassi, for his part, was making the rounds of the schools. But tomorrow was Sunday, the schools would be closed, and Rinaldi wouldn't be on duty . . . Everything would grind to a halt.

The inspector could easily have had one of Badalamenti's photos published in *La Nazione*, the Florentine daily, but he didn't want the girl to encounter any trouble of any sort before he had a chance to talk to her. His only choice was to wait. They would find her sooner or later.

Every now and then his thoughts turned to Fabiani. He tried

to imagine the moment when he would see him again, but kept feeling embarrassed about it. Putting an unlit cigarette between his lips, he took a few empty drags just to taste the scent of the tobacco, then tossed the cigarette on to the desk. He was making progress. He wanted to get to the point of smoking only four a day, five at the most. He might just pull it off.

He took out the ring that Diotivede had recovered from Badalamenti's stomach and rolled it around between his fingers. It looked pretty expensive. Who knew why the loan shark had swallowed it, or whether it had anything to do with the murder.

In late afternoon he dropped by the archives office, an enormous, poorly lit room, the domain of the giant Porcinai. Stacks full of bulging files rose up to the ceiling in the penumbra. Porcinai's lamp illuminated only the top of his desk, which was covered with papers and folders. It was always too hot in there, and the smell of old dust dried one's throat. It was a mystery how Porcinai managed to live there year round without getting sick. Maybe it was all the fat on his body that protected him. He was the largest human being Bordelli had ever seen.

The archivist was typing, and the movements this required made the fat on his neck tremble. He was a very fast typist.

'Hello, handsome, did you prepare those addresses for me?' asked Bordelli.

'I was about to send for Mugnai so he could bring them to you,' said Porcinai, handing him an envelope. He and Bordelli were about the same age and on familiar terms. Porcinai was so fat that they'd had to have a chair made to measure for him, one that he could fit into and that could also bear his weight. His demeanour was always serious. His completely shaven head was always slowly bobbing. And he never stood up. Bordelli had very rarely seen him walk. Whenever Porcinai had to find something in the stacks, he would call a younger policeman and give him instructions.

Bordelli opened the envelope and started reading. It was the typewritten list of Badalamenti's debtors, with the address and birth date of each.

'Did you find them all?' he asked.

'Yep.'

Bordelli leaned against the wall and suppressed a yawn.

'Did you count them?' he asked.

'Look on the back.'

Bordelli turned the page and read: *Men: nineteen. Women: twenty-seven. Total: forty-six.* With Fabiani and Rosaria Beltempo, that made forty-eight.

'How's Piras doing?' asked Porcinai.

'Getting better by the day.'

'Give him my regards.'

'What are you doing for Christmas?'

'The usual dinner with the usual relations. We sit down at the table at seven p.m. and at midnight we exchange presents. How about you?'

'I don't know yet,' Bordelli said curtly, continuing to study the sheet of paper in his hand.

Porcinai spent his life in the dusty heat of the archives, and always kept a handkerchief near by to mop his brow. And he always wore the same white sleeveless T-shirt with red horizontal stripes. Bordelli had never had the heart to tell him that white and horizontal stripes make one look fatter.

'Cigarette?' he asked, offering him one.

'No, thanks, I've never had any interest in smoking,' said Porcinai, raising a hand.

'Sorry, I always forget.'

'I think if I ever started I would prefer cigars.' Porcinai then reached into a drawer, took out a funnel of greaseproof paper and shoved his fingers into it.

'Would you like an olive?' he asked. 'They're pitted and stuffed.'

'Another time, Porcinai. I've still got the taste of coffee in my mouth.'

Porcinai grabbed a handful and put the cornet back in the drawer. Then he put all the olives into his mouth at once and wiped his hands on his trousers. The inspector put the list of addresses in his jacket pocket.

'Porcinai, what sort of Christmas present would you give to a woman who is no longer young but still pure of heart?'

'Is she your girlfriend?' asked the archivist with his mouth full.

'Just a friend.'

'Does it have to be something special?'

'I just want to make her happy.'

Porcinai picked a piece of olive skin from between his teeth.

'Give her something strange. Women like gifts that are strange,' he said.

Bordelli brought his hand to his chin.

'What exactly do you mean by strange?' he said.

'Something nobody else would give her . . . I don't know, sing her a song, make a rabbit appear out of your hat.'

'I get it,' said Bordelli.

'Or write her a poem.'

'Thanks, you've been a great help.'

Suddenly the door opened and Rabozzi appeared with his chained-up-dog face. His shoulders were as broad as a door.

'Hey, look who we have here,' he said. 'Ciao, Bordelli.'

'*Ciao, caro.*'

'I hear you've been working on a nice little murder.'

'Great fun.'

'Getting anywhere?'

'I'm still at square one. Diotivede's still got the body.'

'I've been after a bloke who amuses himself scaring old ladies, and he's even managed to hurt a couple of old maids. The guy's really getting on my nerves.'

'Knowing you, you'll probably end up dressing up as an old lady,' said Bordelli.

Rabozzi chuckled.

'I just might, you never know,' he said.

Porcinai raised a finger to say something. 'I did that search for you, Rabozzi . . .'

'You're looking thinner, Porcinai! Are you eating enough?'

Rabozzi then put a hand on the back of Porcinai's neck and

tried to rock him in his chair, without success. Porcinai didn't like Rabozzi's manner, but let it pass and continued looking for that paper for him.

'It was right here . . .' he said, rummaging through the papers on his desk.

Rabozzi laughed and cuffed his head.

'You probably used it to wrap some sausage, eh?'

19 December

The following morning Bordelli opened his eyes around nine. He snorted and remained in bed, staring at the ceiling. It was Sunday. He would have liked to fall back asleep and not wake up until the next morning. Getting out of bed, he went and put the coffee on the stove. He wanted the day to go by quickly, so it would soon be Monday and he could get back to work on the murder. He was anxious to talk to the girl in the photographs.

The best plan he could come up with was to go out, get in the Beetle and drive to Grassina, where he could pick up the Chiantigiana. He drove slowly, looking distractedly at the hillsides dotted with houses and castles. He'd always liked this road. The sun was out, but the countryside had the dead colours of winter. He liked them too, however. When he was at university, he'd gone several times to Siena on his bicycle, to let his brain unwind before or after an exam.

He passed the Villa l'Ugolino and stopped at the inn at La Martellina, where he ordered a panino with prosciutto. Then he got back in his car and took the road for Impruneta. Every so often a Bianchina or station wagon passed in the other direction. He drove slowly while eating the panino, with the window half open. The air was nice, the bread too. The prosciutto was a masterpiece. He was in a place where he would have liked to spend the last years of his life.

When he got to Impruneta, there was a small market in the church square. He parked the car in front of the town hall and started making his way through the stands of vegetables and cheeses, asking the peasants whether they knew of a farmstead for sale in the area. They all said he should go and talk to the barber or, better yet, the *treccone*, who would know – and if he didn't, then nobody would. Bordelli had once seen a *treccone* as a little boy, when he'd gone to Greve with his father to buy olive oil from a farmer. The *treccone* was a chap who went from house to house on a bicycle, asking people whether they had a ladder in need of repair, a chair in need of a new seat, or a broken tap, things of that sort. But he would also trade things. He would get eggs from the peasants and sell them in town to regular clients, or else swap a pair of boots or a hoe for a chicken, which he might then pass on to someone else for a couple of litres of olive oil or something else. He chatted with everyone and always knew when there was something to be sold or bought.

'Where can I find him?' Bordelli asked a short, squat peasant.

'When there's a market he's always around. He's tall and skinny, with a face that looks like it got crushed in a slamming door.'

Bordelli continued to circulate through the stands, still looking around, but saw no one who fitted that description. While he was at it, he bought some vegetables, a piece of aged pecorino, and some thick slices of *finocchiona*, the Tuscan salame flavoured with fennel seeds, and went and put it all in the car.

He kept on looking around, but there was still no sign of the *treccone*. At last he decided to try the barber at the far end of the piazza. He found him sitting on a bench, leafing through *La Domenica del Corriere*. His hair was as red as an Irishman's.

'There might be a house at Terre Bianche, a nice big one,' he said.

'What you mean, there *might* be?'

'Well, it's there all right, but nobody wants it.'

'Why not?' Bordelli asked, curious.

The barber leaned forward, as if to confide a secret. 'People say that at night . . .'

'Ghosts?'

'Just one, a woman,' the barber explained.

'Is there any land?'

'Five hectares, mixed.'

'Mixed?'

'Olives and vineyards, all in the sun. But it needs some work, 'cause nobody's done anything for a while.'

The former owner, an old peasant, was dead, and his children had all moved to the city. Bordelli had the barber tell him how to find the house, then thanked him and left. As he was heading back to his car, he saw the *treccone* coming out of a bar. It couldn't have been anyone else. Tall, skinny as a rail, with a thin, pointy face. He went up to the man, introduced himself, and asked whether he knew of any houses for sale in the area. The *treccone* said they were practically giving away a beautiful farmstead at Terre Bianche, with a barn and five hectares of land. It was being sold with all its furniture and everything else.

'If you're interested, they're even leaving the fodder-cutter for rabbits,' he said. His breath stank of wine.

'Isn't that the house with a ghost in it?' Bordelli asked. It had to be the same house the barber had been talking about.

'Nah, c'mon, what ghost? It's the deal of a lifetime. If I had the money I'd buy it myself.'

'How much do they want?'

'That I can't tell you, but I know it's a great deal. Old man Antero is dead and the kids don't want to hear any more about pigsties and chickenshit.'

'Yeah, the barber told me they left.'

'All five of 'em went down to Florence to live some time ago, and the owner decided to sell everything. What's he gonna do, stay behind in the country? The man owns a brickworks and has a villa down in San Casciano that's as big as a castle.'

'Thanks. I think I'll go and have a look at the house.'

'Take that road over there downhill, and you'll see that it starts to go up again. Just when it starts to descend again, there's a path on the left . . .'

'Thanks, the barber's already explained it to me.'

The *treccone* raised a hand by way of goodbye and went off in the direction of the vendors' stands. The inspector got back into the Beetle, took the same road he'd come in by, and shortly thereafter he noticed a small dirt road on the left. That had to be it. He turned left and advanced a few hundred yards, and when he came out of the woods he began to slow down. The barber had said the house was big and white, with three tall, beautiful cypresses behind it. He saw it from afar and began to draw near. He was expecting a farmhouse in a state of disrepair, whereas this looked like a fine, solid house with the roof and windows in good condition. To one side there was a sort of garden overgrown with weeds. Both the barber and the *treccone* had said that it was uninhabited, but on the brick pavement in the courtyard there was a Fiat 600 Multipla.

He parked beside it and got out. It was a lovely spot, with an open view of the hills. He walked around a bit, and when he returned, he saw a fat man in jacket and tie standing next to his Beetle.

'Good morning,' he said in a loud voice, going up to the man.

'Hello,' the man said. He was tall and massive but had a high voice. His huge hands stuck out from the jacket's sleeves and hung down almost as far as his knees.

'I'm sorry, the *treccone* told me this house was for sale,' Bordelli said, stopping in front of the man.

'It's true.'

'Could I have a look inside?'

'It's not mine, it's the landlord's,' the man said, looking at Bordelli as if he couldn't wait to be rid of him.

'Where can I find him?'

'He lives in San Casciano, but his mother lives in Impruneta, just above the bar del Piro.'

'How big is the house?'

'Fifteen rooms, plus the sheds and the barn.'

'How much do they want for it?'

'Eighteen million lire for everything, including the land and all the furniture,' said the man, still staring at him without the slightest interest.

'Thanks,' said Bordelli.

He looked one more time at the house's enormous façade, then got in his Beetle and drove off. Eighteen million wasn't really so much for a fortress like that. His flat in San Frediano was worth more or less the same amount. He could sell it and start a new life. But the farmhouse was really too big for him. He had to keep looking.

Back on the main road, he turned left at one point, to go by way of Falciani. There was still half of Sunday left to kill, and when he got to Tavarnuzze he decided to stop at Careggi, where the forensic medicine lab was.

'Are you examining the urine of Lorenzo the Magnificent?' Bordelli asked, going into the lab and seeing Diotivede with a test tube in his hand, looking at it against the light. Though it was Sunday, both of them often paid no mind to the fact.

'To each his own,' the doctor said caustically. He hardly ever laughed. At best his lips curled a little when he was about to say something naughty.

'I went to see Baragli, he sends you his greetings.'

'How's he doing?'

'He's not long for this world . . .'

'One of these days I'll go and see him,' the doctor muttered. He knew Baragli and had always admired him.

They both remained silent for a few moments, as if embarrassed by the sergeant's imminent death. The inspector looked at what Diotivede was doing but didn't understand a thing.

'Did you do Badalamenti?' he asked.

'I said this afternoon.'

'You know I'm not very patient.'

'At any rate, I've finished,' the doctor said.

'You see? I was right to drop by.'

'My first scribbles are over there.'

'May I?'

'If you can manage to make anything out . . .'

'Just a quick look.'

The inspector picked up a small handwritten piece of paper with a number of dark splotches on it. By now he could find his way through Diotivede's notes as surely as an augur through the entrails of a bird. Aside from the time of death and things already said, they listed specific scientific details on the cuts and perforations of tissue. By studying the angle of the cut and other minutiae, it was surmised that the killer was about six feet tall, rather strong, and left-handed. And quite likely a man. The blow had been dealt to Badalamenti from behind, and the point of the scissors had slid between two vertebrae, shattering one of them. Like at a bullfight, Bordelli thought. Within seconds the victim was dead. The traces of adrenalin in Badalamenti's blood might bear witness to great anger, but not to the terror of death. In short, he hadn't been aware of what was happening right behind him.

Bordelli sighed and put the stained paper back in its place. It wasn't much, but it was better than nothing. Diotivede was busy smearing something on a slide for the microscope. Bordelli drew near.

'Forgive me for asking . . . but are you absolutely sure the killer was left-handed?' he asked, defying the pathologist's sensitivity.

'Don't you ever get tired of asking me if I'm sure?' the doctor said.

'Don't take offence. I only want you to explain to me how you arrive at such a conclusion, so I can learn.'

The doctor looked back into the microscope's eyepiece.

'I'm a hundred and ten per cent certain. First of all, the inside cutting edge of the blades goes from left to right,' he said in the tone of someone explaining something very simple to a complete idiot.

'But couldn't he have done it like this?' asked Bordelli, and he raised his right hand over his left shoulder, pretending to have a knife in his hand, and cut the air from left to right. Diotivede observed his gesture without interrupting his work.

'No,' he said.

'Why not?' asked Bordelli. The doctor sighed and came away from the microscope.

'That's impossible for three reasons. First: a right-handed person striking in that fashion will generate much less force and will be considerably more hampered and therefore less precise. Second: he will block his field of vision with his arm. Third: that sort of movement isn't instinctive, and at certain moments instinct is of paramount importance. And there is even, if you will, a fourth reason.'

'And that would be?'

'That never in all my life have I seen anything of the sort,' the doctor concluded.

'So, in short, you have no doubt.'

'Tell you what. If you discover that the killer was not left-handed, I'll retire immediately.'

'Say no more, you've convinced me . . . the killer is left-handed.'

'I'm ever so grateful.'

Diotivede leaned forward again and looked into the microscope, for another glimpse of the wondrous world of bacteria. He sat there motionless, scowling slightly, and turning the knobs. Bordelli stretched and yawned.

'Have you decided about Christmas?' he asked.

'I think I'll accept your invitation. Who else will be there?'

'I still haven't asked anyone else, but I was thinking of Dante Pedretti and Fabiani . . . And if they let him out in time, Botta might also come, that way he would cook.'

'Sounds good,' said the doctor, still engrossed in ogling his orgies of microorganisms.

'If they won't let him out we can bring home some dishes from Cesare's,' said Bordelli.

'How's Piras doing?' the doctor asked.

'He seems well.'

'The boy was really very lucky.'

'That depends on your point of view . . .'

'Don't always say such banal things,' the doctor said, still turning the little knobs of the microscope.

'You're so kind,' said Bordelli, smiling. All at once Diotivede raised his head from the microscope, looking doubtful.

'I'm sorry, what day is it today?' he asked.

'Sunday.'

'The eighteenth?'

'I think it's the nineteenth,' the inspector said. 'And I believe I heard tell that they're casting the second ballot today in France. Who do you think will win?'

'It's already the nineteenth? I could have sworn it was the eighteenth,' said the doctor, still perplexed. Bordelli had picked up a pair of scissors from the table and was fiddling with them.

'Eighteenth, nineteenth, twentieth, what difference does it make, Diotivede? Whatever day it is, you're always in here sticking your nose in the bellies of the dead.'

'Is that a sin?' Diotivede asked without looking at him.

'Perish the thought,' the inspector said, raising his hands. The doctor ignored him and started writing something on a sheet of paper. He then opened a cylindrical glass receptacle and started scraping a yellowish goo from the bottom with a thin iron rod. Returning to the microscope, he spread some of the slop on to another slide. Bordelli couldn't stop yawning. He really hadn't been sleeping very well and always woke up feeling tired.

'What would you like to eat for Christmas?' he asked. Diotivede switched slides and leaned over the microscope again.

'I would love some French onion soup. I've been wanting some for quite a while,' he said.

'For Christmas?'

'What's wrong with that?'

'Well, if Botta's done any time in France, I'm sure he knows how to make it.'

'Then let's hope he has,' said the doctor, looking up.

'We must also hope they let him out before the twenty-fifth . . .'

Piras was eating supper with his parents as they all watched the evening news on television. There was a fire burning, as usual, and the little flames licking the wood were reflected in the ornaments on the Christmas tree.

There was a knock at the door, and Gavino went to open it. It was Pina Setzu, a neighbour. She looked upset. Wrinkling her nose and squinting, she said she was a little worried about her cousin Benigno.

'He was supposed to come by at seven but there's been no sign of him,' she said, arching her eyebrows.

'Maybe he's tired,' said Gavino.

'He always comes every Sunday . . .' she whimpered, huddling up in her shawl.

'Come in,' said Gavino, shuddering from the cold. Pina had been living in the house next door since marrying Giovanni thirty-five years before.

'I just know something has happened, I can feel it,' she said, coming into the kitchen and crossing herself.

'What's happened?' asked Piras. The woman opened her shawl and repeated what she'd just said to Gavino.

'When did you last see him?' Gavino asked.

'He came on Friday to bring us cheese and said he'd come again today . . .'

'You should go and have a look,' said Maria. They all knew that Benigno lived alone in a big, isolated house and didn't have a telephone.

'Maybe he just fell asleep,' said Gavino, pretending not to be worried. He too was beginning to imagine the worst, but he didn't want Pina to get even more upset.

'I'll go,' said Piras, standing up. As he was adjusting the

crutches under his arms, his mother gave him a worried look but said nothing.

'How will you get there?' asked Gavino. Neither they nor the Setzus owned a car or even a motor scooter.

'Ettore's got a Five hundred,' said Piras, taking the torch his father kept over the fireplace. He put on his coat and went out with Pina. It was quite cold outside.

'Is Giovanni coming too?' asked Piras, stopping at the edge of the road.

'He's not feeling well and has a little fever,' Pina said, shaking her head.

They headed towards Ettore's without another word. Pina walked fast, stopping every ten paces or so to let the hobbling Piras catch up. They climbed the street to Ettore's house and knocked at the Cannas family's door. Ettore was having supper with his parents and five-year-old sister, Delia.

'Pina's worried about Benigno,' said Piras, and he explained the situation to everyone. Ettore put the last piece of rabbit in his mouth, took a sip of wine, then grabbed his torch and went to take the car out of the stable. All three got into the tiny vehicle and took the road to Milis. Piras sat in the back. Nobody spoke. After Tramatza they turned on to the Carlo Felice highway in the direction of Oristano. The heating system was blowing very hot air that smelled of exhaust fumes. But it was better than the cold.

Benigno's house was along that same main road, near the ancient Zocchinu quarry, about a mile and a half past Tramatza. It was an isolated farmhouse with half the roof caved in and sat on rocky terrain about fifty yards from the road. Behind it was a sheepfold and a small stall with pigs, which at that time of year must have been nice and fat.

Benigno was forty years old but looked older. He was short, stocky and taciturn. A bear who had never married. He owned several hectares of land around his house, both on this side and beyond the Carlo Felice road. But he also owned other plots of land outside Oristano, which he'd inherited from an uncle many years before. One could almost say he was rich, though he certainly didn't look it.

They turned on to the rocky dirt road that led to Benigno's house, and in the distance they saw a lighted window on the first floor. Everything else was pitch black. Pina crossed herself again, muttering a prayer.

Ettore pulled up in the brick forecourt in front of the house and they all got out. The moon was hidden behind a thick layer of clouds. Piras shone his torch all around. Benigno's Ape, the three-wheeled minitruck, was parked as always under a sheet-metal lean-to that Benigno had built at one corner of the house. At a glance everything looked normal.

'Nino!' Pina cried, knocking at the door. The dog behind the house started barking. He was a sweet little mutt with a heart of gold. At night Benigno kept him on a long chain inside the sheepfold.

'Quiet, Leone!' Pina yelled. The dog gave a yelp and stopped barking. A harsh smell of sheep wafted through the cold air in waves.

Pina called out again, and they waited. But the door didn't open. It seemed completely quiet inside the house. Ettore and Piras yelled Benigno's name three or four times in chorus and banged their fists against the door, but nothing happened. All they heard was the grunting of the pigs behind the house and an occasional bleat and some clanging bells.

'Maybe he went out with a friend,' Ettore muttered without much conviction.

'Nino, open up! It's me!' Pina shouted again, with tears in her eyes. Piras put the torch under his arm and, walking very carefully over the uneven brick surface, went to look at the Ape. He bent down to touch the engine. It was cold. But at that temperature, it wouldn't take long for it to cool, maybe an hour. He turned round and hopped over to the opposite corner of the courtyard.

'Keep calling him, I'm going round the back,' he said.

Proceeding on his crutches, he went behind the house and

heard the flock of half sleeping sheep before he actually saw them. Leone started whimpering again. Piras leaned one shoulder against a picket in the fence, pointed the torch at the dog and went over and patted him on the muzzle. Leone wagged his tail and licked Piras's hand.

'Maybe you know where Benigno is,' Piras said under his breath. He looked around with his torch. The donkey was tied to his post, the sheep were sleeping peacefully, there was nothing that looked strange. He stuck the torch back in his armpit and went on. He could hear Pina still shouting and knocking on the door.

The pigsty was attached to the house. He pulled the bolt open and slipped inside. He peered in over the low wall, shining his torch. The pigs looked at him placidly, sniffing the air. They were enormous and had that strangely astonished look that all pigs have. They must have been stuffed to the gills; there were some leftover apples still on the ground. The pigsty floor was clean. Before sunset Benigno had done what he needed to do; he'd shut the sheep in their fold and fed the pigs. Piras went out, throwing the bolt to lock the door. Hopping back towards the house, he saw the light of Ettore's torch shine in the darkness.

'Find anything, Pietrino?'

'Everything seems normal,' said Piras, going up to him. Behind Ettore he saw Pina's shadow, wrapped in her shawl.

'What should we do?' Ettore asked.

'Let's go inside,' Piras said. He started shining his torch on the windows, one by one, to see which was the most vulnerable. Pina took his arm.

'There's one in front that doesn't close well,' she said, and the three of them went round to the front of the house, where Pina showed them the defective window.

'It's that one,' she said, pointing to a closed shutter. The windowsill was only about three feet off the ground. Pina explained that the shutter was sound, but the fastening on the window didn't work properly.

'Take my torch,' Piras said to Ettore. As Ettore shone the light, Piras inserted his fingers between the slats of the shutter and started yanking violently. But it wouldn't open. Pina was still mumbling prayers. She had always been very close to Benigno, ever since he lost his parents at the age of ten in a terrible accident.

'Let me try,' said Ettore. Passing the torch to Piras, he got a firm grip of the shutter, pulled a couple of times to test its resistance, then started getting serious. After a few fierce tugs, one shutter came off its hinges and very nearly fell on him. But he carried on until he'd removed the whole thing.

'Okay, stand aside,' said Piras. He raised a crutch and thrust the tip of it forcefully at the centre of the window, which opened immediately.

'Ettore, hold these for me,' he said, handing him the crutches and then climbing through the window. Ettore shone the light inside. It was the cheese room. Everything seemed to be in order there too. Piras had Ettore pass the crutches back to him and then stuck the torch under his arm again.

'I'm coming with you,' said Ettore.

'No, you wait there with Pina,' said Piras.

Leaving the room, he found himself at the bottom of the staircase leading to the first floor. He could see the glow of the only light in the house up there, the same light they had seen from outside. He started climbing the stairs. The steps were narrow, and it wasn't easy with the crutches. Halfway up, he called out Benigno's name, but nobody replied. When he got to the top, he walked down the hallway towards the first room, where the light was coming from. The door was wide open.

'Benigno, you here?' he said softly, as if afraid to wake him up. He thought he smelled a pungent odour, similar to gunpowder. When he got to the door, he looked inside.

'Fuck . . .' he said, stopping in the doorway. Benigno was seated in an old upholstered armchair, his right temple blasted off, eyes wide open and seeming to look at the ceiling. A thick stream of blood ran down his neck to his shirt, soaking it. His arms hung at the sides of his body, the hands hidden by the armrests. Piras approached and circled the armchair. There was a pistol in Benigno's right hand, and he bent down instinctively to look at it. If he wasn't mistaken, it was a Beretta 7.65, a regulation navy firearm from the last war. Apparently Benigno Staffa had decided he'd had enough. Standing back up, Piras studied the corpse's now greying face. The blackened tongue was swelling between half-open lips; it looked like a piece of meat ready to be spat out. Extending a finger, he tried to move Benigno's head, but it was stiff. Rigor mortis had already begun. So he must have died at least two or three hours earlier. Thinking of Pina, Piras ran a hand over his face. He couldn't imagine how he would ever tell her. He tried to close Benigno's eyes, pushing the lids down with his fingers, but they reopened at once. He tried again several times and finally succeeded. He looked around to see whether Benigno had left a note, but then remembered that he didn't know how to write. On the floor, beside the chair, was a small radio, turned off, and Benigno's hat, a sort of Basque beret that he'd always had on whenever Piras had seen him. It had almost certainly fallen off when he shot himself. Piras was about to pick it up, but then left it where it was.

He went out of the room and down the stairs, thinking of what he was going to say. He had butterflies in his stomach. He had to make sure that Pina didn't go upstairs. He opened the front door of the house. There were Pina and Ettore. He stopped in the doorway and looked Pina in the eyes, trying to find the right words . . . But she already seemed to understand everything and thrust herself through the doorway, trying to go inside. Piras grabbed her arms and pulled her towards him.

'Don't go upstairs, Pina,' he said. She looked through the open doorway as if she could go through the entire house with her eyes alone.

'Nino . . .' she said, then fell to her knees and buried her face in her hands. She started saying something as she wailed, but it was incomprehensible. Without Pina seeing him, Ettore gestured as if to ask what had happened. Piras mimed the shape of a gun with his hand and pointed his finger at his temple. Ettore opened his eyes wide, then shook his head and looked at Pina.

'Please, Ettore, go and call the *carabinieri* in Milis,' Piras said. He would have preferred to summon the Oristano police, but it would have taken much longer.

'What about her?' asked Ettore, pointing at Pina.

'Take her with you.'

'Pina . . .' Ettore called. He persuaded her to stand up and held her by the arm all the way to the car. Piras watched them drive down the dirt path to the main road, then went back upstairs. He sat down in a chair in front of Benigno and stared at him. With his eyes closed, he looked more serene. If not for the hole in the side of his head, he might be sleeping.

20 December

Bordelli woke up very early that morning. He wanted to start paying calls on Badalamenti's debtors, a first attempt to establish perhaps some more specific leads than what he'd come up with so far. For the moment he'd singled out seven men, all those under fifty. If he could fit it in he would also pay a call on Rosaria Beltempo, the woman who'd written the letter, to give her back the photographs that had kept her shackled to the past and, of course, the IOUs of her blackmail. She would certainly have a more peaceful Christmas without that sword hanging over her head. Ginzillo somehow didn't understand these things.

The previous evening the inspector had also assigned Officer Biagi the tedious task of going to the courthouse to request a check of all the records of the people on that list. Something interesting might turn up, even if he didn't have much hope of this.

He put the coffee on the burner. Waiting for it to bubble up, he went to the end of the hall for no real reason and opened the door to a room he never entered. He turned on the light and stood in the doorway, just looking. A dark wood bookcase full of books he'd read and reread, a carpet from the house in Via Volta, a trunk full of old photographs, an ancient, cast-iron bed with a painted headboard and no mattress. And that was all. He would have liked to turn it into a guest room. Or perhaps a reading room. Or he could even simply leave it the way it was and just go into it every now and then. If he'd had a family, it probably would have been the children's room. A boy and a girl, both as beautiful as their mother . . . Right, and after a maudlin thought like that, he might as well recite Dickens' *A*

Christmas Carol, he thought, trying to laugh at himself. He didn't want to become an old man full of regrets who wept every time he saw a small child. He closed the door with a smile on his lips, but in fact he felt a little sad. It was better not to think about such things. He had only to brush his teeth and go out. He went into the bathroom and splashed some cold water on his face. The plant on a corner shelf was losing its leaves. He didn't even know what it was, only that Rosa had given it to him. He poured some water into the pot and went out of the bathroom. As he was getting dressed, he wondered whether he should buy a Christmas tree, perhaps a small one. He decided against it. Christmas trees were for children or, at best, for sulking police inspectors who were always thinking about the past. No tree.

He was about to leave when he heard the coffee bubbling. He'd completely forgotten about it. He raced into the kitchen. The coffee had been boiling for a while already and smelled burnt. He poured it all into the sink and went out.

The sun was already up, but the neighbourhood's small streets were still in darkness. The sky was the same as the previous day, grey and flat, looking as if it might snow at any moment. There was no wind, so the cold was tolerable.

Bordelli got into his car and drove off. As it was barely half past seven, he hoped to find some people still at home. The newspaper kiosks had bold headlines delaring: DE GAULLE RE-ELECTED. By the thinnest of margins, the liberator of Paris had done it again. Bordelli smiled, thinking that the story of the general with the pear-shaped head wasn't too different from that of Napoleon, though on a smaller scale.

The first person on Bordelli's list was a certain Gino Ercolani, aged forty-nine, who lived at Via Torta 22/C. The inspector parked the Beetle with two wheels on the pavement and rang the doorbell. A few moments later, a window on the second floor opened and a very bald man looked out, his face half covered with shaving cream.

'Who is it?' he shouted.

'I'm looking for Signor Ercolani.'

'That's me.'

'I'd like to talk to you for a minute. I'm Inspector Bordelli, police.'

The man made a worried face.

'What's this about?'

'I'd prefer to talk to you in private,' the inspector said, indicating the people passing by. Ercolani hesitated for a moment, thinking, then closed the window. Seconds later the front door to the street clicked open. Bordelli climbed the stairs slowly and reached the second floor. Ercolani was waiting for him in the doorway in a vest, one cheek covered in foam and razor in hand. He was short and thin, with two sad but placid eyes. On the whole, there was something simian about him.

'Bad news?' he asked, a little anxious.

'I'd say not,' Bordelli replied.

'Then would you mind terribly if I finished shaving? I haven't got much time,' he said.

Bordelli could hear the water running in the bathroom.

'By all means,' he said.

'Please go into the sitting room and make yourself at home. I'll be with you in a jiffy.'

Ercolani left him alone and went off to the bathroom, braces dangling round his knees. The inspector went down the short corridor, glancing into the rooms. It was a modest but dignified home. Hanging on the wall in the bedroom was an old print of Christ carrying the cross on his shoulder, in a frame of black wood. It looked like a small picture his grandmother used to have in the entrance to her flat. The bed was a hospital bed, with an iron frame painted olive green and peeling. The kitchen had a central overhead fluorescent light and was sparkling clean. The bathroom door was ajar, and when passing by, Bordelli saw the razor sliding over Ercolani's face in the mirror. The sitting room featured a threadbare couch and a little glass-fronted cabinet with glasses inside. He went in and sat down in an old armchair. While waiting for Ercolani, he checked to see whether he had his cigarettes, but left them where they were. He'd decided not to smoke that day until after lunch. It was the first time he had tried it. He had to take the bull by the horns. Who knew whether he would make it till then. He looked around. There were reproductions of a number of famous paintings on the wall: Giotto, Leonardo, Raphael . . .

'I haven't got much time, Inspector, or I risk missing the tram,' said Ercolani, poking his head in the doorway.

'Where do you work?' Bordelli asked, standing up.

'In Peretola.' It was on the other side of town.

'If you like I can give you a lift, and we can talk at our leisure in the car,' said Bordelli, suppressing a yawn. The man thought this over for a minute. He didn't understand what was happening, but in the end he accepted. Putting his coat on in haste, he tucked a small brown leather bag with a broken strap under his arm and opened the door.

'What sort of work do you do, Mr Ercolani?' Bordelli asked.

'I'm an accountant in a transport firm.'

They descended the stairs without speaking. Ercolani smoothed down the few hairs on his head. He seemed a little nervous, but appeared to be a very patient man.

They got into the Beetle and left. Bordelli noticed how composed the accountant was. He kept his feet together, bag on his knees, hands on the bag. Perhaps this was the position he assumed while riding the tram. The inspector drove slowly through the nearly empty streets in the centre of town. In Via Sant'Egidio they saw a blond young man with hair down to his shoulders and a beard down to his chest. He didn't look Italian. On his back was a large military backpack as swollen as a balloon, and he was walking towards Santa Croce. The accountant followed him with his eyes, as though unsure of what he was looking at. Then he turned to Bordelli.

'What did you want to tell me?' he said, seeming slightly worried.

'You signed some promissory notes made out to a certain Totuccio Badalamenti, is that right?'

Ercolani sighed, and nodded in affirmation. Bordelli extracted the notes from his jacket pocket and laid them down on Ercolani's bag. The man picked them up and turned to look at the inspector.

'What is the meaning of this?'

'Badalamenti was murdered.'

'I know, I read it in the papers . . . but what about these notes?'

'You can do whatever you like with them.'

Trying to hide his elation, the accountant folded the notes in two and put them in his bag. He sighed again. It seemed almost like a habit.

'I didn't kill him,' he said, staring at the road.

'I have no doubt whatsoever of that.'

'How can you say that?'

'Intuition. I'm very presumptuous,' said Bordelli.

'I have to admit, I'm not at all displeased that the man was murdered,' the accountant said in a whisper, still staring at the road.

'When did you last see Badalamenti?'

'Forty-three days ago.'

'Is this yours, by any chance?' Bordelli took the ring that Diotivede had found in the usurer's stomach out of his pocket and showed it to him. Ercolani barely glanced at it.

'No,' he said.

The inspector turned on to the Viali, and they sat for a while in silence. Every so often Ercolani shook his head and sighed. A very fine, freezing rain started to fall. It stuck to the windows. Bordelli turned down Viale Redi and continued on towards Novoli. There was more traffic than fifteen minutes earlier. In front of them a sleepy little boy was watching them through the rear window of a Fiat 600, and out of the blue he made a face at them. Bordelli replied in kind, and the boy burst out laughing and fell down on to the seat. Then the Fiat turned right. Bordelli continued to the end of Via di Novoli, and they arrived at Peretola.

'Signor Ercolani, I know it's none of my business, and you're perfectly free not to answer . . . but I'm curious. How did you ever end up going to Badalamenti?'

The accountant lightly clenched his fist and, of course, sighed.

'I need money for my sister,' he said.

'What for?'

'She's mentally ill. I didn't like her staying at the mental hospital, so I put her in a private institution . . . Take the next right, please. We're there.'

Bordelli obeyed the accountant's instructions and pulled into a large paved yard with a number of lorries and vans parked higgledy-piggledly. At the far end was a warehouse, and behind it were some now abandoned fields. They were at the margin between city and country. Ercolani glanced at his watch.

'I'm early,' he said. He still seemed a bit astonished by the unexpected news. Bordelli parked the car in a corner of the yard and turned towards him.

'What are you doing for Christmas, Signor Ercolani?'

'We're all getting together at my mother's place. I'll be thinking of you, Inspector. I would never have been able to pay those IOUs.'

'Try not to think about it any more.'

'I would never have been able,' the accountant repeated, eyes searching for the right handle to open the door. Bordelli pointed it out to him. He felt sorry for this mild-mannered accountant with four strands of hair on his head. He seemed like someone who asked for nothing in life, as if it were some kind of sin. Ercolani opened the car door and put a foot outside. Then he turned towards Bordelli.

'Thank you very much, Inspector. Happy Christmas.'

'Happy Christmas to you too.'

The accountant got out of the car, and his leather bag fell to the ground. It was as if he'd never set foot in a car before. Picking up the bag, he waved goodbye, then closed the door and started walking towards the warehouse, head tilted slightly to one side.

Bordelli pulled out his list and crossed out Ercolani's name. According to Diotivede, it could not have been him. He was too short. More importantly, the inspector had seen him shaving with his right hand.

The second man on the list was Benito Muggio, born in 1936 and residing in Via del Canneto, which was an ancient, sloping little street above Via de' Bardi that was too narrow for a car to pass through. Bordelli left the car in Piazza de' Mozzi and walked the rest of the way. It had stopped raining. The sun was stifled by clouds, but the cold was strangely dry. He looked up at a monument to the fallen in the fight against Fascism, erected in '47 to replace a bas-relief of Il Duce. It oozed rhetoric. It might actually have been better to leave a few signs of the reign of Fascism here and there, as in Rome, to keep the memory alive in those who'd lived through it and to let the young see what they'd been spared. Bordelli tried to imagine a public speech by Mussolini in the television age and realised that probably nobody would have gone to hear him.

He started climbing up Costa Scarpuccia, pleased that the desire to smoke hadn't yet become too strong. He liked this area very much. It was close to the centre but already had one foot in the country. A little farther up, beyond the high walls of Via San Leonardo, there were vineyards and olive groves. From the upper floors of the houses one could see Florence below, so close that one could almost touch it.

He turned right down Via del Canneto, passed under the first arch and stopped. He pressed the only buzzer beside a peeling door, and a dull ring echoed within. Hearing a clatter of metal over his head, he took a step back to have a better look. A window protected by a rusted grille opened, and an old woman with a headscarf tied under her chin looked out.

'Who is it?' the woman asked, suspicious.

'Good morning, signora, does Benito Muggio live here?'

The old woman turned round towards the inside.

'Benito! It's for you! Beniiito!' she shouted, then she disappeared inside, leaving the window open. A few moments later a young man of about twenty-five appeared. He had a nervous face and thick, black eyebrows and looked at Bordelli with a questioning air but without saying anything. The inspector started digging for his badge.

'Are you Benito Muggio?' he asked.

'And who are you?'

'Inspector Bordelli, police. I'd like to talk to you for a minute.'

'About what?'

'Nothing serious. Can I come in?'

The young man withdrew from the window. Bordelli was still looking for his badge but couldn't find it. The old woman reappeared.

'He says he's coming down,' she said.

'I'll wait for him.'

Bordelli kept searching his pockets, but the badge wasn't there. He must have left it in his other jacket . . . He wasn't ageing well . . . A policeman never forgets his badge. He looked around, relishing the calm of the ancient little street. It felt like a medieval village at the top of a mountain. He would gladly live in a place like this. A rat walked serenely past him and scurried into the opening of a stone drain. Another rat was walking along the wall as though out for a stroll after breakfast.

He heard a clatter of bolts, and immediately Benito opened the door and came outside. He was tall and fat, with massive arms. They shook hands.

'Could we talk out here?' Muggio asked. 'The house is a little messy.'

He was rather well dressed, though tie-less and wearing very worn-out shoes. But it was clear that he tried to look smart. He kept swallowing and blinking his red eyes as though he hadn't slept. Bordelli didn't feel like standing.

'Could we go sit over there?' he asked, pointing to a low

stone wall on the other side of the arch. They went and sat down. Behind them were six or seven enormous plane trees without leaves. Muggio apparently didn't feel like sitting, since he immediately stood up again. The old woman's head reappeared at one of the windows looking out on to the trees, above the arch. Benito gesticulated impatiently at her.

'Go back inside, Mamma!' he shouted. The old woman muttered something and closed the window.

Bordelli calmly pulled out Benito Muggio's promissory notes.

'I believe these are yours,' he said and, clasping them between two fingers, held them before the young man's eyes. Muggio didn't understand at first. He looked at them for a second, then recognised them and practically snatched them out of Bordelli's hand.

'Tell me the rest,' he said.

'Badalamenti's been killed,' said Bordelli.

Muggio stared at the inspector with eyes flashing. 'I know. I read it in *La Nazione* . . . And I'm glad,' he said between clenched teeth.

'It's not a crime.'

'And these notes?'

'They're yours.'

'Ah . . .' said Muggio, a malevolent smile on his lips.

The inspector put a cigarette in his mouth but didn't light it. 'When was the last time you saw Badalamenti?' he asked.

'Am I a suspect?'

'For the moment I have no choice but to consider everyone a suspect. But if you don't want to answer . . .'

'I've got nothing to hide. I saw the bastard a fortnight ago.'

'Where?'

'At his place.'

'Why did you ask someone like Badalamenti for a loan, Signor Muggio?'

Benito scratched his head.

'It was a woman . . . It was all because of a stinking bitch.'

'Don't you have a job?'

'I'm supposed to get an answer after the holidays.'

'What are you doing for the holidays?'

Benito sneered.

'For starters, I'm going to celebrate like this.' And he started tearing up the promissory notes slowly, one by one, into little pieces, putting the little bits in his trouser pocket as he went along.

The inspector waited for him to finish, then dug into his pocket and pulled out two rings. He showed Muggio the one with the name *Ciro* inscribed on it, but Benito said he'd never seen it before.

'This, on the other hand, I think is yours,' Bordelli said. He handed him a gold wedding ring with the names of the newly-weds and the date inscribed on it. Benito blushed.

'It's my mother's. I would definitely have got it back, even if I had to do a John Wayne . . .' he said, miming a pistol with his hand.

'Why not use a pair of scissors?' the inspector said.

Muggio took a step forward. 'I don't think I would have been able to kill him, Inspector. I honestly don't know. Or maybe I could have, since that southern bastard really did deserve it . . . but I didn't do it.'

The inspector looked at his watch and stood up.

'Don't worry, I know it wasn't you,' he said.

'How can you be so sure?'

'Intuition,' Bordelli lied.

'Aren't you ever wrong, Inspector?'

'Hardly ever.'

Benito bit his lip.

'I don't know who killed him, but whoever it was, he did a good thing,' he said. The sentiment was apparently heartfelt.

Bordelli smiled. 'I have nothing more to ask you, for the moment,' he said.

'Do you believe in God, Inspector?'

'It's a difficult subject,' Bordelli said.

'I do. He's always looking down at us from above,

113

spitting on us. If there was no God, the world wouldn't be this way.'

'What way is that?'

'It wouldn't be such a pile of shit.'

'Goodbye, Signor Muggio, and happy Christmas. And good luck with your work.'

'Thanks . . . and thanks for the IOUs.'

They shook hands and Benito went back towards home. The inspector looked up and saw the old woman at the window. She seemed never to have left. He raised a hand and waved goodbye.

'Happy Christmas,' he said.

'Happy Christmas to you, sir,' the old woman replied, smiling and exposing her gums.

The inspector headed towards his car. Walking back down the street, he took the list and struck out the name of the unemployed Benito Muggio. When imitating John Wayne holding a gun he'd used his right hand. So he wasn't left-handed, and Diotivede had said . . .

Bordelli went back home to fetch his badge, got back in the car, and continued his rounds, knowing he had to be patient. His incentive was simply the hope that sooner or later he would find someone worth pursuing.

By half past eleven he had already struck two more names off the list. Giorgio Parroni was just over forty but too weak and ill even to crack a nut. He was even unfit for work. His wife was a docile, quiet little woman who moved about the house like a ghost. When the inspector gave Parroni the promissory notes, the man had acted strangely, giving a start as if wanting to spring forward and kiss him. Then he'd hidden the notes in a drawer and started weeping in front of a photo of his dead mother. The house was dark and stank of humble cooking. Bordelli had fled with a desire to see the sun.

Mauro Baldi was at home because he was a barber and the shop was closed on Mondays. He was a colossus but wasn't left-handed. The gorilla had crumpled the notes into little balls with gusto, one by one, letting them fall to the floor.

'I'll tear them up later and throw them away, but I've imagined this scene many times . . . I've been wanting for so long to crumple them up and throw them on the floor.'

He'd borrowed from Badalamenti because he needed to make mortgage payments on the shop and had lost a fair amount of money at the races. His wife was out shopping and knew nothing.

'If Manuela ever found out there'd be hell to pay,' he'd said, bringing a hand to his head. Bordelli had reassured him and left after declining a glass of wine.

He'd shown both men the ring with the name *Ciro* inside, but neither had recognised it. He crossed out their names and continued his rounds. There were three names left on that first list, and they all lived in the area between Via Pisana and Casellina. If they worked he was unlikely to find them at home at that hour, but it cost him nothing to try anyway. In less than half an hour he had rung three buzzers and spoken with two wives and a mother, all three rather worried and frightened to have a policeman call on them. The inspector reassured them, saying that it was a simple routine check for firearms permits and that he would return around lunchtime or at the latest between 7 and 8 p.m. He could have asked where the men worked and gone to see them at once, but he didn't want to create any needless problems. He had all the time in the world.

At one o'clock, the sky was still the same dirty white as at eight that morning, uniform all the way to the horizon. Atop the hills in the distance there was a trace of snow. Three degrees less and it might snow in the city as well.

The inspector stopped at Porta Romana to eat a panino and drink a beer, and took advantage of the moment to ring police headquarters. He had them put Rinaldi on and asked him whether there was any news of the girl in the photographs, but neither Rinaldi nor Tapinassi had managed to find her yet.

He got back in the car and went up Via Senese. Driving past Via delle Campora he couldn't help but turn and look down the street. Until the previous spring a cultured, unpleasant man who murdered four children had lived there. After Bordelli arrested him, the man was murdered in turn in prison. All in all, a nasty affair. But he had other memories of that period, such as . . . Milena . . .

He accelerated, as if wanting to leave those memories behind. Continuing past the Due Strade, he went by Galluzzo and the Certosa. About half a mile before Tavernuzze he turned left down a little street that went steeply uphill. He knew it well. It led to Impruneta by way of Le Rose, Baruffi and Quintole.

Rosaria Beltempo, the woman Badalamenti had blackmailed, lived in Le Rose. Bordelli had the compromising photos in his pocket, as well as the promissory notes she had signed to guarantee the blackmail. He couldn't wait to give it all back to her and wish her a happy Christmas. He hoped not to encounter any suspicious husbands or housemates who might create problems, but in her letter to the usurer the woman didn't mention any men, so Bordelli's concern was perhaps unfounded.

It took him a while to locate the house, since out in the country not everyone took the trouble to post their street number outside. In the end, however, he found it. It was an old farmhouse about a hundred feet from the road, with a large brick loggia and an olive grove behind it. There was a narrow, unpaved driveway leading up to it. Bordelli parked the Beetle on the threshing floor in front and got out. It was already half past one. The house wasn't as big as the one he'd seen at Impruneta and, actually, would have been perfect for him. He looked around. It was really a very nice place. He would gladly have lived there. With three or four chickens for eggs, a kitchen garden with a bit of everything in it, perhaps a few fruit trees and a hundred olive trees. He had to start thinking seriously about it.

At first glance the house seemed abandoned. The roof was warped and a gutter had come detached and was dangling in the void. Tall grass was growing through the cracks in the brick pavement of the threshing floor. Opposite the house was a large, half-ruined barn full of wreckage. The shell of an old Lancia Ardea, a pair of rusted Lambretta scooters without wheels and resting on bricks. Bicycle frames, an old Motom that looked as if it had caught fire, and countless other things thrown about helter-skelter.

He entered the loggia and knocked on the door. There was no reply. He knocked again, harder this time. There were motor-oil stains and faint tyre tracks on the tiled flooring, as if someone parked a motorbike there. There wasn't a soul around. The house really did seem uninhabited. Aside from those marks under the loggia, there was nothing to make one think otherwise. He went round to the back of the house. The olive grove was fairly large and sloped slightly downwards. It looked rather neglected, the ground all overgrown with weeds, though the olive trees looked well tended and the olives had been harvested.

Twenty or so paces from the house, under a fig tree, there was some wire fencing enclosing a small wooden shelter. Within the enclosure some twenty-odd chickens were scratching about in the company of a white rooster which looked too old to enjoy all that good luck. A few items of clothing had been hung out to dry on a line, only men's garments, mostly shirts. A bit farther from the house was a sort of large tool shed, as ramshackle as everything else. Here and there Bordelli could see abandoned grapevines, their black, contorted stocks strangling the support posts while the unpruned shoots snaked along the ground for several yards. Beyond the olive grove was a forest of pine and cypress that climbed up the hillside. Here and there in the distance could be seen large yellow farmhouses amid the vineyards, a number of churches, and the crenellated towers of a few fake nineteenth-century castles. It wasn't often that Bordelli saw such open spaces. He liked the countryside more and more, and in an era like the present one, he was perhaps the only person who thought that way. Perhaps he needed to stop thinking about it and finally take the plunge.

Sell his flat in San Frediano and move to a place like this, or perhaps even farther away from Florence . . . To Impruneta, or Strada in Chianti, or even Greve. He started strolling through the olive grove, enjoying the light breeze caressing his face. He tried to imagine himself at one with the land. He didn't know the first thing about it, but he would gladly ask the advice of the local peasants so he could learn. He would try making wine, growing salad greens and tomatoes and raising chickens. It couldn't be that difficult.

He went back to the threshing floor in the forecourt. The sky was a grey dome. Unable to hold out any longer, he lit his first cigarette of the day, thinking he would take the bull by the horns another day. He smoked it while poking about in the barn amidst carcasses of bicycles and motorbikes, pots and pans without handles, glass jars, crates, torn blankets and dismantled bedframes. There were six or seven old tyres stacked on top of one another, and through the holes in the middle stood some pestle-shaped sticks used to crush grapes in tubs. He'd seen them being used once or twice as a child, when he and his father would take the bus out to the country to buy wine from the priest at Montefioralle or some other vintner. Those big sticks had a precise name, but he couldn't remember it just then.

He went back outside. Crushing the cigarette butt on the brick threshing floor, he glanced at his watch. It was almost one o'clock. He didn't feel like waiting any longer and decided to come back another time. He got into the Beetle and turned on the ignition. As he was backing up, a young man arrived on a Vespa. He was wearing goggles that covered half of his face. Bordelli turned off the engine and got out. The lad parked the Vespa under the loggia and took off his goggles. He looked about twenty years old. He was wearing a raincoat that must have once been white. He walked towards Bordelli, a leather bag in his hand, and stopped about ten feet away.

'Are you looking for someone?' he asked. He had a beautiful face, dark eyes and black hair.

'Hello,' Bordelli said provocatively.

'Are you looking for someone?' the youth repeated, slightly annoyed. His expression seemed to be one of eternal resentment.

'I would like to speak with Signora Beltempo,' the inspector said.

'My mother died three months ago.'

This might be the Odoardo mentioned in the letter, Rosaria's son.

'I'm sorry . . . Your mother must have been very young,' Bordelli said.

'Forty-two.'

'What happened?'

'To whom am I speaking, if I may ask?'

'Sorry . . . I'm Inspector Bordelli, police,' said the inspector, pulling out his badge.

The lad's face tensed. 'My mother was hit by a car. Why are you looking for her?' he asked coldly.

The inspector took a few steps forward and stopped in front of him. 'I wanted to give something back to her and talk to her a little,' he said vaguely.

'Whatever it is, you can give it to me.'

'It's a private matter. I don't know if your mother would approve.'

'My mother is dead. Is there anything else you have to tell me? I'm in a bit of a rush,' the youth said, stiff as a tree trunk.

'Do you have any brothers or sisters?'

'No. Why do you ask?'

'To know whether you have any brothers or sisters.'

'Good answer.'

'Does your father live with you?'

'I live alone,' the lad said.

'Oh . . . And where is your father?'

'I don't know, I've never met him.'

'I'm sorry.'

'I stopped thinking about it a long time ago,' said the youth, shrugging.

'Aren't you afraid to be here all alone?'

'Are you referring to the bogeyman or the big bad wolf?'

The inspector smiled. He was amusing himself, but that wasn't why he'd come.

'Do you know someone called Totuccio Badalamenti?' he asked out of the blue.

'No,' the boy said decisively. But Bordelli had seen him give a slight start, with nostrils flaring. Perhaps it was only a coincidence, or perhaps the boy was just nervous because a policeman was asking him strange questions.

'So you live here all alone,' Bordelli repeated, gesturing towards the large house.

'Yes, I live here all alone.'

'It's a nice big place. Is the land around it yours?'

'A few hectares,' the lad said placidly. He'd already recovered his cool.

'You're very lucky . . . Do you tend the olive trees yourself?' Bordelli asked with great apparent interest.

'No.'

'Who takes care of them?'

'An old peasant who lives near by.'

'I can just imagine how good the oil must be . . . The new oil's ready now, you know, the kind that stings on the tongue,' said Bordelli.

The boy's eyes narrowed. He seemed annoyed. 'Do you have anything else to ask me, Inspector? I'm a little busy.'

Bordelli calmly took another step forward.

'No, nothing else,' he said.

'Then, if you don't mind, I'll be going,' the youth said, staring at him with hostility.

'There's no need to hurry.'

'Unfortunately, I happen to be in a hurry.'

'Tell me . . . What are you doing for Christmas?'

'Nothing I have to tell the police about,' the lad said.

'I wasn't asking as a policeman.'

'At any rate I've still got nothing to say.'

Bordelli glanced at the old Ardea.

'Beautiful car. Did it belong to your mother?'

'We found it.'

'In my day it was everybody's dream.'

The lad made a gesture of exasperation.

'Goodbye, Inspector. As I said, I'm very busy.' And he turned away and walked towards the house, keys in hand.

'Just a second, Odoardo,' said Bordelli.

The boy turned round abruptly. 'How do you know my name?' he asked.

The inspector walked towards him with his hands in his pockets. 'I'm a policeman . . .' he said as though excusing himself.

'Why don't you tell me straight out why you came here?'

'Do you know that this same Mr Badalamenti was killed?' Bordelli asked, looking him straight in the eye.

'I don't know him,' Odoardo said indifferently, looking for the right key on the chain.

'Don't you want to know who he was?'

'No.'

'I'll tell you anyway. He was a loan shark . . . A despicable usurer and extortionist.'

'I'm not interested,' Odoardo said impatiently, sticking the key in the lock. With his left hand, Bordelli noticed, but perhaps that was because he had his bag in his right.

'Somebody stabbed him in the neck with a pair of nice sharp scissors, the pointed kind . . .'

'I'm sorry, but I really don't care.'

'The killer searched the whole house, but in my opinion he didn't find what he was looking for.'

Odoardo shot him another exasperated glance.

'I really don't know what you're getting at,' he said, annoyed, letting the key chain dangle from the door.

'I just wanted to have a little chat.'

'What does any of this have to do with my mother?'

'I don't know yet,' said Bordelli. Then he took out the ring with the name *Ciro* inside and went up to Odoardo.

'Does this ring look familiar to you?' he asked, handing it to him.

The boy looked at it for only a second. 'Never seen it,' he said, shaking his head.

'Are you absolutely sure?'

'Of course not, I would need several days to think it over.'

'You see? You can be funny when you want to be,' said Bordelli.

'Let's make this quick. Is this what you wanted to give my mother?'

'Do you know where I found it?' Bordelli asked, ignoring the question.

'Do you want to keep me here until nightfall, Inspector?'

'It was in Badalamenti's stomach . . .'

'So what?'

'The guy swallowed it. When the police pathologist opened him up, he found it in there somewhere . . . Odd, don't you think?'

The youth looked at the ring again.

'I've never seen it before,' he repeated. Then he handed the ring back to Bordelli and turned the key in the lock.

'Have you got a telephone?' the inspector asked absently, eyes narrowing.

'Yes, why?'

'Could you please give me the number?'

'What for?'

'I may need you.'

'You can find it in the phone book.'

'Since we're here, tell it to me yourself . . .'

Odoardo looked at him in defiance, then shook his head and told him the number. The inspector searched his pockets, pretending to be looking for something to write with.

'I haven't got a pen on me,' he said, shrugging. Odoardo couldn't take it any more and just wanted to get the whole thing over with. He set his bag down on the seat of the Vespa, yanked it open, and pulled out a pen and notebook. He scribbled the number, tore the sheet out, and handed it to Bordelli. The inspector noticed he held the pen in his right hand.

'What do you do for a living, Odoardo? I'm not asking as a policeman,' he said, putting the piece of paper in his pocket.

'I work with an architect.'

'Where?'

'In Via Bertelli,' the youth muttered, repressing the urge to tell him to go to hell.

'Ah yes, over by Coverciano . . .' said the inspector.

'No, I'm referring to Via Timoteo Bertelli.'

'I'm not familiar with it.'

'It intersects with Via delle Forbici,' said Odoardo, looking at him with antipathy.

'I don't believe it . . . I was born about a hundred yards away from there. Can you imagine?'

'I can spend the rest of the afternoon imagining it. Now I have to go.'

'What's the architect's name?' Bordelli asked in a friendly tone.

'Why? What do you want with him?'

'I was just curious. Maybe I know him.'

'Do you want to ask him if I go around at night killing people?'

'I just want to know his name,' said the inspector.

'Giampiero Balducci.'

'No, I don't know him. Would you happen to have a cigarette? I've finished mine,' Bordelli lied. The young man pulled out a packet, nostrils flaring. With a brusque flick of the wrist, he made a cigarette pop out. Bordelli took it and thanked him. They were Alfas, matching the ash found in Badalamenti's house. That didn't mean anything, of course. A lot of people smoked Alfas, especially youngsters with no money.

'Would you like a light, too?' asked Odoardo, with feigned courtesy.

'I'll smoke it later, thanks,' said Bordelli, putting it in his pocket.

'Good. Do you need anything else, or can I get on with my life now?'

'That'll be all for now, but I'll be back to see you soon, mind you . . . I like this place,' the inspector said, looking around.

'Goodbye, Inspector.'

'Oh, one last thing, I'm sorry . . . What do you call that big stick in the shape of a pestle used to crush grapes in the—'

'It's called a plunger,' the lad interrupted him, patience at the limit.

'Ah yes, a plunger . . . Thank you so much.'

'Not at all.'

'See you soon,' said Bordelli. He shook the youth's hand and noticed that it was sweaty. Odoardo opened the door and disappeared inside.

Before leaving, Bordelli looked around again. He really did like the place. There was something glorious about the two tumbledown buildings. The carcass of the Ardea and the rusting motorcycles weren't just scrap iron. All piled together like that in the barn, they were as fascinating as an archaeological find. Bordelli had a weakness for those sorts of things. He liked to see that time didn't ravage only living beings.

He got into the Beetle and drove slowly back into town. When he turned on to the Viali, it was almost three. He passed the Fortezza and turned down Viale Lavagnini, which when he got confused he sometimes called Viale Principessa Margherita, as it was known before 1947. He was about to stop by the Trattoria da Cesare to see whether he could get a quick bite to eat, but then realised that Totò would only manage to make him eat more than he wanted. So he skipped it. Every so often one needs a break. He turned down Via Santa Caterina and shortly thereafter stopped in Piazza del Mercato Centrale. He went to the *friggitoria* in Borgo la Noce and had some fried polenta. Coming out, he noticed that the sky was still overcast with dense, grey clouds. At the tavern next door, he drank a

glass of red. After a cup of black coffee, he lit Odoardo's Alfa
. . . Was it the third or the fourth cigarette of the day? He had
to find a way to keep track. Inhaling the smoke, he felt a sort
of thud in his chest. That blend of black tobacco was too strong
for his taste.

While he was at it, he bought a piece of pecorino cheese
at the Casina Rossa, for those rare occasions when he happened
to eat at home. Heading back towards his car, he thought
again of Odoardo. The boy was closed as tightly as a sea
urchin. He seemed to be at war with the world. Bordelli
imagined him plunging the scissors into Badalamenti's back.
The picture seemed right. But he wasn't left-handed, and
Diotivede had said . . .

He put the pecorino in the car and went for a stroll in the
centre of town to do a little window shopping. Everything would
be reopening shortly. He couldn't let himself forget that he also
had another big problem at that moment: finding a present for
Rosa. Porcinai had made it seem so easy. Give her something
strange. What the hell was that supposed to mean?

He stopped to look in all the shop windows but couldn't
make up his mind. Perhaps it was better to go into a shop at
random and ask a salesgirl for advice. He tossed aside the
fag-end and blew the smoke upwards. He was still thinking
about Rosaria Beltempo's son, reviewing the young man's every
gesture and expression in his mind. He'd seen him give a start
two or three times. Was Odoardo lying or was he simply surly
by nature? It was hard to know. Bordelli decided he would pay
him another call soon; it probably wasn't a bad idea to talk a
little more with him. He didn't quite know why, but there was
something about the boy that aroused his curiosity. He
wondered whether he was being guided by his sixth sense or
was simply prey to suggestion. The danger was that he might
be led astray by a false intuition or by his habit of always
interpreting human behaviour no matter what. He had to be
careful. But, all things considered, he liked the kid. He seemed
quite intelligent and had a keen sense of irony.

Meanwhile he continued looking in the shop display windows, but didn't see anything for Rosa. In the end he surrendered and slipped into a gift shop full of useless knick-knacks. He put himself in the hands of the saleswoman, a blonde of about thirty-five in spiked heels. Luckily he got away after almost spending a fortune on a tiny blue horse in Murano glass. He'd escaped just in the nick of time. The saleswoman had already started to wrap it up when he suddenly came to his senses and said he was no longer convinced, rushing out of the store under the nice lady's angry glare.

Piras was lying in bed, resting after his long afternoon walk. He wanted to hurry up and mend. He'd gone out early that morning and taken the street past the church, on the left, which climbed steeply towards the vineyards. He'd arrived at Pavarile with his lips dry from the north wind, then come back down, passed his house and decided to continue walking. He went almost all the way to Seneghe, through the pastures and thickets of scrub oak where pigs roamed wild. Behind the village, at the foot of the Montiferru, lay the olive groves. In all he'd walked over six miles. He felt in better and better condition. His legs were stronger and the back pains had almost disappeared. But he couldn't bear hopping about on crutches much longer. If he'd had sound legs he could have run all the way to the pond of Cabras.

It was past five o'clock. He started reading another Simenon novel, but kept getting distracted by the thought of Benigno in the armchair with his tongue hanging out.

His father had gone back to the field, where he'd gathered a mountain of *cavolo nero* that he'd piled on to the kitchen table. The cabbage was to be prepared for the following morning. That was always Maria's job, since she had two hands. She would clean the vegetables while watching television, tying them together into little bundles to be sold at the market. She would sometimes start with children's TV in the afternoon and then resume work after supper.

The telephone rang, and from his room Piras shouted that he would answer it. Getting out of bed, he grabbed the crutches and headed for the entrance hall as fast as he could. At that hour, it was almost certainly Sonia. To spare her the inevitable questions, he always managed to pick up the phone before his mother could. The telephone kept on ringing. Piras leaned against the wall to free one hand and then picked up.

'How's our little convalescent?' Sonia asked.

'Better and better, but to fully recover I need the cure I mentioned,' said Piras.

'Well, if you're wrong I'll scratch your eyes out.'

They carried on in this fashion for a good while, needling and desiring each other. Piras had decided not to tell her about Benigno's suicide, so as not to put a damper on their pleasant banter. Now and then Sonia would lower her voice and recall some details of their first night together. Piras would feel a wave of heat rise up from his belly to his brain. Her words were the best possible incentive for a speedy recovery.

Maria was in the kitchen, already preparing the bunches of *cavolo nero*, sitting in her low chair in front of the embers in the fireplace. The instant the phone started ringing, she had run to turn down the volume of the television, hoping to over-hear a few words of their conversation. With the ease of habit, she stripped away the yellowed cabbage leaves, or those half eaten by snails, and threw them into a basket. When she'd cleaned four heads, she bound them together with a rubber band, all the while thinking of Benigno and poor Pina, who loved him like a brother. Such thoughts did not, however, prevent her keeping her ears pricked to try and catch a few words of Nino's telephone call, even though her face showed none of this. Her curiosity was whetted by the secrecy of her son, who hadn't revealed a blessed thing about this girl. But she could do nothing about it. Nino was a grown-up now. Soon, by the grace of God, he would be fully recovered, and unfortunately he would go back to the big city to resume his dangerous job. She had tried to change his mind, saying there were so many other things he could do for a living, perhaps in Oristano. But Nino was as stubborn as his father, and when he'd made up his mind, it was final. Being shot by criminals hadn't sufficed to make him change his mind. In fact, he seemed more determined than ever to carry on, the mule.

Piras whispered a last goodbye to Sonia and hung up. He glanced at his watch – half past five – and went into the kitchen. *Felix the Cat* was on the telly, with the volume turned down almost all the way. His mother looked at him dejectedly.

'Poor Benigno,' she said, still stripping away the damaged cabbage leaves, 'what a terrible thing.' She didn't have the courage to ask about the mysterious girl who had called.

'Where's Dad?' asked Piras.

'He's behind the house. The handle on the hoe's broken.'

'I'm going to Pina's to see Benigno.'

'Tell her we'll be there shortly.'

'All right,' said Piras. He went into the entrance hall, leaned the crutches against the wall and put on his overcoat, buttoning it up to the collar. The moment he opened the door the phone rang again.

'Shall I get it?' his mother asked, taking the cabbages out of her lap.

'No, never mind,' said Piras, walking over to the telephone. It might be Sonia again.

'Hello?'

'Hello, Piras, how are you feeling?'

'I'm feeling fine, Inspector, and yourself?'

'Not too bad. Doing anything interesting?'

'Nothing very interesting, but I'm going to pay my last respects to a neighbour who died,' said Piras, and he told Bordelli in a few words what had happened. Then he asked about Baragli.

'He hasn't got much time left,' said the inspector.

'Does he know that?'

'He seems to, at certain moments.'

'I hope I can make it in time to see him,' said Piras.

'Well, you never know . . .' said Bordelli. The phone call was slipping into gloomy territory. They said goodbye and Piras went out.

The Setzus lived next door. Parked on the street were a couple of cars and a few three-wheeled vans. Some scooters and bicycles were propped up against the wall. He knocked on the door and Adele, the young daughter of Sergio Minnai, a cousin of Giovanni's, came to the door. She was seven years old and had a big mop of black hair on her head. Piras had never heard her say a word. He stroked her cheek and went inside. The children were all in the kitchen, having a snack and quietly playing.

Piras climbed the stairs, one step at a time, as Giovanni started coming down slowly, arms dangling. They met halfway and stopped. Giovanni's face looked tired and his bald head was glistening with sweat. Piras asked him how his wife was doing. Giovanni shook his head and in a whisper told him what had happened over the past few hours . . .

Pina had spent the night pacing about the house, reciting the rosary. At dawn she'd collapsed and lain down on the brick bench next to the hearth. Early that morning Giovanni had gone with the *carabinieri* to their Oristano station to complete the formalities. They asked him about Benigno's pistol, which turned out not to be registered, but neither he nor Pina knew a thing about it. The report stated: 'weapon of unknown origin not registered by owner'. They also told him that in such cases the judge declared the weapon illegal and ordered it destroyed. Then they told him that Benigno had died around 6 p.m. on Sunday and that his mortal remains could now be returned to his next of kin.

And so Giovanni had gone to buy a coffin for Benigno and returned to Bonarcado with a hearse from the funeral home. A little while later an ambulance arrived, and the body was laid in state in the house. Benigno's body had been brought to their house because his parents were no longer alive, he was an only child, and he had never married. Pina was his closest relation as well as his sole heir. Pina's and Giovanni's sons had been alerted, but they both worked 'on the continent', had very young children, and unfortunately could not come, not even for Christmas. The journey was too expensive to make every single year. They would come the following year.

'What's happening with Benigno's sheep and pigs?' Piras asked.

'Barraccu's looking after them.' He was an old friend of the deceased who lived in Tramatza.

'I'm going to go say hi to Pina,' said Piras.

Giovanni went downstairs, and Piras went up. He quietly entered the death chamber, which was illuminated only by candles. There were some whispers of greeting, then silence. The children downstairs could be heard making noise, but nobody paid any attention. There were some twenty people in the room, relatives and friends. Piras knew most of them. His eyes searched for Pina in the penumbra and found her sitting in a corner. He went over to her, trying not to make any noise with his crutches.

'Ciao, Pina,' he whispered.

She looked up, and a smile appeared on her face swollen with grief. 'Ciao, Nino.'

'Why don't you go and rest for a while . . .'

'Do you think he'll go to hell?' she asked.

'Hell doesn't exist, Pina.'

'I don't think God will send him to hell, I really don't think so . . .'

'God doesn't send anyone to hell, Pina. I'm going to go say goodbye to Benigno.'

He went up to the deceased. The coffin lay on the bed, sinking into the mattress. The lid was propped up in a corner of the room. Benigno looked at peace, which he had never done when alive. The head wound was hidden by a large square dressing. His cheeks had fallen back towards his ears, and the skin on his face was shiny, as if someone had oiled it. A dark wooden rosary was threaded through his fingers, with the crucifix in plain view. He'd been dressed up in a fine black suit and his Sunday shoes. Piras sent him his best wishes. He remembered when, as a child, he used to go fishing with Benigno in a rough torrent near an old abandoned mill at the foot of the Montiferru. They would go to a spot where the water formed a peaceful cove and sit on a rock, watching the cork on the surface, waiting for it to go under. At times they didn't say a word for hours at a stretch. The sound of the torrent filled their ears, and when he went to bed at night, he thought he could still hear it . . .

He felt something graze his elbow and turned round. Pina was beside him, approaching the coffin. She looked at Benigno and smiled. Then she reached out and caressed his face, first the cheeks, then the forehead, nose, mouth. To leave her undisturbed, Piras took a step back, then felt someone squeeze his arm. It was Giacomo, Giovanni's older brother, his face carved by his seventy years.

'Where are Maria and Gavino?' he asked in a whisper.

'They're on their way. Do you know anything about the funeral?'

'Nine o'clock tomorrow morning,' said Giacomo. There was a buzz in the room. Piras turned round and saw his parents come in.

That evening Bordelli went to have a bite to eat in Totò's kitchen and ended up chatting with him until almost eleven. It was easy to talk to Totò. He always had something to say about everything. But it was also easy to eat and drink too much in that kitchen. As he was leaving, the inspector swore that he would not set foot back in that place for at least a week. But he said this to himself often and didn't really believe it. It was just a way to ease his conscience until he had finished digesting.

Getting into the car, he thought he would drop in on Rosa but then changed his mind. He felt like being alone. He'd been feeling strange lately, and he didn't know why.

He went home, poured himself a glass of grappa and turned

on the television. He was just in time to watch the last national news report. The most important news item seemed to be Christmas. What presents Italians were buying for one another, how much they spent, who had a tree and who a crib, what they would be eating for Christmas Eve supper and Christmas Day lunch. All one saw were smiling faces. Apparently those who didn't smile weren't worth interviewing. The poor and unhappy were not part of the celebration. But perhaps the poor and unhappy no longer existed and were now extinct; maybe everyone was now rich and happy and bought each other gifts and tons of meat and tortellini. And he was just like everyone else, except for the fact that he laughed less than them. Bordelli shook his head. He felt like an old Scrooge letting bitterness get the better of him.

He emptied his glass, put the cigarette he'd been holding between his lips back in the packet and went into his bedroom, where he lay down in bed and turned out the light. Staring into the darkness, he started thinking about the girl in the photographs, the beautiful Marisa. What the hell were Rinaldi and Tapinassi up to? How long was it going to take them to find her? He could hardly wait to talk to her and learn the whole story behind those photos.

Then he thought again of Odoardo. He could see the young man's grim face, his nervousness at the mention of Badalamenti's name. It might mean nothing, of course, but why indeed had he given a start? If he'd never before heard of the man, why did he have that expression? True, he might never have met him. His mother would certainly have had no good reason to tell him about the man blackmailing her with those scandalous photos. Still, the boy gave him something to think about. That afternoon the inspector had checked the phone book and found Giampiero Balducci, architect, at Via Timoteo Bertelli 29. He'd felt tempted to call him then and there, but on second thought had decided not to. Given where the case stood at that moment, what point would there have been in talking to the architect?

What more could the man have told him about Odoardo? The inspector rolled on to his side, head full of vague impressions and useless questions. He kept coming back to the same point: Odoardo wasn't left-handed. He even reviewed Diotivede's explanations again, and found nothing to object to. The doctor had been quite clear about things. Asking him to confirm them yet again might make him turn nasty.

Bordelli changed position again, thinking he had to be very patient. Sooner or later something would turn up. But his brain kept on whirring. At supper time he'd gone back to call on the three men on the list who hadn't been there in the morning, and he'd returned the promissory notes to all three, unbeknownst to mothers and wives. Each had thanked him in his way. One with tears in his eyes, another with a hearty laugh. Mario Cambi had given him a bottle of farm-fresh olive oil and a jar of home-made tomato sauce . . . None, however, was left-handed. It was as if there were no left-handed people left in the world . . .

The inspector sighed deeply and buried his head under the pillow. For the moment the list was the only lead he had. He turned on to his other side, thinking he had to stop obsessing about his job. He was always turning something or another over in his head. He swept it all away, but a second later the shadowy face of Odoardo returned. The boy had a hardness in his eyes that certain sensitive people sometimes have, as if always leery, always careful to probe the world around them to avoid being tricked. He seemed quite emotional, yet able to pull himself back together in a hurry. When Bordelli told him that Badalamenti had been killed, his lips had hardened like a fist, but only for a second. But Odoardo wasn't left-handed . . .

21 December

He was woken up by a dull thud. It must have been a rubbish bin crashing against the truck while unloading. He remained in bed a little longer with his eyes closed, listening to the sounds of the morning. He heard the creaking of some vendors' carts on their way to the small open-air market in Piazza Tasso and realised that it was seven o'clock.

He took a long hot shower. After making coffee, he sat in the kitchen and drank it while leafing through the previous day's newspaper. He stopped on the cinema page. Perhaps one of these evenings he could take Rosa to see a film. They hadn't been to the pictures for several months. The last time they'd gone to see a James Bond film replete with shoot-outs and corpses painted gold like church candelabra, but the main attraction was Sean Connery, who was able to elicit a sigh even from the finicky Rosa.

'Did you know he looks like you?' she'd whispered in his ear in the packed cinema, during a close-up of Connery. The people seated closest to them heard everything and turned round to stare at them, to Bordelli's great embarrassment. Good thing it was dark.

'Talk softly, Rosa,' he'd whispered back, face burning red.

'What did I say?'

'Easy now . . . You're supposed to be quiet at the cinema . . .'

'Shhh!' enjoined a number of people all around.

'See, it's you they're upset at!' Rosa had said in all innocence. She'd liked the film immensely, not least because of the handsome actor. Another time he'd taken her to see a Western with endless shoot-outs and dead men who didn't bleed. She'd had great fun anyway, because one of the bandits was a blond guy with long hair and a face wicked enough to make you quiver. But Rosa's favorite films were the ones with Totò.

Bordelli went out at eight and got into his Beetle. The streets were still wet with the night's rain, but at that moment the sky was clear, and the sun shining through the car windows almost managed to warm him up. He crossed the Arno and minutes later turned on to the Viali. There was already a bit of traffic. When he got to Le Cure he turned down Via Volta and drove past the house where he'd grown up. As always he turned his head to look at the ground-floor windows. The shutters were open and some light shone through the living-room windows. He remembered every detail of that room the way it used to be. There was a large walnut cabinet with a glass front, full of antique glasses, a Flemish painting with sheep and clouds, and decorative floor tiles. It always gave him a weird feeling to know that another family now lived in that house.

The day he'd returned from the war was etched in his memory. He'd got back one morning, after a long train ride, holding a large German shepherd dog on a leash. He'd found the dog a few months earlier, lying down in a hole carved out by a mortar shell, with a serious wound in its side and breathing with difficulty. It was almost as big as a calf, and if anyone approached, it started growling. It had fangs as long as Focke-Wulf bullets. It was a Nazi dog, seemed fatally injured, and war was raging all around it. Too much trouble to bother with. Bordelli had pulled out his pistol to finish it off, taken aim, and was about to shoot . . . when it occurred to him that the dog wasn't guilty of anything and that he could try to save it. With some cunning he had managed to bring it back to camp without getting bitten and had decided to try to win its friendship. A week went by and he still was unable to approach it to attend to its wound. Once a day he would throw it something to eat, but the dog wouldn't touch anything, leaving it all to the flies. The animal was weak and had lost a great deal of blood. At moments it lay on its side with eyes closed, immobile, and looked dead. But if anyone approached it would start growling again. Then one morning Bordelli noticed that the beast had eaten everything around it, even the biscuits, and seemed much calmer. He managed to put a rope muzzle on it and treat its wound. After another week, it had turned into a big puppy. It was called Blisk, according to the tag on its collar, and he continued to call it Blisk. Then the war ended and it seemed only natural to bring the dog home with him. When, a year later, he moved out of his parents' house to the San Frediano quarter, his mother was almost happy. She couldn't stand having the great beast about the house any longer, leaving fur everywhere and practically knocking her down when it wanted to express affection.

Blisk was used to sleeping at the foot of its master's bed and following him wherever he went. Bordelli usually took the dog around with him, but when he couldn't, he needed only to say, 'Wait here,' and the ferocious beast of legend would sit down in front of the door with expectant eyes. When Bordelli returned, he would always find it in the same position.

Blisk eventually got old and tired, and Bordelli stopped taking the dog everywhere with him. One evening about ten years ago, when returning home, he'd found it lying in front of the door. It was weak and could hardly move. Blisk died with his muzzle in Bordelli's hands, after a long sort of whimper. It was almost as if the dog had waited for him to come home before dying. That same night, Bordelli had gone into his mother's garden in Via Volta, dug a deep grave, and buried the animal . . .

Thinking about that night, he realised he'd slowed down too much, and so he downshifted and stepped on the accelerator. In that area the streets were almost deserted. Just before the avenue started its ascent to San Domenico, he turned on to Via di Barbacane and climbed up that equally steep, old street. After a few curves, he pulled up in front of Fabiani's house and got out. The laurel hedge that ran along the iron grille had been trimmed. Bordelli went up on tiptoe to look into the garden. Fabiani was pruning the rose bushes in front of the glass door of the living room and wearing a blue work smock and rubber gloves. There was a bit of wind, and the doctor's white hair rose from his head like flames. Bordelli rapped on the gate to get his attention. Fabiani turned round, waved hello, and went to open the gate.

'You read my mind, Inspector. I was going to ring you tomorrow to wish you a happy Christmas,' he said, inviting him in. Fabiani had a beautiful voice, deep and warm, and eyes as clear as certain animals'.

'Telepathy,' said Bordelli, shaking his hand. Remembering what he had in his pocket, he felt a little uneasy, and perhaps it showed. It was different with the other people on his list, since he didn't know them or anything about them but was only a sort of postman delivering a letter.

'My dear Bordelli, you didn't come here to wish me a happy Christmas,' said Fabiani, half smiling and lightly shaking his head.

'Why do you think I've come, then?' Bordelli asked in a mutter.

'Perhaps to tell me the tale of the big bad wolf.'

Fabiani closed the gate and headed towards the house, with Bordelli following behind. The garden looked the way it always did, well tended but not too much so. Trees and plants were arranged in such a way as to create hidden nooks and shady corners. It seemed like the ideal place for seeking solitude, which was probably exactly what old Fabiani wanted.

'What can I get you, Inspector?'

'Nothing, thank you, I've just had some coffee.'

Before going inside, the psychoanalyst took off his dirt-covered boots, and they went and sat down in the living room in front of the closed glass door. At a distance of about ten yards from the house was an iron pagoda, overwhelmed by an age-old wisteria that was completely bare at that time of year. In the middle of the pagoda was a round marble table with four wrought-iron chairs around it. Bordelli had taken tea there several times.

Fabiani looked expectantly at the inspector without saying anything. His face was as small as a child's and covered with very fine wrinkles. Bordelli reached into his pocket and took out the photo of Fabiani's house and a stack of promissory notes, held together with a clip, and laid them down on the table. Fabiani adjusted his glasses on his nose, took the notes, looked at them, then set them back down without saying a word. He looked again at Bordelli, as though waiting for him to speak. The inspector put a cigarette between his lips but didn't light it.

'As you've probably read in the papers, Badalamenti was killed,' he said.

Fabiani took his glasses off and ran a hand over his head to tame his unruly white hair. 'I imagine you were surprised about me, Inspector,' he said, smiling faintly.

'Well . . .'

'You wouldn't have expected it, would you?'

'I'm sorry, Dr Fabiani – you don't have to tell me anything,' Bordelli said, feeling awkward. He then rose to his feet, to leave the doctor to his thoughts. He didn't want to give the impression he had come there expecting an explanation.

'Are you in such a hurry?' the old man asked in a sad tone.

'I just didn't want to attach too much importance to the matter.'

'You act as if I should be ashamed.'

'You're wrong . . .'

'Inspector, do you know exactly what the work of a psychoanalyst involves?' asked Fabiani, gesturing for him to sit back down.

'I'd like to say yes, but I'd probably be wrong,' Bordelli replied, obediently sitting down.

'Do you feel like listening to a rather sad story?'

'Only if you feel like telling me one.'

Fabiani remained silent for a moment, then began to speak calmly.

'In two words, the psychoanalyst has to bring into contact, so to speak, the different levels of the patient's inner life, which for some obscure reason remain divided or are even at war with one another.'

'What exactly do you mean by "levels"?'

'Or the different planes, if you prefer – that is, emotion, sentiment, reason, and so on. Some individuals experience tremendous inner conflict precisely because of this disharmony. What can happen is that reason will condemn the emotion, and thus the sentiment is broken in two, or else for some unknown reason these three levels live separately from one another out of mutual fear. There might be a whole range of causes: mistaken ideals, groundless fears, traumatic experiences, or a thousand other reasons related to the personal life of whoever is in that unpleasant condition. And that's where the psychoanalyst comes in. With the patient's help, which is absolutely essential, he will try to liberate him or her from the invisible illness that prevents him from living in peace. He will try to re-establish a certain harmony inside him. Even though, in the final analysis, it's an adventure in which both doctor and patient run a certain risk. This must never be forgotten.'

'It seems to me a fine profession,' said Bordelli.

'It's wonderful, even though it's based on entirely hypothetical assumptions. You're forced to proceed by trial and error, pretty much in total darkness. It requires a great deal of sensitivity, even delicacy. But tremendous detachment above all . . . Because it's perfectly normal, and beautiful, to grow fond of people; it happens to everyone. But it *must never* happen to a psychoanalyst . . . Vis-à-vis his patients, that is. Otherwise he risks contaminating the therapy with personal feelings and problems. It's even possible that the doctor will live out his own conflicts through the patient, and when that happens . . .'

The old man shrugged and shook his head, smiling with resignation.

'And when that happens?' Bordelli asked, curious.

'When it happens, things can go very badly. Do you remember when I told you some time ago that I had stopped practising because of a sort of work-related accident?'

Bordelli nodded. He had a strong hankering for a cigarette but decided to resist. Fabiani got up, went towards the glass door, and started looking outside. The sun was out, and a few blackbirds were hopping about on the lawn in search of worms.

'I won't tell you the whole story, because it involves other people as well, and that wouldn't be right. I'll only say that I made a very serious, professionally unacceptable mistake, which had very painful consequences.'

Bordelli finally lit his cigarette, eyes focused on the back of Fabiani's neck, and inhaled deeply. He would forgo the next one, but this one he wanted to smoke. The old psychoanalyst looked very thin, his smock draped over his body like a rag hung from a nail. He kept on looking outside, hands resting lightly on the glass door.

'I'm not guilty by any law, of course, but I can't escape my own judgement. It's true that there's a limit to the responsibility one can have for the life of another, and this is exactly what psychoanalysis teaches ... That everyone is fundamentally responsible for his own life, especially the inner life. But after that horrible episode I had nevertheless decided to stop practising, as you know. I was afraid I might make the same mistake again, and I didn't want to take that chance.'

The glass in front of Fabiani's mouth had fogged up, making a white spot which the doctor quickly erased with a sweep of the forearm.

'When did it happen?'

'About ten years ago. I took as long as I needed to set my former patients up with some colleagues of mine, then closed my office. I was already getting on in years, and it wasn't easy to change jobs. After trying unsuccessfully for a few months to find something, I started to get discouraged. I did do some odd jobs for publishers and wrote a few articles for a magazine, but it was never enough to live on. I have no family, no close relatives, but luckily I wasn't poor. I had a few valuable possessions ... furniture, paintings, objects ... Now and then I would sell something, though, truth be told, I never got much in return, since I'm not very good at that sort of thing. Little by little, my savings ran out. I must say I got scared. I wasn't used to counting my spare change to buy food. I was still trying to find something more stable, and finally things changed. I managed to find a job as a consultant, and I still give seminars at the University of Pisa. Come January I may even have a job at the courts. And I'm actually thinking of resuming practice, though starting with only two or three patients. All these things are very well remunerated, but since they're sporadic, so are the payments. I've had some big expenses with the house, and I must say that my dentist's bills have been considerable as well . . . And so I thought that a small loan might help me catch up with these things. I would have all the time in the world to pay the money back. So I went to my bank, but the only way I could get a loan would have been to mortgage the house, and I didn't want to do that. This house is all I have left. I spent many happy years here with my wife, and I would like to die here. But I urgently needed some money, and so . . .'

'You turned to Badalamenti.'

'And I would even have managed to pay the gentleman back, albeit with some difficulty.' Fabiani hadn't said a single word condemning the usurer.

'How did you know about him?' Bordelli asked.

'A clerk at the bank gave me his name.'

'Nice favour.'

'He told me that if the bank couldn't satisfy my needs, he knew a gentleman from whom I could obtain a loan without much trouble.'

'Who exactly was it that gave you this advice?' Bordelli asked, feeling a strong desire to drop in at that bank.

'I'm sorry, Inspector, but I'd rather not say. It's water under the bridge.'

'As you wish.'

'Thank you.'

'Forgive me for changing the subject, Doctor, but might I ask what you're doing for Christmas?'

'Normally I go for a walk in the morning, all the way to Fiesole, and then I return. As long as it's not raining, of course.'

'Would you like to come to dinner at my place on Christmas Eve? It'll all be people you know . . . though Piras, the Sardinian lad, won't be there.'

Fabiano looked at him with the hint of a smile on his lips.

'Let me think about it. But thank you,' he said.

Bordelli stood up to leave.

'If you decide to come, give me a ring,' he said.

'I'll call anyway to wish you a good Christmas.'

'Ah, I almost forgot. Is this yours, by any chance?' Bordelli pulled out the same ring he'd been showing to everyone, the one with the name *Ciro* inscribed inside, and held it between his fingers. Fabiano looked at it.

'Never seen it before. Why do you ask?'

'Nothing important. I'll let you get back to your roses, Dr Fabiani.'

Benigno's coffin was sealed at ten o'clock, and four men carried it out of the Setzus' home. Friends and relatives waited out in the street, silent and dressed in black under a blanket of dark clouds. The coffin was lowered and then slid on to the open flatbed of a light truck, which drove off at once. The small gathering of people then headed off to the Corso, walking slowly. Piras hopped along on his crutches beside Ettore and Angelo, who had skipped work to attend the funeral. The wind was blowing from the south, bringing with it not only an increase in temperature but a very fine, reddish sand that stuck to the windows of houses and cars.

They climbed the broad stone staircase leading up to the church, then entered in silence. It was as cold inside as outside, but more humid. The coffin had already been laid before the altar. It was a dark day, and the church was in penumbra. Through the tall windows as narrow as loopholes there entered just enough light to prevent one from running into the pews. Everybody sat down and waited for Don Giuliano, the priest.

Some exchanged a few words in subdued voices, steam escaping from their mouths. A buzz of whispers filled the church. Piras and his friends sat in the back, on straw-bottomed chairs. Gavino and Maria were farther up, next to Pina.

Collu's son came through a door, dressed in altar boy's garb, ringing a bell. Behind him was the priest, wearing funeral vestments. Don Giuliano was short and broad and looked like a true shepherd. His face was as sunburnt as everyone else's. He had been born in Gonnosfanadiga, a secluded village at the foot of Mount Linas, and was always saying he wanted to return there to die. He talked constantly about the steep steps that led from Gonnos to the top of the hill, from where one could see the whole plain all the way to the horizon.

He began the mass, and all rose to their feet. A few minutes later, they all sat down again. Piras could scarcely remember the liturgy and looked at the others to see what he should do. He couldn't quite manage to follow the service; it reminded him too much of how oppressed he felt as a child in that same church. In the end he started thinking again about Sunday night, when he'd found Benigno sitting in that armchair . . .

The *carabinieri* had arrived from Milis, followed by an ambulance. There were two of them. The older of the two looked like a smaller version of Amedeo Nazzari and may have even cultivated the resemblance by growing a moustache exactly like the actor's. The other officer was a skinny, stony-faced youth of about twenty. (Piras played the whole scene again in his mind.) The *carabinieri* had written out the report, starting from the moment Ettore's Fiat 500 arrived at the Zocchinu quarry. The stretcher-bearers then took away Benigno's corpse and loaded it into the ambulance. The *carabinieri* put the pistol in a sack and took it away. Benigno's beret remained on the floor. Piras picked it up and gave it to Pina. He'd then locked up Benigno's house, and the 500 had driven off to Bonarcado. Pina didn't say a word until they'd reached town.

He felt someone tug his shoulder and awoke from his reverie. It was Angelo, telling him to stand. The priest was about to bless the deceased. Piras rose to his feet and started watching Don Giuliano, who was raising a brush dipped in holy water over the coffin, but before he had finished murmuring the Holy Benediction, Piras's mind had slipped back to the evening of the suicide. He had the sensation that something had eluded him and was therefore continually reviewing in his head everything that had happened . . . The arrival of the *carabinieri* . . . the report . . . the pistol . . .

Angelo tugged at his sleeve. The mass was over. They all filed out of the church, and the coffin was loaded back on to the truck. The cemetery was just outside the town, at the opposite end to the church. It was a nice cemetery, orderly and clean, with high walls and dark cypresses. The priest mingled with the group, and everyone began to follow the truck, which now proceeded at a walking pace. Piras remembered the funerals of his childhood, with the coffin on a wooden cart pulled by a donkey. Ettore was walking beside him, telling him an old story about Benigno, but Piras had heard it many times before and wasn't listening. He was still thinking of that Sunday night and trying to bring into focus the thing that eluded his grasp.

They arrived at the cemetery. The hole in the ground was ready. It had been dug by Mattia Magliona and his son. Magliona had been a gravedigger since adolescence, alongside his father, and was now teaching his son the trade. His graves all had perfectly vertical walls and right angles.

Unloading the coffin from the flatbed, they lowered it with ropes into the hole, as everyone approached the edges to watch. The priest said something, not as a priest but as a friend. Pina stared at the coffin as if she wanted to jump into the grave herself. Giovanni had his hands on her shoulders. Then Mattia and his son began shovelling the earth back into the hole . . .

At that moment Piras realised what it was that had been dancing around in his head, and he pressed his lips together. Perhaps it was only his policeman's obsession that made it seem so important. Perhaps it was only a useless detail. But the thing gave him no peace.

★   ★   ★

At one o'clock, Bordelli's Beetle was parked in Piazza della Vittoria. He was sitting inside with the window open, smoking a cigarette as he watched the Liceo Dante. The limpid sky had only one large Flemish cloud in it, immobile as a mountain. There were already a few parents' cars in front of the school. Along the pavement were long queues of bicycles, Vespas and even a few Solexes, those strange motorised bicycles whose engines sat atop the front wheel.

Earlier that day, Tapinassi had come into the inspector's office, flourishing a sheet of paper in the air. He'd found the girl in the photographs.

'She's called Marisa Montigiani, Inspector.' She lived in Viale Don Minzoni, was seventeen years old, and attended the Liceo Dante.

Bordelli had asked for the photos back, since they were no longer needed. Tapinassi readily obeyed, but with a certain regret. It was almost as if he were breaking up with his girlfriend.

The inspector didn't want to call on the girl at home. He didn't want to risk causing any trouble in the family. He was hoping that nobody came to the school to pick the girl up, since Viale Don Minzoni was just round the corner from where she lived. Informing himself as to the schedule, he'd gone to wait outside just before classes let out.

He heard the bell ring inside the building and recalled the days when he'd attended the same *liceo* many years before. A dark time, with strict rules for all children starting at the age of eight. He got out of the car, tossed aside his cigarette, and waited on the pavement. Moments later the boys and girls started coming out. They created quite a commotion around them. The girls were colourful and full of smiles. When Bordelli had gone to school there weren't many girls, and what few there were dressed in black and came out silently, in orderly single file.

Little by little, the bicycles and Vespas started to move. Car doors slammed and the vehicles drove off. The inspector scanned the groups of girls, looking for ones with long black hair, and at last he saw her. She was walking beside a chubby blonde and laughing. Marisa looked even more beautiful than in the photographs. She was wearing a navy-blue overcoat and white woollen gloves. Bordelli crossed the street and went up to her.

'Miss Montigiani?'

'Yes?' she said, stopping. Her friend also stopped.

'Could I speak with you alone for a moment?' Bordelli asked, looking her in the eye. She was really very beautiful. She looked like an actress.

'And who are you?' Marisa asked, a furrow in her brow. The friend stood still, watching.

'I'll tell you as soon as we're alone,' said Bordelli, with a reassuring smile.

Marisa turned to her friend. 'I'll be right back,' she said.

'Don't take all day,' the little blonde said, staring at Bordelli. Then she went towards the street corner swarming with boys and girls.

'What is it?' Marisa said, frowning. Her dark eyes sparkled like wet stones.

'I'm Inspector Bordelli, police . . .'

'What?' the girl said in a quavering voice, looking at the badge the inspector had thrust under her nose.

'No need to worry. I just want to ask you a few questions.'

'What's happened?' she said, upset.

'I want you to tell me about Totuccio Badalamenti,' Bordelli said calmly.

The girl opened her eyes wide and blushed all the way to her ears. 'I've never heard of him.'

'I found the photos.'

'What photos?'

'Signorina Marisa, I beg you please to cooperate . . .'

The girl's eyes strayed, looking for her friend, and when she spotted her she gestured as if to say not to wait for her. The friend waved goodbye and left. The throng of kids was thinning out.

'I hope you don't think *I* killed him,' Marisa said in a soft voice.

'I just want you tell me quite honestly what your relationship with him was.' By this point they were almost alone, and the few remaining kids in front of the school were watching them with curiosity, perhaps trying to understand who the man in the dark trench coat talking to Marisa was.

'I don't want to stay here,' she said, looking around.

'Shall we walk a little?'

'Don't you have a car?'

'It's over there,' said Bordelli.

They crossed the street and got into the Beetle. The girl set her books down at her feet and sighed. She moved very naturally, like a wild animal. She was very different from how she appeared in the photos.

'When I saw on the telly that the guy'd been killed I thought, "Good! He deserved it!" I know that's not very nice,' said Marisa.

'Just tell me everything, slowly, from the beginning,' the inspector said.

Marisa breathed deeply. She seemed a bit agitated. 'He told me he could get me into a film . . . with Mastroianni,' she said, looking outside. She felt embarrassed for having fallen into the trap like a chicken.

'And that was why he asked to take those photographs?' the inspector enquired, sniffing the air. The compartment had filled with the girl's lovely scent. Even the car's dusty interior seemed to look better.

'He was very insistent. He said he had to send some photos at once to Cinecittà, because Mastroianni was looking for a girl just like me.'

'It's a rather old trick.'

'I was a fool, I know. At first I didn't want to do it, but then I started thinking I was passing up a unique opportunity . . .'

'Do your parents know?'

'Noooo,' said the girl, waving a hand in the air. She had slender fingers that looked as fragile as breadsticks. Bordelli studied her attentively. She was truly very beautiful. She had a finely drawn mouth and two red lips that looked made for kissing. She looked a little like a famous French actress he liked a great deal . . . What the hell was her name?

'When did he take those photos?' he asked.

'And to think that you've seen them . . . I'm so embarrassed . . .'

'Don't think about it. When did he take them?'

'Late last month. I skipped school one morning and went to the guy's house. He said he had a very good camera and the right clothes, and would do it for me for free . . . And I fell for it, like a complete idiot.'

'How did you meet him?' Bordelli asked.

'By chance, at the UPIM department store. He'd been staring at me for a while and always seemed to be appearing right in front of me. Then he came up to me and introduced himself. He started in immediately with that story about the movies and gave me his telephone number. He even said he was good friends with Celentano and Little Tony. Right then and there he seemed like a cool guy . . . Jesus, what an idiot!'

'And then?'

'Do you swear never to tell any of this to my parents?' Marisa asked with fear in her eyes.

'You have my word that I have no such intention whatsoever,' said Bordelli. The girl thought about this for a moment, then resumed speaking.

'I went to his place and he gave me some things to put on, and we started taking pictures. He would tell me how I should stand, that sort of thing . . . He seemed to know what he was doing . . . How am I supposed to know how these things are done?' She paused for a moment, seeming increasingly tense, as if the memory of those things made her feel very uneasy and ashamed.

'At a certain point he told me to take off my bra and cover myself with my arms. I turned round and took off my bra. When I turned round again, he'd put the camera down. He started saying he couldn't control himself, and he was in love with me . . . He

148

put his arms around me and started kissing me. I tried to push him away, but he was holding me tight . . . I felt his mouth on my neck . . . I was really scared . . . He kept saying, "Come on, be a good girl." He seemed like a different person, he had a wicked look in his eyes and was breathing heavily. He was holding my head and trying to kiss me. I kept pushing him away, but he was a lot stronger than me. Then I tried to scratch his face, and he got angry and threw me down on to the bed . . . and then he jumped on me and touched me all over. I started screaming and he put his hand over my mouth. He said that girls like me were made for this . . . and that I shouldn't play the prude, because he knew I did it with everyone . . . and he kept repeating that I would like it, because a man is different from a boy . . . He seemed like an animal. I kept on kicking, and then he started slapping me. He would slap me and then bend down to kiss me. He said I was just a silly girl who would never amount to anything anyway . . . And then at a certain point I noticed . . . I don't know how he did it . . . he'd opened his trousers . . .'

She stopped talking and pulled her overcoat tightly around her.

'Did you manage to get away?' Bordelli asked, impatient to know. Marisa didn't answer. She closed her eyes and two tears, as big as grains of maize, rolled down her cheeks. When she resumed speaking, her voice quavered a little.

'. . . I tore off his glasses and threw them against the wall . . . He couldn't see without them . . . And so I smashed my head against his nose . . . and I was finally able to get him off me . . . I put my coat on and grabbed all my stuff in a hurry and ran down the stairs . . . When I got outside I started trembling from the cold, because I had hardly any clothes on under my coat . . . So I went to a bar and got dressed in the bathroom . . . I felt so stupid I wanted to die . . .'

Bordelli was trying to imagine the scene as she was recounting it, and suddenly found himself with a cigarette between his lips. Unlit. He bit it. He wished Badalamenti were still alive so he could have a few words with him, man to man.

'Was that the last time you saw him?'

'Yes,' the girl said, wiping her face with her fingers. Then she added that a week later she had phoned him from a public place to ask him for the photos back, and Badalamenti had replied that she could come and get them whenever she liked . . . But he'd said it in a tone that left little room for doubt . . .

'What was the date?'

'I dunno, the fifth or the sixth.'

'Have you told any of this to anyone?'

'I'm sorry, but could we go closer to home?' Marisa asked, looking at her watch. Bordelli started up the car and drove off.

'Have you told this story to anyone?' he asked again.

'No . . . I mean, yes . . .'

'To your boyfriend?'

'No,' she said, staring at the street.

'Don't you have a boyfriend?'

'I told my brother,' Marisa said, blushing.

'And what did he say?'

'He got really pissed off,' said Marisa, eyes widening.

'At you?'

'At me too . . .'

The inspector was driving slowly to buy time, and perhaps also because it was pleasant having so much beauty right beside him.

'Did your brother ever go to Badalamenti's house?'

'Surely you aren't thinking . . .'

'I'm not thinking anything, I'm just trying to understand,' Bordelli said, smiling placidly.

'It wasn't him,' Marisa said.

'Did your brother ever go to Badalamenti's house?' the inspector repeated.

'Yes, but . . . all they did was quarrel.'

She explained what had happened. When she'd tried calling *that guy* again, he'd only laughed in her face and called her a 'whore'. And so, to get it all off her chest, she'd told the whole story to her brother, and that same afternoon, rather late in the day, they'd gone together to a bar in Piazza della Libertà, where there was a booth with closing doors, and called Badalamenti. Hearing a man's voice, Badalamenti had an even worse reaction and started insulting Marisa . . . 'Slut, prostitute, cunt, and even worse,' she said, blushing. And her brother, for his part, was not about to be outdone. Badalamenti then said he didn't want to be bothered any longer and threatened to send the photographs to some men's magazine . . . At this point her brother had got pissed off in earnest and told Badalamenti that if he didn't turn the pictures over of his own accord, he would go there and get the bloody things himself. Marisa thought her brother was saying this just to frighten him, but the following day he'd actually gone to the guy's house. And they'd nearly come to blows . . . But nothing more of this sort had happened after that. And her brother had never managed to get the photos back. She hadn't learned about it till afterwards, otherwise she would have tried to prevent her brother from going . . . Because *that guy* was crazy.

'So your brother never went back there after that?'

'No . . . I don't think so,' Marisa said, unsure. She added that her brother had wanted to report Badalamenti, but she'd begged him not to, because she was terrified at the thought that her parents might find out about the whole thing. There really seemed to be no easy solution to the problem, and in the end she had almost thought of letting it all drop. At a certain point, however, she couldn't stand it any longer. Knowing that Badalamenti had those photos and could look at them whenever he wanted made her feel too terrible. And so she'd tried calling him again, hoping to convince him one way or another, even if she didn't quite know how. But he hadn't answered the phone. She'd kept on calling for a few days more, at all times of the day, but he was never in . . . Then one evening she'd seen the newspaper . . .

'What does your brother do?' Bordelli asked.

'He plays electric guitar,' she said.

'And that's all?'

'He's very serious about it . . .'

'Where can I find him without going to your parents' place?'

'He's hardly ever at home, anyway. He's always at a friend's house,' said Marisa.

'What the friend's name?'

'Guido Fontana.'

'Is he related to the lawyer?' asked Bordelli, who knew the man by reputation.

'He's his son.'

'Where does he live?'

'In Via Stoppani.'

Bordelli knew the street well. It was a cross-street off Viale Volta. A private, rather posh street at that.

'I think I'll go and look for him straight away,' he said.

'What are you going to do?' Marisa asked anxiously, perhaps imagining an interrogation of the kind she'd seen in American movies.

'I just want to talk to him.'

'Pay no attention to his manners . . . He's a lamb.'

'What's his name?'

'Raffaele, but we call him Lele.'

'Does he have a girlfriend?'

'I don't think so . . . You can let me out here,' said Marisa, at the corner of the Ponte Rosso. Bordelli pulled up to the kerb but left the engine running. She opened the door, put a foot outside, then turned round.

'Could I have those photos back some time?' she asked, embarrassed.

Bordelli opened the glove compartment and pulled out an envelope. 'Here you are. The negatives are there, too,' he said.

Marisa opened her mouth in surprise, hastily checked to verify that they were really the photos, then hid them in her satchel.

'I'm going to burn them,' she said, a flash of joy in her eyes.

'I cut up two of them to help my patrolmen find you.'

'Thank you,' she said, blushing.

'How old is your brother?' Bordelli asked.

'Twenty-six.'

'So he saw the war through the eyes of a small child '

'He hardly remembers anything . . .' Marisa said, shrugging. She seemed more relieved since he'd given her the photos. She'd even managed to smile . . . A beautiful smile, full of little white teeth surrounded by soft lips fresh as cherries.

'Did you hear me, Inspector?'

'Eh?'

'I said goodbye,' Marisa said.

'I'm sorry . . .' Bordelli said, coming to, and he blushed as if the girl could read his mind. He'd been spellbound for a few long moments in a dream . . . where he was twenty-five and had just met Marisa and was trying to arrange a date with her.

'My brother hasn't killed anybody,' said Marisa, shaking her head. She seemed to be talking as much to herself as to him. The inspector pulled himself together and tried to assume an impassive expression.

'Is your brother left-handed?' he asked.

'Yes, why do you ask?'

'Nothing, just curious,' said Bordelli, feigning indifference.

'Lele likes to act tough, but it's all put on,' Marisa said. Then she gestured goodbye and got out and ran across the piazza. When she reached the pavement, she slowed her pace and turned round for a second to look at the Beetle. Then she quickened her pace again. Bordelli sat there and watched her. She looked like a filly agitated by a storm. She was as beautiful as the full moon, he thought. She had to be more careful than the other girls.

Right after the funeral, Piras asked Ettore and Angelo to take him to Benigno's farmhouse, saying he wanted to check something. He'd asked Pina for the keys, with the excuse that they ought to turn off the electricity. She'd given them to him without batting an eye.

Ettore drove fast, and fifteen minutes later they were already on the dirt road that led to the Zocchinu quarry. When they pulled up in front of the house, the sun was high in the sky. There was a rusty Motom motorbike propped up against the wall. It must have belonged to Gioacchino Barraccu, the shepherd who'd been looking after Benigno's animals since his death. At that hour he was out in the pasture.

They entered the house and went upstairs. Going into the room in which Benigno had shot himself, Piras started pacing back and forth, looking at the floor.

'What are you looking for?' Ettore asked.

'The shell.'

'The shell?' Angelo asked.

'It must be around here somewhere. Give me a hand, you two, if you don't mind,' said Piras.

All three of them started searching. They looked in every corner of the room and under the furniture and even dug their fingers into the folds of the armchair. But they didn't find it.

'It's not here,' Ettore finally said, throwing his hands up.

'Shit,' said Piras, still circling about the room with his eyes on the floor.

'What the hell do you need the shell for?' Ettore asked, having already grown bored.

'Can't you figure it out for yourself?' Piras said without looking at him.

Ettore thought about it for a moment, staring into space, then shook his head. 'No . . . What do you need it for?'

'It's not possible . . . it has to be here. Let's keep looking,' Piras said, getting agitated.

'Maybe it got tangled up in his clothes,' Angelo said blithely. Piras thought about this for a second, then shook his head and continued searching the room. The others exchanged a glance and raised their eyebrows, resigned, then resumed looking for the shell without much conviction, just to make their policeman friend happy.

'C'mon, Nino, there's nothing here,' Angelo finally said, putting his hands in his pockets.

'I'm hungry,' said Ettore. They were fed up. Piras looked at his watch. It was almost one o'clock.

'All right, let's go,' he said, walking towards the door. There was no point in carrying on the search. The goddamn shell just wasn't there. Piras turned off the electricity and then locked the main door. He remembered that on the night of the suicide it had been closed with only the spring-lock, not with a turn of the key or bolted. But that, of course, might be perfectly normal, since Benigno was about to go out to Pina's place for dinner.

'So?' said Ettore, seeing that Piras's thoughts were elsewhere.

'Wait, I just want to have a quick look behind the house,' said Piras.

'*Arrazze 'e segamentu,*'[14] Angelo muttered between clenched teeth. The other two followed Piras behind the house. The fold was empty, the sheep out to pasture along with the dog. The pigs had plenty to eat, and the sty had been cleaned that morning. The donkey was placid. Everything seemed in order. Barraccu was doing a good job looking after everything. Piras checked the windows of the house and made sure the back door was locked tight.

'All right, we can go,' he said.

'Yes, sir, General, sir,' said Ettore.

They circled back to the front of the house, got into the car, and drove to the main road. The little Fiat's motor whirred like a fine watch. Piras sat in silence, rehashing the question of the missing shell in his mind, while his two friends chatted about the upcoming Christmas dinner, discussing which relatives would or wouldn't be coming.

'Don't tell anyone what we went to do there,' Piras said when they were within sight of Bonarcado. Angelo and Ettore swore to keep their mouths shut, though from the way they said it, it was clear that they thought that all this mystery was a bit overdone.

Ettore dropped Piras off in front of his house, then continued on his way with Angelo. Piras glanced at his watch. He looked over at the Setzus' house, hesitated for a moment, then made up his mind and went and knocked on the door. When Pina appeared, he returned the keys to her and asked her whether he could please have a look at the clothes Benigno was wearing when he died. Pina was so tired she didn't even ask him why. She let him in and led him upstairs to the room where they had changed Benigno's clothes. She opened a wardrobe and took out some clothes.

'Here they are,' she said.

Piras asked her please to lay them out on the bed, then propped a crutch against the wall and with his free hand began to squeeze the sweater and trousers. He then held them up in the air and shook them. There was no shell.

'All right, I'm done. Thanks,' he said.

'What were you looking for?' asked Pina without much interest.

'Nothing. I'm going to go and eat. If you need anything, don't be afraid to ask. Come whenever you like.'

'I'm going to lie down for a while,' she said.

'Why don't you come over tonight and watch some television with us?'

'No, not tonight,' said Pina, her eyes lifeless.

'Then tomorrow. There's going to be a film on Channel Two.'

'All right, maybe . . .' she said.

They descended the stairs in silence, gestured goodbye at the door, and Piras went home. His parents had waited for him to start eating. The pasta water had been boiling for a long time over a low flame, but in the end Maria had turned off the gas.

'It's almost two o'clock,' said Gavino. The television was turned off.

'Go ahead and put the pasta in,' said Piras, 'I'll be right there.'

'What are you doing, Pietrino?' his mother asked, lighting the flame under the pot.

'I have to make a telephone call.'

'A girl called about an hour ago, asking for you,' Maria said in a neutral tone.

'Oh, really?' said Piras, studying his mother's face. Normally Sonia never called at that hour.

'I'm hungry,' said Gavino, but nobody paid any attention.

'She said her name . . . but I've already forgotten it . . .' said Maria, trying to remember.

'Francesca?' asked Piras.

'Yes, Francesca,' Maria said, smiling.

'And what did she say?'

'It's not true, nobody called. I just wanted to know what her name was,' she said with satisfaction.

'Well, now you know,' Pietrino said curtly, having already guessed his mother's game.

'The water's boiling,' said Gavino.

'But why won't you tell us anything about this girl? Is she really so ugly?' Maria asked, finally getting it off her chest.

'She's a monster,' said Piras, thinking of Sonia's face. He could hardly wait to hold her in his arms.

'Maria, put the pasta in,' said Gavino, getting tired of their banter.

At last the spaghetti were lowered into the pot. Pietrino limped to the hall and closed the door behind him. He phoned the *carabinieri* in Milis and asked whether anyone had perhaps picked up the shell of the bullet that had killed Benigno, but nobody knew anything.

'It must still be in the dead man's house. But I don't think it really matters,' said Amedeo Nazzari.

Piras thanked him and hung up. He stood there staring at the closed kitchen door, wondering about the missing shell. Nobody can kill himself and then make the shell disappear.

'It's almost ready, Nino,' Gavino shouted.

At three o'clock Bordelli went into his office and opened the window. It was cold outside, but the room was warm and stank of smoke. He sat down without taking his trench coat off. As usual, he'd eaten too much in Totò's kitchen. Every time he went through that door, he would swear to himself not to overdo it, and every time he forgot his solemn vow. He stuck a cigarette in his mouth and was about to light it, but then he decided to wait and set it down on the desk. He thought again of Marisa, her dark eyes that looked like living stones, and all at once Milena's face came back to him . . . She had black hair like Marisa, and the same colour skin . . .

Enough of this crap. He'd best get down to work. He had to ring Marisa's brother, who was the first left-hander he'd come across in the investigation. The prospect excited him a little. Marisa had said her brother was always at his friend's house, and Bordelli grabbed the phone book and looked for the number of Gustavo Fontana the barrister. While searching he thought that if he could go back in time, he would throw caution to the winds and put a tap on Badalamenti's phone, without authorisation . . . Had he done so, he might now have a better lead to follow to get to the bottom of this affair. Well, let that be a lesson. Whatever the case, somehow or other he would find the person who had killed the loan shark. He was absolutely sure of this. And he said it so often to himself that he started to doubt his own certainty. At last he found Fontana's home phone number.

'Hello?' said a young man's voice. In the background Bordelli could hear music being played at high volume, but he didn't recognise it.

'Good afternoon, I'd like to speak with Raffaele Montigiani,' he said.

'I'm Raffaele, who's this?'

'Inspector Bordelli, police. I need to talk to you. When could we meet?'

'What's this about?' asked the young man, but the inspector could tell from his tone that Marisa had already told him everything.

'I just want to ask you a few questions,' said Bordelli.

'Is tomorrow all right?'

'I'd prefer we did it straight away.'

Raffaele was silent for a moment. Somebody turned the music down.

'Would five o'clock be okay?' asked Raffaele.

'Where?'

'In Piazze delle Cure, in front of Cavini's *gelateria*.'

'All right. Don't be late.'

They hung up. Playing around with his unlit cigarette, Bordelli tried to picture Raffaele's face based on his voice, and he imagined a boxer. He liked to amuse himself with such speculations, and often he was close to the mark. A moribund fly was flying slowly from one end of the room to the other before landing on the wall and staying there without moving. With realising it, the inspector lit the cigarette, blowing the smoke upwards while thinking again of Odoardo. The sensation that the kid was hiding something was still strong, and he felt that he needed to talk to him a little more. Actually, he liked Odoardo. The boy had a beautiful face and clear eyes. Except that, perhaps . . . he wasn't telling the truth.

When he looked outside and saw the sky darkening, he glanced at his watch and stood up. He slapped his paunch and screwed up his mouth. He had to lose a few pounds, he thought, but with Totò in the neighbourhood it wasn't easy.

He left the station, taking his time, then drove slowly to Piazza delle Cure. It was already dark outside. There were a lot of people in the streets. He parked near Cavini's, in front of a bunch of cut fir trees stacked against the wall. It was cold and rather windy, and he decided to wait in the car. Children passed with their woollen caps pulled down over their ears, and some of them stopped to look at the trees. Their mothers dragged them away, walking fast, hand on their collars and eyes closed against the wind.

A few minutes later a young man on a big motorcycle came round the corner of Viale Volta. The bike looked like a BSA. He slowed down and drove on to the pavement, then parked the motorbike against the wall and went and stood in front of the ice-cream shop. He had on a close-fitting black leather jacket, zipped up to his neck, and looked around impatiently. He wasn't very tall but had broad shoulders. His long chestnut hair covered his ears. He didn't look at all like Marisa, but it was definitely him. Bordelli got out of the Beetle and went up to him. The young man took off his gloves, and they shook hands.

'Nice bike,' said the inspector.

'It's not mine,' the youth said, working his chewing gum. Bordelli had been wrong. He had nothing of the boxer about him. He looked more like a medieval knight. He had a rather singular face, quite virile but also a bit feminine, and the contrast worked well. The wind was cold, and the inspector invited him to come inside the car. They got into the Beetle. Raffaele, needing space, pushed the seat all the way back.

'I already know what you want to ask me,' he said. He didn't move, but Bordelli could sense his nerves rustling under his skin.

'Your sister told me—'

'My sister has the brains of a chicken,' said Raffaele.

'I think she's only a little naïve.'

'Nobody else would ever have believed that bullshit.'

'Tell me about the time you paid a courtesy call on Badalamenti. When was that?' Bordelli asked.

'A couple of weeks ago, maybe less.'

'You don't remember the exact day?'

'I remember that it was a holiday.'

'The Immaculate Conception?'

'Bah, perhaps . . .'

'What time of day did you go there?

'I feel like I'm back at school,' said Raffaele.

'It's not a difficult question.'

'It was night, round about ten o'clock, I'd say.'

'Did you go alone?'

'Yes.'

'And you never went back?'

Raffaele shook his head.

'I was sure that if I ever went back, something bad would happen. The guy had lard in his head instead of brains. I really don't understand how Marisa could have trusted such a piece of shit.'

'Apparently he could be polite and persuasive.'

'With a face like that, it's hard to believe. I would have reported him except for the fact that my sister didn't want me to,' said Raffaele, shrugging.

'Exactly what happened when you went to his place?'

'Let's get straight to the point, Inspector . . . I didn't kill him.'

'I think I've heard that statement before.'

'You're like my father. You never say things openly.'

'What does your father do?' asked Bordelli, ignoring the provocation.

'He has a car dealership, earns tons of money but lives a shitty life. I'd rather clean cesspools than work for him.'

'And what do you do?'

'I make music.'

'What sort of music?'

'Nothing that you're familiar with, and at any rate you wouldn't like it,' said Raffaele, avoiding the subject. He was playing tough, and succeeding, in part. The inspector dropped the musical discussion and came to the point.

'How did you spend the day of the tenth of September?' he asked.

Raffaele started laughing. 'I really don't know. I didn't know I would have to remember,' he said.

'Try.'

'Listen, Inspector, that bastard deserved to die, and if I had rid the world of him myself I certainly wouldn't feel guilty about it. But the fact is, I didn't kill him. It's as simple as that,' said Raffaele, looking him in the eye. They were more or less the same words Benito Muggio had used.

'Did you come to blows?' Bordelli asked.

'Almost.'

'Did you threaten him?'

'When he said I had to pay him to get back those pictures of my *whore* of a sister, I flew off the handle and told him that if he didn't give them back to me . . . Well, anyway, I wanted to scare him.'

'But he didn't get scared.'

'I haven't told this to Marisa, but her little friend pulled out a switchblade and started counting to ten, and not very quickly, either. I realised he was just a little prick who made up lies so he could fuck young girls. He seemed much more relaxed with that knife in his hand.'

'And then?'

'Well, I didn't feel like getting my belly cut open over my fool of a sister . . . So when the guy reached the count of ten, I spat a nice big gob on his floor, wished him an early death, and left.'

'You were prophetic.'

'Maybe I have magical powers,' Raffaele said with a cold smile.

'So you gave up on the photos?

'I would have had to kill him to get them back, and, as I said, I didn't kill him.'

'But you can't remember what you did that Friday.'

'No, I can't. Do you remember what you did that Friday?' the young man countered. Bordelli smiled . . . He couldn't remember.

'What was that music I heard over the telephone?' he asked, offering him a cigarette.

'I don't smoke that stuff,' said Raffaele.

'Only marijuana?'

'Give me a break. Marijuana. I obey the law . . . I drink a bottle of grappa a day and smoke three packs of cigarettes with the government's seal on them, all healthy, legal stuff,' Raffaele said with the sneer of a gangster.

'So what was that music?' Bordelli asked again.

'It's not for you.'

'I used to say the same thing to my father when I listened to Duke Ellington.'

'The difference is that I know the Duke better than you do,' said Raffaele.

The inspector lit a cigarette, rolling the window down an inch or two. He was getting a little tired of being treated like an old codger incapable of understanding new things. He thought about what he'd gone through in the war and wondered whether this kid had any idea what had actually happened . . . Whether he knew who Mussolini and Hitler were, whether the name Buchenwald meant anything to him. Bordelli didn't want to play the part of the old pain in the arse trying to give lessons in life, but the question slipped out of him anyway.

'Does the name Buchenwald mean anything to you?' he asked, fully expecting the answer to be no.

Raffaele looked at him and shook his head. 'Treblinka, Sobibor, Birkenau, Mauthausen, Auschwitz, Majdanek . . . I know every piece of shit that ever rained down upon the earth, never mind that we're drowning in it. You Methuselahs think you know everything,' he said all in one breath.

'Methuselahs?' Bordelli wondered, never having heard the word before.

'Old fogeys,' said Raffaele.

'We all get old sooner or later.'

'People like you and my father are old inside. Age's got nothing to do with it. I see twenty-year-old kids who are older than my grandmother,' Raffaele said disdainfully. Bordelli didn't know what to say. It had never occurred to him that he might be *old inside*, and he tried to understand what this could mean. But, looking at Raffaele, he started to get an idea. The kid was made of a different *material* which Bordelli had never before seen up close. He wasn't arrogant or offensive. He was just a young man full of anger and rancour, as if the world had done him a great wrong by not being the way he wanted it. Seen from the outside, he was very different from Odoardo, and yet the two youths had something in common. Perhaps it was their attitude. It was as if they never had enough breathing room, were disgusted by just about everything, and their patience was at its limit.

Tiny drops of rain started to dot the Beetle's windscreen, and Raffaele slapped his thigh.

'Fuck,' he said in a low voice, thinking of the motorbike.

'Pay close attention, Raffaele, it's all very simple. A murder has been committed and I, unfortunately, am a policeman. You went to the victim's house, and it wasn't for a candlelight dinner. Badalamenti was killed on Friday the tenth. All I want is for you to tell me what you did that day, and if you have an alibi I'll have to verify it . . . Does that seem so strange to you?'

The young man sighed.

'I almost certainly spent the whole day with Guido, but I can't remember exactly what we did minute by minute,' he said, looking outside. Every so often a strong gust shook the car, as the wind gained in intensity. Pages of newspapers and plastic bags started to fly across the pavement.

'Is this yours?' Bordelli asked, taking out the ring found in Badalamenti's stomach.

'No,' said Raffaele.

'All right, then, I guess that's all for now.'

'I only ask that you don't call on me at home. My parents would make a tremendous scene. And, at any rate, I'm always at Guido's.'

'So there wouldn't be any problem if I came to your friend's place?'

'There's never anybody there.'

'All right.'

'Now it's my turn to ask you a question,' said the youth.

'Go ahead.'

'Are you really so interested in finding out who killed that guy?'

'It's my job.'

'Don't you have a less banal answer than that?' Raffaele asked, without malice. Bordelli thought about it for a moment. Not so much about what he should say, but about what words he should use. He was suddenly feeling anxious about not being *modern* enough. It was the first time this had ever happened to him. In his youth he'd been quite aware that his father had grown up in another era, but it was nevertheless an era he recognised. This young man, on the other hand, seemed to look at him as if he were from another planet. There was an abyss between them. Maybe it was all due to the fact that Bordelli had never had children and therefore didn't know this new race from up close. But Raffaele was waiting for a less banal answer, and he had to give him one.

'If we accept that it's all right to kill arseholes, there's a little detail that must be clarified at once: who decides which people are arseholes? It may all seem clear to you now, but things can change, as happened only a few decades ago . . . You said you know all about those things,' said Bordelli.

Though it had come out as a little speech, the inspector felt he'd expressed the concept fairly well. He took a last drag and crushed the cigarette butt in the ashtray. Raffaele sat for a few seconds in silence, thinking it over.

'Somebody always decides,' he said. Then he shook the inspector's hand and got out of the car. It was still drizzling, but very little. The young man straddled the BSA, kicked the starter a couple of times, rolled off the pavement, and went off, raising the front wheel. He disappeared round the corner of Viale Volta, but the noise of the bike could be heard for a good few seconds more.

As he was driving on the bridge over Le Cure, the inspector thought of Baragli and felt his stomach tighten. He decided to go and pay him a visit. Every time he went there, he was afraid he would find him dying or already dead. Reaching the end of Via Lorenzo il Magnifico, he turned right. As he was driving down Via dello Statuto, he pulled out his cigarettes, and as he lit one he thought seriously about the possibility of quitting for good. He could do it; he only had to find the right moment. Or else he only had to stop making all these excuses and go cold turkey. But it wasn't easy. Perhaps he could reach a compromise. Three or four cigarettes a day, and some exercise. If he'd been younger he would have gone back to Mazzinghi's gymnasium and sparred a little, but at his age, he no longer felt up to it.

He drove slowly through the irritating drizzle, which forced him to activate the windscreen wipers every thirty seconds or so. If he left them on the whole time, the glass dried up at once and the wipers dragged noisily; if he left them off, after a few minutes he could no longer see anything. It was one of life's little annoyances.

Halfway down Via Alderotti, he saw a man on the pavement walking briskly, hat pulled down over his eyes. He thought he knew him. Turning the car around, he drove past him again. It was him, in fact: Clemente Baroncini, known as 'The Baron', a con artist nobody'd ever been able to nab. A great one, in his way. The inspector stopped the car and got out. The man was coming towards him.

'Hello, Baron,' Bordelli said, accosting him. Clemente stopped dead in his tracks, looked him straight in the eye, and his face broadened into a smile.

'Bordelli! What a lovely surprise!'

They embraced, slapping each other on the back. The Baron was tall and well built, and rather handsome.

'You're looking good,' said the inspector.

'You don't look too bad yourself.'

They were on familiar terms, having attended elementary school together.

'What are you up to these days?' Bordelli asked.

'Oh, nothing much, the usual stuff.'

'Are you about to rob another dunce of his millions?'

'Bordelli! You know well that there are certain things I don't do any more,' said the Baron, pretending to be offended.

'Ah, sorry, I'd forgotten.'

'It's all water under the bridge.'

'Of course it is . . . Did you hear about that Milanese collector who bought a fake Cézanne a couple of months ago?'

The Baron narrowed his eyes, trying to recall.

'Yes, that does ring a bell.'

'Sixty-five million,' said Bordelli, raising his eyebrows.

'Damn!' said the Baron with a look of amazement.

'You should have seen how angry he was . . .'

'I can imagine.'

'Just think, the gentleman was even a great connoisseur of art, especially French Impressionism. I do wonder how he could have fallen for it.'

The Baron was staring at Bordelli with a twinkle in his eye, but said nothing. The inspector was sincerely curious to know how it had been done. He couldn't understand how one could so deceive an expert in French art. And if the unfortunate Milanese man could realise the Cézanne was fake after buying it, why not before? Bordelli would have paid a hundred thousand lire to know the whole story.

'It's not so easy to make a monkey out of an expert like that,' he said.

'I realise that,' said the Baron, repressing a smile.

'How would you have done it, Clemente?'

'How would *I* have done it?' said the Baron, with the same barely repressed smile in his eyes. Bordelli put a hand on his shoulder and squeezed it amicably.

'I know it wasn't you . . . I'd just like to know how you *would have* done it, that's all.'

'I really don't know,' said Clemente with a satisfied air.

'I'm sorry, you're quite right. You'd really have to be a genius to pull off something like that.'

The Baron seemed stung by these words, and his smile vanished. His vanity was bleeding.

'Well, actually, I can imagine *one* way it could be done,' he said, massaging his chin. He knew he was giving in to a provocation, but he couldn't help it.

'How?' asked Bordelli, feigning innocence.

'Well, you would need two paintings, a real one and a fake . . . But a good fake, a fake with bollocks. At the first meeting, you show the sucker the real one, and then, at the moment of payment, you bring the fake, making sure to arrange the meeting in a room without good lighting. It's a classic bait-and-switch, requiring manual skill and a touch of psychology. But it could work.'

'And where did you— I mean, where *would* you get the original?'

'I would borrow it from another collector, replacing it temporarily with the fake. And obviously on the sly.'

'I'm sorry, I don't understand . . . If you've got the original in your hands, why not sell that?'

'Well, in my case, because I'm not a thief.'

'Ah, I see. I hadn't thought of that.'

'But there might be another reason too.'

'And what would that be?'

'Sentimentalism,' said the swindler. They exchanged a glance of understanding and smiled.

'Thanks, Baron, that's a load off my mind. Got any plans for Christmas?'

'I was thinking of going up to Paris. It's quite a village. Apparently people sleep with chickens there . . . but I don't know in what sense, so I thought I'd go and check.'

'Keep the purse-strings tight, Baron. In Paris you can spend seventy-five million in a hurry.'

'I'll keep that in mind, copper.'

'Take care of yourself.'

'Ciao. I'll send you a postcard from Montmartre.'

They embraced again and the Baron went on his way. Bordelli got back inside the Beetle and watched his friend in the rear-view mirror, giving him one last look.

Baragli looked well that day. Some colour had returned to his face, and he was no longer in pain.

'I'm feeling much better, Inspector,' he said. He was sitting on the bed, in excellent spirits, and more confident in his movements.

'Maybe you'll even be able to spend Christmas at home,' said Bordelli.

'The doctor's against it, but if I keep feeling this way I'll lower myself out of the window,' the sergeant said. Bordelli was well aware that it was the morphine that made him feel that way. He looked at Baragli with the knowledge that these were probably his last days, and felt very sad.

'Diotivede came by to see me today . . . and the moment I saw him I thought he'd come to cut me open,' said the sergeant, smiling

'From him, it would be an act of friendship,' Bordelli said to keep them both smiling, though deep down he wasn't smiling at all.

With one hand, Baragli reattached a corner of the adhesive bandage holding the needle of the intravenous tube in the hollow of his elbow, then looked up to see whether the bottle was empty, but in fact it was still half full.

'And how's our Sardinian boy?' he asked.

'He's spending Christmas in Sardinia, but then he'll be back, just wait and see.'

'Is he still with the pretty Sicilian blonde?'

'Apparently.'

'What a beautiful girl,' said Baragli, staring into space.

'I agree,' said the inspector.

Baragli stopped smiling, leaned forward, away from the pillows behind his back, and brought his head close to Bordelli's.

'See that bed there, Inspector?' he whispered, gesturing to the bed opposite his.

'There was an old man there, no?'

'He died last night,' said the sergeant, raising his eyebrows and drawing a cross in the air. Bordelli sighed in commiseration. He really wanted a cigarette. He looked Baragli in the eye and tried to smile. It was embarrassing knowing more about his death than he did.

'A game of cards?' he enquired.

'Sure,' said Baragli, rubbing his hands together. He was in a good mood. The inspector took the deck and dealt, and they started playing.

'Any news about the loan-shark case, Inspector?' the sergeant asked.

'Diotivede is certain the killer is left-handed.'

'Well, if he says so . . .'

'Anyone can make a mistake.'

'Except Diotivede,' said Baragli in a knowing tone.

'I haven't seen any evidence to the contrary,' said the inspector.

'Have you called on any of the people on that list?'

'I've made a first round.'

'You'll have to be patient, Inspector.'

'I've got patience to spare,' said Bordelli. As they played he started telling Baragli about his visits to the usurer's various debtors, going into considerable detail. Then he told him about the post-mortem and the ring. They both joked about it a bit. Baragli laughed and the inspector forced himself to laugh along, but he was feeling more and more dejected. Bordelli even told the sergeant about Marisa, and how the beautiful young girl had fallen for Badalamenti's lies about the movies. Baragli shook his head.

'Today's kids want to do things too fast, Inspector. It's as if they're snakebitten.'

'Maybe we just don't understand them . . . Maybe we're too old,' said Bordelli.

'Have you ever gone into one of those dance clubs where the kids go? I have, when I was on the job . . . You get a headache just watching them.'

The inspector also told him about Raffaele and Odoardo, again in great detail. He said that Raffaele was left-handed and could not remember what he'd done that Friday. Then he told him about his difficult conversation with Odoardo and his suspicions about the reticent and seemingly fragile youth. Thinking aloud, he said that putting a tail on either Odoardo or Raffaele, or tapping their phones, would probably serve no purpose, and the same was true for any other potential suspect. The murder was not the sort of crime that would be repeated. There wasn't anything to keep watch over. Baragli listened to the inspector with the attention of a child. Bordelli fully satisfied his curiosity, and shook his head when he had finished.

'That boy, Odoardo,' he said, 'made a very strange impression on me.'

'But he's not left-handed.'

'No, but the other one is, Raffaele,' said Bordelli.

Baragli distractedly threw down a card. 'Whatever the case, Diotivede can't be wrong,' he said, shrugging.

'If you say that again I'm going to start thinking you don't really believe it.'

'Your turn, Inspector.'

'Three and four makes seven,' said Bordelli, picking up the seven of diamonds.

'*Scopa* . . .'[15] And how old is this kid?' Baragli asked.

'About twenty, I'd say.'

The sergeant looked lost in thought, eyes staring at the bed opposite. The empty one.

'Shall we stop playing?' Bordelli asked.

'No, I'm sorry . . . Whose turn is it?'

'Yours.'

At that moment the brunette nurse came in and greeted the two policemen. It must have been time for more morphine.

'Sleep well, Sergeant?'

'Very well, and I even had a dream about you,' said Baragli, turning on to his side and exposing a buttock.

'About me? And what did you dream?' asked the nurse.

'I'm afraid I can't tell you.'

'Ah, I get it,' she said, shaking a finger at him. Baragli was like a child in the woman's hands. She rubbed some cotton on his bottom and administered the injection.

'We'll be eating shortly,' she said.

'Can I invite you to dinner?' asked Baragli, grabbing her wrist.

'I never dine without champagne,' she said, then left humming to herself.

'If your wife could see you, she'd drag you home,' said Bordelli.

'With my feet tied to the rear bumper,' Baragli said, laughing. For Bordelli it was a relief to see him smiling, though his good humour had something macabre about it. They finished their card game and immediately started another.

'You know what I think, Inspector? I think you're planning to go and see that boy again, whether or not he's left-handed.'

'You mean Odoardo?'

'Yes.'

'You're right.'

'And I know why.'

'And why's that?'

'Because,' said Baragli, and he burst out laughing.

Bordelli woke up in the middle of the night wanting a drink of water. He'd fallen asleep with the light on and a book lying open, face down, on his belly. He could hear a light rain falling in the street. As he sat up, the book fell off the bed. He was rereading Beppe Fenoglio. He liked listening to another tell stories about partisan fighters and things that were happening at the same time as he was fighting the same enemy in another part of the country. He often wondered how certain Italians could remember the Nazis so well and the Fascists so poorly.

His throat was parched. He had forgotten to fill the basin on the radiator, and now the air was too dry. But it was also the fault of those delicious anchovies *alla piemontese* he'd eaten in Totò's kitchen. He always kept a bottle of water beside the bed, and he set upon this avidly, drinking almost all of it. Then he lay back down and turned off the light. With a little patience he would soon be asleep again . . .

Actually, he himself had encountered very few Fascists during those years, from '43 to '45. All in all, he was happy he had never shot an Italian, but if he'd found himself in a situation where he had to, he would not have hesitated. One October morning in '44, he was out on patrol with three of his comrades in a mountainous area in northern Tuscany. They were all very tense, and nobody breathed a word. They'd been hearing terrible things about the Nazi retreat. A few days earlier there had been rumours of a massacre in the Apennines. They told of some two thousand civilians killed by the Nazis, but nobody in the San Marco camp wanted to believe it.

They were advancing abreast of one another, about a yard

between them. There was some sunshine, and a few birds were screaming in the treetops. When they came out of the dense wood, they heard a burst of machine-gun fire and immediately fell down flat into the high grass. A cluster of bullets slammed into the trunks of the trees over their heads, throwing up a rain of splinters. Dragging themselves along on their elbows, they crawled quickly back into the woods. A strong smell of resin and fresh wood lingered in the air. But the shooting had stopped. A minute went by.

'Come out with your hands on your heads,' a voice shouted in the local accent. It sounded about a hundred feet away, and seemed to come from a long strip of low shrubs dotted with a few isolated trees. But nobody was visible.

'Are you Italian?' Bordelli shouted, trying to buy time.

'You can't get any more Italian! Who are you?' the same voice called out.

'San Marco.'

'Shit, so are we!' cried a shrill voice. Bordelli exchanged a glance with his men.

'Who's your commander?' he shouted towards the clearing.

'Who's yours?' shouted another voice. Nobody wanted to be the first to answer.

'We're with the king,' Bordelli said at last, winking at Gennaro, who lay on a bed of moss beside him. Nobody replied. A couple of more minutes passed. Then a fourth voice said:

'We're coming out, don't shoot.'

'Okay,' Bordelli shouted.

A few seconds later six men rose up from the earth like ghosts and started walking towards the wood. They came forward with their machine guns under their arms, pointing downwards. They were wearing clean uniforms and the same black berets that Bordelli and his men had on. It seemed sort of eerie. Bordelli and the others stood up, their machine guns pointing down, fingers on the trigger, and came out into the small clearing. The other six were still advancing, and they all looked rather young. The shortest one must have been the captain. He had a round face and eyes too small for even a child. But his gaze was sharp and alert. The others followed him like chicks.

'The little midget can go fuck himself! Italy belongs to Mussolini!' he said, with the passion of one whose only consolation lay henceforth in words. Bordelli waited for them to come nearer.

'Let's forget about that,' he said calmly. The Fascists stopped about twenty feet away. One of them was tall and fat and looked like a woodcutter. He had a gentle face. Another, tall and hollow cheeked, had a blade of straw in his mouth and was chewing it nervously. Four against six, thought Bordelli. They all looked each other in the eye, studying one another like animals. One of the six Fascists was smiling, and it wasn't clear whether he was afraid or just wanted to start shooting.

'Your king is a traitor,' the short one said, and spat on the ground beside him. Deep down, however, he seemed untroubled. Bordelli put on the safety catch on his weapon, then slung the gun over his shoulder. He turned towards his men and gestured for them to do the same. He waited till all their guns were at rest, then turned back towards the six Fascists.

'So why do you like the Germans so much?' he asked. Nobody answered. They didn't even change expression. But, one by one, they slung their machine guns over their shoulders. The short guy lowered his head.

'And yet you look exactly like us,' he said, 'from the outside.' The other five punctuated the quip with some throaty laughter.

'Disappointment is part of life,' said Bordelli.

'So is death,' said the other, rather dramatically. Bordelli didn't reply. The whole situation was very unpleasant and dangerous, actually like the whole shitty war itself. On one side stood those who were about to lose everything, and on the other were those who had nothing left to lose. Somebody could get seriously hurt. Bordelli looked at the Fascists' boots; they were clean and fairly new. He hadn't seen such shiny boots in quite a while.

'We're going to go now,' he said, looking their commander

in the eye, 'and we're going to forget we ever saw each other
. . .' Everyone remained silent for what seemed a long time,
staring hard at one another . . . When he thought about it now,
it reminded Bordelli of the final scenes of one of those Westerns
he'd seen at the Aurora cinema . . . After a few bars of music
and some extreme close-ups, the biggest bastard would draw
his pistol and a slaughter would take place.

But the commander only smiled in the end, even though he
had the face of someone about to howl in pain.

'That's fine with me,' he said.

'Let's hope we don't meet again,' said Bordelli. He wanted
to head back to the woods, but before turning his back on
them he wanted to be sure he could trust them. They might
be Italians, but they were still Fascists allied with Nazis. He
continued staring at the short one. He hoped he wouldn't have
to start shooting. He was used to doing so against Germans,
but this situation seemed strange. And yet they were the same
people, he kept repeating to himself. Whether Nazis or Black
Brigades, it made no difference. But if he had any say in the
matter, he would rather leave and forget he'd ever seen them.
The commander cleared his throat and spat again.

'We made Italy, and we'll take her back, that much is certain
. . . But I don't shoot at Italians in uniform,' he said.

'Goodbye,' said Bordelli, his thumbs hooked into his belt.

'*Viva il duce!*' said the commander, making the Fascist salute,
but it came off as a rather lifeless gesture. It seemed less an
affront than a habit. Bordelli nodded one last time, then turned
and started walking back towards the cover of the forest, flanked
by his men. They walked calmly, without turning round, but with
their ears pricked. And they were in a cold sweat. After they'd
walked about a hundred yards, they heard the captain yell again.

'Give my regards to your dickless king!'

They heard the other five laugh.

'The bastards are right,' Respighi said in a low voice,
frowning.

'Let's first get the hell away from those buffoons, and we

can worry about the king later,' said Bordelli. At that moment he couldn't imagine what would happen in Italy after a defeat was transformed into a victory. Because one thing alone was certain: the Allies were going to win the war, and it wasn't going to take them very long, either.

'Go and suck Kesserling's arse!' yelled Gennaro at the top of his lungs. But there was no reply.

22 December

The telephone rang. Bordelli took a few moments to emerge from his dream, then reached out in the darkness and picked up the receiver.

'Yeah . . .'

'Inspector, it's me. Did I wake you up?'

'Piras . . . what's happening?' Bordelli asked, pressing his eyes with his fingers.

'I'm sorry, but I had something to tell you.'

'What time is it?'

'Eight o'clock, Inspector.'

'So what is it?' said Bordelli, yawning. It wasn't really so early, but he'd slept poorly and felt tired. Piras, on the other hand, was wide awake and talking too fast for the inspector's foggy head.

'That person I know who shot himself . . . I went back to his house, because I suddenly remembered to check for the shell . . .'

'The shell . . .' Bordelli muttered, trying hard to grasp the concept.

'I searched the room from top to bottom, Inspector, but there was no shell.'

'That's not possible,' said Bordelli, finally awake.

'I searched Benigno's clothes, and I even asked the *carabinieri* who wrote up the report. No shell. It's vanished. I thought about it all night, Inspector, and I could think of only one possible explanation . . .'

'Murder?' Bordelli interrupted him, sitting up.

'Find me another and I'll change my mind,' the Sardinian said.

Bordelli turned on the light and put his feet on the floor. 'I won't say you're wrong, Piras.'

'Bullet shells don't just fly away, Inspector.'

'What do you plan to do?'

'What would you do?' asked Piras, breathing hard into the receiver.

'If you're really convinced of what you say—'

'I'm convinced,' Piras interrupted him.

'Then carry on,' said Bordelli, standing up.

'For the moment I'd rather not say anything to the *carabinieri*, but I want you to agree,' said Piras.

'Do what you think best, Piras, you have my full support.'

'I was very fond of Benigno, Inspector. And if someone killed him, I want to find them,' said Piras.

'Just be sure not to do anything stupid, and keep me informed.'

'All right.'

'Good luck, Piras.'

'Thanks, sir.'

They said goodbye, and Bordelli dragged himself into the bathroom. He washed his face in cold water and then looked at himself in the mirror. Piras's phone call was still echoing in his head. A pistol is fired and the shell can't be found. It wasn't normal, in any sense. If someone had actually shot this Benigno, hoping to make it look like a suicide . . . getting rid of the shell could not have been part of his plan.

He brushed his teeth and spat the night's bitterness into the plughole. Looking at himself again in the mirror, he saw something dark trickling from one nostril. He thought it was blood. He blew his nose and looked at the results. There were black spots on the handkerchief. But it wasn't blood. The tar in his lungs was beginning to break up. Smoking less was starting to bear its first fruits . . . Even if they were disgusting to look at.

He went out and got into his car. A few clouds floated lazily across the sky, but the night's rain was gone and the sun showed its face from time to time. Every time his thoughts turned to Odoardo, he heard a great big fly buzz in his head. Actually it was a bee in his bonnet, to be more precise. He had to go back soon and have another little chat with the lad. Let's wait for Christmas to be over, he thought, and then I'll go back.

When he got to the office, he sent Mugnai to fetch him some coffee. He put an unlit cigarette down on the desk and looked at it from time to time. But he was able to resist.

Around mid-morning there was a knock at the door. It was Mugnai again. He had in his hand a couple of letters for the inspector and a cardboard box with a slot on top.

'What's the box for, Mugnai?'

'Signora Attilia's Christmas bonus, Inspector. It's your turn.' Attilia was the woman who'd started cleaning the offices a few months before, following old Rosalia's retirement. She came every morning by train from Vicchio. Bordelli pulled out a couple of thousand-lira notes and slipped them into the box.

'What are you doing for Christmas, Mugnai?'

'I'm working, that's what.'

'Well, that certainly must make you happy.'

'Don't get me started, Inspector.'

'At least you know you won't have to do it next year.'

'I think I'll go and celebrate right now,' Mugnai said, walking away with his Chaplinesque waddle.

Bordelli opened the first envelope. It was the complete report on Badalamenti's post-mortem. As usual, Diotivede had typed it up himself on his Olivetti Lettera 22. And, as usual, the results were awful. Diotivede made a lot of mistakes, and to correct them, he merely typed over them ten times. The paragraph indentations never lined up, and the paper always had a few stains on it. The contents, however, were clear and precise. Diotivede had a great passion for his work, and he always inspected the bodies one millimetre at a time, inside and out.

The inspector read the report very carefully, and when he'd finished, he heaved a long sigh. It contained nothing new that might be of help, at least for the moment. He dropped the sheets of paper on to his desk. Almost without realising it, he picked up the cigarette and lit it. Still thinking about Odoardo, he became spellbound watching a fly walk on the handle of the paper-cutter. It was going round in circles, a bit like himself at that moment. Let's wait for Christmas to be over, he repeated to himself, and then I'll go back and talk to the boy . . .

When the fly flew away, he roused himself and opened the other envelope. It was the order for the seizure of Badalamenti's possessions, signed by Ginzillo. Inside there was also Badalamenti's gold key-chain, with the keys to the Porsche. He was about to call Mugnai to have him take care of it, but then changed his mind and decided to see to it himself. He'd never driven such an expensive car before.

He left the office and went to the police garage to pick up the Beetle. He'd left it there early that morning to have the oil and spark plugs checked. Entering the garage, he saw a raised bonnet in the distance, with the lower half of a human body hanging out of it. Sallustio, the police mechanic, was working on the motor of a black Maserati, Rabozzi's patrol car. He seemed deeply engrossed. Bordelli stopped beside him.

'Hello, handsome,' he said.

Sallustio looked up with a jolt and very nearly bashed his head against the bonnet. 'Bloody hell, Inspector! You frightened me.'

'I wonder if there's really any difference between you and Diotivede.'

The mechanic emerged in full from the car's bowels. He was short and broad, with the proud, sort of blustery face of one who knew he did his job well. He stretched his cramped back, keeping his oil-stained hands far from his oil-stained overalls.

'I wouldn't trade places with Diotivede even for a Ferrari, Inspector. We work hard here, but then we get to see the engine running again. It's like we've brought it back to life. Diotivede, on the other hand . . .'

Bordelli was always amazed that a massive man like Sallustio could have such delicate hands.

'But the passion for poking around inside someone's or something's guts seems the same to me,' he said.

'Ah, well, as for that, either you've got it or you haven't,' the mechanic said, laughing. The inspector bent over to have a look at the Maserati's dismantled engine. He had trouble believing that all those greasy parts could come back together and make a car run.

'Have you had a look at the Beetle?'

'I changed the oil. The plugs should be all right for a while yet.'

'Thanks.' Bordelli took out a thousand-lira note and, ignoring Sallustio's protests, put it in the pocket of his overalls.

'Thank you, Inspector. The keys are in the glove compartment.'

'What are you doing for Christmas, Sallustio?'

'I'm going out to the country with my brothers to see our parents. They'll be killing a goose for the holiday. All the uncles and aunts and cousins will be there too. Usually there're more than fifty of us.'

'All right, then, I'll be on my way. Have a happy Christmas.'

'A happy Christmas to you, too, Inspector.'

Around eleven o'clock, after his walk, Piras went and knocked at Pina's door again. He wanted to tell her he needed to talk a little more about Benigno.

'Why, did something happen that you didn't tell me about?' she asked, alarmed.

'Nothing important, Pina. I would just like to understand why Benigno did what he did,' Piras lied.

'Come in,' she said, not quite convinced. When they entered the kitchen, Piras smelled a strong aroma of cooked apples. Pina went and turned down the flame under a large aluminium pot, then lifted the lid and stirred the hot jam. Spread out on the table was some dough for making *papassinos*.

'My mother's making some, too,' said Piras, just to say something ordinary.

Pina didn't reply. She took two ornate glasses from the cupboard and grabbed a bottle of Vernaccia that Giovanni had made himself.[16] 'A little wine?' she asked.

'Just a drop, thanks. What are you doing for Christmas?' asked Piras. He was anxious to ask her some questions, but pretending to be calm so as not to arouse her suspicions. Pina poured a little wine into both glasses, and they took a sip.

'My sons are staying in Italy this year,' said Pina.

'I know, your husband told me.'

'Only Giovanni's cousin will be coming from Solarussa with his wife.'

'Ah, good,' said Piras.

'What are your family doing?'

'We've got some relatives coming over,' said Piras.

They sat for a few moments in silence. Pina seemed absent, as if forever in the grip of an obsession. Then she shook her head.

'I always told Benigno, find yourself a wife, you can't live your life always alone,' she said.

'How did he seem, the last time you saw him? Did he seem strange?' Piras asked.

'Don Giuliano always says that only God can take your life away, and it's a mortal sin if you do it yourself,' said Pina.

'There are always exceptions . . .'

'Nino wasn't a bad man.'

'I'm sorry, Pina, but do you remember if he was worried or upset about anything the last time you saw him?' asked Piras, anxious to talk about Benigno.

'He was the same as always,' said Pina.

'Do you know if anything bad had happened to him?'

'He didn't say anything to me.'

'I dunno . . . Did he quarrel with anyone, or receive some bad news?'

'He didn't say anything.'

'Do you know if he had any enemies, or if he was involved in some old feud or vendetta?' Piras pressed her, hoping to find something to grab on to, even though that sort of murder had little of the style of traditional Sardinian feuds. Pina frowned at him.

'What's this got to do with vendettas? He wasn't murdered!'

'I was just . . . you know, asking . . . Sometimes, with those things, you never know what can happen,' Piras lied with the straightest face imaginable.

'I don't know anything about any vendettas. I think he would have told me. When I last saw him, he was fine and didn't seem to have any troubles. I really don't understand why he went and did such a terrible thing,' she said, staring at the table. Then she stood up and went over to the cooker, lifted the lid on the pot again and stirred a few more times, looking grim. The smell of apples was growing stronger and stronger. Piras stood up and, leaning on his crutches, went over to her.

'Think hard, Pina. Had Benigno been doing anything . . . unusual lately?' he asked.

'He was doing what he always did. Tending his sheep, making cheese . . .' Pina muttered, still stirring the hot jam.

'Where did he sell his cheese?' Piras asked.

'He gave most of it to a man who sold it at the market at Oristano.'

'Did Benigno bring it to him, or did the man come and get it himself?'

'Nino would bring it to him once a week.'

'Did Benigno have any shepherds working for him, lending a hand? Or did he do everything alone?'

'He did everything alone,' said Pina.

'And did he by any chance meet anyone new these past few weeks?'

'I have no idea,' she said, shrugging. Piras ran a hand over his head, increasingly discouraged.

'What sort of things did he say to you the last time you saw him?' he asked.

Pina raised the ladle and let the jam drip slowly out. It was still too liquid. She put the lid back on the pot and turned round. 'He talked about a lot of things,' she said.

'Try to tell me everything you can remember,' said Piras, convinced he was getting nowhere.

Pina thought it over for a moment. 'He said he was tired of looking after all those sheep. He wanted to buy a vineyard and start making wine, like Giovanni.'

'And?'

'He'd decided he was going to fix the roof, because it rained inside the house . . . He also mentioned some land he wanted to sell,' said Pina, seeming tired of all these meaningless questions.

'What land?' asked Piras.

'I don't know.'

'Did he want to sell it, or was he already in the process of selling it?'

'I really don't know, but I'm sure Giovanni does. He talked a lot more about these things with him.'

'And where's Giovanni now?'

'He went out to chop some wood, up past the orange grove. He should be back pretty soon.'

'I'll go and look for him. That way I'll get a little exercise,' said Piras, heading for the door. Pina shuffled behind him with a weary step. She was taking Benigno's death very badly, especially the fact that it had been a suicide.

'Will you two be coming over to watch the film tonight?' Piras asked at the door.

'If we're not too tired . . .'

'A little distraction might do you good.'

'I don't know . . . Tell your mamma we'll see her on Christmas Eve around midnight for the mass.'

'All right.'

''Bye, Nino,' she said, trying to smile.

'Pina, if you need any help with the declaration of succession . . . don't hesitate to ask.'

She was the sole heir of the deceased's estate.

'You can talk about it with Giovanni. He does everything,' said Pina.

'Goodbye, Pina.'

Piras nodded and went out. The Setzus' wood was a little over half a mile outside town, towards Sulacheddu. It was all uphill, and it took Piras a good half-hour to get there. Without crutches it would have taken him less than half that long. A large, motionless cloud covered the sun, but all around it the sky was blue. When he turned down the path that led into the wood, he saw Giovanni coming towards him on a cart full of wood. He waited for him at the end of the path, leaning on his crutches.

'Hey . . .' Giovanni said as he drew near, and the donkey slowed down and came to a halt.

'A lot of wood, eh?' said Piras.

'And it's never enough!' said Giovanni.

'I've just been to see Pina. We talked a little about what happened.'

'Lately that's all she ever talks about . . .'

'She told me Benigno wanted to sell some land in Oristano,' said Piras, as if it were the most natural thing in the world to say.

Giovanni looked at him, scratching his face with his fingernails. 'That's right. Why do you mention it?'

'I dunno . . . I'm just trying to understand what sort of reason Benigno might have had . . . for doing what he did,' said Piras.

Giovanni spat from the cart and shook his head. 'I kept telling him he should keep that land, that it was a gold mine, but he never listened to anybody,' said Giovanni.

'Was it suitable for building?'

'Benigno used to tell me you could build two buildings as tall as the bell tower on it,' he said, raising his hand to the sky.

'Maybe he needed money to repair the roof.'

'He should have kept it,' said Giovanni, still shaking his head. The donkey was immobile, staring into infinity.

'Now it's all yours. You can do whatever you want with it,' said Piras.

'It's all Pina's. I've got nothing to do with it.'

'Was there already someone interested in buying it?'

'I don't know. Benigno had put it all in the hands of some lawyer in Oristano.'

'Do you know his name?' Piras asked, taking a step forward.

Giovanni rearranged the hat on his head and searched his memory. He seemed to be looking at the donkey's ears. 'Musillo,' he said at last with confidence.

'Musillo . . .' Piras repeated softly.

'He's half Pugliese. Benigno trusted him.'

'Can that donkey pull both of us?'

'Climb aboard.'

Piras set his crutches down on the cart and sat at the end of the flatbed.

'Are you going to need any help with the succession papers? Angelo works at the town hall and knows about that sort of thing,' he said.

'We can talk about it after Epiphany . . . Ho!' said Giovanni, and the donkey resumed walking.

Around midday Bordelli turned down Via Stoppani, a private road with no exit, which started at the corner of Via Volta and went up the Camerata hill, where Fontana the barrister lived. At the corner of Via Barbacane, there was a niche with a painted Madonna, peeling in spots but still solemn, in the stone wall marking the boundary of the garden of a large house dressed up as a castle. Across the street was an immense, abandoned villa surrounded by a park overgrown with weeds. It no longer had any windows, and the black rectangles gave the house a lugubrious atmosphere even during the day. If someone had told him there were ghosts between those four walls he would have had no trouble believing it.

He drove slowly up the street. There were a few cars parked along the pavement, almost all of them fancy. Big Fiats, Lancias,

even a black MG and an extremely long Jaguar. A pot of money
on four wheels. He'd never been inside a car like that. Proceeding
another hundred yards or so, he stopped at last in front of
Fontana's villa. He got out and peered through the gate. The
villa was enormous, apparently deserted, and surrounded by
high-trunked trees that towered above the roof. It must have
been built in the late nineteenth century, though it didn't look
as unwieldy as some buildings from that period. The garden
was well tended, the flower beds nicely hoed and raked, the
grass mown. Earthenware jugs and vases were scattered taste-
fully about on the lawn and along the steps leading up to the
villa. The street was completely silent, but when he pricked up
his ears, he could hear a sort of indecipherable refrain. It
seemed in fact to be coming from Fontana the barrister's villa.
A bit farther on, there was another, larger gate for cars. Bordelli
looked in through the bars. Beside the house was a paved lane
that led to a garage with its broad door open. Visible inside
were Guido Fontana's BSA and a Solex.

He went back to the smaller gate. He pressed the doorbell
and heard two chimes ring inside the house. He waited for at
least a minute, but nobody came out. He rang again and, while
waiting, put a cigarette between his lips. He looked around a
little. Every so often he could hear a car drive past in Viale
Volta, but it was only a distant, almost pleasant hiss. In spring-
time the place must be a cacophony of bumblebees and songbirds,
he thought. The villas were only on one side of the street; the
other was lined with an old stone wall a good ten feet high
with bottle shards cemented on top. Beyond the wall one could
see a small hill covered with centuries-old trees and tall, bare
acacias. It was the wild part of the Parco del Ventaglio . . . The
very place where a young girl of eight had been found strangled
to death the year before. The inspector remembered the scene
well. That day was the beginning of one of the worst nightmares
of his career . . . Then he unfailingly remembered that he had
also met, during the same period, a beautiful Jewish girl who
had set him dreaming for a few weeks . . .

He rang the Fontanas' bell again and waited a while longer. But no one came to the door. He was about to leave when he saw the curtain to a first-floor window move. For a brief second a head appeared behind the panes, and then the curtain closed again. A few seconds later the front door opened. A tall, slender young man came out. He was wearing a brown leather jacket and had a fringe of black hair over his eyes. An old German shepherd that looked rather gentle came out with him. The youth crossed the garden with the dog at his side and stopped in front of the gate. Through the still-open door to the house came some music that seemed to be rising up from underground.

'Good morning,' said the young man, suspicious. The dog stuck its muzzle between the bars and sniffed the stranger.

'Inspector Bordelli, police,' said Bordelli, flashing his badge. 'I'm looking for Guido Fontana.'

'That's me,' said Guido, hands in his pockets. He made no move to open the gate. He had a gaunt face and nervous, slightly bloodshot eyes.

'Aren't you going to let me in?' asked the inspector. 'I'm unarmed.'

Guido turned to the dog.

'Go lie down, Poldo,' he said. The dog went a few yards away and lay down on the ground. The youth opened the gate.

'Are you looking for Raffaele?' he asked, shaking Bordelli's hand.

'Is he here?'

'Yes, he's inside.'

'First I'd like to have a few words with you,' said Bordelli.

'Now?' said the youth, impatient. Bordelli nodded. The dog calmly got up and came forward to have a closer look at the inspector.

'It seems Raffaele has already told you everything,' said Bordelli.

'He mentioned a couple of things,' said Guido. The dog started sniffing the intruder's clothes. The inspector patted the animal's head, and Poldo began wagging his tail. He was a fine specimen, but a bit short compared to Blisk.

'If I've understood correctly, you see each other often,' Bordelli said.

'Every day.'

'Do you remember what the two of you did on the tenth of December? It was a Friday,' said Bordelli, hand still stroking Poldo between the ears.

'We spent most of the day indoors, because it was raining,' said Guido.

'Good memory,' said Bordelli.

'I remember it clearly because at one point we went into town to buy a record and got all wet,' Guido said as if bored.

'What was the record?' Bordelli asked, like a meticulous police detective. Actually, however, he was merely curious to know what sort of music those two listened to. The youngster shrugged.

'You wouldn't know them.'

'Aren't you being a little prejudiced?

'The Rolling Stones,' Guido said curtly.

'You're right, I don't know them.'

'I told you,' the lad said. He was the opposite of Raffaele. He acted as if speaking cost him a great deal of effort. The dog lay down and rested its muzzle on its forepaws, as if expecting a long, boring conversation.

'At what time on that Friday did Raffaele come here?'

'He always comes round about ten o'clock.'

'In the morning?'

'Yes.'

'And on that day, too, he came at ten?'

'Yes.'

'And you were together the whole time . . . Is that right?'

'Yes.'

'Aside from going and buying that record, what did you do?'

'We played music, listened to music, talked, breathed . . . that sort of thing.'

'I asked you a serious question,' said Bordelli.

'We were together the whole time. Isn't that what you wanted to know?'

'At what time did Raffaele leave?'

'Late at night, as always.'

'Meaning?'

'Around two, half past two,' said the youth, tired of all the questions.

'And from ten in the morning till two at night, you were never apart?'

'No, that's what I just said.'

'Not even for, say, an hour?'

'No.'

'Would you repeat these same things under oath in a court of law?' the inspector asked, looking him hard in the eye.

'Of course.'

'I have to tell you something,' said Bordelli.

'What?'

'I have the feeling that in about a minute your nose is going to start growing like Pinocchio's . . . Do you know who Pinocchio is?'

'I told you the truth.'

'It's very good of you to want to protect your friend, but it's also a mistake.'

'I'm not protecting anybody.'

'So much the better. Could I talk to Raffaele?' Bordelli asked with a cheerful smile.

'He's inside,' said Guido.

'Are you inviting me in?'

'Do as you like.'

'I wouldn't want to trouble you.'

'No trouble at all,' said Guido. He closed the gate behind the inspector, and headed towards the villa with the dog beside him. Bordelli followed behind.

'Is there anyone else in the house?' he asked.

'No.'

'Don't you have a cleaning woman?'

'She's out shopping.'

'And what about your mother?'

'My mother doesn't live here.'

'Where does she live?'

'Milan.'

'Are your parents separated?'[17]

'Yes, but we're not supposed to say so,' said Guido, shrugging his shoulders, as if the matter didn't concern him.

They went into the house, followed by the dog, and Guido closed the great door behind them. The music was more audible inside. They climbed three more steps and found themselves in the entrance hall, a majestic space full of paintings and sculptures with a number of dark wooden doors opening on to it. There was also a staircase in *pietra serena* with a carved balustrade leading to the first floor. It was all very solemn and not very welcoming. It looked like something grandiose in miniature.

The inspector walked beside Guido down a broad corridor full of pictures and antique furniture, followed by the clicking sound of the dog's claws on the marble floor. The slender, silent youth moved through all these things like a shadow, ignoring them. He had no connection to anything around him, like an outsider who had ended up there by chance.

The music was getting clearer and clearer. There was an electric guitar, endlessly repeating the same notes, and a voice yelling over it.

'What is this music?' Bordelli asked.

'It's the record I mentioned,' said Guido.

'What did you say it's called?'

'It's by the Rolling Stones, a British rock group,' Guido said with a sigh, as if he'd been forced to say that pigs have four feet.

'And what does it mean?'

'Well, you know the saying; "a rolling stone gathers no moss". It's like calling yourself "the Ne'er-do-Wells" or "the Hooligans".'

'Interesting,' said Bordelli.

The lad went through an open door and they entered a relatively small room with an entirely different atmosphere from the rest of the house. Raffaele wasn't there. The walls were papered over with posters . . . Very young men with hair down to their chins and electric guitars in their hands. Scattered about on the bed was a bit of everything: clothes, books, dust covers of 45 rpm records. The music was very loud and blaring out of a light blue portable gramophone. Guido went and turned down the volume, ever so slightly bobbing his head to the rhythm of the song.

'I liked that,' said Bordelli, curious. In that song he heard a power that seemed to carry the listener away with it. The dog went and lay down in a corner, resting its muzzle on its paws. The floor was covered with a carpet full of cigarette burns, and through the window, which gave on to the garden behind the house, the inspector saw the trunks of a few age-old pines and a stone fountain covered with moss.

'Raffaele must have gone downstairs,' said Guido.

'To the cellar?'

'He's obsessed with my electric train set.'

'You two play with electric trains?' asked Bordelli, repressing a smile.

'Come,' said the young man. They left the room, walked back through the whole house, and entered a large kitchen. There was a wooden table so long that it could have seated twenty. Behind a small dark door was a staircase. As they descended, Bordelli heard a noise that sounded like potatoes frying in a giant pan.

'Raffaele, there's a policeman here looking for you,' Guido called out in a loud voice. Nobody replied. When they got to the bottom of the stairs, Bordelli's jaw dropped. In the dimly lit room, he saw a complicated network of railways with level crossings, tunnels, waterfalls, tree-covered hills . . . and six or seven trains with headlights on, travelling through the night. He felt like a giant looking on. On the other side of that miniature world was Raffaele, smoking, with great clouds of dense smoke swirling round his head. He waved hello to the inspector and started walking round the model trains. Taking a last puff, he threw the butt on the floor. He walked like a gunslinger, legs sheathed in black leather trousers. He came up to the inspector and shook his hand.

'Have you come to arrest me?' he said, smiling. His eyes were also bloodshot.

'It might not be a bad idea,' the inspector said, sniffing the air. There was a strong smell vaguely similar to that of burnt rosemary.

Raffaele shrugged and turned to look at the trains penetrating the darkness with tiny headlamps the size of lentils. 'When I get bored I come down here and watch,' he said.

'I'm going back upstairs,' said Guido, heading for the stairs.

'I won't bother to ask what you two have been smoking,' said Bordelli.

'Whereas I know what drug *you've* been smoking,' said Raffaele. 'It's the strongest of them all.'

'It's hardly a drug,' Bordelli said defensively.

'Just try going a week without smoking your government-stamped cigarettes.'

'What's your point?'

'My point is that *we* are sick and tired of having to deal with your hypocrisy . . . We are unsatisfied, very unsatisfied,' Raffaele said calmly.

'Who's "we"?'

'I was waiting for you to ask that. You know perfectly well what I'm talking about and are only pretending not to understand . . . And that's exactly what we're sick and tired of.'

Raffaele's tone was not terribly aggressive. In fact, it was rather serene, if, perhaps, a bit disillusioned. He spoke as if he were repeating the most obvious things for the hundredth time. Bordelli said nothing. He didn't know what to say. It was hard to give a name to what he was feeling, but there was no question that he had never before found himself in a situation like this. The young man could have been his son, and with his manner he seemed to be asking for a clout on the head . . . And it was he, Bordelli, who felt ill at ease. He who had fought the war against the Nazis and the Fascists, suffered the cold, risked his life for his country . . . Jesus bloody Christ, he was turning into an old dodderer spewing rhetoric!

Raffaele turned off the power switch for the trains, and all railway traffic stopped at once. He then gestured to Bordelli, inviting him to go back upstairs with him, and started up the steps. The inspector followed behind.

They went back into Guido's room. The dog looked at them without bothering to raise its head, thumping its tail. The gramophone was playing the same disc as before, at a more acceptable volume. Guido was sitting on the bed, holding a guitar and trying to keep up with the music. Raffaele sat down on the carpet and leaned back against the wall. The inspector went over to the record player and picked up the empty dust jacket for the disc. He read the title: 'Satisfaction'. Under it were three boys with hair over their ears and faces like tough guys. But they also had something feminine about them, too, like Raffaele, and, like him, seemed to belong to a different race. The inspector thumbed through some of the other records, all with English names he didn't recognise.

'What do the words say?' he asked.

'They say what I was saying before,' Raffaele quipped.

The inspector dropped the records and put his hands into the pockets of his trench coat. He started fingering his packet of cigarettes, without making up his mind to take it out. He didn't want the two children to see that he was a drug addict.

The song ended, and for a few seconds there was only the scraping of the needle on the record, but then the arm rose with a click and went backwards. After the music, the silence seemed absolute. Guido was holding the guitar strings still with his fingers. The inspector calmly looked over at Raffaele, even though he still had that strange sensation of being a foreigner in a faraway land. He had come for a specific reason, and here he was wasting time.

'Your friend told me that on Friday the tenth the two of you were together the whole day. Can you confirm that for me?' he asked Raffaele.

'Will it serve any purpose if I reply?'

'That depends,' said the inspector.

Raffaele made a wry face. 'I think I understand. You plan to keep badgering me with your little questions until I throw myself on the ground, weeping, and confess to my sins.'

'That does happen sometimes,' said Bordelli, smiling. But little by little he was beginning to realise he had more or less reached a dead end. Raffaele had a good motive to kill, was left-handed, and did not have an ironclad alibi. But, aside from these facts, there was no evidence against him. If something concrete didn't turn up soon, the murder case's file would end up on a courthouse shelf with a nice long number on it and be soon forgotten.

'I didn't kill the bastard,' said Raffaele. His friend started playing and wailing something very softly, head bent over the instrument's resonance chamber. What was happening in the room seemed of no concern to him at all.

'Maybe you both did it,' said Bordelli. Guido stopped his strumming and looked up.

'Did what?' he said.

'Killed Badalamenti.'

'I don't know him,' said Guido, who kept staring at him.

Raffaele calmly went up to Bordelli. 'I've already told you what I think, Inspector . . . The sewer rat deserved to be murdered.'

'Then tell me the rest.'

'Somebody gave him what he had coming to him, but it wasn't me. I have nothing else to add,' said Raffaele.

'I foresee a lot of long conversations with you, Mr Montigiani.'

'All right, then, Inspector, I did it, I killed him, I stuck those scissors in his neck . . . but this is only the beginning, I'm going to kill a lot more shitbags like him,' said Raffaele, crossing his arms over his chest. For the first time, Guido's face broke into a smile.

'I'll be seeing you soon,' said Bordelli, not knowing what else to say.

'I'll show you out,' said Guido, laying the guitar down on the bed.

'No need,' Bordelli said, stopping him.

'Happy Christmas, Inspector,' said Raffaele, giving him a military salute, then turning round and going over to the record player.

Bordelli left the room. A few seconds later the sound of the same electric guitar burst out, soon followed by the voice.

He walked through the house without looking around, then closed the main door behind him with the feeling of having been through an ordeal. At the gate he ran into the cleaning lady, who was returning with the shopping. She was tall with broad shoulders and thin white hair.

'Good morning,' said Bordelli. The woman looked at him with suspicion and muttered a reply. She had a large mole on her chin, bristling with hair. She set her shopping bags down on the ground, waited for the stranger to leave, and then made sure the gate was locked. She remained there, watching Bordelli through the bars. She looked like a cloistered nun from Santa Verdiana.

The inspector got into his car, turned it round and went back towards town. It was time to go see Totò and eat something.

Piras closed the kitchen door and looked in the directory for the telephone number of a lawyer called Luigi Musillo. He found it and dialled the number.

'Yes?'

'I'm looking for Musillo, the lawyer. My name's Piras.'

'I'm Musillo.'

'I'm a friend of the family of Benigno Staffa, sir,' Piras said in a soft voice, so his mother wouldn't hear.

'I heard about the tragedy,' said Musillo.

'I would like to speak to you. When do you think we could meet?' Piras asked. He didn't want to stay on the phone too long.

'Is there some problem?' the lawyer asked.

'I'm sorry, but I'd rather discuss this in person.'

'All right, then. Call me right after Christmas.'

'I'm sorry, sir, but it's quite urgent. I forgot to mention . . . I'm with the police.'

'Has something happened?' asked Musillo, slightly alarmed.

'I don't know yet, but I would like to see you as soon as possible.'

Musillo heaved a long sigh and remained silent for a few seconds.

'Would tomorrow morning at eleven be all right?' he finally said.

'That would be perfect, thank you.' Piras said goodbye and hung up.

He went into the kitchen and saw the table already set. He was very hungry. His mother was cooking something in a skillet. It had to be pork.

'How long till we eat?' he asked.

'Not long,' said Maria. Gavino was hammering away at something in the tool shed behind the house.

'What's he doing?' asked Pietrino.

'Fixing the chicken-coop door.'

'Again?' he said in surprise.

'He found another dead hen with her bottom bitten off.'

'It's a lost cause when you're dealing with martens,' said Pietrino.

'You know what Dad's like. He's stubborn like you,' said Maria, who went and stirred the meat.

'Pina says she and Giovanni will come by on Christmas Eve, before mass,' said Pietrino.

'Poor Pina . . .'

'Maybe they'll come tonight for the movie.'

'The Faddas are coming too,' said Maria. That evening there was an American musical on the telly. The Piras's kitchen had become a sort of cinema, especially on Mondays and Wednesdays, when there was a film on TV. Piras waited for his mother to put the pasta in the water, then hopped on his crutches to the telephone and dialled Sonia's number.

At half past seven the sky was as black as the bottom of a well. The inspector left the station and got into his car with the intention of going and getting Badalamenti's Porsche. Then he changed his mind. Driving slowly through the back streets of Florence, he arrived at the hills at the edge of town. He was lost in thought, patiently chewing the end of an unlit cigarette. The song with the guitar he'd heard at Guido's house was still playing in his head, though he would never have been able to sing it. He turned up another small street and came out at Via Senese. He turned left, drove past Galluzzo and, a few minutes later, down Via di Quintole. He'd failed to resist the temptation to go to Odoardo's house.

He entered the unpaved driveway and parked on the threshing floor. The house was in total darkness. There wasn't even a light on under the loggia, and so he left the headlamps on. He got out and went to see whether the Vespa was there. It wasn't. It was very cold outside. He got back into the car, turned off the headlamps, and settled in to wait for the boy. There was a bit of moonlight. The dark silhouette of the Lancia Ardea reminded him of a dead whale beached on the sand.

He decided to wait until nine for Odoardo. If the kid didn't show up by then, he would return the following morning. He wanted to see him as soon as possible, there was no getting round it. By now he was convinced the lad was hiding something, and he had an overwhelming desire to find out what. Getting more comfortable in the seat, he lit a cigarette. It must have been his fourth, but he wasn't sure. If he wanted to count them in earnest, he would have to mark a notch in pen on the packet each time he lit one. Too much trouble.

Suddenly a light shone in the distance. It was the headlamp of a motorbike coming up Via di Quintole, and he hoped it would be Odoardo's Vespa. Every so often the light would disappear round a bend and then reappear. When it was opposite the house it slowed down and then turned towards the farmstead. Odoardo drove across the threshing floor wearing his motorcycle goggles and a red scarf that covered half his face. When he passed by the Beetle he slowed down for a moment, then went on. He took the Vespa up under the loggia and turned off the motor. A few seconds later two lights came on, one shining on to the threshing floor, the other above the front door of the house. The inspector got out of the car and went towards the youth. Odoardo was wearing an oversized coat and holding the usual bag. He seemed chilled and was shivering slightly. Bordelli went up to him, holding out his hand.

'Hello, Odoardo,' he said.

The boy removed a glove and shook his hand. He looked at Bordelli without surprise but seemed quite irritated. 'What brings you out this way, Inspector? Are you on the trail of a wild boar?' he said with a straight face.

'If you've got a minute, I'd like to have a little talk with you.'

'What about?'

'Why don't we go inside? I can see you're cold, too.'

Odoardo sighed and turned the key in the door.

'I don't have much time, I have to go out again in half an hour.'

'I'll take only ten minutes of your time.'

They entered a large unfurnished room, then the inspector followed Odoardo up some stone stairs. The inside of the house was not in the same state of abandon as the outside. The air was warm, and it all smelled clean.

They entered a big room with a great fireplace charred black and full of ashes. Beside it was a box for fruit now full of old newspapers; the firewood was stacked in a corner. The terracotta-tiled floor was almost entirely covered by an enormous oriental carpet. There was little furniture, but one could see that this was by choice.

'I like this house,' said Bordelli.

'My mother did everything,' said Odoardo.

On the opposite side of the room there was a dark doorway leading into a corridor. Bordelli looked around a little more. The couch and armchairs were from the twenties, their fabric a bit worn, and in the middle of the room was a low table of burnished wood. On the walls were some pictures, a functioning pendulum clock and a map of the world. The walls were yellowed with age but in good condition. It was the kind of house one could quickly grow fond of, thought Bordelli. Odoardo took his hat off and tossed it on to the back of an armchair. He seemed calm, as if resigned to the intrusion.

'No television?' Bordelli asked.

'No.'

'It's amusing sometimes.'

'I'm sure it is.'

'At other times, however . . .'

'Do you mind if I change my clothes?' Odoardo asked, though it wasn't really a question.

'Just act as if I wasn't here,' said Bordelli.

'That's asking too much. Meanwhile, if you'd like something to drink . . .' said the young man, pointing to a glass-fronted cabinet. Bordelli thanked him, went over to the cabinet and opened it. In the first row he saw a dark bottle with a hand-written label on it that said: *Nocino 1962*.[18] He took it and held it in the air.

'May I?' he asked.

'Please do, the glasses are below.'

Bordelli took a small glass and filled it to the brim. Odoardo was unbuttoning his shirt.

'What was it you wanted to say to me?' he asked calmly.

'This *nocino* is excellent,' Bordelli said. 'Did your mother make it?'

'How'd you guess?' said Odoardo in the tone of someone

who knew how to ignore provocations. Then he went down the dark corridor and disappeared behind the first door. Bordelli started walking about the room, sipping the *nocino* and poking about. On the mantelpiece he noticed an old hand grenade. It was Italian, a model he knew well. He unscrewed it, made sure it was empty, then closed it again.

'Did your mother like hand grenades?' he asked, raising his voice to be heard.

'That's mine,' the youth yelled.

'I've seen quite a few of these explode. They do a lot of harm.'

'What did you do during the war, Inspector?'

'I was in the San Marco brigades.'

'They were Fascists, if I remember correctly.'

'Only a minority, up north. I was with Marshal Badoglio's San Marco.'

'What did you do?'

'We paved the way for the American advance. We were putting salt on the Germans' tails almost daily.'

Odoardo reappeared in the room, buttoning up a white shirt.

'Did you kill of a lot of them?' he asked.

'I tried my best.'

'The bastards deserved it.'

'Killing is never fun, but in that case I felt I was ridding the world of an infection.'

'I agree,' Odoardo said coldly.

'Maybe killing a loan shark gives you the same feeling,' said Bordelli, looking him in the eye.

Odoardo stiffened a little. 'You should ask that question of someone who can answer it,' he said, disappearing again into his room.

Having finished his glass of *nocino*, Bordelli went back to refill it. He really felt like smoking, but as usual tried to resist. With the little glass in his hand, he went slowly down the corridor and poked his head into Odoardo's room. He found him seated and tying his shoes.

'I'm seriously thinking about finding a house like this to live in,' said Bordelli, looking up at the ceiling rafters, riddled with woodworm holes.

'Lucky you . . .'

'Why do you say that? Do you think it's such a bad thing to move to the country?'

Odoardo stood up, turned off the light and left the room, passing by the inspector and looking annoyed.

'I'm sorry, Inspector, but I still haven't understood what this urgent thing was that you needed to talk to me about.'

Bordelli followed him into the great room with the fireplace and set his empty glass down on the table.

'I like you, Odoardo. But don't take it the wrong way. I mean it man to man. I'm convinced I'm dealing with an intelligent person, and I'd like to talk to you a little more.'

'I don't understand what about,' said Odoardo.

'Well, for example, I'd like to give you some of the details of that murder. I still remember them clearly . . . Did I mention that Badalamenti lived close to me?'

'I don't know who he was and I couldn't care less that he was murdered.'

'I haven't heard a single nice thing about the man. Don't you think that's sad?' the inspector asked.

Odoardo put on his coat and sighed impatiently. 'I have to go now,' he said, finger on the light switch.

'Of course,' said Bordelli.

The youth turned out the light and started descending the stairs, followed by the inspector, who was humming an aria of Rossini. They went out into the loggia and Odoardo closed the front door with a swift tug before turning the key. The air was freezing cold.

'Goodbye, Inspector,' said Odoardo, shaking his hand more firmly than usual. He then started up his Vespa and straddled it. Revving the engine a couple of times, he pushed it off its kick-stand. Bordelli came up to him, waving away the oily white smoke that had invaded the loggia.

'I'll be coming back to see you, Odoardo. I've still got something that belonged to your mother.'

'You can give it to me now.'

'Not yet,' said the inspector.

'This is far too mysterious for my taste.'

'I've got my reasons.'

'I'm sure you have.'

'Why don't you ask me why I won't give it to you straight away?'

'Because I know you would just answer me with a question,' Odoardo said with a malicious smile. He turned the Vespa towards the courtyard and revved it again. The engine was misfiring and emitting a great deal of smoke.

'Maybe it's flooded,' said Bordelli.

'Maybe.'

'When you've got a little more time, I'd still like to have that talk with you.'

'Didn't we just have it now?'

'You didn't give me enough time,' said Bordelli, smiling.

Odoardo looked at him, eyes flashing with hatred. He arranged the scarf around his neck, put on his goggles, and put the scooter into first gear. Making a final gesture of goodbye, he left, leaving a cloud of white smoke in his wake.

Bordelli didn't leave straight away. The place gave him a feeling of peace. Odoardo had left a light on, and it shone on a little Madonna built into the wall at the corner of the house. The dim lamp cast a lunar glow across the threshing floor. He put a cigarette between his lips, lit it and stood there listening to the sound of the Vespa heading down towards the Certosa. As he blew the smoke out of his mouth, he looked up. The sky was black and riddled with stars.

'Do you know, my dear Inspector, where the word *assassin* comes from?'

'No, Rosa, I don't think so.'

'And you're supposed to be a policeman?' she asked.

'Should I be ashamed?'

'If you like, I'll tell you myself.'

'Okay.'

'Wait for me here . . .'

'Who's going anywhere?' said Bordelli, with a glass in his hand and his feet propped up on the coffee table. Rosa ran into her bedroom and returned with a small book decorated with arabesques. She turned off all the lights except for a small reading lamp beside her. The coloured lights on the Christmas tree flashed on and off in clusters and created a sense of peace in the dimly lit room. Putting on her glasses, Rosa looked for the page and started reading in a fairy-tale tone of voice . . .

'"In the year 1000, in a great oasis there lived a very powerful Arabian prince who was the envy of all. He had many enemies, and wanted an army of devoted followers in whom he could place his blind trust. For months he thought day and night how he might do this. He paced back and forth, and back and forth, without rest . . ."' – Bordelli closed his eyes, the better to listen – '"until, one day, he had an idea. He summoned his most faithful servant and ordered him to dissolve a great deal of hashish in his men's wine, and when they fell asleep he had them transported to a beautiful garden, full of flowers and fountains and lovely, sweet women, and food fit for a king, and great jugs of scented wine. The men enjoyed all these pleasures and felt happy. But that wine, too, was mixed with hashish, and soon they fell asleep again. When they reopened their eyes, they were back in their familiar world, and they felt sad. The prince had them summoned to him, and he looked them in the eyes and said: 'You have been in the garden of valorous men, the place that awaits you if you die for me in battle. But for as long as you are alive, every time you kill one of my enemies, you shall return to that garden for a few hours.' And so, in the hope of tasting those pleasures again, the prince's men became ferocious, ruthlessly killing anyone who dared threaten the prince. They would go out in groups and return with scimitars dripping with blood. Soon people began to call them the *hachchaachii*, that is, the hashish drinkers, and from this derives the word *assassin* . . ." Did you know that?'

'No, I didn't. But it's a nice story.'

'Have you ever smoked the stuff?' Rosa asked, a little smile on her lips.

'No, I've never come across any.'

'And what if your Rosina happened to have a little bit of weed?'

Bordelli gave her an amused look.

'Finish your sentence.'

'Would you smoke it with me?'

'I should warn you that I'm a policeman.'

'Would you arrest me before or after we smoked the joint?'

'Where did you get it?

'A girlfriend of mine gave it to me, but don't ask me who, because I'm not a snitch,' said Rosa, crossing two fingers over her lips.

'What's it like?' asked Bordelli, curious.

'It makes you feel light headed.'

'So I would need some every day.'

'It's fun, and then you get hungry like you wouldn't believe . . .'

'That's never been a problem for me.'

'Do you want to try it or not?' she asked impatiently.

'Well, I guess, as a policeman, it's my duty to get to know certain things from up close,' said Bordelli, trying to remain serious. But he really was rather curious to know what sort of effect the stuff had. He didn't want to remain in the dark on the subject, especially when dealing with people like Raffaele.

'Yes or no?' said Rosa, as insistent as a little girl.

'All right.'

'I knew it! I knew it!' Rosa turned on a light in the corner and ran back to her room, hands fluttering. She returned a second later with a small wooden box.

'Okay, now I'll show you how you do it,' she said. 'My friend taught me.'

She kicked off her shoes and sat down on the carpet, crossing her legs like a fakir. Then she opened the box and took out the necessary items. Marijuana, rolling papers, and tobacco. Bordelli observed the procedure. Rosa took a small strip of cardboard about one third the length of a cigarette, rolled it up tightly and set it aside, then picked a magazine up from the table, placed it in her lap, and dumped some tobacco on it. Then she mixed some of the marijuana into the tobacco and slid the blend into a cigarette paper, put the little roll of cardboard at one end, and rolled it all up into a joint.

'*Voilà!*' she said, holding it up in the air. It was all crooked, with clumps of tobacco sticking out of one end.

'Now we only have to light it,' said Bordelli.

'I'll let you have the honour.'

'If you insist.'

Rosa handed him the cigarette and struck a match.

'You have to inhale the smoke and hold it in for a few seconds. It works better that way,' she said in the tone of an expert. Bordelli obeyed and, after taking three or four puffs, passed the joint to Rosa. It had a nice smell, and the taste it left in one's mouth wasn't bad, either. Rosa took a drag and coughed.

'Do you like it?' she asked, passing it back to him.

'I certainly like the smell.'

'It takes a few minutes before you feel the effect.'

Taking puff after puff, they finished the cigarette. Rosa got up to put a record on the gramophone at low volume. It was *Famous Symphonies of Rossini*, directed by Toscanini. Then she went and sat down comfortably on the sofa.

'Where's Gideon?' Bordelli asked. He hadn't seen him yet.

'Out roaming the roofs,' said Rosa.

'There must be a female involved.'

'Don't you feel anything yet?' she said, giggling.

'I guess not,' said Bordelli, listening to *The Thieving Magpie* with his eyes closed. But the moment he'd said it he realised that the music was entering his head differently . . . as if the melody were forming inside his brain and then coming out of his ears. He didn't know how else to explain it. Without opening his eyes, he made a gesture to Rosa, to let her know that the stuff was starting to work.

'The music . . .' he said.

'What about the music?' asked Rosa.

'I'm imagining it . . . it's like a great big snake moving around.'

'A snake?' she asked.

'It seems all . . . I don't know how to say it . . . but it's very interesting . . .'

'And what's this great big snake doing?'

'It's as if . . . it were coming out of my ears . . .'

'What ears?'

'It's as if . . . as if I can see the music . . . and . . . see it turning into the snake,' said Bordelli.

'Your face looks strange,' Rosa said in a serious tone.

He opened his eyes and looked at her. 'What do you mean?' he said, touching his cheeks.

'It's as if . . .'

'What?'

'It's like y . . .' but she couldn't finish her sentence and burst into laughter. When she caught her breath and tried to speak again, another even greater fit of laughter overcame her, and she flopped back on to the sofa. Bordelli kept touching his face, worried. And she kept laughing to the point of tears, not recovering her breath for a good minute. Sitting up, she pointed a finger at Bordelli and started laughing even harder than before. Her face turned all red, and at one point she seemed to have gone so long without breathing that it appeared as if she could die. She tried two or three more times to speak, but couldn't even manage to get out the first consonant. At a certain point Bordelli caught the giggles too, and started laughing for no reason at all. Or perhaps there was a reason, but he didn't know yet what it was. He was laughing, full stop. And more and more. It was hard to speak.

'You say . . . my face . . . is it . . . the snake? . . .' he managed to say between hiccups. Rosa was rolling around on the couch, shaking her hands as if to tell him to stop. She was squeezing her legs together and seemed in danger of peeing her pants. They both carried on laughing and laughing like idiots, weeping from the strain.

'M . . . my . . . face . . .' Bordelli said with great effort, but didn't have the breath to continue. Rosa rolled off the couch, holding her stomach, then managed to bolt to her feet and, running on tiptoe, raced to the bathroom. Bordelli flopped back in his chair, letting the *William Tell* Overture enter one ear at a gallop and exit the other just as fast. He couldn't recall ever having laughed that way before. Rosa kept on laughing in the bathroom, then took a deep breath, and all fell silent. She returned a few moments later, reeling. She looked serious. She sat down like a good girl, then raised her eyes, looked at Bordelli, and opened her mouth . . .

'Your face . . . looks like it's falling down,' she managed to say, then burst out laughing so hard that Bordelli almost thought he should somehow help her. But he wouldn't have had the strength, because he too then started laughing again like a simpleton.

Little by little they regained their senses. Rosa got up and, light as a butterfly, went and put a more 'modern' disc on the gramophone.

'You were right, Rosa. Now I feel hungry,' said Bordelli.

'Me too . . .'

They ate a bit of everything, drinking wine and listening to Modugno. As soon as the song '*Vitti 'na crozza*'[19] ended, Gideon started scratching at the pane of the French door. Rosa went to let him in, and he replied with a miaow. He allowed her only one caress, then, tail wagging, ran to the far end of the room and hopped up on to the sideboard. Lying down at once, he licked a paw three or four times, yawned, and then closed his eyes, with the two of them looking on.

'All he ever does is sleep,' said Rosa.

Bordelli looked at his watch and stretched his back. 'I think I'll go to bed too,' he said.

'It's barely half past two,' she complained.

'I need to sleep, Rosa.'

'Oh, poo . . . *'a donna riccia non la voglio n-no . . .'* she started singing along with Modugno.[20]

'I don't suppose you could give me a bit of that stuff?' asked Bordelli, gesturing towards the little box with the marijuana inside. 'I'd like to continue my investigation of its effects.'

'Only if you don't leave . . .'

'I'm sorry, Rosa, but I'm a wreck. And tomorrow I have a very busy day.'

'You're mean,' she said. Then she tore a page out of the magazine, put a little grass and a few rolling papers in it, wrapped it all up in a little package, and slipped it into his jacket pocket.

'You're a dear,' said Bordelli. He drank his last drop of wine and stood up. Rosa followed him to the door, still huffing in frustration. When she didn't feel like sleeping, it bored her to be alone. On the wall in the entranceway hung a sort of small bowl with the face of Pope John XXIII on it. Rosa ran her finger over it.

'Look how dirty. I really need to dust the place,' she said, frowning.

'Goodnight, Rosa.'

'Will I see you again before Christmas, monkey?'

'I'll come on Christmas Eve with your present.'

'Oh, goody! You've already bought it?' she asked, her expression changing.

'Of course,' Bordelli lied.

'What is it? No, wait, don't tell me!'

'I wouldn't dream of it,' said Bordelli. He opened the door

and lowered his voice. 'Let's be quiet,' he said, gesturing towards the door of Signora Anichini, an old maid born not long after the unification of Italy who still liked to spy and eavesdrop on other people. Rosa stood up on tiptoe and kissed the inspector on the chin.

'Goodnight, Rosa, thanks for everything.'

'You're leaving me all alone, you wicked man.'

He kissed her hand, as in the old days. He knew she liked it. A last wave goodbye and he vanished down the stairs, quiet as a burglar, followed by Rosa's incomprehensible whisperings. As he was descending the last flight, a rapid-fire burst of kisses came down through the stairwell. When he was already at the main door, he heard Rosa's voice.

'Tell me what the present is, since I'll forget anyway.'

'Sshhh . . .' said Bordelli, closing the door behind him.

The weather had taken a turn for the worse. It was raining. The car seat was cold, but Bordelli barely noticed. He drove distractedly, grinding the gears. When he got home, he went straight to the kitchen. He was still hungry. He wolfed down a slice of the pecorino he'd bought at the market in Impruneta and finished what little was left of the *finocchiona* salami. All without bread, since there wasn't any. He even scarfed down half a banana and a week-old piece of mozzarella. Then he rolled himself another cigarette of that stuff and smoked it pacing slowly about the flat. He really liked the smell of it. He went and poked his head back into the room he never left open. Nobody had ever slept in it. Which was sad, when you came right down to it. He decided that he would fix it up a little by the end of the month. He might even sleep there himself from time to time, just for a change. Closing the door again, he went into the bathroom to brush his teeth. He couldn't quite grasp how he actually felt. His face in the mirror looked back at him with an amused expression, and he felt as if he was being watched. He'd never felt that way before. But, still, he also felt calm and relaxed.

He went into the bedroom and got undressed. He folded

his clothes, which he had never done before, and arranged them tidily on a chair. Then he got into bed, switched off the light, and turned on to his side. He felt as if he were floating in the middle of the room and let his mind drift away. He fell asleep thinking of the hashish drinkers who woke up in a pleasure garden.

23 December

He was still asleep when the phone rang at his bedside . . . but he did not wake up in a pleasure garden. He picked up the receiver without turning on the light.

'Yes . . .?'

'Inspector . . . am I disturbing you?'

'Who's this?'

'Don't you recognise me? It's me.'

'Ennio . . . but what time is it?'

'Seven o'clock, Inspector. I just got out of the hotel.'

'That's excellent news.'

'You told me yourself to call as soon as I got out . . . for that little job.'

'Thanks, but I don't need you any more for that. The guy I wanted to nab was killed.'

Botta huffed into the receiver.

'Too bad, I was really keen on doing you a favour,' he said, disappointed.

'Next time, Botta.'

'Who was the guy that got killed?'

'A loan shark.'

'Fantastic. Don't tell me you're desperately looking for the killer, Inspector.'

'It's my job, Botta. But it's true I'm not really so desperate, when you come down to it.'

'Will you dump the body in the Arno or feed it to the pigs?' Botta asked in all seriousness.

'Let's talk about something else, Ennio. Are you hard up?'

'What do you think, Inspector? Have you ever seen Botta rolling in dough?'

'Well, if you hadn't pissed away all that money from Greece at the races . . .'

'I've sworn off the horses for ever . . .' said Ennio, sighing into the receiver.

'If you feel like dropping by, we can have coffee together,' said Bordelli, already thinking of the Christmas dinner.

'Sure, I'd be glad to come by. Need anything?'

'I'd like to ask you to get me a carton of cigarettes, but I'm trying to quit.'

'A nice little watch?'

'Just come and we'll see.'

'I'm on my way.'

Botta hung up, and the inspector got out of bed. From the chair he picked up the trousers he had carefully folded just a few hours before and slid his legs into them. He went into the bathroom barefooted, braces dangling. Leaning over the sink, he looked at himself in the mirror. He grabbed the flesh on one arm. It didn't seem so old, really; the skin was still rather smooth. At fifty-five and counting, it could be a lot worse. It seemed like the start of a rather positive day. He barely had time to splash some water on his face when the doorbell rang. Drying himself in haste, he went and opened the door, waiting on the threshold. Botta arrived out of breath and dripping with rain. He gave the inspector a sad smile. He'd lost a lot of weight, cheeks looking hollower than usual.

'Hello, Inspector. As you can see, they let me out for Christmas.'

'You didn't take very long to get here. Were you close by?'

'No, I was in Bologna, but I told the chauffeur I was in a hurry.'

'You look well,' Bordelli lied, shaking his hand.

'Cut the shit, Inspector, I've lost fifteen pounds. They don't know how to cook in that fucking prison.'

'I'll send a memo to the ministry and demand that they hire a French chef for the Murate.'

'Shall I make the coffee, Inspector?'

'Good idea.'

Botta then took two false Bulova watches out of his pocket.

'First get a load of this stuff. Only six thousand lire. There's even the little window with the date.'

'You're barely out of prison and already loaded with rubbish?'

'I could make a lot more money with cocaine, Inspector, but I don't like that sector . . .'

'I know, I know.'

'You like this one?' said Ennio, holding up another watch.

'Put that shit away, Botta.'

'Forget I ever mentioned it.'

'Let me finish shaving and I'm all yours,' said Bordelli, slapping him on the back.

'I'll go and make the coffee.'

'Everything's out on the counter, there's nothing to break open.'

'Too bad,' Botta said, chuckling, and then disappeared into the kitchen.

He prepared the moka in strict accordance with the rules, and while the inspector was shaving, he started milling about the flat. Nothing had changed. Along the wall in the entrance were the same stacks of newspapers and dusty boxes he'd always seen there. It looked like the home of someone who'd just moved in and hadn't yet decided where to put things.

'What are you doing for Christmas, Botta?' Bordelli asked loudly from the bathroom.

Ennio appeared in the doorway. 'What was that, Inspector?' They looked at each other through the mirror.

'I was asking what you're doing for Christmas.'

'Didn't you know? I'm going to my house in Monte Carlo,' Botta said with a wry face.

Having finished shaving, Bordelli splashed some aftershave on his face. It burned like fire, and he liked the feeling. 'Feel like putting together a dinner here with me?' he asked. He could still remember the dinner of two years before, in the middle of the summer, when Botta had outdone himself by making a multilingual meal.

'Who else is coming?' Ennio asked, frowning.

'Diotivede, Fabiani, Dante . . . all people you already know.'

'What about the Sardinian kid? Has he recovered?'

'He's still in Sardinia. He's doing all right, says he'll be back in January.'

'If you hear from him, give him my best.'

'Will do,' said Bordelli, trying to tame some overgrown hairs in his eyebrows. Hair is weird, Rosa had said to him one evening . . . The older you get, the more you've got on strange parts of your body.

'I've already got something in mind for your dinner,' said Botta, looking thoughtful. Bordelli looked at him through the mirror.

'I like people with a sense of initiative. The only thing . . .'

'The only thing?' Ennio asked, concerned.

'Diotivede would like some French onion soup. Do you know how to make it?'

'Are you kidding, Inspector? Right after the war I spent a year in a Marseille prison. I know all about French cuisine.'

'Then you'll make the pickiest corpse-cutter in Italy a happy man,' said Bordelli. Realising he hadn't shaved properly, he lathered his face up again.

Ennio was already at the organisational stage. 'It would probably be a good idea to start doing some shopping today.'

'I'll give you the cash straight away.'

'Now if only I can manage to find what I need . . .'

The inspector was taking his time with his face, and in the end Botta went and sat down on the toilet lid.

'How much do you need?' Bordelli asked.

'Ten thousand should be enough.'

'When will you need the kitchen?'

'I need to start today, Inspector, and I should probably hurry.'

'All right, then, I'll leave you the house keys so you can come and go as you please.'

Bordelli thought about what he'd just said and started laughing. Botta looked at him as if he felt slightly offended.

'Why are you laughing, Inspector?'

'Do you even know how to use keys any more, Botta? Do you remember how you do it? You stick them in and turn . . .'

'Look, I'm not just a burglar, you know. In my day I even went to school . . .'

Bordelli at last finished shaving and put the fiery aftershave on his face again.

'How's the coffee coming along?' he asked. Ennio leapt to his feet and ran into the kitchen. Bordelli heard him yelling and, drying his hands, went to see what he was doing.

'Who you yelling at, Botta?'

'You know what they say in France, Inspector. *Café boilé café fouté*. I'll make a fresh pot.'

'I haven't got the time, Botta. I'll get one outside.'

'It'll only take a minute.' Botta immediately got busy. The inspector went to look for a shirt and was putting it on as he returned to the kitchen. The coffee pot was already on the fire.

'You were saying you went to school . . .' said Bordelli.

'I even did a year of university.'

'And how did you pay for your studies?'

Ennio had rinsed off two espresso cups and was looking for something to dry them with.

'My father was still around. I don't know how he did it, but we almost always had money for food and study. And when we didn't . . .'

'It was your job to find some.'

'What else was I supposed to do? To learn a profession you have to study, Inspector, and to study you need a lot of money. Do you think it's right for the poor to remain ignorant?'

'I agree with you, my dear Botta, but apparently someone else likes things this way.'

'Anyway, I'm not ashamed to be a thief, because I've never

robbed anyone who had less than me. I go and take from the rich what I haven't got but am entitled to. What's wrong with that?'

'You talk like a Sardinian bandit.'

'Even Don Bencini says that whoever robs because he's hungry goes to heaven.'

'Who's Don Bencini?'

'A priest with bollocks, and a man who doesn't talk much but takes action.'

'The one who goes around to prisons talking to crooks like you?'

'That's the one . . . One time he told me that if Jesus Christ could see the way Italy is today, he'd ring his daddy and tell him to drown the place.'

'I think he's right.'

'We could use a lot more priests like that . . . instead of those fat puppets with double chins in gold vestments . . .' Ennio was standing with the two wet cups in his hands, waving them around in the air as he spoke.

Bordelli buttoned his shirt sleeves. 'So, what exactly did you study?' he asked.

'I did nearly a year of Letters.'

'You don't say.'

'My father wanted me to become a teacher or something like that.'

They both smiled. The inspector pulled up his braces and took out his wallet.

'Let's get to more serious matters, Ennio,' he said, putting a ten-thousand lira note in Botta's pocket.

'Oh, shit . . . I forgot the wine, Inspector.'

'In what sense?'

'To do things properly, we should have French wine, which costs a lot of money . . . But if you like, I could get something from the Piedmont.'

'You're the chef, and if you've decided on French wine, there must be a reason. Here's another five thousand.'

The coffee started bubbling up, and Botta still hadn't found anything with which to dry the cups. He waved them around in the air another couple of times, with gusto, then set them down on the table. Using the sleeve of his sweater as a pot-holder, he picked up the coffee pot and filled the little cups.

'Not to brag, but get a whiff of this coffee,' he said.

The inspector opened a cupboard, took out a sugar bowl, set this down on the table, then took a teaspoon out of a drawer . . . Ennio followed his movements with a look of concern. When he saw the inspector about to put the sugar in his cup, he jumped.

'What are you doing, Inspector?!' he yelled.

'Shit, Ennio, you scared me.'

'Just tell me one thing: do you want to drink coffee or slop?'

Bordelli was still holding the teaspoon in midair. He emptied it back in the sugar bowl.

'Did I do something wrong?'

'I thought you took it bitter, Inspector, otherwise I would have sweetened it myself.'

'What, do you want to be my mother now?'

'So you refuse to understand! The sugar must be put in the cup *before*, not *after* . . . And no spoons, either. If you move the sugar, it can do damage. At the most you can make a little circling motion . . . like so.' And he started gently swirling the coffee in the little cup. Ending the demostration, he grabbed the inspector's coffee and dumped it back into the pot. Bordelli was watching him with curiosity.

'And what difference does it make?'

'The same difference there is between beer and cow piss,' said Ennio. He put half a teaspoon of sugar in Bordelli's empty cup, then poured the steaming coffee on top of it.

'Here, Inspector. This is probably the first proper cup of coffee you've ever had in your life.'

'And where did you learn that?'

'I spent a couple of months in Naples as a kid.'

'Inside or outside?'

'Inside. Circulation of false banknotes.'

Bordelli took a sip of coffee.

'Not bad,' he said.

Ennio seemed satisfied. 'You see, Inspector, putting the sugar in *first* doesn't get rid of the bitterness, and what kind of bloody coffee is it if it's not bitter? But it does get rid of the really bitter part that tastes like . . . I dunno . . . I mean . . . it leaves the good bitterness and gets rid of the bad.'

The inspector drank the last of his coffee and went to put his cup in the sink.

'You're right, it gets rid of the nasty bitterness, the one that tastes burnt,' he said, heading out of the kitchen. Ennio followed him to the front door.

'One of these days I'm going to teach you how to make pasta with butter and Parmesan, Inspector. It sounds like a piece of piss but it's actually one of the hardest. It's all a question of timing.'

'One is never done learning . . . Ciao, Botta. We're in your hands for Christmas dinner.'

'Just leave it to me.'

'But don't forget the onion soup.'

'It's pronounced *onyònh*, Inspector, *onyònh*.'

The sky was purple and looked as if it were about to fall down on to the city at any moment. The needle on the barometer was practically horizontal, and Bordelli had the impression that he could feel the air weighing down on his shoulders. The moment he entered the office he grabbed the telephone and dialled a number. He let it ring at least ten times, and at last he heard someone pick up.

'Yes?'

'Good morning, Odoardo. Were you asleep?'

'Who the hell is this?'

'It's Bordelli. Did I wake you?' He heard a sigh at the other end, then silence. 'You still there, Odoardo?'

'What do you want this time, Inspector?' asked Odoardo, thick-tongued with sleep.

'I've got something to show you.'

'What?'

'You'll have to do me the favour of coming here.'

'Where's *here*?'

'Police headquarters. Ask for me at the guardhouse.'

'I really don't understand why,' said Odoardo, annoyed.

'It'll only take a minute. But don't go back to sleep. I'll be waiting for you.'

Bordelli hung up, confident he would see him soon. He rang Mugnai on the internal line and asked him if a parcel had arrived from the courthouse. The inspector had phoned De Marchi the previous day and asked him please to send him the scissors used in the Badalamenti murder the following morning.

'They've just arrived this minute, Inspector. I'll bring them up.'

A minute later Mugnai entered the room.

'Here you go, Inspector. I also brought the post,' he said, setting a flat cardboard box and a few envelopes down on the desk.

'Thanks, Mugnai. In a little while a young man should be arriving, and he'll ask for me. His name is Beltempo—'

'Well, let's hope he stays for a while . . .' Mugnai chuckled.[21]

The inspector sighed. 'You really ought to work on your witticisms, Mugnai. You seem to be the only one who laughs at them.'

'Just making a little light conversation, Inspector, since I'm shut up all day long in that bloody little boo—'

'You're forgiven, Mugnai, but let me finish what I was saying,' Bordelli said, interrupting him.

'Sorry, sir, go ahead.'

'When the kid arrives, I want you to let me know, but don't let him in immediately. Create some sort of obstacle for him, make him wait a little . . . I'm sure you can think of something . . . Just make him a little nervous before you bring him here.'

'Don't worry, Inspector, I'll take care of it.'

'But don't overdo it, mind.'

'I know exactly what to do,' said Mugnai with a knowing air. He liked having a mission to accomplish. After he left, Bordelli settled a few bureaucratic matters, signed a few documents, made a few phone calls, but most of the time he was thinking about Odoardo. He could hardly wait to have him there in front of him.

He went over to the window and started looking outside, head full of useless thoughts. The sky was darker than ever. A dense, fine rain started to fall. The drops left long streaks on the glass which looked like cuts. After only a few minutes he could already hear the dripping of the broken gutter pouring water on to the cobblestones of the courtyard. Bordelli was also thinking about the left-handed Raffaele, his cowboy-like grit and his dreams. Perhaps he ought to have summoned him to the police station too, but he didn't feel the need to do so yet. For the moment he wanted only to have a little chat with Odoardo. There was something about him that didn't add up, and he wanted to have a better sense of whether or not the kid was lying. He heard the internal phone ring and ran to pick up.

'He's here, Inspector,' Mugnai said in a mysterious whisper.

'Good, now it's down to you,' Bordelli said, hanging up. He still had a little more time. Opening the box, he picked up the transparent plastic bag that held the murder weapon. Attached to one of the scissor holes was a little card that said: *Exh. no. 1*. The depth to which the blades had sunk in the victim's neck was still visible, marked by a line of dried blood. The inspector made room on his desk surface by pushing the disorder to one side with a sweep of the arm, then placed the scissors right in the middle. Waiting for Odoardo, he started pacing back and forth in the room, fiddling with an unlit cigarette. From time to time he would start humming a tune without knowing what it was. It was certainly true that music had changed a great deal from the time he was young. There was something angry in the music of today, and there must be a reason for it. But it wasn't just the music that was changing, it was everything. It seemed as if young people had suddenly become fed up with everything that had anything to do with the older generation. Perhaps it was their way of throwing off the burden of a past that they themselves had not suffered, and looking forward. One thing was certain: they could no longer bear hearing the older people's complaints about the war and having to queue up for bread. The tears to be cried had already been shed. Now it was time to start living again, and having fun. Maybe they were right . . .

There was a knock at the door, and Bordelli gave a start. Mugnai poked his head inside.

'Inspector, there's a young man here to see you,' he said, winking.

'Let him in.'

Mugnai turned round.

'You can go in,' he said.

Odoardo came forward with a hard face and stopped in the doorway.

'You took such a long time to get here, I thought you'd gone back to sleep,' said Bordelli, gesturing to Mugnai to close the door. The youth approached the desk. His hair was wet with rain and he looked quite cross.

'That policeman is an animal,' he said, looking back at the closed door.

'He's just doing his job,' the inspector said.

Odoardo looked down, saw the bloodied scissors, and his eyes seemed to light up . . . Or perhaps it was only an impression of Bordelli's. Perhaps he was watching him too intensely or had already made up his mind. And the fact remained that the killer was left-handed, and Odoardo was not.

'What is it you have to tell me, Inspector?' the youth asked.

'Sorry about the rain. Would you like something to dry yourself with? The bathroom's right here next door.'

'I just want to make this brief,' Odoardo said curtly, shooting a cold glance at Bordelli.

The inspector made a friendly gesture, indicating the chair. 'Please sit down.'

'I'm perfectly fine standing, thank you. What did you wish to tell me?'

Bordelli started patting himself all over as if looking for something.

'You wouldn't happen to have a cigarette? I seem to have finished mine,' he said. This time it was true.

'I never smoke in the morning,' the youth said. Bordelli shrugged.

'Good. That way, I won't smoke either.'

'I don't have much time, Inspector.'

'Don't worry, I'll get to it. Have you ever been in a place like this before?'

'I've never had the pleasure.'

The inspector got up, calmly circled his desk, stopped in front of Odoardo, and spoke almost into his face.

'In your opinion, Odoardo, am I a good policeman?'

'What kind of question is that?' said Odoardo, taking a step back.

Bordelli smiled serenely. 'Why don't you sit down?'

'I'd rather stand.'

'Suit yourself.'

As if he had nothing more to say, Bordelli started pacing about the room, hands in his pockets, looking out the window. The rain was coming down more insistently. He heard the boy huff with impatience behind him.

'What do you want, Inspector? Just tell me without beating around the bush, so we can get it over with.'

Bordelli turned towards him and looked at him thoughtfully.

'I'd like to go over something with you,' he said.

'I can hardly wait.'

'Listen to me carefully. We're going to pretend that a certain young man, whom we'll call Odoardo for the sake of convenience, committed that murder . . . You know what I'm talking about, don't you?'

'No.'

'Totuccio Badalamenti, the loan shark who lived in Piazza del Carmine.'

'I've already told you I don't know him,' said Odoardo.

Bordelli raised a hand and smiled.

'And I believe you. Do you believe me when I say I believe you?'

Odoardo's eyes looked darker than usual.

'I just want to know clearly what you want from me. I think it's my right,' he said, trying to remain calm.

'Look, you have no reason to get upset . . .'

'I'm not upset. I just want to know what I'm doing here. Is that so unusual?' he said, slowly turning his face away.

He *is* upset, thought Bordelli, starting again to pace slowly back and forth.

'Let's say that I'd like for us to reconstruct, together, the narrative sequence of that murder, and perhaps even make a few conjectures as to the killer's motives and psychological make-up. What do you say, do you feel like trying?'

'Will it make any difference if I don't?' asked Odoardo.

The inspector stopped pacing.

'I'm asking you as a personal favour, Odoardo. You can't refuse.'

'Let's be quick about it.'

'Don't worry. There's a time for everything, my grandfather used to say.' Bordelli saw a flash of hatred in the boy's eyes and resumed his pacing, utterly relaxed, hands in his pockets.

'Certainly this hypothetical Odoardo had serious reasons for killing Badalamenti, and that is probably where we should start,' the inspector said, but then he stopped and waited for the lad to make the next move.

'I'm listening,' said Odoardo, looking indifferently at the bloodied scissors. He already seemed calmer. Bordelli took one hand out of his pocket and hooked it behind his neck.

'Let's take a step back. Let's imagine that after his mother's death, our imaginary Odoardo received a visit from a guy he'd never seen before. A nasty bloke with a "fuck you" attitude . . . Are you following me?'

'I'm all ears.'

'Don't worry, it's not a long story, but it's worth our while to tell it slowly. Now listen closely. This nasty bloke tells Odoardo that his mother signed some promissory notes made out to him, and that, by law, the debts of the deceased are passed on to the heirs . . . He tells him that the payments are in arrears and that there will be trouble if they are not made at once. He might take away Odoardo's country hovel, but even that may not be enough to pay off the debt. And if he won't pay it off, there'll be hell to pay. It really sounds like a threat. Odoardo feels crushed by this news . . . But that's not the end of it. The usurer also says something offensive about his mother and mentions some compromising photographs which, if made public, could sully her memory. And, in fact, Odoardo realises that it was because of those photographs that his mother was forced to sign those promissory notes in the first place. A sort of blackmail to be paid off in instalments . . . It's enough to piss a man off, wouldn't you say?' the inspector asked, stopping in front of the lad.

'What the hell are you talking about? What photographs?' said Odoardo, newly upset.

The inspector took advantage of this to look him straight in the eye. 'You're not interested in the promissory notes?'

'I'm not interested in anything you're saying,' said Odoardo, clenching his teeth.

Bordelli smiled. 'Wait before you say that. But let's get back to our story . . . Odoardo thus comes to know some unpleasant things, and he comes to know them from a man like Badalamenti, with that ugly face . . . You remember Badalamenti's face, don't you?'

'I believe I've already told you six or seven times that I don't know him.'

'You're right, I'm sorry, I got a little distracted there . . . But are you sure you never went to Badalamenti's flat? Not even once?'

'Is that a serious question?'

'I should think so.'

'Then I will answer in all seriousness: no, I never went there. Not once. I didn't know him, I never saw him, I have no idea what kind of face he had, I've never even heard mention of him. Have I left anything out?'

'Excellent. To continue, let us imagine that our friend Odoardo is rather frightened by this visit and promises Badalamenti that he will pay off the debt as soon as possible. Naturally, however, he wants the photographs of his mother in return. The blackmailer tells him he will get them back only when he has paid everything in full, down to the last lira. So the young man asks how much his mother's debt amounts to, and is given a figure with so many zeros that his hair stands on end. Badalamenti is in a hurry, sets the due dates, and leaves, telling the lad not to do anything silly . . . Everything clear so far?'

'Crystal clear,' said Odoardo, folding his arms over his chest.

'Good. Now we'll pretend that one day our imaginary Odoardo goes to see Badalamenti to pay off one of the promissory notes, and he suddenly gets the idea to ask the shark for the photos of his mother, which he has never even seen. Badalamenti counts the money and then shakes his head. He is adamant. No photographs until Odoardo has paid up. Odoardo swears he will pay off his mother's debts and continues to ask him for the pictures, but Badalamenti laughs in his face. Odoardo insists further and says he would at least like to see them. But Badalamenti won't listen to reason and orders the kid to get the hell out of there and, as if that weren't enough, says something unpleasant about his mother. Then something happens. Odoardo's face changes, he feels overcome with rage. Badalamenti *invites him* to clear out, but he doesn't budge. Try to imagine our Odoardo . . . On the outside, he seems calm, but inside he's furious. All he can see is a fine pair of scissors in the pen-holder on the desk, a big pair of pointed scissors, nice and long . . . the very same ones you see over there . . . Had you noticed them?'

'Go on.'

'I can see you're warming to the story yourself . . . I'm glad.'

'I'm just waiting for it to end.'

'I can picture the whole scene . . . Try to do so yourself . . . Badalamenti turns to open the door to chase Odoardo away, but the boy has something else in mind. All at once he grabs the scissors, raises his hand in the air and . . . thrusts them deep into the man's neck . . . like this.' Bordelli mimed the motion, left hand in the air, then resumed pacing calmly back and forth and talking.

'With Badalamenti dead, our Odoardo now has the time to look for the photographs. Not exactly calmly, mind you. He's just killed a man and can't wait to get out of there. And so he ransacks the whole flat in haste, searching every corner, even the bathroom, but finds nothing. In the end he gives up and leaves. What do you think? The ending's a little weak, but we can work on it.'

'It would make a bad movie,' said Odoardo.

'You can help me make it better.'

'Listen, Inspector, I've been a good little boy and listened to your story through to the end. But now I'd like to leave.'

'Why is it that everyone your age is always in such a hurry?' asked Bordelli, stopping in front of the window. The boy didn't reply. 'What are all these important things you have to do?' the inspector continued, watching the rain, which showed no sign of letting up.

'It's not just the important things,' said Odoardo.

Bordelli looked at him, feigning great surprise. 'That's a very interesting reply,' he said. 'I knew you were an intelligent lad. Perhaps all we'd need to understand one another would be a common language . . . Are you familiar with Plato's example of the fisherman and the fishing line?'

'No.'

'But I'll bet you like Kafka . . . Do you remember that horrific story about the penal colony?'

Odoardo looked at him as if he were dealing with a madman.

'I'll make you a complete list of all the books I've read and post it to you,' he said, voice hoarse with irritation.

'That's another interesting reply. What do you think, Odoardo? Is killing Badalamenti a crime or isn't it? I mean from a moral perspective.'

Odoardo clenched his teeth so hard that, for a moment, his cheeks trembled.

'That's enough, Inspector. If you wish to indict me, please do so, but this charade makes no sense at all,' he said, trying to control his anger.

He's very upset, Bordelli thought again, then he made a face of utter astonishment.

'Indict you for what?' he asked.

'That's exactly what I've been wondering.'

'My dear Odoardo, I told you, all I've just said is mere conjecture. I used your name only to help you identify with the main character. I would, however, like you to tell me how a—'

'I didn't kill him,' Odoardo interrupted him.

'And I believe you.'

'Then leave me alone.'

'Just a minute,' said Bordelli, and he resumed pacing back and forth. Then he stopped in the middle of the room, forefinger on his brow.

'As I was saying, there's something I would like to understand . . . How is it that an alert, intelligent lad like Odoardo was unable to find Badalamenti's secret hiding place under one of the living room tiles? Don't you think that's odd?'

'What are you talking about?'

'What you were looking for, Odoardo, was under the floor . . . That is, if you were Odoardo the killer, of course . . . We're still in the realm of hypothesis. It *is* odd, though. I mean, I myself, who am less intelligent than you, I found the hiding place in no time at all . . . In short, in case you haven't yet understood, *I* now have those photographs of your mother.'

Odoardo changed colour but said nothing. Bordelli pointed at the desk.

'They're right there, in a drawer. I imagine you must be quite anxious to see them.'

The boy said nothing, but only stared at the inspector with eyes as cold as ice.

'But I'm afraid I can't grant your wish . . . I'm sorry.' Bordelli sighed histrionically.

'I don't know anything about those photos . . . In fact, I'm convinced they're just another of your lies,' the boy said, stone faced.

'My dear Odoardo, you're free to think whatever you like.'

'And if they really do exist, they belong to me now, since my mother is dead.'

'You're better off not seeing them, believe me,' said the inspector.

Odoardo curled his lips as if wanting to smile, but he looked more like a dog baring its teeth.

'Inspector, why don't you drop all the bullshit?' he said.

'You think I'm just pulling your leg?'

'Worse. You've got it into your head that it was me who killed that guy, and you're making up all manner of bollocks to confirm your belief. You don't know which way to turn, and so to bring the case to a close, you're happy to find any culprit at all . . . Unfortunately you've landed on me. You policemen do this sort of thing all the time . . . You think I don't know?'

Odoardo gave a sort of half-smile, as if he'd finally found the right way to defend himself. But it was clear he couldn't stand being shut up in that room any longer.

Bordelli let out another long, slow sigh. 'You know something, Odoardo? I've seen killers who were extremely anxious to confess, as if admitting to their crime gave greater meaning to what they had done. There's one I remember well. He was sitting right there, in the same chair as you. His name was Guido . . . Guido Mecocci. He looked me straight in the eye and sweated . . . And sweated . . . It was very hot, too, it must have been July . . . July '56, I believe—'

'Do you know what time it is, Inspector?' Odoardo asked, annoyed, tapping his watch with his finger.

'Let me finish telling you about Mecocci, it's quite interesting. Mecocci was short and stocky, practically illiterate, but he had a very intelligent face. You know what I mean? The kind of person who has . . . How do you say it? Well, intelligent eyes. You know what I'm trying to say?'

'No, these concepts are too difficult for me,' said Odoardo. He could no longer stand all the chatter.

Bordelli was satisfied. He felt he'd played the part of the oddball inspector rather well.

'Have you ever noticed, Odoardo? That people who are lucky enough to have those eyes, even if they're short and ugly, well, it doesn't even matter . . . Have you ever noticed?'

'I'm sorry but I really don't give a fuck about any of this.'

'Don't worry, I'll only take up another minute of your time . . . At any rate we've established that Guido Mecocci was that sort of man , short and ugly but with all the pride of a handsome one. But let's get to the point, otherwise I risk boring you . . . Mecocci had clubbed his brother-in-law to death because he couldn't bear seeing him mistreat his wife, who was Mecocci's only sister. He was a prime suspect and had no alibi. I interrogated him. He didn't say anything for quite a while, though I could see that he was squirming. At a certain point, though, his expression changed, and without my having to ask him anything, he started telling me everything from A to Z. He was glad to tell me how and why he'd killed his brother-in-law or, actually, "that great big son of a bitch of a brother-in-law", as he put it. And when he was done, he actually thanked me for having listened to him. Interesting story, don't you think?'

Odoardo looked as if he were carved out of wax.

'And where do the three little pigs come in?' he said.

'Oh, I've got dozens of stories, if that's what you want. For example, I remember the time I had to climb up to the top of a roof to catch a multiple murderer. I managed to bring him down without firing a shot but, boy, did that ever cost me some effort. I won't even mention how hungry I was afterwards. I ate like a pig, then I went to bed and fell asleep straight away, without reading even a page . . . Whereas normally I always read. What about you? Do you read before falling asleep?'

'No, I can't because at night I have to go around killing people.'

'Not to be indiscreet, but . . . what was the last book you read?'

'*Crime and Punishment*, and I loved it. Especially when Raskolnikov splits the pawnbroker's head open with an axe.'

Bordelli folded his hands behind his neck.

'And have you read any Lermontov?' he asked with an air of great interest.

'Inspector, I'm going to go now. If you're going to arrest me, I suggest you do it for a specific reason and, above all, with a stamped and signed arrest warrant,' said Odoardo, heading for the door.

Bordelli waited for him to open it, then said calmly: 'You may not realise it, but I am your friend.'

The lad turned round. His face was pale.

'Enemies are quite enough for me, thank you,' he said.

'Well, I'm going to have to write that down,' said Bordelli. Odoardo went out and closed the door behind him. It was still raining outside. He was going to get soaked to the bone.

The inspector went and sat down, sighing for the thousandth time. In the end he hadn't liked the charade either. Perhaps Odoardo was right. Perhaps he was evaluating things with his mind already made up. He'd got it into his head to torment the boy in every way possible and observe his reactions. He didn't have the slightest bit of proof against him. Still, that great big fly kept buzzing in his brain, not allowing him a moment's peace.

Another fly, a real one, fat and hairy, flew in. It kept trying to land on his face, in always the same spot, right beside his nose. He would wave it away with his hand, and the fly would buzz about for a moment, making that tiresome drone, and a few seconds later would land in the same place, beside his nose. It seemed a little groggy. He shooed it away again, and the bastard got as far as the wall opposite Bordelli and then turned back. The inspector got his open hand ready, waited for the fly to return to home base, let it relax, then dealt himself a powerful slap. He struck himself square in the face, but the fly was faster than him. He could hear it buzzing away, and saw it land on the ceiling. His cheek and nose burned from the slap, and he felt like taking his gun out and shooting the damned thing. If God created flies, there must be a reason. That much he agreed with. What he did not understand was why God had created that particular reason. It was a subject that could take him far, very far . . .

By mid-morning the sky was completely overcast with grey clouds. A fine, granular snow started to fall. Even the pigeons looked chilled, huddling together in groups along the buildings' highest cornices, sheltered by the eaves.

Bordelli stuck the customary unlit cigarette between his lips. It was too hot in his office, and he'd already taken off his jacket some time before. When he felt a drop of sweat roll down his cheek, he went and opened the window and started gazing outside. The snowflakes were tiny and icy, but the snow didn't stick. Little by little, his memory started whirring . . . A similar snow was falling at Christmas in '43, at Torricella Peligna. And a shitty Christmas it was, with Nazis encamped on the hillside opposite them, barely six miles away. Bordelli felt nervous that day, smoking one cigarette after another while awaiting orders from the rear lines. Because it was Christmas, nobody was shooting, like the good Christians they all were . . .

Late that morning two of his men returned from patrol with Christmas dinner on a leash, a nice fat pig with a rope round its neck. They said they'd found it wandering about the countryside, and they were as happy as children. Everyone in the camp gathered round the beast, already tasting its roast flesh on their tongues. Battle-knives were drawn and the pig started to get nervous. Like everyone else, Bordelli too wanted a good hot meal; he was sick and tired of Italian biscuit spread with American tinned meat. But the whole thing seemed fishy to him. He told the men to hold their knives and asked for a more precise explanation of how they'd come by the pig. In the end it turned out they'd taken it away from a peasant.

'But the bloke had another pig, Captain!' the two men said, trying to minimise the offence. Bordelli could practically smell the roast pork already, but he was the commander and could not tolerate pillage, and so with an effort of will he told them they had to take the animal back to its rightful owner. And he felt that a little speech was in order.

'This is robbery. Bloody hell, we're not Germans, after all!' he'd said.

The pig was taken home, with heartfelt apologies and a few bars of dark chocolate. At camp that evening, they spread more American meat on Italian biscuits, but it tasted worse than ever. They had no way of knowing at the time, but they would have to wait more than six months before they had a decent meal, six long months during which several of Bordelli's comrades would die. And they died not only from the increasingly sophisticated safety catches the Germans kept inventing to prevent removal of their mines. One morning Bordelli had to go out to recover the bodies of four of his men, killed in a basement when a defective hand grenade had gone off while they were playing cards. The small room was flooded with still-fresh, sticky blood. Their boots stuck to the floor. One piece of shrapnel had sliced Gaetano's belly in two, and under his torn uniform one could see the mass of intestines moving. Bordelli bent down to pick up a blood-soaked playing card. The queen of spades. He put it in his pocket. They loaded the four bodies on to a lorry and returned to camp. Bordelli was the only one who vomited when, as they were taking a curve, Gaetano's intestines fell out on to the flatbed . . .

After a while the granular snow turned to a freezing drizzle. Only up in the hills did it continue to snow. The inspector sat back down behind his desk and lit the cigarette he'd had in his hand for the past few minutes. He smoked it while reading the list of Badalamenti's debtors for the umpteenth time. There were nineteen men. Almost all of them were over seventy, and one over eighty. Diotivede had been quite clear about that, too. It was highly unlikely that an elderly man could have the strength to thrust a pair of scissors so deeply into another man's neck, to the point of shattering a vertebra. He thought about this, blowing the smoke up towards the ceiling. The big fly seemed to be gone. Maybe it was already dead.

The killer might be the son or grandson of one of the debtors, he supposed, though a person like Badalamenti usually operated without the knowledge of his victims' families. Still, there were always exceptions. This line of reasoning also brought the sons and husbands of the female debtors into the picture, complicating the whole matter quite distressingly. But if he stuck strictly to the list, obviously the youngest men were the most likely suspects. And Odoardo Beltempo was also a young man, the youngest of them all, intelligent and highly strung, shut tight like a sea urchin, and the son of a woman blackmailed by the shark. But he wasn't left-handed. Diotivede be damned. Then there was Raffaele, who was rebellious, a big talker and, most importantly, left-handed. But it may have been another person not even on the list, someone who'd gone to see Badalamenti for the first time . . . a killer nobody would ever find, who had no need of the promise of pleasure gardens in order to kill.

While following these useless conjectures Bordelli had started doodling on a sheet of paper, almost without realising it. And a rather strange figure had emerged, with pig's feet and two swastikas instead of eyes. He crumpled the page and threw it into the wastepaper basket. He yawned with his whole mouth, accompanying it with a kind of groan. He thought he would return the promissory notes to the others on the list after the holidays . . . But then he changed his mind. The following morning he would send two police officers out to give back all the remaining IOUs, telling them to use maximum discretion and to speak only to those people directly involved. He had all the time in the world to call on them in person, but with those notes under the Christmas tree, they would sleep easier that night.

He knocked on Patrolman Biagi's door. An envelope had just arrived from the courthouse with a reply to his enquiry as to the criminal records of all the loan shark's debtors. He read it at once. They all had clean records except for two men, the same two whom De Marchi had found when investigating the fingerprints he'd taken.

Deep down he'd never expected that search to produce any earth-shattering new developments. He wondered whether he really believed he would ever discover the truth of the murder, and he shook his head. He felt he'd reached a dead end. Of course, he'd told himself more or less the same thing many times in the past, and in those instances he'd decided, as a last resort, to follow his instinct. And in the end he had always succeeded in finding the killer. Almost always, that is. One time he'd failed, when a hunter had found, in the countryside near Cerbaia, the corpse of a woman of about forty of Nordic appearance, literally hammered to death and then dumped in a torrent that had carried her some several hundred yards over the rocks in the stream. No lead, no suspects, no nothing. He'd never even managed to identify the victim. The poor woman's

235

face was in a pitiful state, and there was no point in publishing a photo of it in the papers. Actually he would rather not think too much about that case. It was a nasty affair that didn't exactly do wonders for his self-esteem.

He started fiddling with an unlit cigarette, still thinking about Odoardo Beltempo and Raffaele Montigiani. He was trying to figure out what his next move should be. He repeated to himself for the hundredth time that there was no hard evidence incriminating either of the two youths. There weren't any real suspects, actually. And yet that big fat fly wouldn't stop buzzing round one name: Odoardo.

The office of Musillo the lawyer was in Via Parpaglia, near the corner of Via La Marmora, on the first floor of an ancient palazzo. Piras got to Oristano at a quarter to eleven, drove the entire length of Via Tirso and parked near the Tower of Mariano. After some insistence, he had succeded in borrowing Ettore's Fiat 500, which its owner usually left at home for fear of damage, taking the bus to work instead. To calm his worries Piras had shown him that, despite the crutches, he could drive safely, and in the end Ettore had tossed him the keys, telling him to drive slowly because the engine was still being broken in.

He stopped at the Ibba bar and drank a cup of coffee, then covered all of Via Parpaglia on foot, ringing Musillo's buzzer at eleven o'clock sharp. The great door giving on to the street came open. Piras took the lift, and when he got to the first floor, he saw the lawyer waiting for him in the doorway. He was a short man of about fifty, with a great deal of hair that was still black, and thick glasses. Noticing the crutches, Musillo seemed momentarily embarrassed. He greeted Piras with a very firm handshake, showed him in and closed the door. The vestibule was empty but for a coat rack, an umbrella stand and an old upholstered chair. They went into the office.

'Are you sure you're an active-duty policeman?' Musillo asked wryly, seeing him limp. He had two penetrating eyes like a nightbird's, enlarged by his glasses.

'Not to sound rhetorical, but a policeman is always on duty,' Piras said with a smile.

The lawyer nodded and went and sat down behind his desk, which was covered with folders and documents stacked in orderly fashion. The room was not big and had one wall entirely covered by a bookcase full of tomes and a glass-fronted cabinet overflowing with files. Piras collapsed with relief into a chair and leaned his crutches against the chair beside him. Just so there should be no doubt, he took out his badge and showed it to Musillo.

'I had no doubt,' the lawyer said with a mendacious little grin.

'But now you can be certain,' said Piras, putting the badge back in his pocket. The lawyer closed his eyes, and for a moment his face seemed vacant.

'I have to confess that I would never have expected a man like Benigno Staffa to do such a thing,' he said, head swaying slightly.

'Why do you say that?'

'I don't know, it's just a feeling.'

'It's hard to know what goes on in other people's minds,' said Piras, not wanting to reveal his own suspicions about the mysterious suicide.

'Please give the family my condolences,' said Musillo.

'Thank you.'

'So, tell me, Piras, what did you want to ask me?'

'Well, I was told that Benigno had hired you to sell some land here in Oristano.'

'Yes, that's right.'

'Land suitable for building, correct?'

'Yes.'

'Was there already a buyer?'

'An offer had been made, but negotiations were just beginning,' said Musillo, looking for a folder among the many on his desk.

'A developer, I imagine?' said Piras.

'That's right. One of those who are in the process of changing the face of Oristano,' Musillo said with a bitter smile.

'What's his name?' asked Piras.

By way of reply, the lawyer passed him the file, which he had finally found. On the cover were the names *Staffa-Pintus*. It contained a map of the land in question, a cadastral survey, the declaration of succession by Benigno's uncle, and a page from a notebook with the builder's vital statistics, written in hand: *Agostino Pintus, Eng., born at Custoza di Sommacampagna (Verona province), 16 July 1912, residing in Oristano at Via Marconi 33 bis.*

'The son of émigrés?' Piras asked, looking up.

The lawyer nodded and smiled. 'I asked him the same thing. I was curious because he has a Sardinian surname but talks with a Veneto accent.'

'And what did he say?'

'He said he was born and raised in the Veneto, but his parents came from a town in Cagliari province,' said Musillo. 'He lost both parents when he was thirty, and after the war decided to come and live here in Sardinia.'

'He's done well for himself.'

'He certainly has.'

'And had anyone else shown interest in that land?' Piras enquired.

The lawyer leaned back slowly in his chair. 'Mr Staffa asked me to take only one offer at a time. He didn't like confusion.'

'You were saying he hadn't fully reached an agreement with Mr Pintus . . .'

'Pintus made me a verbal offer and asked me to refer it to Benigno. But Benigno wouldn't agree to the price. He wanted to get as much as possible for the land and was in no hurry. I must admit, however, that the payment terms were quite attractive.'

'I guess developers can afford it,' said Piras.

'Of course, but just to make sure I informed myself as to

Mr Pintus's solvency. The banks treat the man with kid gloves. He seems to be one of the richest developers in the region.'

'So everything was in order.'

'It seemed like a good deal to me, and I said so to Mr Staffa.'

'May I ask how much the engineer offered?'

'Thirteen million five hundred thousand lire. Half upon signing the contract of agreement, the balance upon settlement, payable within six months.'

'A tidy sum,' commented Piras.

'And practically in cash. But our friend Benigno wanted five hundred lire more per square metre, and he dug in his heels. And Pintus wouldn't budge from his price of forty-five hundred.'

'And you tried to make them meet halfway . . .?'

'I was trying, but it was all very complicated. Not least because Signor Benigno didn't have a telephone at home. He would call me from the bar in Tramatza, once every couple of days, more or less,' the lawyer said, shrugging.

'When was the last time you saw him?'

'Last Sunday, actually, the day of the tragedy. He'd come here to see me,' said Musillo.

'At what time of day?'

'Around five. I'd been trying for some time to arrange a first meeting between him and Engineer Pintus, hoping to get things moving again. It wasn't easy, because Benigno was very stubborn and didn't even want to hear about anything under five thousand per square metre. Pintus, on the other hand, said he wouldn't pay one lira more, had checked his books carefully, and simply couldn't pay more than that. By bringing them together, I had hoped that one of them would give in.'

'Why on a Sunday?' Piras interrupted.

'My meetings with Benigno were always on Sundays, because he said he had too much to do during the week. It wasn't really a problem for me, since I live close by.'

'And how did the meeting go?'

'Badly ... and something happened that I still don't understand.'

'What was that?' Piras asked eagerly.

'The engineer arrived early. When Benigno rang the doorbell, I went to let him in and whispered to him not to be pig headed, because he was being offered a very good deal. He made a joke and seemed to be in a good mood. I thought he'd finally decided to accept the engineer's terms and felt pleased at the idea of pocketing all that money. Everything seemed settled, in other words. And so we went into the office. But when I introduced him to Pintus, Benigno's expression changed. He looked at Pintus very strangely ...'

'What do you mean, "strangely"?'

'I don't know how to put it ... At first I thought he simply didn't like the man.'

'And after?'

'Then we all sat down. Pintus said he could move up the settlement date to four months, and if they agreed on the deal he could make an immediate down payment of two million. But his offer was still forty-five hundred per square metre, and not one lira more. Benigno just kept staring at Pintus in that strange way, without saying anything ...'

'As if he was angry?' Piras interrupted.

'Not really angry, but ... astonished.'

'Then what?'

'Pintus seemed a little irritated by Benigno's silence, but in the end he smiled. He pulled out his chequebook and asked me for a pen. I didn't even have the time to hand him one before Benigno stood up, said he'd changed his mind, and was out the door. It was almost as if he was running away from something. Pintus said something to try to make him stay, but Benigno didn't even turn round, and before we knew it, we heard the front door close downstairs. I was terribly embarrassed. It had taken me a long time to set up that meeting, and everything seemed to have gone up in smoke ... But of course it turned out to be much worse than that.'

'And how did Pintus take it?'

'He was very upset. And he didn't understand what had happened, either. He merely said that his offer was good for another week, put his chequebook back in his pocket, and went away frowning.'

'And a few hours later Benigno shot himself,' said Piras.

'I still have trouble believing it,' said the lawyer, big eyes blinking behind his glasses.

'Has Pintus got a telephone?'

'The number's in the phone book, but I'll write it down for you, if you like,' said Musillo.

'No need to bother but, if you don't mind, I'd like to copy the personal information on Pintus.'

'Just take the piece of paper from the folder.'

'Thank you, sir, and have a good Christmas,' said Piras, standing up.

'And a happy Christmas to you and your family as well.'

The lawyer showed him out, and at the door they shook hands.

'If Pintus should happen to call you . . . please don't tell him you talked to me,' said Piras.

'Don't worry, I won't mention it to anyone.'

'Thank you very much, sir. I'm afraid I'll have to bother you again if I need you.'

'*A mellus biri*,'[22] Musillo said with a smile.

Just before one o'clock Bordelli parked the Beetle in front of the Trattoria da Cesare, but instead of going directly into Totò's kitchen, he started walking towards the Mugnone. He wanted to see Marisa again, to ask her . . . well, some important questions. Sort of.

In front of the *liceo* were the usual mothers, sitting in their cars, waiting. It had just stopped raining, and the benches in Piazza della Vittoria were wet. As it was cold, Bordelli started pacing back and forth under the trees. The sky was in motion, and the dark clouds gathering promised more rain.

He heard the bell ring inside the school, and the kids started pouring out. He looked for Marisa, without crossing the street. Everything was the same as the last time. People waving to one another, kids getting into cars. Scooters and bicycles leaving. Small groups of students formed up and down the pavement, then stood around laughing and talking. Bordelli got distracted looking at a girl dressed and coiffed exactly like her mother, who had come to get her, and he didn't spot Marisa until she was turning the corner of Via Ruffini. He calmly crossed the street and started following her. Marisa was alone and walking fast. When she disappeared round the corner of Via XX Settembre, he quickened his pace and, once round the corner, saw her hurriedly crossing the lawn along the bank of the Mugnone. On the road parallel to the grass was a fire-red Fiat 850 coupé following her at the same speed. Every so often she turned to look at the car and shook her head. Then the car accelerated and came to a stop farther up. A tall youth got out and leaned with his back against a tree, trying to look tough. When Marisa reached the boy she stopped and they started talking. When she tried to leave, the youth grabbed her arm. At that moment Bordelli arrived on the scene, out of breath.

'Hello, Marisa,' he said.

The girl turned round and, seeing the inspector, blushed up to her ears. The boy let go of her arm. He was tall and thin with short hair, but had the same attitude as those English tough guys he'd heard at Guido's house. Under his open leather jacket he was wearing only a light T-shirt. A real superman. He stared at Bordelli without saying anything, chewing gum.

'Everything all right?' asked Bordelli.

'What the hell is it to you?' the youth said.

'I had the impression the young lady didn't want to be bothered.'

'Mind your own fucking business, Grandad.'

'I can't. I have a Robin Hood complex.'

'She's my girlfriend,' he said.

Marisa said nothing, but merely stood there, holding her satchel and looking annoyed. Her dark eyes were like two stones just removed from the embers.

'Is that true?' the inspector asked her. She looked at the boy as if she wanted to set him on fire, then shook her head.

'I don't know him.'

'Marisa . . .' the youth said impatiently. He tried to come closer but she took a step back.

'Don't touch me.' She was absolutely beautiful so angry.

'Could I talk to you alone for a minute?' Bordelli asked the girl.

'You want to tell me what the hell you want?' the youth said threateningly.

'I'm Inspector Bordelli, police. I'd simply like to talk to the girl for a moment.'

'Police?' the boy said, changing expression. Bordelli nodded.

'Don't leave, I may need you too,' he said.

The youth looked at Marisa. 'Would you tell me what the hell is going on?' he asked incredulously.

'Nothing,' she said with a shrug. She seemed a little calmer.

'What do you mean, nothing?'

'It's nothing serious,' said Bordelli.

'I didn't ask you,' the youth said, agitated.

'Come on, Marco . . .' Marisa took the boy by the arm and pulled him a few yards away. They spoke in low voices for a couple of minutes, then Marco went towards his red car, got inside, and sat there as though waiting.

'Was it just a quarrel?' the inspector asked.

'I don't trust him. He's a cad,' said Marisa, casting a nervous glance in the direction of the little sports car.

'Have you been together a long time?'

'I left him this summer, and today he reappeared.'

'Sounds like the opening of an interesting film,' said Bordelli.

'Not with me.'

'You never know.'

'He flirts too much with other girls, and I don't like it.'

'Does this Marco know anything about the photographs?'

'This is the first I've seen of him since August,' she said under her breath.

'So only your brother knows about them?'

'He's the only one . . . And I know you talked to him.'

'Yes.'

'Lele wouldn't hurt a fly, I know him too well,' Marisa said softly.

'Most killers have mothers and sisters.'

'Lele is not a killer.'

'I didn't say he was,' said Bordelli. At moments he fell under the spell of the girl's face, noticing the tiniest movements of her eyebrows and lips . . . And he felt like a drooling old goat. That black pearl wasn't even eighteen years old. He had to keep repeating it to himself: she's a child, she's only a child . . .

'Inspector?'

'Eh?'

'I asked you why you came looking for me . . . I'd like to go home,' the girl said, a bit coquettishly.

'Of course . . . I wanted to ask you if . . . perhaps you'd forgotten to tell me anything important.'

'I've told you everything I know.'

'Are you sure? Think it over carefully.'

'I'm pretty sure,' she said.

'One final thing. That boy, Marco . . . Do you swear he knows nothing?'

'I swear it,' Marisa said without batting an eye.

'What's his surname?'

'Bandinelli.'

'Where does he live?'

'On the Lungarno Torrigiani . . . Why do you ask?'

'No specific reason,' the inspector said. At that moment he suspected he'd gone to talk to Marisa simply because he wanted to see her again, and was worried he might blush.

'Can I go?' she asked.

'Yes, of course, sorry to have bothered you.'

Marisa shook his hand to say goodbye and started walking home without turning round to look back at Marco. Bordelli approached the youth's sports car and bent down at the window.

'How long has it been since you last saw Marisa?' he asked.

'Not since the summer, more or less. Why? Would somebody please tell me what's going on?' the youth said.

'A fly ate a cypress,' the inspector said, and walked away. His mother used to answer him that way when he was a child, and it always made him angry. The 850 started up, and he heard the tyres screech on the asphalt. Apparently the lad didn't like that answer any more than he had. He'd decided to let him go because he was certain that Marisa had told him the truth. Marco knew nothing of the whole affair and didn't even know who Badalamenti was.

Bordelli turned round. Marisa was gone. Shivering in his trench coat, he kept on walking along the Mugnone, pleased that he felt quite hungry. The touch of Marisa's handshake was still palpable in his hand, and he thought again of Milena, dark Milena, over whom he'd lost his head the year before . . .

Bordelli was in Totò's kitchen, having managed to erase the image of Milena's face from his mind by dint of *pasta al forno* and *spezzatino di cinghiale*.[23] In his hand he held a little glass full of illegal grappa. It was cold outside, and the alcohol gave him hope. Totò had earned a minute of rest and filled two demitasses with black coffee, but only *after* having put the sugar in, as the inspector had asked him to do. It was only right to share knowledge that made life better. The cook sat down beside him. Bordelli finally lit his third cigarette of the day, holding it far from the grappa.

'So, Inspector, what are the police up to these days? Any difficult murders?'

'I'm trying to find out who killed a loan shark,' Bordelli said.

'How was he killed?'

'Stabbed in the neck with a pair of scissors.'

'Ah, yes, I read about it in *La Nazione*, but they didn't say the guy was a loan shark.'

'Proof of his "profession" was found later.'

'Well, I can see why you people have it in for us Southerners, when you've got pricks like that coming up here . . .' the cook said scornfully.

'You win some, you lose some, Totò. But if all the Southerners who came here were like you, we'd all be fat.'

'And what are you gonna do when you find the killer, Inspector? Kiss him on the forehead and slip him a few ten-thousand-lira notes?'

'I see it the same way as you, Totò, but we can't always do as we please. There's the law.'

'Oh, don't give me the law, Inspector! When I was a wee lad this big, there were a couple of those gentlemen in town and an uncle of mine ended up shooting himself. I remember it like it was yesterday . . .'

'Drink with me, Totò,' Bordelli interrupted him. The cook filled the two little glasses with grappa and made a sad face.

'To my uncle Nicola whom I loved like a father, Inspector, maybe even more. He used to take me with him night-fishing and poaching in the game reserves, and I would practically pee my pants for happiness. And then, one day . . . boom! He shot himself. Back home they show little kids the dead, you know, to teach them about life. Zio Nicola'd shot himself in the throat with his boar rifle, and they'd stitched him up as best they could . . .'

'How old was he?' Bordelli asked.

'Same as me now . . . an overgrown kid. They'd laid him out on the bed, all dressed up, with black socks on his feet and a white rose in his hands. I just looked at him and wondered why he wouldn't talk. I was just a nipper and didn't know a bloody thing, but I could tell it wasn't a happy occasion. At one point I heard a buzz of voices and in comes Don Vito, the loan shark who'd ruined him. He was a guy who owned a lot of land, and cows and pigs, but it was like he never had enough money, and so he would lend out money at really high rates of interest. He was wearing a fancy black suit with a gold clasp as big as a smith's pliers. He'd brought a couple of his lads with him, and everybody knew they were armed to the teeth. Everybody was too scared to breathe a word. Nobody'd ever heard it so quiet. You could hear the flies shitting. I can still see the brute now, in his big black overcoat, with his big fat face that shook when he walked. Little kids remember those kinds of things. Don Vito didn't have to push anyone aside to make his way through the crowd. Everybody'd already stepped aside 'cause they didn't want him to touch them, and that was fine with him. When he got to the coffin, he took off his hat, prayed for a few seconds, made the sign of the cross, and even kissed my dead uncle's face. Before leaving, he also kissed my auntie, Zio Nicola's wife. Said some nice things about the deceased, and she thanked him. That's how they do it, down in our parts, Inspector. First they kill you, then they come to pay their respects. But everyone knew Don Vito had come to make sure my uncle was good and dead and hadn't just pretended to die to screw him. Afterwards, it was down to my family to pay the rest, all of it . . . I swear, Inspector, if I ever found your killer, I'd give him free lunch and dinner for a whole year, wine included, without asking him for a single lira . . .'

'What a sad story, Totò.'

'I've got many more just like it, Inspector, each more disgusting than the next. Down south people don't joke around. The worst you've got here up north is sissy stuff compared to us.'

To Totò, anything above Rome was the 'north', and he talked about his native Apulia as some sort of mythical Far West.

'To the Milanese, my dear Totò, Florence is already the south.'

'And the rest of us are Africans, I know, but they're just envious. All the beautiful things we've got down there, they can take 'em and stick 'em straight up their arses, those polenta fiends. Eh, Inspector . . . Boy, would I love to see olive and orange groves right now. And the peppers! Up here you haven't got the kind of peppers I need, the long, green kind . . . And the sausages? You ever tasted a ginger sausage with sun-dried tomatoes?'

Having just eaten, Bordelli wasn't exactly in the mood to hear talk of sausages and peppers, but there was no stopping Totò.

'You take the peppers, punch some holes in them with a fork, then roast them over hot coals . . .'

'They're calling for you, Totò,' Bordelli said. A waiter had stuck his head inside the serving hatch but said nothing, out of respect for the inspector. Totò gestured for him to wait. In the kitchen, he was the boss.

'To cut it short, Inspector, if my relatives ever bring me any peppers, I'll put one aside for you, and hopefully they'll even bring some sausages . . . Now there's some flavour with balls!' he said, clenching his fist and walking away, grieving for the lost beauty of the south. He exchanged a word with the waiter, then sent him away with a wave of his hand. Opening the refrigerator, he took out a piece of dark, quivering meat that seemed to be still bleeding. It must have been liver. The cook cut two slices with a very sharp knife, then put the meat back into the fridge. Yuck, thought Bordelli. Liver was one of the few foods that disgusted him. Olives were another. The mere thought of them could make him vomit. Once, when he was a boy, four of his friends had decided to stick an olive in his mouth as a joke. When they tried to restrain him, he ended up unintentionally breaking three or four of their ribs and two noses. The struggle had left blood on the ground, but the five of them just kept on laughing like bollock-brains. One of the noses belonged to Binazzi, a great big lad full of energy and socialistic ideas who was a couple of years younger than him. He died in Spain fighting the Falangists in '39. It all seemed like centuries ago. Things had changed more than in the previous hundred years . . . Look where a disgusting piece of liver has led, thought Bordelli. As he watched the liver slices being covered in flour and lowered into the skillet, he still had Binazzi's face before him. Totò began to fry the meat in boiling oil; he let it brown, then turned it over, then lowered the flame and covered the pan. Tearing a clump of sage from a fresh plant in a carafe, he chopped the leaves very fine and left them on the cutting board. When he turned towards Bordelli, he saw a grimace of disgust on his face.

'Too bad you don't eat liver, Inspector, you're missing a bit of heaven,' he said with compassion.

Bordelli threw his hands up. 'I don't think I'll ever go to heaven, Totò.'

'Another grappa, Inspector?'

'Thanks, Totò, but I have to go,' Bordelli said, standing up. His head was full of old memories, and they weighed on him more heavily than Totò's wild boar.

'One of these days I'll take you for a spin in my Six hundred, Inspector. I've had the engine souped up by a friend who makes Abarths . . .[24] On the motorway to the shore I can get it up to ninety miles an hour! Damn!'

'Be careful, Totò.'

'Don't worry, I know what I'm doing.'

'Happy Christmas, if I don't see you before.'

'You too, Inspector, take care of yourself.'

When he got to the office he could still smell the grappa on his breath. Flopping down in his chair, he set a cigarette down on his desk. He swore not to light it before an hour had passed. Above the blazing radiators one could actually see the dust dancing. He picked up the phone and rang his home number.

'Ciao, Ennio, how are things going?'

'Your kitchen is a disaster, Inspector,' Botta said gravely.

'What do you mean?'

'There's nothing here . . . I had to go home and get pots and pans from my place.' It was as if someone had asked him to build a bridge out of playdough, and he had to explain why that wasn't appropriate.

'All taken care of now?' asked Bordelli, to move on to positive matters.

'Of course . . . But now I have to go, or else I'm going to burn the onions.'

Ennio hung up without another word, and the inspector was left there holding the phone. He glanced at his watch and thought he would ring Dante Pedretti to invite him to Christmas dinner. It had been a while since he'd last talked to him. He'd liked the old giant since the first time he'd met him a couple of years before. Dante lived at Mezzomonte in an old turreted house and spent his days in the basement, inventing complicated and mostly useless gadgets.

The telephone rang for a long time, but there was no reply. While he was at it, Bordelli decided to phone some relatives to wish them a happy holiday: aunts, great-aunts, first cousins and second cousins. All of them people he never saw. He saved for last his cousin Rodrigo, a chemistry teacher at the *liceo* and a pedant by nature. They had never spent much time together, and in the last two years had entirely lost track of one another – ever since, in fact, Rodrigo had found a woman who had changed him completely, a woman Bordelli had never met. Perhaps the poor thing had even managed to make Rodrigo less boring, though this was hard to believe. He'd talked to her only once, over the telephone, and had liked the sound of her voice. Maybe she would answer the phone this time, too, he thought. But no.

'Hello, Rodrigo, I thought I'd call to wish you a happy Christmas.'

'All right, then do so.'

'I thought I just did.'

'I hadn't noticed.'

'How are your students doing?' Bordelli asked, to drop the subject as quickly as possible.

'I'm sorry to let you go, but I have a lot of things to do,' said Rodrigo.

'Homework to correct?'

'If I say I have a lot to do, it probably also means I don't have time to say what it is I have to do, wouldn't you say?'

'If you'd answered *yes* or *no*, you would have saved time,' Bordelli said playfully.

'I'm going to hang up . . .' Rodrigo said gloomily.

'All right, then. See you soon.'

'I really don't see why.'

'What are you talking about?'

'About why we should see each other soon.'

'It's just an expression, Rodrigo.'

'People who use "expressions" like that have nothing to express.'

'Well, I wouldn't go that far . . .'

'I would. Sorry, but now I must go.'

Rodrigo hung up without adding anything else, not even a burp. He had never been an easy person to talk to. But deep down Bordelli found it all rather amusing, a bit like going to the theatre. Apparently the mysterious woman had not succeeded in completing the transformation. She had either already dumped him, or Rodrigo had become even more of a bollock-brain than before.

Bordelli tried ringing Dante again. He waited a long time, and in the end he heard someone pick up.

'This is Dante,' the old man said in his basso voice.

'Dr Pedretti, do you remember me?'

'Greetings, Inspector! It took me a moment to answer because I couldn't find the telephone.'

'How are you?'

'Like the leaves on the trees. And you?'

'Not bad, thanks. What are you doing for Christmas?' Bordelli asked.

'I haven't given it any thought yet.'

'Would you like to come to my place tomorrow evening? Ennio will be serving French dishes.'

'I couldn't ask for anything better.'

'Then I'll expect you tomorrow evening around half past nine.'

'*À demain, Commissaire.*'

Only two days remained until Christmas. Streets in the centre of town were full of people and money. Bordelli still hadn't found a present for Rosa and was beginning to feel a little anxious about it. He told her he'd already bought it, when in fact he was still at sea and simply couldn't think of anything acceptable. He'd thought of getting her a new blender, but it seemed to him like the sort of gift a husband would give. A pair of slippers? Perfume? The ring of the telephone interrupted his meditation. It was Piras, speaking softly and seeming excited.

'What's happening, Piras?'

'Nothing serious yet, Inspector. But I'd like you to do me a favour.'

'Why are you speaking so softly?'

'I don't want my parents to hear.'

'What do you need?'

'I need some information on a man. I want to know everything you can find about him.'

'Who is he?'

'It's a bit too complicated to explain, sir, and anyway, I can't really talk.'

'Hang up, and I'll call you back, so your parents won't have to pay,' said Bordelli.

'Thanks.'

Piras hung up and the inspector called back immediately.

'How long do you think it'll take, Inspector?' asked Piras.

'I'll get on it straight away. What's the man's name?' Bordelli asked, searching for a pen.

'Agostino Pintus. He's an engineer. Born at Custoza di Sommacampagna, Verona province, on 16 July 1912, but his parents were Sardinian. He now lives in Oristano, at Via Marconi 33 bis.'

'Don't you want to tell me even a little about him?' Bordelli asked, his curiosity aroused.

'Wait just a second,' Piras whispered. He left the phone on the little table and went to see where his parents were. His father was already out in the field, and his mother was in the courtyard behind the house, washing sheets. In winter she couldn't go down to the river, and it was a rather long operation in which she had to wash the linens with ash in a large earthenware washtub. Going back to the phone, Piras thought that one day he would buy her a washing machine. He picked up the receiver.

'Here I am . . .'

'Don't start me worrying, Piras.'

'Have no fear, sir.'

'Who's this Pintus?'

'It's a long story.'

'I have all the time in the world, Piras,' the inspector said, suppressing the desire to light a cigarette.

'He's an engineer who wanted to buy a parcel of land from Benigno. They were negotiating but hadn't yet agreed on the price . . .'

'Nothing strange about that.'

'Wait. I went to talk to the lawyer in charge of the negotiation. He'd just succeeded in arranging a first meeting between Pintus and Benigno the same Sunday as the suicide, a few hours before Benigno killed himself. And he told me something . . .' Piras then told the inspector what he'd learned from Musillo, repeating all the details of that failed encounter. 'The lawyer told me that Benigno had seemed to be in a good mood when he arrived, and that the moment he saw Pintus, his expression changed.'

'As if he'd recognised him,' said Bordelli.

'Well, if that's the case, they could not have been very good friends.'

'I'm starting to get curious myself, Piras . . .'

'I have to find out who this Pintus is as quickly as possible, Inspector. Something might turn up.'

'I'll send out some telexes straight away.'

'Thanks, Inspector, and happy Christmas, by the way.'

Piras hung up, and when he turned round he saw his mother standing in the kitchen doorway.

'Has something happened?' Maria asked, brow furrowed.

'No, no, nothing's happened,' said Piras, hopping towards the clothes stand.

'What are you doing, Nino? Has something bad happened?'

'No, Mamma, stop worrying.'

'You must never hide anything from me, Nino,' said Maria.

The matter was taking a dramatic turn. Piras put on his coat and smiled. 'I'm just trying to help a friend find a job, up in Florence. But I'm trying to keep it quiet . . . there are certain things a policeman isn't supposed to do.'

'That's all?'

'That's all, Mamma.'

'Swear it,' said Maria.

Piras looked her straight in the eye. 'I swear,' he said, thinking that any god would have forgiven him.

His mother went up to him and stroked his face. 'I only want what's best for you,' she said with a sad smile.

Piras couldn't stand that whingey tone of hers. He sighed. 'Apart from these crutches, I'm fine, Mamma. Don't make that face,' he said with irritation. Then he felt guilty and kissed her forehead.

'God bless you,' she said.

'I'm going out for a walk,' Piras said. He went out of the house and headed in the direction of Milis. Trying at first to advance on one crutch alone, he decided it wasn't time yet. The usual children were playing in the road. There weren't many of them in Bonarcado. Almost all the young people moved away to work in the cities or in Italy proper. There weren't even many people around the age of forty. Many had died in the war and in German labour camps.

Round about three o'clock, Bordelli parked in Via dei Benci, near Rosa's. He'd already had telexes sent to the police headquarters of Verona and Oristano, and only had to wait for the replies. A fine rain was falling, but to the west the sky was clearing. The medieval façade of San Miniato, at the top of the hill, looked as if it were lit up with floodlights.

The inspector hardly ever called on Rosa at that hour, but that day he had a good reason. He hadn't yet bought her a present, and he had to come up with something quickly. It was a serious problem that had to be resolved before evening. He hoped that going to see her might suggest something to him, perhaps when he saw what she had in her flat, or if she mentioned something she liked. But he had to take care not to show his hand. It was a difficult mission.

Before going up to Rosa's he stopped to have a coffee at the bar next door, which belonged to Carlino, a former partisan fighter who was still angry at the way things had turned out.

'Ciao, Carlino.'

'*Eia eia alalà*, Inspector.[25] I feel like I'm back in the old days,' said Carlino, hands on the counter. Two big hands full of 'Fascist scars', as he called them.

'I wouldn't paint it so black,' said Bordelli.

'It's blacker than a coal miner's lungs, Inspector. The other day in the newspaper I saw the picture of an MP from the MSI, and you know who it was? A little Fascist from Salò who used to shoot women and shake his bum behind Pavolini . . . And now I see him in the paper making speeches about social policy.'

'What's so surprising about that, Carlino? We've had Almirante since '46.'

'We should have killed them all on 26 April, Inspector.[26] Fuck the so-called pacification. Togliatti was a bleeding fool.[27] The bastards will be back sooner or later, and they've already tried several times. One fine day we'll find the doors to Parliament locked and a general on the telly . . .'

'Let's hope not, Carlino. But if it does happen, it will only mean we have to get busy again.'

'Coffee, Inspector?'

'Thanks.'

While preparing the coffee, Carlino kept on raving against the things he didn't like about Italy . . . Which was everything, except for the women and the wine. Bordelli found it amusing. It pleased him to see that not everyone had forgotten. Carlino might exaggerate at times, but there was always something sound behind his arguments.

'It's on me, Inspector,' Carlino said, setting the little cup down on the counter.

'Thanks.'

'But there's one thing I have to tell you: I'd be a happier man if you weren't a policeman,' said the former resistance fighter.

'You always say the same things, Carlino.'

'I must've picked up the habit watching TV.'

Bordelli gulped down his coffee and found himself mysteriously with a cigarette in his hand.

'Going up to see Rosa?' Carlino asked.

'Yes.'

'Give her this.' Carlino handed him a pink rose in a pink pot, the whole thing wrapped in pink paper. Bordelli would never have imagined that a permanently pissed-off woodsman like Carlino could think of such a thing, and he made an admiring face.

'It's not from me, Inspector. A whore friend of Rosa's left it with me,' said Carlino to clarify.

'Ah, I see . . .'

'I gave her a bottle of grappa.'

Now it all made sense.

''Bye, Carlino, have a good Christmas.'

'You too, Inspector, though the best Christmas we ever had was in '45,' the barman said, putting the empty cup into the sink.

'Did you like the cake, monkey?'

'Loved it.'

'I made it with my own two hands.'

'Congratulations.'

'Just look at this lazybones . . .' Rosa said, going towards the cat. Gideon was sleeping with his head turned upside down and his hind legs dangling off the edge of the chair. Rosa picked him up and laid him against her neck like a baby, then held him in the air and swung him around the room without the animal moving a muscle, then set him back down in the same place she'd picked him up. The cat slept through the whole thing as if nobody had touched him.

'It's almost revolting,' said Bordelli.

'I was the same way when I was a child. You could throw me out of bed and I wouldn't wake up,' Rosa said with a giggle. Then she filled two glasses with *vin santo*. Bordelli lit his sixth cigarette . . . or maybe it was already his seventh. He had to remind himself that he'd decided to quit. He would pay more attention starting tomorrow.

'Shall we have one of my cigarettes?' Rosa asked, with a naughty, childish smile.

'I'd probably better not, at this hour. I have to go back to the office.'

'But we *will* smoke it next time . . .'

'Of course.'

'It's no fun alone,' she said, shrugging.

Bordelli looked at her and tried to imagine her as a little girl. He pictured her at age ten with her lips smeared with lipstick and wearing her mother's high heels. 'What are you doing for Christmas, Rosa?'

'What are *you* doing?'

'A dinner with old friends.'

'Jerk. You could have come here with us.'

'Who's us?'

'Five women, all fabulous cooks,' said Rosa in an alluring tone.

'I would only get in the way,' said Bordelli, crushing his cigarette butt in the ashtray.

'What a lame excuse . . .' said Rosa.

'Anyway, I would feel awkward in the company of five women.'

'Why?'

'I don't know. I was the same way even as a child.'

Rosa sniggered.

'And what were you like as a child, Inspector?'

'Always sad and snotty-nosed.'

'You must have been so cute . . . I can picture you, you know. With scabs on your knees . . .'

'Shall we have another little glass?' he asked.

'I'm not used to it at this time of day. I already feel drunk.'

'You'd rather make me drink alone?'

'Poor dear . . .'

Rosa filled his glass, then sat down on the carpet in front of the coffee table and started writing the last of her gift tags. She tried to think of something funny, perhaps mischievous, for each. She would stare into space and concentrate, then giggle and start writing. Gideon woke up, jumped down from the chair and walked slowly into the kitchen to eat. The inspector kept looking around for an idea for Rosa's present, but felt more confused than ever. A corkscrew? A cup? A succulent plant?

The cat returned full of energy from his snack. He played a little with a Christmas-tree bauble and almost made it fall. Then he changed his mind, leapt up on to the sideboard and approached a ceramic fruit bowl. Rosa looked up.

'Gideon, leave the hazelnuts alone,' she said in the tone of a mother scolding her son. The cat stuck a paw into the bowl and, after a few swipes, made a hazelnut fall out, then knocked it off the sideboard and headed off in pursuit of it. He started dashing round the room, swiping at the nut and sending it off in every direction.

'That's become a bad habit of his,' Rosa said with resignation, still writing her gift tags. Every so often Gideon would stop, circle round the hazelnut with apparent indifference, then pounce anew on that strange little ball, batting it away and then running after it. Bordelli watched the scene in amusement, hypnotised by the sound of the hazelnut rolling across the floor, pursued by that sort of miniature white bear . . . He was falling asleep, glass in hand, eyelids drooping, head falling to the side. All at once he started snoring.

'Did you know I'm taking tennis lessons?' Rosa asked, slapping him lightly on the head. Bordelli gave a start. He opened his eyes and realised the glass in his hand was gone. The cat was no longer playing, having gone back to sleep in an armchair.

'Eh?' said the inspector, dazed. Rosa was sitting beside him, sticking her fingers in his ears.

'Look at all this hair, monkey.'

'Come on, that hurts.'

'Did you hear what I said?'

'I think I heard something about *tennis*. Where's my glass?'

'Here, monkey, you were about to spill it all over yourself,' said Rosa, handing it to him.

'Rosa, if I didn't have you . . .' he said.

Rosa kept touching his ears and giggling. 'Do you think I'm too old for tennis?'

'Old? You're still a child . . .'

'Liar! At any rate, Artemio says I have a natural talent.'

'Who's Artemio?'

'My teacher.'

'Ah, well, if he says so . . .'

'He's also a good-looking lad.'

'Then he must be a champion.' Bordelli imagined Rosa running across a clay court in stilettos, arms jangling with bracelets, and started laughing.

'Are you laughing at me?' she asked.

'I wouldn't dare.'

Rosa ignored him and ran into her bedroom. She returned with a racket in one hand and a tennis ball in the other, jumping all over the place. Moving the coffee table with her knees, she planted herself in front of him with her legs apart.

'I'll give you a little demonstration,' she said.

'You're going to hit a ball in here?'

'No, silly, I'm going to show you the motions. It's not easy, you know. But I learn fast. Artemio says I'm a natural.'

'Didn't you already say that?'

Rosa shrugged and reached back with the racket, got up on tiptoe and swept the air with her stroke. The upshot was an absurd motion, and she ended up clipping Bordelli's foot with the end of the racket.

'Oh, I'm so sorry!' she said, hand over her mouth, laughing like a little girl. Bordelli, however, was not laughing. He sat bolt upright, then stood up. His face had turned very serious.

'But Rosa, you're—'

'Come on, monkey, I didn't do it on purpose. Does it really hurt?'

'What?'

'What's wrong, dear?'

'But you . . . you're left-handed.'

'Of course. Why?'

Bordelli's eyes were bloodshot, and he stared at her.

'But you write with your right hand, or am I mistaken?' he said.

'Ah, what a good policeman . . .'

'So you're left-handed but you write with your right hand?'

'Of course, darling.'

'And why's that?'

'Because the nuns forced me to. The left hand is the devil's hand . . . didn't you know?'

'Oh, shit.'

'What's got into you?'

'Nothing, I was just thinking of something.'

Bordelli sat back down, looking absent, downed his glass and lit a cigarette. Rosa was still holding her racket.

'Did you see how well I *hit*?' she asked, letting out a shrill giggle. She kept waiting for her monkey to laugh with her, but Bordelli seemed completely out of reach.

'I have to go,' he said, standing up again.

'What's the hurry?'

'I'll come back tomorrow with your present,' Bordelli said, heading for the door. Rosa followed him, racket in hand.

'You could have brought it today,' she said.

'It wasn't possible.'

'Why not?'

'Well . . . you'll understand when you see it,' Bordelli lied, smiling.

'Jesus, I'm so curious,' said Rosa, squeezing the handle of the racket.

'You'll like it, just wait and see,' the inspector said, feeling more and more mired in his unsolvable case.

Outside, he got into the car and went straight to Odoardo's house. The Vespa wasn't there, and all the lights were off. He decided to wait inside the Beetle on the threshing floor, hoping the lad would come. He didn't want to go looking for him at the architect's office; that would only create an unpleasant situation.

The sleet had stopped some time before. A few frozen puddles were visible here and there. To the west, just over the snow-spotted hills, the sky had cleared a little, and below the cover of black clouds, a luminous band of sunlight poured out across the countryside. It looked as if God and his court of angels might appear at any moment.

Bordelli couldn't believe he'd been so stupid as to fail to realise that a left-handed person might be able to write with his right hand. Even though, in fact, he'd never personally known of such a case. He'd known only left-handed people who wrote with their left hands and had never stopped to wonder about it . . . But he could at least have imagined it might be otherwise. A policeman is supposed to think of certain things. Maybe he was ageing badly.

He waited until half past four, watching the fire-red sun setting behind the snow-whitened hills of San Casciano. But no Odoardo.

Driving back down by way of Via di Quintole, he remembered his promise to Rosa about her Christmas present. He had to forget about Odoardo for a while and concentrate on this other serious problem. He simply could not come up with an idea. Clothes were out of the question. Rosa had very particular tastes of her own and was hard to please. What, then? A vase? Coffee pot? Pressure cooker? . . . Who knew? Maybe he could get her something related to tennis . . . a racket, some balls or an outfit. But then he thought this wasn't such a good idea, either. He simply couldn't see Rosa running after a tennis ball. And her interest would probably soon fade, as with everything else . . . the guitar, skiing, horseback riding, painting . . .

What had he given her the year before? He couldn't remember. Maybe the antique nutcracker he'd found in his flat . . . or was that in '62? And what had he done for all the other Christmases? He recalled that it had always been difficult, but in the end he'd always come through. Whereas this time . . .

Driving past Galluzzo he felt quite discouraged, and by the time he reached Porta Romana, he thought that chasing down killers was easier than buying a present for a woman.

Heading back towards the station, he found himself in a traffic jam on the Viali. He'd never seen anything like it. At Porta al Prato he saw a police car stopped near the traffic signal with its lights flashing. When he began to draw near he saw old Sergeant Di Francescantonio, trying to restore some order to the traffic with the help of a very young officer whom he knew only by sight. When he was within a few yards of them, he rolled down his window.

'What's going on, Tonio?'

'There was an accident in Piazza Beccaria, sir,' Di Francescantonio shouted.

'Serious?'

'Apparently not, but there's a bus blocking the junction.'

'Damn . . . Listen, could I leave you my car? I can move faster on foot.'

'Try to put it over there, Inspector, and then leave me the keys.'

'Thanks, Tonio.'

With some effort and a lot of patience, Bordelli managed to pull up along the wall and park the Beetle there. Wending his way slowly through the cars, he went and handed the keys to Di Francescantonio, who was going mad in the middle of all the exhaust fumes.

'You can leave them with Mugnai,' he said, putting them in Tonio's pocket.

'Very well, Inspector . . . Come on, signora, move!' Di Francescantoio shouted at a woman driver. Bordelli thanked him again and left him to the pandemonium. He headed off to the police station on foot. It was very cold outside, but walking fast he managed to warm up a little. He went through the centre of town, taking the smallest streets with the fewest shops. The main streets were a cacophony of car horns, and on the pavements one couldn't take more than two consecutive steps without colliding with somebody. It was like trying to exit a stadium at the end of a match.

He turned down Via San Gallo and a few minutes later arrived at the station at last. Mugnai was rubbing his hands together and stamping his feet. Bordelli greeted him with a slap on the guard-booth window and went upstairs to his office. As usual, it was very hot there. The radiators paid for by his fellow citizens were blazing, and the air was dry. He took off his trench coat and jacket and rolled up his shirtsleeves. Then he went and sat down and started staring at the wall in front of him, an unlit cigarette between his lips. Following the cracks in the yellowed plaster, he tried to put his thoughts in some sort of order. He made a few observations, ventured a few hypotheses, turned it all over a few times and . . . the ideas were all useless, but they did help to calm him down a little.

He felt again like smoking, and to avoid lighting the cigarette, he tried phoning Odoardo's house. There was no reply. No hurry, he thought, we can wait till after Christmas. But deep inside he desperately wanted to know as quickly as possible if the youth was . . . well, that's enough now. He was getting tired of all these *ifs*. Besides, he had something much more urgent to attend to. Lighting the cigarette he had between his lips, he got up to go hunting for Rosa's present, but at that moment there was a knock at the door. It was Tapinassi.

'A couple of telexes for you, sir.'

'That was fast,' Bordelli said, sitting back down. Tapinassi handed him the two sheets of paper and left the office in a hurry. The telex from Verona said:

Our research has found no individual corresponding to the name of Agostino Pintus, born at Custoza di Sommacampagna (Verona province) on 16 July 1912, in any records available at the Sommacampagna Town Hall. It must be added that in 1945 the Official Registry of the Commune of Sommacampagna was destroyed in a fire along with the entire town hall building and did not return to full functioning capacity until February of 1946. Further research for possible traces of said Pintus, carried out at the Registry Archives of Verona and bordering municipalities, yielded no results. Still other research through the records of Verona police and local school archives likewise yielded nothing. End of message.

The telex from Oristano:

Agostino Pintus, born at Custoza di Sommacampagna (Verona province) on 16 July 1912, was found to be residing in Oristano at Via Marconi 33 bis as of 17 November 1945, having come from the Commune of Sommacampagna, according to a sworn statement by the subject. No document bearing his name has ever been received by the Town Hall of Oristano from said commune, owing to the destruction of the Registry Office of said commune in 1945. Also according to the subject's sworn statement, he is the son of Pietro Pintus, born at Armungia (Cagliari province) on 12 July 1882, and

*Maria Giuseppina Gajas, born at Armungia (Cagliari prov-
ince) on 6 November 1887. Said subject is unmarried. Sole
proprietor of the firm bearing his name, Pintus has practised
the profession of property developer in Oristano since 1949.
No charges pending, no prior convictions. End of message.*

The inspector rang Piras at once. Maria picked up.

'Nino has gone out for a walk, Captain.'

'Do you know by any chance when he'll be back?'

'It's already dark. He may have dropped in on a friend.'

'Please ask him to call me at once. It's rather urgent,' said
Bordelli, snuffing out his cigarette.

'I'll tell him the moment he returns, Captain,' said Maria.

'Thank you, and please give Gavino my regards . . .'

Bordelli hung up, and while waiting for Piras's call he tried
ringing Odoardo's house again, but there was still no answer.
He went into the bathroom to wash his face. It really was too
hot in that office. As he was drying his hands he heard the
telephone ring. He raced back to pick up. It was Piras.

'I've got some information on your man,' said Bordelli. 'Hang
up and I'll call back.'

He redialled Piras's number and read him the telexes, trying
to give the right intonations to their strange bureaucratic
language.

'And there you have it,' he said when he was done.

'So we know even less than before,' said Piras, disappointed.

'It's strange, however, that there are no traces anywhere
around Verona.'

'Maybe Pintus's declaration was false.'

'You run fast, Piras.'

'Don't use that word, Inspector, I've just about had it with
these crutches.'

'Pretty soon you'll be using them for firewood,' said Bordelli.

'We have to keep searching, Inspector,' Piras said impatiently.

'I'll ask Verona to do an immediate check at the Custoza
parish church and to interview a few of the town's inhabitants

to see if any of them remember this Agostino Pintus. We can also ask Cagliari to do similar checks at Armungia. Maybe we'll come up with something on Pintus's parents.'

'We can try. But what's the use?' said Piras, sceptical.

'Well, we can find out in the meantime whether Pintus told the truth.'

'Even if we find nothing on his parents, it doesn't mean anything, Inspector. They were born in the nineteenth century, and Armungia is a village of three hundred souls . . . Nobody will say anything. Sardinians don't talk.'

'You never know. I'll also have a telex sent to the Ministry of Education. If Engineer Pintus is registered with the Order, we'll have our first lead . . . But at this point, we'll have to wait till after Christmas for all this.'

'And what if Pintus changed his name?' asked Piras, following a hunch.

'One thing at a time, Piras. Let's wait for the replies to the telexes first. Then we'll see.'

'And what if we don't come up with anything?' Piras continued pessimistically.

'If we don't come up with anything, I'll ask all the police commissaries of Italy to research your man. Registries, parishes, school archives, university secretariats, the works . . . You'll see, sooner or later something will turn up.'

'If he's living under an assumed name it'll all be in vain,' said Piras, continuing down the same path.

'You have to be patient . . .'

'We're going to have to be lucky, Inspector.'

'You've already had your share of luck, Piras, don't complain,' said Bordelli, alluding to the firefight in which the Sardinian nearly ended up dead.

'I just hope the bitch doesn't abandon me right now,' said Piras.

'Keep me posted and don't do anything without telling me first.'

'I want to pay a call on Engineer Pintus. I'll ring you afterwards.'

'Not to discourage you, Piras, but there's certainly no shortage of mysteries in your neck of the woods . . .'

'You're thinking of sawn-off shotguns and knives, Inspector. But if my hunch is correct, a murder disguised as a suicide is a little too sophisticated, and even a little too low, for the proud bandits in this neck of the woods.'

'There's always someone ready to to blaze new trails,' said Bordelli, countering Piras's arguments. Over the years he'd learned that during an investigation one can form certain preconceived ideas that will compromise the search, and it's always best to be very careful. He himself needed to take heed of this, especially concerning the Badalamenti murder.

'Whatever the case, I'll get to the bottom of this, Inspector, even if it means I have to throw away my crutches like Enrico Toti.'[28]

'Fine, but don't ever forget to think before you act,' said Bordelli.

'I'll do my best,' said Piras.

The moment they hung up, the inspector sent for Tapinassi. When he arrived, Bordelli gave him pen and paper and dictated three new telex messages to him, one for the Minister of Education, another for Verona police and the third for Cagliari police.

'Write *Extremely Urgent* on all three,' he said to Tapinassi.

Then he rang Mugnai to find out whether the Beetle's keys had arrived. Di Francescantonio had called via radio to say he was on his way.

Pietrino went into the kitchen, mixed himself a shandy and went and sat down in the armchair in front of the fire. His mother had just started making dinner and was talking to him. He replied in monosyllables. A column of steam rose up from a big pot sitting directly on the coals. It was the *cavolo nero* for the soup. Gavino was busy in the shed behind the house. He always had something to repair or modify. If he had two arms he would build another house, thought Pietrino. Without getting up, he took two small logs and put them on the fire. The television's blank screen reflected the flames. His mother carried on complaining of the cold and the snails that kept eating the cabbages, but he wasn't listening. He felt somewhat agitated, and not only about the Pintus business. He had another equally serious problem on his hands. When, late that morning, he'd returned Ettore's car to its stall, he'd noticed a dent in the door on the passenger's side. It must have happened when he left it at the Tower of Mariano; some arsehole must have hit it while manoeuvring . . . Shit. He could only imagine how pissed off Ettore would be. He knew him too well. He could already hear him yelling *'I knew it! I sensed it! I should never have lent it to you! A cop on crutches shouldn't even try to drive a cart!'* SHIT! He would make him pay dearly for this, and Piras could kiss the little Fiat goodbye. There wasn't any point in arguing that it could have happened to Ettore himself. It was a stinking mess, but Piras would rather tell him before he discovered it himself. After leaving the car in the stable he'd knocked on the Cannas' door and asked Ettore's mother whether she would kindly tell her son, as soon as he got home, to come to his place at once on an urgent matter. Ettore worked down in the plain, far from town, and wouldn't be back on the bus until evening.

Piras looked at his watch: almost seven o'clock. Ettore might arrive at any moment.

'Shall I turn on the set?' Maria asked, pointing at the television.

'I can do it,' said Pietrino. Without getting up, he pushed the 'on' button with the tip of his crutch. He was getting good at it. The National channel was showing cartoons. He started watching them somewhat distractedly, head full of worries. As Popeye was beating up Brutus, there was a knock at the door. Piras got up.

'I'll get it,' he said, and he hopped to the entrance and opened the door. It was Ettore, just as he'd expected. He seemed calm. Piras assumed he hadn't seen the car yet.

'Dad said you were looking for me,' said Ettore.

'Yeah . . .'

'What's with the long face?'

'Nothing . . . there's something I have to tell you.'

'What happened?'

'The Five hundred . . .'

'Don't tell me you got a flat tyre,' said Ettore.

'No, but . . . this morning, when I got back, I noticed that—'

'Shit, d'ya see that dent in the door?' Ettore interrupted him.

'Calm down, I just wanted to say—'

'Damn that fucking pole and whoever put it there!' said Ettore bobbing his head.

'Ah . . . so it was you . . .'

'It's gonna cost me a good thirty thousand lire . . .'

'It *is* a pretty nasty dent,' said Piras, relieved. He even smiled.

'You go ahead and laugh . . .'

'Sorry.'

'So what was it you wanted to tell me?' asked Ettore.

Piras stopped laughing. 'I just wanted to tell you that the car's tyres . . . are a little low,' he said, all serious.

'And you had me come all the way here for that?'

'You shouldn't take it so lightly, you know. When the tyres are low you can end up in a crash . . .'

'Is that all?' asked Ettore.

'Yes, that's all.'

'I'm gonna go eat . . . *A si bière.*'

'*A si biere.*'

Ettore waved goodbye and walked away shaking his head.

The air was dry, and the wind chilled the hands. And the Beetle's heating system parched the throat. Around 8.30, Bordelli parked in Piazza Piattellina and got out. Sniffing the air, he had the impression the whole quarter was imbued with the smell of onions. All the shops were already closed, the neighbourhood nearly deserted. In the dim light of a lamp-post, a group of young boys were playing football in the middle of a crossroads, steam rising from their skin. The goalposts consisted of bricks 'borrowed' from some nearby worksite. When Bordelli walked through their 'playing field', they stopped and glared at him. He quickened his pace, and as soon as he hopped on to the pavement, the kids resumed running and shouting.

'What's the score?' Bordelli asked, digging in his pocket for the house keys. The goalkeeper cast him a rapid glance.

'Three–one,' he said. And at that moment a ball flew between the bricks, and a little boy with almond eyes started yelling.

'That doesn't count! It doesn't count!'

The others crowded around him.

'What do you mean it doesn't count?' they shouted.

'It doesn't count! The goalie was distracted! Bloody hell! He was talking to that man!' And he pointed to the intruder without looking at him, eyes still on his opponents. A row seemed about to break out, and Bordelli decided to intervene.

'He's right, the goalie was distracted,' he said, walking towards them. One of the bigger boys turned round. He looked to be about ten, with long, curly hair.

'And what do *you* want? We can work it out ourselves,' he said, playing tough.

A little boy with rabbit-teeth pulled the kid aside.

'He's with the police,' he said softly, but not enough. The others all turned towards Bordelli.

'Is it true you're a copper?' one of them asked.

'I'm afraid so,' said Bordelli.

'Are you one of those cops that arrests criminals?'

'I certainly am.'

The children all changed expression, dropped the ball and came towards the inspector.

'Did you catch any killers today?' asked Rabbit-teeth.

'Not today, but I have been looking for one these last few days,' said Bordelli.

The boy with the long hair stepped forward, hands in his pockets.

'The one who bumped off the newcomer?' he asked with the hoarse voice of a smoker.

'Good guess.'

'And will you catch him?' another one asked.

'Of course,' said Bordelli.

'And what if you don't?'

It sounded like a challenge. Bordelli needed to free up his mind a little, and was beginning to like this game.

'Shall we bet that I catch him by the end of the year?' he said.

'What do you wanna bet?' asked one.

'If you win, I'll bring you a new ball, a real one, made of leather . . .'

'Wow!' two or three of them cried.

'And if I win, you have to wash my car every Sunday for a year. Is it a deal?'

Bordelli held out his hand. After a moment of reflection, one boy after another shook on the bet. The biggest boys tried to impress Bordelli by shaking his oversized hand hard.

'And what if you still haven't caught him by Epiphany?' asked Rabbit-teeth, like someone with a nose for business. Bordelli thought about this for a moment.

'Well, then I'll have to bring you all some coal.'[29]

'Look, if you lose you have to pay, you know,' said the tough one.

'Cop's word of honour,' said Bordelli.

About twenty yards ahead, a third-floor window opened, and a woman stuck her head out.

'Nino! Come home this instant!' The window closed again with a thud.

'Ouf! . . . See you guys tomorrow.' Nino broke away from the group and started walking home with his hands in his pockets. The game was over. Rabbit-teeth went and picked up the ball, then came back to Bordelli clutching it to his belly.

'How many killers have you caught in all?' he asked.

'I've lost track.'

'Could we see your gun?'

'Another time, I have to go now.'

'Aww, come on!'

From a first-floor television somewhere came the theme music of the evening news.

'Pretty soon there'll be *Carosello*,' said one of the kids.[30]

'And then there'll be the clowns,' said another.

They all hastily said goodbye to the cop and ran home. The street was left deserted. The inspector went into his building and while climbing the stairs thought he was wrong not to have had children. But now it was too late and there was no point crying over it.

Entering his flat, he found Botta in a greasy apron stirring an earthenware pot. There wasn't a single free hob on the cooker. The kitchen had been turned upside down, but it smelled divine. Bordelli especially loved the aroma of cooked onion.

'Ciao, Ennio, I can see you're getting serious here.'

Botta was too engrossed to reply. Bordelli went up to him.

'Ciao, Ennio,' he repeated.

'Don't distract me, Inspector, I'm at a difficult point.'

'Then I'll leave this very instant. I just wanted to tell you that I've heard from Dante and he said he'll be coming.'

'Fine,' said Botta, without turning round.

'Think you can manage to throw something together for tonight as well?'

'I think we should probably go out, Inspector. But later; I can't right now.'

He lowered the flame under a sizzling saucepan and added some red wine. There was a brief, violent burst of smoke. Ennio sniffed it with satisfaction, then broke a stick of butter in two with a spoon and put one half in a frying pan to melt. At the same time he raised the lid of a large pot, looked inside, and took a big ball of steam square in the face. Lowering the lid, he wiped his hands on his apron. He looked like a great international chef, and perhaps he was. But one would have to wait another day before knowing for certain. French cuisine was no joking matter.

Bordelli left him to his labours and went into the living room with a glass of wine. He turned on the television, sat down in an armchair, and watched the end of the evening news on the National station. And he left it on afterwards as well, for the *Carosello* adverts programme, hoping that the 'Colgate with Gardol' spot, starring Virna Lisi, would air . . . It was worth waiting for.

Linetti hair cream, Calindri sitting in the middle of traffic, Paulista coffee . . . There were still two more to go . . . Arigliano with Antonetto, the digestive liqueur, and then . . . the Papalla family waiting for a Philco appliance. No Colgate. Too bad.

He got up and switched to Channel 2, then sat back down. The evening news was just starting. He hadn't yet decided whether or not he liked television, but he found himself watching more and more of it. He'd bought the set in '58 and it had never broken down. A day didn't go by without him watching at least one news broadcast, but he watched other things as well. He especially liked it when those two jokers Tognazzi and Vianello were on, not to mention Walter Chiari, Manfredi, Gaber, Pinelli . . . and, of course, the great Totò. After a day on the job it was a little like sitting next to a warm fire. But there was also something about that magical object that bothered him, though he couldn't quite put his finger on it. Sitting there smoking or drinking and silently watching the greenish screen fill with images . . . when he thought about it that way, it almost seemed ridiculous. But at this point he couldn't even imagine his home without the big luminous box, and every time he turned it off he felt a twinge of sadness. And that was precisely what bothered him, that subtle sense of dependency.

When the news report was over, Giorgio Gaber's programme began. During the theme tune Bordelli started think about Odoardo again. He was tempted to ring him, but decided against it. At any rate, he didn't feel like going out there that evening. He was too tired and needed to relax a little. The screen filled with Gaber's huge nose. By now the man was more famous than the Pope. The inspector was about to succumb and light a cigarette, but was saved by the ring of the telephone. It was Fabiani.

'I wanted to thank you for the other morning, Inspector.'

'Why, what did I do?'

'You listened to an old man's complaints . . . which is quite a lot in itself.'

'Sooner or later I'll have to ask you to listen to mine.'

'Whenever you like, Inspector.'

'What have you decided about tomorrow, Dr Fabiani?'

'I've decided to accept your invitation, thank you.'

'Do you like French cooking?'

'Do you know anyone who doesn't?'

'Then I'll expect you around half past nine.'

They said goodbye, and Bordelli went straight into the kitchen to let Botta know. He found him dicing garlic with a mezzaluna.

'We're a full house for tomorrow, Ennio. Fabiani just called to say he's coming.'

'Didn't you already tell me that half an hour ago?' asked Botta.

'No, that was Dante.'

'Don't distract me, Inspector.'

Botta stopped chopping and went over to the cooker to stir something delicately with a wooden spoon. He sniffed the air and said nothing. He had a very serious expression on his face, like Diotivede when he was bending over one of his corpses. The lid of one pot started dancing about, pushed up by the steam.

'Ennio, I need to ask you one more thing. For tonight, what do you say we have something delivered from Alfio's?' Alfio's *rosticceria* always closed late.

'Whatever you say,' said Botta.

'What would you like?'

'You decide. Everything in a rotisserie tastes like roast chicken anyway.'

'Then roast chicken it is. That way we can't go wrong.'

Bordelli phoned Alfio's *rosticceria* and ordered half a roast chicken with potatoes. While waiting for the delivery boy, he went and sat back down in front of Giorgio Gaber. He felt very tired, and even though he was quite amused, he couldn't stop yawning. Some sort of circus music was booming from the apartment above . . . and who knew where the snatch of the song that won Bobby Solo first prize at Sanremo was coming from . . . The kid wasn't bad, actually . . . the other one, too . . . what was his name? And those young roughnecks Raffaele and his friend were listening to . . . the singer had a pretty good voice . . . and then maybe . . . what was I thinking . . . music . . . in my day . . . when you came right down to it . . .

After Alfio's delivery boy had rung the buzzer at least five times, Botta at last went to open the door, wooden spoon in hand.

'Inspector! Didn't you hear the buzzer?'

No reply. Ennio paid for the chicken and went to look for Bordelli. He found him asleep, lying on the couch as Gaber sang on the telly. He went and turned the set off, and while he was at it, he took a look around to decide how he would arrange the room for the Christmas dinner. When he had found the solution, he turned off the light and closed the door gently. Returning to the kitchen, he continued cooking while eating his chicken and potatoes with his hands.

At midnight he turned everything off and put on his overcoat. Before leaving, he poked his head inside the living-room door, to see whether the inspector was still asleep. Hearing him snoring, he closed the door and left. Out in the street it was cold as hell. The pavements were covered with frozen sleet. He headed home with his hands in his pockets, whistling a song by Rita Pavone.

24 December

The inspector woke up very gently. He thought he could hear pigeons on the roof, but it may just have been a drainpipe upstairs. The room was completely dark, and there were no signs of life outside. He remained immobile for a few minutes, bogged down in sleepy, useless thoughts. He yawned so broadly that he nearly dislocated his jaw, then stretched and heard his bones crack . . . Only then did he realise that he was fully dressed and not in bed. And then he remembered he'd fallen asleep on the couch with an empty stomach. He'd collapsed like an idiot. Apparently he'd really needed some rest.

He stood up, groped his way to the window and opened the shutters. The street lamps were still on, raindrops streaking like flares in the cones of light. It was pretty cold, but he remained at the window, elbows on the sill. The street was wet and shiny. There was nobody about. It was a wet December morning, but it was also the 24th. The schools and many offices were closed. The only people working on Christmas Eve were shop-keepers in the centre of town and grocers, taken by storm by last-minute shoppers. There was a mad desire to spend in the air. Everyone wanted everything, even if they had to pay in instalments. Only fools get left behind: this seemed to be the message. The eyes of the young were full of desire, while the elderly tried their best to shake off the smell of the past. But everyone was anxious to shake a leg and get busy in any way possible. The cities seemed like gigantic but not very well-organised ant colonies. The mere thought of ants made Bordelli's body itch all over. He stopped thinking about it and went into the kitchen to make coffee. There were a number of

pots lined up on the table, with a large sign on top: ATTENTION:
DO NOT TOUCH. He searched for the coffee pot and put it on
a burner. While waiting for it to bubble up, he peeked into one
of the pots. What he saw and smelled seemed not bad at all.
He looked around for the wine. In a corner was a large cardboard box, but he didn't look at the labels. He would rather
be surprised, same as when he was a child. He still remembered
certain Christmas dinners with all the relatives together and a
feeling of solemnity that no longer existed, not even in church.
The presents were different in those days . . . Useful things
for the grown-ups and a few wooden or cloth toys for the
children. But the best toys were the ones he built himself out
of pieces of wood, nails, scrap metal and string . . .

The coffee pot started whistling, spewing steam through the
spout. Maybe it was time to change the gasket. Following the
gospel according to Botta, he put the sugar in an empty espresso
cup, *then* poured the coffee. No spoon, of course. He took a
sip. Indeed, it was something else altogether.

He was already in his office before eight. The first thing he
did was to summon two officers and assign them the task of
returning all the remaining promissory notes to Badalamenti's
debtors. He enjoined them to use the utmost discretion and to
turn the envelopes over only to the persons in question, and
quietly. The patrolmen left and Bordelli started drumming his
fingers on the desk. He thought of ringing Odoardo and asking
him straight out whether he was right- or left-handed, but
didn't want him to realise that it was an important detail. No,
it was better to find out some other way . . . But now it would
have to wait till after Christmas, he thought. He tried to think
of a cheap ruse that would enable him to find out, with
minimum effort, whether the lad was left-handed or not. And
what if he was? It obviously didn't necessarily mean he was
the killer. Raffaele was also left-handed. The world was full of
left-handed people . . .

He sat there, glassy eyed, for a good half-hour, engrossed
in these rather abstract thoughts, then finally bestirred himself.

Sticking a cigarette between his lips, he got into the Beetle and left police headquarters, heading for the Viali. There was a good bit of traffic for that time of day.

'Are you ready for this evening?' Bordelli asked.

Diotivede was lovingly cleaning his microscope, and the whole lab stank of disinfectant. It was time for the Christmas clean-up.

'And the onion soup?' the doctor asked without looking up.

'Not to worry. Ennio did time in a Marseille prison.'

Little brush in hand, Diotivede stopped what he was doing.

'Is onion soup a Marseillais dish?' he asked gravely.

'Never fear, Ennio knows what he's doing.'

'Just wondering,' the doctor said, going back to cleaning the tools of his trade.

'You spend all your time face to face with corpses. What do you care where onion soup originally comes from?'

'Don't start with your usual rubbish.'

'Just wondering,' said the inspector. Diotivede paid no attention. Having finished cleaning the microscope, he took off his smock.

'I'm done here. I have to go into town to buy a present for my granddaughter,' he said.

'You have a granddaughter?' Bordelli asked, surprised.

'In a way. She's the daughter of my sister's son.'

'You have a sister?'

'I've got two. Haven't I ever told you?'

The inspector was dumbfounded.

'How long have we known each other, Diotivede? It must be fifteen years . . .'

'Fourteen and a half.'

'Precisely . . .'

'So what? Do you think I know whether you have any brothers or sisters?'

'But I haven't.'

'That's a hypocritical answer,' said Diotivede.

'How old is your "granddaughter"?'

'Five, but she's already in school . . . And she learned to read a long time ago. She's quite intelligent.'

'I'm not surprised, with the blood she's got.'

Diotivede put on his overcoat.

'Cut the comedy,' he said.

'I'm not joking. I consider you a sort of genius, you know.'

'Shall we go?'asked Diotivede, buttoning the top button on his overcoat and then turning out the lights. It was raining outside, but not too hard. Diotivede opened his umbrella, and they stopped in front of the Beetle.

'Need a lift into the centre?' asked Bordelli.

'No thanks, I'll take the tram.'

'See you later.'

They said goodbye on the pavement, and the doctor headed for the tram stop. The inspector drove off, turning left at the end of the avenue and passing through the entrance gate of the hospital. He wanted to see Baragli and wish him a happy Christmas. The lanes were completely full of parked cars and motorbikes.

He climbed the stairs in leisurely fashion, getting ready to put on a serene face for the dying sergeant. He was about to enter the room smiling, but at the last minute it seemed too insincere and he dropped the pretence. As soon as Baragli saw him he raised a trembling hand in greeting. The other patients also had visitors, and a murmur of voices filled the room. The sergeant had taken a serious turn for the worse. The morphine killed the pain, but his body was drained of reserves. He was lying down, with the usual tube in his arm.

'Inspector, I've started reading that book you brought me,' Baragli said in a faint voice.

'Do you like it?'

'It takes my mind off things.'

'How are you feeling?'

'I can't breathe.'

The sky outside was a slab of darkness. There was a rumble

of thunder, and a few seconds later the rain started coming down hard. Bordelli suggested a game of cards, but Baragli wasn't up to it.

'Any news of your son?'

'He arrived two days ago. He comes to see me often.'

'Give him my regards, and best wishes to your wife as well.'

'Thanks, Inspector. Any news about that murder?' Baragli asked in a weak voice.

'Nothing important . . . Come on, let's play a round.'

'All right.'

The inspector picked up the deck and shuffled it.

'*Briscola?*'

'*Briscola,*' said Baragli.

Bordelli dealt him his cards, and the sergeant picked them up, then discarded one.

'Have you gone back to see that boy, the one who's always angry?'

'Which of the two?'

'The one who lives out in the country.'

'I've seen him another couple of times.'

'How'd it go?' Baragli asked, looking him in the eye.

'We chatted a little,' Bordelli said vaguely. He didn't want to tire the sergeant out with too much detail.

'Tell me everything, Inspector. It'll do me good, I can feel it,' said Baragli.

'There's really nothing of great importance to tell, Oreste. I did, however, discover something that put a flea in my ear.'

'What was that?' The sergeant's curiosity was growing.

'There are left-handed people who write with their right hands, thanks to the nuns,' said Bordelli.

'The left hand is the devil's hand . . .'

'Exactly.'

Baragli raised a hand and let it fall back down on to the sheet, shaking his head faintly.

'How could I not have thought of that? I even knew it . . . I'm getting soft in the head,' he said.

'Me more than you.'
'Whose turn is it, Inspector?'
'Mine, I think.'

Piras went out early that morning. He'd woken up and been unable to fall back asleep. When he set out, the sun was still below the horizon, the street lamps still on. A few lights shone inside the houses. To the east the sky was beginning to lighten. He took the dirt road that descended towards Paulilatino, to go and meet the rising sun. Passing by the cemetery, he thought again of Benigno's coffin being lowered into the hole, and for a moment he felt that nobody would ever know what really happened that Sunday.

A short distance past the cemetery there was a miserable little stream where the women still went to wash linens in the warmer seasons. They would rub their sheets against the great stones lined up at the water's edge. Soap and elbow grease. When Piras was a little boy his mother used to take him with her to the river, and as she beat the linens along with the other women, he would play in the water with the other children.

He walked by with his head full of memories, like an old man. The sound of the crutches was a music he knew well by now and was anxious never to hear again. He felt a little apprehensive and breathed deeply to calm himself. The previous evening he'd phoned Engineer Pintus, introducing himself as a close friend of Benigno and the family.

'I heard the sad news,' Pintus had muttered in a hollow voice. 'Please give the family my condolences.' Piras had told him that Benigno Staffa's heir had given him the task of resuming negotiations over the sale of the land.

'I'm sorry to call you at Christmas, but I don't live in Sardinia and will be leaving after the holidays,' he'd said. Pintus wasn't the least bit bothered by this, and even seemed pleased that he could now continue the negotiations. They'd agreed to meet at the engineer's home at half past eleven the following morning. With some effort Piras had managed to persuade Ettore to lend him the Fiat again, and he already had the keys in his pocket. Obviously Pina knew nothing about any of this.

At nine o'clock he returned home and sat down in the armchair by the fire. He'd walked for over two hours. His parents were already out, working. To make the time pass more quickly, he tried reading but was unable to concentrate. Shaking his head, he let the book fall to the floor. He turned on the television with his crutch, and a moment later a man appeared, writing something on a large blackboard. Piras watched the images but didn't follow. He closed his eyes, trying to calm down, but reopened them every other second to check the alarm clock on the mantelpiece.

In the end he gave in to impatience. He got up and went out of the house. Turning left before the church, he climbed up the narrow street to Ettore's house. There he entered the old stable. The first thing he did was look at the dent in the car's door, and he couldn't help but smile. The tyres seemed to have exactly the right amount of air in them. He got into the car and left. When he reached the high street of Bonarcado, it was only half past ten. Even if he drove slowly, he would still arrive early.

Heading south, he drove past the orange groves of Milis and then turned towards Tramatza. When he got on the Carlo Felice highway, he accelerated to 45 mph. The little Fiat's engine was whirring nicely, and he thought he'd look into buying one himself when he got back to Florence. As for the colour, he would ask Sonia, since women were better at that sort of thing.

Some twenty minutes later he was already in Oristano. He turned on to Via Sardegna, drove all the way to the end, through the intersection with Via Ricovero, and entered Via Marconi. He stopped the car near number 33 bis and got out. Pintus's house was a small, contemporary villa, and there were two cars parked on the lawn: an Alfa Romeo convertible and a black Fiat 1100. There was also an old Rumi motorcycle near the front door. Piras glanced at his watch. He was early. To kill a little time he took a walk in the neighbourhood. There was hardly anyone on the streets. He was walking better and better and thought he would soon hang the crutches up in the shed. He turned down Via San Marco and walked round the block. A cold wind was blowing, but the sky was blue.

At half past eleven he was back in front of Pintus's house. He rang the doorbell. Two German shepherd dogs appeared out of nowhere and rushed to the gate, barking and spraying spittle. Pintus came out of the house, called the dogs and chained them up. He came towards Piras with a strange smile on his face. He was short and burly, with a head that looked too big.

'They make a lot of noise but they're really two big puppies,' he said, opening the gate. He had thick, moist lips and a strong Veneto accent.

'They may be two big puppies but they're pretty scary,' said Piras.

The engineer smiled coldly and escorted him in. His eyes seemed to reflect a sort of disdain for everything, but deep down he seemed like a rather untroubled chap. It was too hot inside the house, and there was a smell of cooking in the air. They went into the living room. A modern bookcase, two brown leather sofas, a fancy television and a record player set inside a wooden chest. Outside, the dogs continued to bark.

'Please,' said Pintus, gesturing to the sofas. They sat down facing each other. Everything seemed a little dusty, but every object spoke of wealth. There were even a few paintings hanging on the wall, though they were nothing special.

'You have a Sardinian surname but a Veneto accent,' Piras said to break the ice. Pintus told him in a few words the same thing he'd said to Musillo the lawyer about his Sardinian parents having emigrated to the Veneto and then dying during the war, and his own decision to return to his native land. It was clear he didn't really feel like talking about it.

'Were your parents from Oristano?' Piras asked, like someone wanting to make small talk.

'No.'

'I was born in Bonarcado. Do you know it?'

'No.'

'You should come and see it some time. There's a beautiful medieval church in town, with the sanctuary of Santa Bonacatu right beside it . . . There are a lot of nice things to see,' Piras said with a friendly smile.

A vertical furrow had formed in the engineer's brow. He sighed and closed his eyes for a second, and when he reopened them, he had a different, less cordial look.

'I don't want to take up too much of your time, Signor Piras. My offer for that land remains the same as what I proposed to Signor Staffa,' he said in a rather brusque tone.

'Thirteen million five hundred thousand lire . . .'

'That's right.'

'I know that Benigno wanted five hundred lire more per square metre.'

'You see, Signor Piras, when I decide to make this sort of investment, I don't like to leave anything to chance. I make precise calculations to determine the maximum amount I can pay for a plot of land. Even one hundred lire more per square metre means an increased risk for me, and I can't afford that. If I want to keep building houses I have to set rules and limits for myself.'

'That makes perfect sense. And what about the payment?'

'Half upon agreement and the remainder six months later, upon the signing of the deed. Those are excellent terms. Normally, for land suitable for building, one makes a down payment of twenty per cent, with the finalisation of the contract hinging on approval of the construction project. I assure you that you don't see an offer like this very often,' said the engineer, pleased with his little speech.

'It must mean your business is doing well,' Piras said with a smile.

'Don't make me wait too long, Signor Piras,' Pintus said coldly.

'It's not my decision to make. I need to discuss things with the heir.'

Pintus flashed another of his bloodless smiles.

'A son?' he asked.

'A cousin.'

'Please tell this cousin that I can only wait one more week,' said Pintus, rocking his crossed leg with an untroubled air.

'I shall repeat your offer and let you know.'

'If I haven't heard from you by the New Year, you can consider my offer null and void,' Pintus insisted. He had nothing else to add.

Piras put his crutches under his arms and stood up. 'I'll ring you right after Christmas,' he said.

Pintus walked him to the gate without saying another word, ignoring the barking dogs. He shook Piras's hand by way of goodbye and stood there watching as he got into the Fiat 500.

A short distance outside the city, Piras got on the Carlo Felice highway in the direction of Macomer. Engineer Pintus certainly wasn't the most likeable person he'd ever met, with his cold, pragmatic way of talking, but, all things considered, he'd been cordial. Out of habit, Piras tried to imagine that Pintus was indeed Benigno's killer, then formulated some conjectures. As far as the land for sale was concerned, Pintus would have had no interest whatsoever in committing murder. Benigno's death was in no way advantageous to him. But the strange meeting between the two men in the lawyer's office led Benigno to think he was looking at someone he'd met before and would rather never have seen again. And so he'd got up and left. Pintus must have realised he'd been recognised . . . There he was, wealthy and leading a peaceful life, but he had a past he needed to keep secret, a past which, if it ever came to light, could cause him great harm. And so, for fear of being unmasked, he killed Benigno, making it look like a suicide.

Good. Well done, Nino, case closed . . . He had a good imagination, but without any evidence his hypotheses weren't worth a fig.

Driving along, he tried to draw some conclusions. He realised that, if this really was a case of murder, there wasn't much hope of catching the killer, even if Pintus himself had done it. He started listing the reasons for his pessimism . . . Benigno's house was in a secluded area along an infrequently travelled main road, about fifty yards from the road, a couple of miles from Tramatza, three miles from Màssama, and seven from Oristano. Next to the house was the old Zocchinu quarry, abandoned decades ago. The nearest house was almost two miles away, just outside of Tramatza. It was hard to imagine how there could be any witnesses, and even if there were only one such person, it was anybody's guess whether he would talk.

He saw Benigno's farmhouse from afar, low and broad, with its curved roof. It looked as if some giant had slammed his open hand down on it. When he was right in front of it, for no reason in particular, he turned on to the driveway and parked the 500 in the space in front of the house. Barraccu's Motom was propped against the wall, as it had been the previous time. Piras went behind the house. The sheep weren't there; apparently Barraccu had taken them out to pasture. The donkey was tied to his tree, and he could hear the pigs moving about in the pigsty. Taking a deep breath, he got a strong whiff of manure. It was something he missed in Florence, like the taste of certain of his mother's dishes.

He started poking around near the house, looking on the ground. He wasn't searching for anything in particular, only hoping for a little luck, something that might put him on the right track. But he found nothing. The forecourt was paved with old bricks, and the ground all around was hard and rocky. One would have needed a pickaxe to leave any tracks, and the same was true of the driveway leading to the Carlo Felice road.

He got back into the Fiat, thinking that perhaps it was true that he'd used up all his luck on the day of the shoot-out with those bandits. He couldn't expect much more. For the moment he would have to make do with his imagination. He turned on to the main road and pressed the accelerator. The road was as straight as a board, with flat land all around.

An insect kept flying around the desktop lamp, the shadow of its wings fluttering along the walls . . . until it got too close to the bulb and fell down senseless, little legs in the air. Bordelli was sitting in his office, thinking of Odoardo, which he seemed to be doing more and more. From time to time, however, his thoughts turned briefly to Botta's French dinner.

It wasn't yet midday. After the downpour, a bothersome light rain was now falling as if it would never let up. There was a knock at the door and Officer Di Lello stuck his head inside. He was a strapping lad who'd arrived a few months earlier from the Pescara province in the Abruzzi. His dark eyes gleamed in his broad face like two roast coffee beans.

'Could I bother you for a minute, Inspector?'

'Come in.'

Di Lello entered, closing the door behind him.

'We arrested a bloke last night . . . He was about to steal a Fiat Eight fifty.'

'Is that all?'

Di Lello seemed embarrassed.

'No, it's just that . . . well, the bloke says . . . he wants to talk to you . . . says he knows you . . . Give him a little more time and he'll say you're great friends,' Di Lello muttered with a compassionate smile.

'What's his name?' Bordelli asked.

'He hasn't said, and he didn't have any papers on him.'

'Where is he now?'

'Just outside the door. He's been kicking up a row . . . threatening not to eat and to—'

'Bring him in,' the inspector cut him off. Di Lello opened the door and stuck his head out.

'You can come in,' he said.

When Bordelli saw the man enter in handcuffs, he slapped himself on the forehead.

'Damin! What sort of mischief have you been up to this time? And at Christmas, no less . . .'

Damin shrugged his shoulders and said nothing. Di Lello was still in the doorway, slack jawed, and the inspector gestured at him.

'Di Lello, please take his handcuffs off.'

The young cop immediately freed Damìn, then looked at Bordelli again, awaiting orders.

'You can go, Di Lello, thanks. I'll take care of this.'

The patrolman gave a last perplexed look at Damìn and then left. Bordelli leaned back in his chair.

'Sit down, Damìn. How is it you're always getting arrested?'

'I almost pulled it off, Inspector, I already had the cables in my hands . . .'

'That's not what I meant.'

'With an Eight fifty I can get by for a whole month,' Damìn continued gloomily. He flopped into a chair, making it creak. Damìn was from Massa, broad as a wardrobe, and had old scars on his face. He claimed to have spent five years in the French Foreign Legion, and to look at him it wasn't hard to believe. Bordelli started drumming his fingers on the desk, trying not to think of the cigarette he felt like smoking.

'You're a great big guy, Damìn . . . how old are you?'

'Thirty-three, Inspector, same as Jesus Christ when they eliminated him.'

'They didn't "eliminate" him, they crucified him.'

'What's the difference? He stepped on a few bastards' toes and they did away with him. That's the gist of it, ain't it?'

'I guess so.'

'And if he ever comes back, they won't wait thirty-three years this time around. They'll get rid of him a lot sooner.'

'Don't change the subject, Damìn.'

'I'm not changing the subject, Inspector, I'm saying that the poor have got no future . . . and Jesus was a poor bloke just like me.'

'But he didn't go around stealing cars.'

'That's another matter, Inspector.'

'Why on earth can't you manage to find a regular job, Damìn?'

Damìn squirmed in his chair. He was as unlucky as he was

good hearted, being the kind of person who might spend a whole day treating an injured sparrow.

'And what would I do, Inspector? I've got all kinds of ideas, but nobody's ever gonna hire a bloke like me . . .'

'Well, if you spend your life in jail you can be sure you'll never get anywhere,' the inspector said.

Damìn shook his head. 'Just my bleedin' luck . . . in the slammer for Christmas,' he said.

'What do you know how to do, Damìn? I mean, what kind of work?'

'I can work as gardener . . . watching the plants grow . . . I like that sort of thing.'

'You like it, or you know how to do it?'

'My father was a gardener and a forester. He worked like a dog and earned less than a bleedin' slave.'

'If I managed to find you a job as a gardener, would you take it?' Bordelli asked.

'Who's gonna hire me?' Damìn said with a shrug.

'Let me give it a try. After the holidays, I want you to go to Palazzo Vecchio, to the employment office, and ask for this person . . . I'll have already phoned him and explained the situation.' Bordelli wrote a name down on a piece of paper.

'How am I gonna do that if I'm inside?' asked Damìn, brow furrowed.

'I'll have the charges dropped,' said Bordelli, passing him the piece of paper. Damìn read the name: Dario Fumagalli.

'So I'm free to go?' he asked. He wasn't sure he'd heard right.

'Only if you behave.'

'Blimey!'

'Did you damage that Eight fifty?'

'No, Inspector.'

'Look at me, Damìn. This is the last time I'm going to help you.'

'After Epiphany I'll go and talk to that guy, I swear to God,' said Damìn, putting his fist over his heart.

'I'm counting on it. Come on, let's go. I'll walk you out of the fortress. They'll never let you leave alone.'

The inspector saw Damìn out of the station, shook his hand, and watched him stomp away in the rain. The luckless lug walked as if trampling on the world in revenge for something.

Bordelli returned to his office and put an unlit cigarette between his lips. Then he picked up the phone to call Dario Fumagalli, the city hall clerk. He had to do it straight away, and he hoped to find him at home. Dario was the son of an old friend of his who'd died a few years earlier. Bordelli had known Dario since he was a baby. He was a smart kid who would understand the situation immediately.

Dario picked up the phone. Bordelli could hear his young son screaming in the background, though it was hard to tell whether he was crying or shouting for joy. He wished him and his family a happy holiday and then explained what he had in mind. He didn't hide anything and said he would vouch for Damìn. Fumagalli said he would see to the matter personally and keep him informed.

'Thanks, Dario.'

'A happy Christmas again, Inspector.'

They hung up. Bordelli set the still-unlit cigarette down next to the telephone and, as every Christmas, decided that the least he could do was to tidy up his desk a little. He studied the situation. Papers stacked high, disorderly piles of scraps, little earthenware plates overflowing with clips, empty envelopes, pen-holders, three ashtrays, and tons of other objects put there who knew when and who knew why. He stared at the disorder for a few seconds. He didn't know where to start. And then he thought that, in the end, that desk, in that state, was a familiar sight and, as every Christmas, he decided to skip it.

It was past one o'clock. Looking out the window, Bordelli noticed that it had almost stopped raining. He went out on foot and, walking under the long, overhanging eaves of Florence, went into Cesare's trattoria. After exchanging greetings with the waiters, he slipped into Totò's kitchen.

'Hello, Inspector! How hungry are you today?' the cook asked. Bordelli dried his hair with a handkerchief and collapsed on to his stool.

'I'd rather eat lightly today, Totò. I've got a French dinner waiting for me this evening.'

Totò looked shorter and darker than usual.

'Well, if you prefer, I can just give you a glass of water,' he said, sneering.

'Don't go overboard. Haven't you got some side dish of vegetables?'

'I've got aubergines Parmesan. What do you say?'

'And for starters?'

'You decide, Inspector. Tagliolini in a truffle crème sauce, *penne all'amatriciana*, pappardelle with wild boar, tortelloni in a sauce of—'

'Never mind, Totò. Just bring me a slice of bread and some olive oil.'

The cook threw up his hands and brought the inspector a serving dish with three slices of bread on it.

'The oil's behind you,' he said.

'Perfect.'

Totò looked at him with pity.

'Would you like some garlic? I've also got some sun-dried tomatoes and a *peperonata* I made today, or I could give you—'

'This is fine, Totò, I'm a happy man.'

'As you wish, Inspector.'

Bordelli prepared his starvation diet. He poured a little oil on to the bread, then added a drop of vinegar and a pinch of salt. Totò, meanwhile, had got back to work. He was wrestling with a rabbit, in a sort of hand-to-hand combat. Then a pan started to smoke, and the cook poured a tinful of tomatoes into it and started crushing them with a fork.

'Tell me a little about this French stuff, Inspector . . . What've they got up there that's so special compared to here?'

'Don't take it personally, Totò, but I think French cooking is the best in the world.'

Totò smiled compassionately.

'Sure, sure, I can believe it. But how do they do pork, these French? Eh? And sausages? And aubergines? And *fegatelli*? I'd really like to see how they do *fegatelli*.'[31]

'I seemed to have touched a sore spot, Totò.'

'Why do you say that?'

'Because I think that the best fate a liver can have is to end up in the hands of a French chef.'

'Oh yeah? And what about pizza? Have they even got pizza, those potato-eaters?'

Bordelli realised he was treading on thin ice and tried to beat a retreat.

'I'll buy you a good book for Christmas, Totò. It's called *France at Table*; I saw it in a shop window.'

'You're wasting your time, Inspector, I don't know how to read,' Totò lied, since he read *La Nazione* daily.

'You could just look at the pictures.'

'I guess I'll have Nina read it to me.'

'Who's Nina?'

'Haven't I told you, Inspector? I've got a girlfriend now.'

'Since when?'

'Ah, that's asking too much . . .' the cook said, flashing a manly smile.

Bordelli asked for some wine to celebrate, and ended up eating a couple of sausages with peppers. They talked about Nina and love in general, took coffee together, drank some grappa, and smoked a cigarette. When the inspector finally came out after three, after struggling to refuse to go for a spin in Totò's souped-up Fiat 600, he felt like sleeping. Luckily it had stopped raining, and so a long walk was in order. To avoid the Christmas crowds, he went towards the Mugnone, crossed the river, and turned right. Odoardo's face came and went in his mind . . . Was the lad left-handed or not? But there was another problem nagging him: Rosa's present.

Pyjamas? A teapot? Or maybe that little blue horse in Murano glass?

Walking under the bare plane trees, he thought of Marisa. Beautiful Marisa. That was where he'd last seen her, with that Marco chap who was bothering her. But who knew whether the young rascal had really been bothering her. Perhaps Marisa was only being a little coquettish that day, as befitted a spoilt girl well aware that she was as beautiful as the sun . . . That's quite enough, Inspector. You're like one of those old codgers who always repeat the same things.

Before the Ponte Rosso, he crossed the street and went into the Garden of the Locomotive. He hadn't been there for a long time. It was a lovely place, and at that hour it was empty. The old steam engine parked on the lawn was as impressive as ever. Big and black with red wheels. Bordelli collapsed on to a bench in front of the large art nouveau greenhouse. He lit a cigarette and tried not to think about Marisa . . . as a way of not thinking about Milena . . .

The sky was one dark cloud, and it was almost night outside. The Christmas atmosphere filtered into his office, even through the closed windows. The flickers of a few flashing lights passed lightly through the panes, and at moments he could hear the sad laments of the *zampogne* in the distance. Bordelli ran a hand over his face. He couldn't wait until Epiphany put an end to it all.

He rang Taddei and asked him to fetch a coffee, and while he was waiting, he imagined for the thousandth time Odoardo stabbing the loan shark in the neck with the scissors . . . Odoardo with his face as hard as stone and his hate-filled eyes that looked as if they were about to explode . . . and with the scissors in his left hand.

'Shit . . .' he said suddenly, slapping his forehead. Rosa's present! He'd forgotten all about it, distracted by his pointless daydreams. He glanced at his watch. Only three hours left before the shops closed. Dashing out of his office, he ran into Taddei in the corridor, coffee in hand.

'Drink it yourself, I haven't got time,' he said, walking past him. Taddei mumbled something and just stood there, watching him hurry away.

Bordelli got into the Beetle, waving at Mugnai as he drove out of the courtyard. The poor cop looked gloomy . . . not surprising for someone who was about to spend Christmas Eve in his guard booth with *La Settimana Enigmistica*,[32] trying to finish at least one of those bloody crossword puzzles.

To avoid getting struck in traffic, Bordelli steered clear of the centre of town and passed by way of the Viali, where things were moving fairly well. It had been only a few years since traffic signals had replaced the cops on pedestals who used to wave their arms all day, rain or shine, and go crazy during the Christmas season. At Epiphany they would receive gifts from the shop-owners, like town doctors in times gone by. It was all different now. The cars and motorcycles had all grown enormously in size, and in their place there were now automatic traffic cops.

Bordelli wanted to leave the car outside his home and walk to the centre of town. At this point he was practically resigned to buying that stupid little blue Murano horse . . . and hoping it hadn't already been bought by someone else. Maybe Rosa would even like it. He wondered whether the saleswoman in boots still resented him. Maybe she wouldn't even recognise him.

He drove past the suspension bridge of San Leopoldo and saw there was quite a bit of traffic bottled up at Porta San Frediano, so he went straight on in order to pass by way of Piazza Tasso, but Viale Raffaello and Viale Aleardi were also fairly blocked. Little by little he managed to get close to home, but he couldn't find a parking spot. It was the first time this had ever happened to him. Crowds of people burdened with colourful packages walked up and down the pavements. Some looked rather tired, as if they'd just finished breaking up the ground with a hoe. It was as though the entire province had descended on the centre of Florence at the very last minute and decided to park in San Frediano. It didn't seem like the same neighbourhood. He kept driving slowly down the narrow streets, searching for a hole in which to stick his car. The little coloured lights were giving him a headache. After fifteen minutes of reconnoitering, he finally found a spot in Piazza del Carmine, not far from Badalamenti's place. It was already half past five. He locked the Beetle and instinctively looked up at the usurer's windows. The shutters were open, and the windows looked dark. Until a month ago, whenever he walked by he would look up, see the windows illuminated, and think: 'Sooner or later I'm gonna get you, you bastard.'

He walked briskly towards the little blue Murano horse, dodging all the bodies coming at him from all sides. But then he turned round and stopped dead in his tracks . . . And he smiled . . . At long last he knew what to give Rosa for Christmas . . . To hell with the little horse . . .

The red Porsche looked like a sculpture that had fallen out of the sky into the piazza. It was freezing outside, but the north wind had carried the rain away. Bordelli walked up to the Porsche and reached for the keys, which he still had in his pocket. He felt slightly embarrassed to be seen in a rocket like that . . . And it was the *newcomer*'s car to boot. In the end he got in and closed the door. He started studying the steering wheel, the instrument panel, the gearstick, the seats. Classy stuff, he thought. At last he started it up. The mere sound of the engine spoke volumes. He turned on the headlamps, and the dashboard lit up with a restful green light. He had a little trouble finding reverse, but in the end he manoeuvred out of the car park and drove off. He immediately liked the feel of all that power under his bottom. Working his way to the Viali, he turned towards Porta Romana. He got there after getting stuck in a couple of jams, and then took the avenue up to the hills. The moment he found a little breathing space, he stepped on the accelerator. It was like grabbing hold of a passing train. He passed the piazzale and started descending towards the Arno. A few moments later he parked in Via de' Benci, blocking a vehicle entrance, and went the rest of the way to Rosa's place on foot. Via dei Neri was also rather crowded. The electricity of Christmas Eve was palpable in the air.

He rang Rosa's buzzer, and when the door clicked open, he buzzed another couple of times. It was a sort of signal to tell Rosa that he wouldn't be coming up. He went into the building's entrance hall and looked up into the stairwell. A few moments later Rosa's head appeared over the top-floor banister.

'Aren't you coming up, monkey?'

As usual, she thought she was whispering but in fact was yelling, and the echo did the rest. Bordelli gestured for her to come down.

'I'll wait for you,' he said softly.

'Why?'

'Stop yelling, I can hear you perfectly well.'

Rosa changed her expression, thinking perhaps that this somehow affected the volume of her voice.

'Why do you want me to come down?' she shouted.

'Sshhh! I'm taking you out.'

Rosa got excited and emitted a little scream.

'Yippeee! I'll be right down!'

'Don't take too long.'

Rosa had already vanished. Bordelli knew he had a long wait ahead, and, pacing back and forth in the entrance, he lit a cigarette. He felt he deserved it, having smoked very little so far that day.

Twenty minutes later, he heard a door close and recognised Rosa's steps on the stairs. No other woman made the same kind of noise. She arrived, all smiles in her stilettos and wrapped in a violet, hooded cape. She took Bordelli's face into her red-gloved hands and kissed it repeatedly.

'Where's my present?' she asked.

'It's outside.'

Rosa giggled with curiosity, then stopped in front of the door, waiting for Bordelli to open it for her. She then linked her arm with his and let him lead the way, striding confidently on cigarette-thin heels that even a Parisian stripper would have had trouble walking in. They turned the corner of Via De' Benci, and when Rosa saw the Porsche, her jaw dropped.

'Ooh, it's so adorable! Don't tell me . . .'

'No, it's not mine. I'm only taking you for a ride in it. Do you like your Christmas present?'

'Oh, you're such a dear . . . And what's a car like this called?'

'It's a Porsche.'

'Ah, it's French . . .'

'German.'

'How odd,' she said, unconvinced. They got in and drove off. Rosa pretended not to see the people looking on. She felt watched, and she loved it.

'Where are you taking me, monkey? Look at all those pretty lights . . .'

'You decide. We have over an hour.'

'Let's see . . . First, I'd like to do the entire circuit of the Viali . . . then we'll go up to Fiesole, then come back down and make a quick tour of the centre and . . . we'll stop at the Giubbe Rosse. I feel like a good cappuccino.'

'The Giubbe Rosse?' said Bordelli, alarmed, imagining the sea of people who would surely be there.

'It's my Christmas present, isn't it? So I decide. You just hush up and drive.'

'Well, I can see you know what you want . . . And where's my present?' the inspector asked, turning down Via Scipione Ammirato.

'I'll give it to you when it's time,' she said. Bordelli downshifted and passed a couple of cars in second gear. It felt as if they were being drawn by dozens of crazed horses. When he slowed down, Rosa let out a little cry.

'Oooh, what fun! I had butterflies in my stomach, just like on a swing!'

'I can do it again, if you like.'

He circled round Piazza Alberti and, when turning on to

the Affrico viaduct, executed a nice downshift to second that made the tyres screech.

'It's a monster,' said Rosa, pressed back into her seat.

'It's a work of art.'

'Why don't you ditch your old heap and buy yourself one of these?' Rosa asked.

'Better yet, I could get two, in two different colours, to match my socks.'

'Marvelous! I would get one pink, and one baby blue.'

'Perfect. I'll order them tomorrow.'

By 7.30 the Porsche was already resting in the courtyard of police headquarters, waiting to be taken to the courthouse depot. Rosa had liked her tour of Florence in the red monster very much. She said it was the sweetest gift any man had ever given her, and after a lipstick-smeared kiss, she had run off to her ladies-only dinner.

'But not all whores,' she was keen to point out again.

Bordelli left the keys to the Porsche on his office desk and went back out on foot to fetch his car in Piazza del Carmine.

When he got into the Beetle it felt as if he were driving a tractor. He turned on to Via Cavour. The same useless question kept popping up in his head: was Odoardo left-handed or not? There was no point in wondering. He simply had to find out. And soon.

He parked in front of his block of flats. The usual boys were playing in the crossroads. They turned to face Bordelli and started staring at him.

'If you're a policeman, why don't you wear a uniform?' asked Nino.

Rabbit-teeth slapped him on the shoulder. 'I *know* he's a copper,' he said with the air of an expert.

'Not all policemen wear uniforms,' said Bordelli.

'And what about your gun?' asked Pippo.

'It's doing fine, thanks.'

'Could we see it?'

'I left it at the office.'

Rabbit-teeth started sniggering.

'He's pulling our leg! He's pulling our leg!'

Bordelli tried to change the subject.

'Aren't you going to go home and wait for Father Christmas?'

'Not now! He's not coming till midnight!' they all said.

They heard a window open over their heads, and Bordelli made a gesture of resignation.

'I think it's time you all went home, boys. Your mamma's calling you.'

But the voice that spoke sounded quite masculine.

'Is that you, Inspector?'

Bordelli looked up and saw Botta's face. He looked worried.

'What is it, Ennio?'

'Come up here at once, Inspector, I've got a problem.'

'I'll be right there.'

'Hurry, Inspector, it's urgent!' Ennio shut the window with a thud, and the little boys all broke out laughing.

'Hurry up, now, Mamma's calling!' they started saying in turn.

Bordelli threw his hands up in defeat, waved goodbye, and went into his block. A second later he heard the boys kicking the ball around again. He climbed the stairs calmly, thinking what it might be like to have a son, see him grow, talk to him ... But he didn't have time to imagine anything, because Ennio was waiting for him on the landing with a big carving fork in his hand. The sweet smell of cooked onions wafted down the staircase.

'What's going on, Botta?'

Ennio's wide eyes burned a hole in him.

'There's no nutmeg!' he said.

'That's not possible. I bought some last year.'

'Maybe you're confusing it with coconut,' Botta said nervously.

'I know I bought some, I'm sure of it,' Bordelli insisted. They walked shoulder to shoulder all the way to the kitchen. On the table were several platters ready to be eaten, covered with yellow paper. Ennio's fists were clenched.

'How could I have forgotten to bring nutmeg? Bloody hell!'

'I've got some, I tell you. We only have to find it.'

'I've gone through everything, Inspector, looked everywhere. There's everything, there's even Idrolitina[33] . . . there's just no nutmeg.'

'Is it serious?'

'Very serious, Inspector. It would be like making *spaghetti alla carrettiera* without parsley.'

'Will we go to hell . . .?'

'You can joke because you don't know anything about cooking, but I can assure you, it's not the least bit amusing.'

Bordelli felt more implicated in this drama than he would have liked. He opened every drawer and cupboard in search of the precious nuggets, but almost immediately closed them without even looking. Something told him he would never find them. He clearly remembered the little glass jar with a red cap, with three nuggets inside, along with a little grater. He'd bought it a year ago, he was absolutely sure of it. He even had the impression he saw it rather often.

'You're going to have to go out at once and buy me some,' Botta said impatiently.

'At this hour on Christmas Eve?'

'It's not even eight o'clock yet. If you hurry, you'll find something open.'

'Wait, I think I know where it is,' Bordelli said, brightening. He went out of the kitchen in long strides and came back immediately with a smile on his face.

'O ye of little faith,' he said.

Ennio snatched the tiny jar from his hands, looked inside to make sure it had what he needed, and kissed it. Then he went over to a large pot gently simmering, raised the lid, sniffed . . . and grated a hint of nutmeg into it. And that was it. All that pandemonium for three grains of nutmeg, thought Bordelli.

But he didn't dare say anything. He'd realised that cooks are even touchier than corpse-cutters.

'Where was it, Inspector?' Ennio asked.

'Where was what?'

'The nutmeg . . .'

'Over there,' Bordelli said vaguely. He was a little embarrassed by the disorder in his flat.

'Where over there?'

'Over there . . . in the bathroom.'

Ennio turned to look at him.

'And what were you keeping it there for?'

'I don't know. I must have mistaken it for something else.'

'When it comes to cooking, Inspector, you're hopeless,' said Ennio, shaking his head. He lifted a lid and a ball of steam came out and rose to the ceiling.

'Have you opened the wine yet?' Bordelli asked, to change the subject.

'I opened all the bottles this morning.'

'This morning? What kind of bloody wines did you get?'

Botta kept shuffling from one pot to another.

'Let's just say that the youngest is from '58,' he said proudly.

'French?'

'From first to last.' Botta lifted a dishtowel. Under it were the still-empty vol-au-vents.

'Now please go into the living room, Inspector. Someone like you can ruin things just by looking at them.'

'Let's not exaggerate . . .'

'I'm not exaggerating. I actually believe it.'

'I'll go and watch the evening news,' said Bordelli. He was still in time to see the national report. When he went into the living room, he found it transformed. Everything served as background for the round table that Ennio had put in the middle of the room. A snow-white tablecloth, dishes and glasses he'd never seen before, embroidered napkins. Bordelli wondered where all that stuff had come from. Atop the radio cabinet were all the wines, resting on a clean dishcloth. The bottles were individually wrapped in newspaper so as not to reveal the surprise.

Bordelli turned on his Majestic television set, plopped into the armchair and patiently waited for the screen to come to life. He felt he had just the right amount of appetite for a dinner like this and could hardly wait to sit down at table.

The news report showed how people spent their Christmas in other countries, then broadcast the Pope's speech, a few items of political news, some sport, and other curiosities . . . Then came *Carosello*, the advert sequence. Maybe Virna would be on today, he thought. During the *Dindondero* jingle, Botta rushed in with the tray of vol-au-vents all ready.

'Do you like the way I've arranged the table, Inspector?'

'Magnificent . . . Where'd you get all these things, Botta?'

'All this stuff is yours, Inspector.'

'Mine? Where'd you find it?'

'I dunno, here and there,' Botta said a little impatiently. He didn't have time for small talk. He disappeared again into the kitchen, and the inspector went back to watching *Carosello*. Calimero turning white, *Carmencita amore mio*, Mulè with his nightmare belly-ache . . . but no Virna . . . In her place was Odoardo with a pair of scissors in his hand . . . raising them high and lowering them forcefully into Badalamenti's neck . . . Shit, what a bore . . . There was no point in rehearsing that little bit of theatre. One step at a time, all in due course. For the moment it was best to get that murder out of his head and enjoy the Christmas dinner in peace . . . He could think about Odoardo tomorrow. The blonde in the Peroni spot wasn't bad, but not worth a fingernail of Virna Lisi. He waited for '*du du du du du du Dufour*' to end, then went into the bathroom to wash his face.

At 9.20, the doorbell rang. It was Fabiani. He crossed the threshold timidly, sniffing the air.

'Good evening, Inspector, this is for you,' he said, handing him a small wrapped parcel with a ribbon on top.

'You shouldn't have.'

'Oh, it's nothing.'

Fabiani took off his coat and, with hands trembling, hung it on the coat rack. Bordelli opened his present immediately. It was Primo Levi's new book, *The Truce*.

'You read my mind,' said Bordelli. After the war he'd bought Levi's first and found it very moving. He thanked Fabiani and led him into the living-dining room. The television had lost reception and was crackling. Bordelli turned it off. Fabiani noticed the beautifully laid table and made a gesture of appreciation. Ennio came in with a dish full of grated Gruyère and set it down on the table. Fabiani held out his hand to him.

'Not a good idea,' said Ennio. 'My hands smell like onion.' And he wiped his hands on his apron. Bordelli glanced at his watch, and at that moment the doorbell rang again. It was 9.26, so it couldn't be Diotivede. He said he would come at 9.30, as agreed.

'I'm going back into the kitchen,' said Ennio, running out of the room.

Bordelli went to open the door. It was Dante with an unlit cigar in his mouth. He looked taller and fatter than usual. From his coat pocket he extracted a small package about the size of a bar of kitchen soap and rather sloppily wrapped.

'This is a little present for you, but if you don't mind, I'll open it myself after dinner,' he said, putting it back in his pocket.

'As you wish.'

They went into the living-dining room. Dante and Fabiani greeted each other, and the inventor immediately began to explain to his fellow guest how to stop the electrical meter at his home from advancing. He'd recently invented a simple, sure method for this and was spreading the good news. He said that electricity had long been an indispensable necessity of life and therefore cost too much. Self-defence was a right.

At 9.30 sharp the doorbell rang, and Bordelli went to open the door for Diotivede. He waited for him in the doorway, listening to his regular footsteps in the stairwell. When the doctor arrived he wasn't the least bit winded. He was very smartly dressed in light grey. Seventy-two years old, thought Bordelli.

'Hello, Inspector,' said Diotivede, with the usual frowning face. He sniffed the oniony air and gave a sort of half-smile. He too had a little present for Bordelli, handing it over to him with the air of someone getting rid of something. Bordelli unwrapped it. It was a fossilised seashell.

'I didn't buy it; I had it in the house,' the doctor said.

'Such delicacy,' said Bordelli.

'I hope you won't use it to put out your foul cigarette butts,' Diotivede said in all seriousness, hanging up his coat.

'Let's eat,' said Bordelli.

Dante's booming voice could be heard all the way from the entrance. They went into the living-dining room, and Bordelli set the seashell down on the television. After shaking hands, everyone sat down at the table. Botta had worked out the lighting arrangement and was now checking the results. The white tablecloth was bathed in restful light, while a lamp in a corner served to give depth to the room. Everything else was in penumbra . . . Yes, that would do.

As Diotivede studied the table settings, his eyes gleamed with curiosity behind his round lenses. Fabiani gazed pensively at some invisible horizon. Ennio reached out for the first bottle, removed the sheet of newspaper in which it was wrapped, and showed everyone the label: Saint-Emilion, 1958. Then he served everyone.

'Let us thank God for this French dinner,' said Dante, proposing a toast. They clinked glasses and took a sip. Bordelli then asked Botta the names of all the dishes they would eat that evening. Ennio couldn't have asked for more. He stood up and presented the menu in the original language.

'*Pahté de fwah grah, volovahn de freedemair, soupallonyònh, dendo mahronh*. And for wine, we have three different vintages of *San Temillion*. I'll tell you the pudding later . . . *Ehwahlàh!*'[34]

'Aside from your French, this all seems very serious,' said Bordelli, stealthily loosening his belt a notch. Botta served the starters, and they all began eating in total silence, except for Dante, who was able to talk even when swallowing. Drinking the Saint-Emilion, Fabiani raised his eyebrows in pleasure. Very soon all trace of the pâté was gone from their plates, and when the last vol-au-vent disappeared from the tray, Dante proposed a round of applause for the cook. To avoid the embarrassment, Botta started removing the dirty plates and slipped into the kitchen to prepare the famous onion soup.

The mood became increasingly more relaxed as the meal continued with a great deal of wine and no more neckties. Bordelli loosened his belt another notch. Diotivede was very pleased with the soup and did not turn down a second ladleful, or even a third.

'Like it?' asked Ennio, fishing for compliments.

'Magnificent,' said the doctor, rubbing his steamed-up spectacles with his napkin.

Bordelli looked at him in amazement. 'Diotivede, what is happening to you? This is the first time I've ever heard you say the word "magnificent" – except, of course, when talking about corpses.'

'It may not look like it, but I *am* laughing, I assure you,' the doctor said with a serious face.

More dishes arrived, each more delicious than the last. When the third bottle was unveiled, Bordelli proposed a toast to all the years Botta had spent in the 'hotel management schools' of half the world. Dante stood up and went and kissed the cook on the head. Ennio downplayed his glory, saying that, all things considered, it was all pretty easy, though one could tell he was fibbing.

By the end of the meal, they were all a bit light headed from the wine. The voices had increased in volume. The tablecloth was covered with stains and crumbs. There had been a great variety of toasts – to life, to psychoanalysis, to all the world's prisons, to women . . .

Ennio changed everyone's drinking glass and brought two bottles of Sauternes to the table. Then he quickly left the room and returned with a great dome of savoy biscuits steeped in a white cream streaked with chocolate.

'*Sharlò o shocolah*,'[35] he said, and then filled the dessert plates. Everyone set to, mooing with pleasure. The cream melted in the mouth and left behind flavours that were probably even beneficial to the mind.

'Ennio, you're a disgrace,' said Bordelli. The Sauternes needed no comment, but unfortunately was finished almost at once. The empty bottles – the corpses, as Ennio called them – were taken away, and in their place came the Calvados. Ennio was the drunkest of all of them, but held it pretty well.

'In Paris they call it just "*calvà*", and I bought two bottles of it,' he said.

They toasted in silence, then Dante called them to attention. He took the present for Bordelli out of his pocket, unwrapped it, and set it down in the middle of the table.

'Guess what it is,' he said. He turned it around several times so everyone could get a good look at it. Then he lit his cigar and leaned back in his chair, making it creak. The other four looked hard at the strange object. It was about half the size of a cake of Sole soap, made of wood, with two cavities shaped like half-eggs on top and, on one side, two holes through which one could see some little mirrors.

'No idea . . .' said Ennio.

'An egg-holder?' Bordelli guessed. Dante shook his head.

'Binoculars,' said Fabiani, and the inventor shook his head again. Diotivede said nothing, but one could see that he was thinking.

'Something for seeing underwater,' Botta said without much conviction.

'You're all way off. I'll give you a hint. I've baptised it *The Infallible*,' said Dante, shaking the ash off his cigar. Everyone sat there in silence for a few moments, staring at the little wooden box with holes in it.

'I give up,' Bordelli said finally.

'Me too,' Botta echoed him.

Fabiani also threw in the towel.

Dante blew his smoke upwards and laughed. 'All right, I'll tell you. It's a—'

'Wait,' said Diotivede.

'Don't tell me you've figured it out,' said Bordelli.

The doctor emptied his glass and set it down on the table. 'It's to let you know whether eggs are fresh or not,' he said.

Dante burst into laughter and clapped his hands, then explained to the ignorant how it worked. You put the eggs in the appointed cavities, then placed the device under some light source, and through the holes, with the help of the mirrors, you could see the colour of the yolk through the shell. If it was bright orange, the egg was fresh; if it was pale orange, it wasn't so fresh, and if white, the egg was rotten.

'Without needing to break the egg . . .' Bordelli said in admiration. It was the first invention of Dante's he'd seen that actually served a purpose.

'I want to patent it,' Dante said under his breath.

'So the thing's mine now?' asked Bordelli, holding *The Infallible* in the air.

'Entirely yours. Now you can conquer any woman you want,' said Dante, laughing. Seeing that the inventor's glass was empty, Botta refilled it. Bordelli kept turning the brilliant invention round in his hand.

'Ennio, have you got any eggs left?'

'I used them all, Inspector.'

'Too bad,' said Bordelli, curious to see the device at work. After they had drunk another round of Calvados, the inspector suggested they each tell a story, as they had done at their dinner two years before.

'What do you think?' he asked, looking at the others.

'It's fine with me,' said Ennio. Fabiani was also in agreement, and Dante nodded, half closing his eyes. Diotivede sighed, as if he didn't feel like participating, but in the end he also consented. Ennio asked if he could go first. And they all agreed.

'In February of '44 I was here in Florence, and I wasn't a Fascist at all. The city was full of Germans and *repubblichini*.[36] To tell you the truth, I had no idea what had happened, because I'd just got out of l'Asinara after a couple of years inside. They didn't send me off to war because of a defect in my leg which I'd managed to invent and even got a certificate for, and when I walked I pretended to limp. There was a strange atmosphere in town, and people in the streets looked at each other with suspicion . . . Of course, I'm sure you all know what kind of atmosphere there was, but I'm just telling you this to set the mood . . .'

The night had barely begun and already seemed well advanced. Ennio spoke slowly and softly, as if the act of telling a story calmed him down.

'I lived alone. My parents had been evacuated to a village in the Val d'Orcia and were living in a convent. A family had moved into the flat next to mine, dad and mum and a little girl. They were nice but very reserved. It was almost like they were in hiding. They never made a peep. People said the father was a watchmaker but for some reason had lost his shop. The little girl was about ten years old. I often ran into her in the morning, queuing up for bread. One time we were in queues right next to each other. I said hello and noticed she was sulking. "What's wrong, dear?" I asked her. She shrugged and said nothing, but turned red in the face as if she was ashamed of something. She was very pretty and had black, sort of curly hair. My queue moved forward a step, and she stayed back, so I turned and smiled at her. "Are you sad?" I asked, and she snapped at me angrily and said: "Don't you know it's bad to talk to Jews?" Her eyes were red. People started staring at us. "Are you Jewish?" I asked. Her face was livid with rage. "Leave me alone!" she shouted. "It's bad to talk to Jews!" Even the people far down the line started looking at us, and it made me uncomfortable. I couldn't just leave it at that. So I said to the girl, "No, come on, why would it be bad?" But she stamped her feet. "We're wicked . . . we're wicked and dirty!" she shouted, even angrier than before. I heard two or three men laughing. I got out of my queue and went and knelt in front of the girl. "What's your name?" I asked. She stepped away as if dodging a kick. "Don't touch me!" she screamed. "You mustn't touch me!" And she ran away without buying any bread. I felt very bad about the whole thing, and so I left, too. When I got back home I felt almost like knocking on the watchmaker's door, but I didn't. A few days later I saw the little girl again on the street. She was carrying a big sack with bread in it and frowning as usual. "Ciao!" I said. "You still haven't told me your name." She kept on walking for about ten yards, and then she turned round and said, "My name's Rebecca. What's yours?" "My name is Ennio," I said, going up to her, "but all my friends call me Botta." "Why Botta?" she asked. I made a serious face and said, "Because wherever I go, everything explodes."[37] I said that because I didn't know what else to say. Then the girl looked at me and said: "I don't believe you, I don't believe you," and she ran away giggling. I was happy, because I'd made her laugh. So I started walking faster and caught up with her. She had a pretty blue ribbon in her hair. "What a pretty ribbon," I said, "do you think a ribbon like that would look as nice on me too?" She thought about this for a minute, then burst out laughing with her hand over her mouth. "Why," I said, "do you think I would look better with a red ribbon?" At that moment a lorry of militiamen came out from a side street. The little girl got scared and ran away to hide. The Fascists drove on, singing one of those songs of theirs at the top of their lungs. When they disappeared round the corner, the girl came out of her hole and looked at me as if she wanted to spit on me. Then she ran away. It hurt me to see her in such a state. A few days later somebody denounced her family to the authorities and the Fascists came to get them. I wasn't there but was told about it by a neighbour. "They're taking them to Germany," he said. "What do you mean, Germany? Who told you that?" I said to him. "Everybody knows that," he said. I asked about the little girl. He mumbled something, calling her a "little spider", and slammed the door in my face. The next morning I went to talk to an acquaintance of mine who knew a lot of people. I asked him if he could help me save a Jewish family. He raised his eyebrows and mentioned the name of a certain monsignor at the basilica of Santa Croce. That priest might be able to do something, he said. I could ask him on his behalf, he said. And so I went to see this monsignor, and he listened to me with a sad smile on his face, as if he'd heard the same story a hundred times before. And I asked him if he could help me. The monsignor said he would try but couldn't promise me anything. He said our best hope was to find a Fascist officer with a sense of decency, but the surest thing would be to supplement our request with some money. "These are terrible times," he said, raising his eyes to the heavens. I asked him how much money we would need, and he said we could try with a hundred thousand lire. He also said I had to move fast, because all the Jews were being rounded up and might be shipped off to Germany any day now. I went back the next day with eighty thousand lire. I won't tell you how I got my hands on it . . .'

Ennio and the inspector exchanged a glance of understanding and a wry smile.

'The monsignor put the money in a drawer and said to come back the next day. I couldn't tell if the cash was for him or some Fascist, but I didn't really care. When I went back, the priest pulled me inside and quickly closed the door behind me. "I tried," he said. He'd done his best, he said, but the whole thing was very dangerous. The operation risked upsetting our German allies, especially since Italy had signed specific agreements regarding the turning over of Jews arrested by the Republic. "It's politics," he said, looking at me wide eyed. But he would make one last attempt that same night. When I went back, the monsignor looked very serious when he saw me.

"What did they say?" I asked. He shook his head. "Only the girl," he said. "They won't give us the parents." I said I could try to find more money, and he collapsed into a chair. He said money was of no use. That wasn't the problem. It was very dangerous, he repeated; it was a delicate situation. Nobody wanted to be shot for treason, he said. The treaties between the Axis powers were the problem. I had to accept it. We could save the child, but not the parents. "It's abominable, but it's better than nothing," he said, shaking his head. I realised that the man was sincere, that he wasn't the one pocketing the money, and, to be honest with you, I was happy to know this. Two days later the little girl was released, and the following morning I went to the priest's at dawn to get her. She was thinner and seemed tired, and she looked at me with hatred. Her clothes smelled dirty. I tried to stroke her hair, but she stepped back. The monsignor wished us luck and pushed the two of us out the door. I started walking, and she followed behind me like a puppy. It was very cold outside. I was afraid of running into some German patrol and had my ears pricked for the slightest noise. "Give me your hand," I said. "That way you'll seem like my daughter." She gave me her hand, and it felt as small as a peach stone. I realised I didn't know where to take her. I hadn't thought of that. Letting her live at my place was out of the question. Too dangerous. Somebody might denounce me, and then they would come and take her away. And I couldn't be looking after her all day. I had to work . . . I really didn't know which way to turn. The little girl was getting more and more nervous and wasn't paying any attention to me. Then I stood in front of her and asked: "Do you think *I* denounced your parents?" She just stared at me. Her eyes looked sunken, as if someone had pushed them back inside her head. I decided to leave her in peace and try to come up with a solution. I thought of a convent near San Casciano. "I'm going to take you to a nice place," I said. We got on a bus. I was afraid we might get stopped by a German or Fascist patrol, but it went without a hitch. The bus let us off on a country road. And so we started walking, me in front and the girl behind. The convent was in a secluded spot full of cypresses. It didn't look like the most cheerful place. I knocked and knocked at the door, and finally a nun came to a window grating. I explained the whole story to her in a few words, and she opened the door for us. But I couldn't go in, she said. Convent rules. No men. So I put my hand on Rebecca's back and pushed her in. "Goodbye," I said. She went in without turning round, and the door closed behind her. I waited for a few minutes outside, listening. I heard the nun say: "What is your name, my child?" And Rebecca's answer made me laugh. "My name is Botta," she said. "Because wherever I go, everything explodes.""

Ennio paused to empty his glass, then said:

'I never saw her again.'

The first bottle of Calvados was almost finished. Ennio opened the second and refilled everyone's glass. All five of them sat in silence, as if to digest the story of the little girl.

'Now it's someone else's turn,' Botta said at last.

'Would you like to continue?' Bordelli asked, looking at Fabiani. The psychoanalyst's eyes were red from all the smoke in the room.

'If nobody minds I'd like to talk for a minute about my wife. She died twenty years ago, right after the Liberation. She'd survived the bombings and round-ups, and on 25 October 1945, she was run over by an American jeep. She'd spotted from afar an old friend she hadn't seen since the start of the war and was so excited that she crossed the road without looking. She was a wonderful woman. Gemma was her name. It hadn't taken her long to discover all my weaknesses. But she loved me very much and accepted me just as I was. She never tried to change me. And in this way she showed me a strength I never had. She was very beautiful; she looked like an actress. I still remember her smile . . . It was like seeing a light come on . . . But, I'm sorry, I only mentioned Gemma because I wish she was here with me tonight. I don't want to ruin your evening with an old man's sorrows.'

'To Gemma,' Ennio said softly, raising his glass.

'To Gemma,' they all repeated, and drank.

Diotivede set down his glass and, with a pensive expression, started breaking a toothpick into little bits. He seemed to be brooding over a none-too-cheerful story. But then again, he nearly always had that same expression. Dante puffed hard on his cigar and blew the smoke upwards.

'Would you like to go next?' Bordelli asked, looking at him.

'First I need more fuel,' said Dante, pushing his already empty glass to the middle of the table. Ennio took care of refilling it. The inventor thanked him with a nod, took a little sip of Calvados, and started talking.

'In '57 an important developer commissioned a job from me. A very long time ago I took a degree in civil engineering. I'm not sure I've ever told you that. And for this project I was supposed to do the necessary calculations for adding a fourth floor to an already existing building that had been lived in for years. The building was to be reinforced with a new support pillar at the centre of the underground garage. I specialised in techniques of pre-stressed concrete but had never actually put them into practice. I'll spare you the technical explanations, but with that system one could make pillars ten times smaller than the conventional ones with the same load-bearing capacity. So I got down to work and a few weeks later, I brought my design to the builder. By my calculations, using pre-stressed concrete we could make a square pillar forty centimetres by forty, leaving the usable garage space essentially unchanged, whereas with the traditional materials, that same pillar would have been two metres square, perhaps even more. The builder gave me a puzzled look. The new technique wasn't very well known yet. I had to explain everything in detail several times, and in the end he accepted my idea. And so we ordered the pillar, and only after having set it perfectly in place did the construction on the new fourth floor begin. The weeks went by. I went often to that basement to check my beautiful pillar. Sometimes I would look at it and think that it really was too small for all the

313

weight it was carrying. But everything seemed to be going well. When the fourth floor was finished I felt immensely satisfied. But then one evening, around supper time, I got a phone call from the builder. He said there were problems, and he seemed rather upset. Great cracks had appeared all around the pillar. Not little fissures, mind you, but cracks big enough to stick your finger in. I felt my hair standing on end. We arranged to meet at once. I felt terrible. I'd had too much faith in that bloody pre-stressed concrete. So I dashed into town and found the builder gloomily pacing back and forth in front of the building. When I approached him, he shot me a dark glance. He wouldn't even shake my hand, and we set off for the garage in silence. My heart was racing. When the builder opened the door, it was pitch black inside. We walked towards the light switch, and when the light came on, do you know what I saw?'

'Had it all collapsed?' Ennio asked, looking worried.

Dante took a big drag on his cigar and shook his head. 'All around the pillar there were tables laid out for a feast, and all the workmen and foremen stood up and started applauding.'

'Fuckin' hell . . .' Botta said for everyone.

'I turned to look at the developer beside me and saw him beaming with satisfaction. He slapped me on the back and said: "Well done, engineer." I looked them all in the eye, one by one. When they'd stopped applauding they told me to sit down and celebrate. But I didn't move, I didn't breathe. I felt like killing them all. Then I took a deep breath and found myself howling at the top of my lungs: "Fuuuck youuuu aaaall!" All the tension dissolved in those words, and everyone burst out laughing. A minute later we were all at table, and we ate and drank late into the night,' Dante concluded, laughing and spewing smoke.

'What a dirty trick,' said Bordelli.

'And where's this building?' Botta asked.

'Down by the suspension bridge, at the corner of Piazza Gaddi and Via Bronzino . . . Every time I go past it I blow it a kiss,' said Dante, rubbing his paunch.

'It's been called Ponte della Vittoria for quite a while now,' Diotivede muttered.

'Oh really?' Dante and Bordelli said in unison.

In the Piras household, Christmas Eve dinner had just ended. There were fourteen of them, not counting three little boys and two girls. As every year, they'd had to put two tables together to accommodate everyone, and as usual Maria had prepared so much food that there were enough leftovers to last three days. Now they were eating chestnuts, tangerines and dried figs while waiting for the midnight bells. A big log burned in the fireplace. The moment had come to exchange gifts. The kitchen sink was stacked with dirty dishes. On the table were sweets and several bottles of aged vernaccia, just opened, two of Gavino's and the rest brought by guests.

They unwrapped the gifts, and soon the room filled with a long murmur of thanks. The children ran at once into the entrance to try out their new toys. Maria stood up and kissed her son on the cheek.

'Thank you, Nino.'

'It's nothing,' he said. He had made a portrait of her in pen and put it in an old frame he'd found in the tool shed.

'You made me too pretty,' his mother said, moved. She set the small picture on the mantelpiece and looked at it. There was a knock at the door. It was Pina and Giovanni, and they'd brought a tray of *pirichittus*[38] and a bottle of wine. A short while later Pina asked whether they could all say a prayer together for Benigno, and without waiting for a reply she started slowly reciting the paternoster. The others joined in with her in soft voices, setting their glasses down on the table one by one. Giovanni hid his cigar with his hand. Pietrino couldn't remember all the words and simply moved his lips randomly. When the prayer was over, they all made the sign of the cross. Giovanni put his cigar back in his mouth and they all picked up their glasses. The children were getting louder and louder, but nobody paid any mind.

Pietrino sat down in the armchair and started watching the fire. He let himself be lulled by the others' voices, paying no attention to the words, and meanwhile thought back on Sonia's phone call. He'd talked to her right before dinner, and the sound of her voice had touched him. He'd whispered sweet nothings to her the whole time, and she'd only laughed, telling him to stop . . .

After a few minutes' distraction he roused himself to the sound of Costante, his father's cousin, telling a story. He started listening without taking his eyes off the fire. Costante was talking about a guy from Abbasanta, a certain Mario Zedda, who had a three-year-old daughter who fell ill one unlucky day.

'She had a high fever and strange blisters on her face. All she did was cry. Zedda had called the doctor, who told him to give her six injections a day. But the little girl wasn't getting any better – in fact, she was getting worse, and in the end she died. She was Zedda's only child. That night he went into the barn and hanged himself. His wife found him the following morning. The poor thing ended up in a mental hospital.'

Pina lowered her head and started crying.

'Nice going,' Gavino said to Costante.

'Why? What did I do?'

'Did you have to tell that story at Christmas?'

'You're such a blockhead,' said Grazia, Costante's wife.

'I'm sorry. From now on I'll keep quiet,' said Costante, offended.

'Never mind,' said Pina, wiping her eyes with her fingers. 'It's nothing.' She then reached out for her glass and took a sip. In the silence they heard only the fire crackling and the clock ticking. The bells of Santa Maria started ringing, and Pina stood up.

'The mass is beginning,' she said. They all stood up to leave. Maria looked at Pietrino to see what he intended to do. He smiled at her but did not move. He waited for them all to leave, then went and got the grappa from the liquor cabinet and poured himself a small glass. He sat back down by the fire. A small flame was slowly devouring the big log of olive wood that Gavino had put on the fire for Christmas Eve night. It would burn until morning.

One after another, the church bells in town started ringing. Bordelli and Diotivede looked at each other to see who should go next. The doctor was biting his lips like a child. To all appearances he wanted to go last. Bordelli got the message and gave in. He lit another cigarette. It must have been already his sixth.

'In April of '44 I was encamped with a few men in a little town a few miles from the front. The weather was nasty, and we were tense. While awaiting our orders we played silly games, such as priming a percussion bomb and passing it back and forth like a ball, trying to catch it as delicately as possible so it wouldn't go off . . . I shudder when I think about it now, but we were in a war, and we measured fear differently. At night we slept in an old primary school. We'd taken up residence in the gym. One evening I was very tired and went to bed before the others. I fell asleep with the feeling that I had forgotten something. When I woke up the following morning, I found all my men standing before me. I scarcely had time to rub my eyes before they started singing "Happy birthday to you" and clapping. Who the hell had told those jailbirds that the second of April was my birthday? When I stood up to thank them, they stepped aside and I saw a drawing in coloured chalk on the wall in front of me, a war scene with life-sized figures and Commander Bordelli in the foreground. For a few seconds it was a little like being at home. I thanked them and embraced them, and right after that began one of the worst bombardments we'd ever seen. Of those six men, three died in the bombing, another one a few days later, while de-mining a bridge, and the other two just one month before the end. I can still see them now as if they were right here. And I remember that drawing well.'

They all remained silent for a spell, exchanging glances. Bordelli downed his glass and refilled it.

'You're the only one left, Diotivede,' he said.

'Well, you're all going to have to be patient, because if I tell my story, I'm going to tell all of it,' said Diotivede. He ran a hand over his head and asked for a cigarette.

Bordelli lit one for himself and passed him the packet. 'I didn't think you smoked,' he said.

'Indeed I don't. Would you give me a light?'

The doctor lit his cigarette and blew the smoke across the table.

'In 1919 I wasn't yet thirty years old, and I was working at a hospital in Turin. The Spanish flu was making a shambles of Europe, and you could smell the insignificance of life in the air. One morning I saw a woman, a very beautiful woman, at the hospital. She was sleeping in a bed with her fists clenched. I asked a nurse who she was and whether she was sick. She told me the woman was South American and had been hospitalised after fainting, probably from hunger. I kept on looking at her. What was a South American doing there? I wondered. Even with her eyes closed, she looked like the most beautiful woman I'd ever seen. Nobody knew her name, as she'd had no identification papers on her. I told the nurse I would attend to her myself. But the following morning she was gone. We thought she'd run away to avoid having to give explanations, and soon afterwards nobody gave her another thought. Nobody except me, that is.'

Diotivede stopped for a moment to smoke. The others watched in silence, waiting for him to resume.

'Five days later, as I was going home on the omnibus, I saw her get on. It was her, I was sure of it. My heart started racing. Even though the omnibus was empty, I gave her my seat. She smiled at my rather blatant courtesy and accepted my offer. We started talking and almost immediately used the informal *tu*. Her vitality almost frightened me. She said she was Colombian and had come to Italy for work. When she stood up to get off, I summoned my courage and asked if I could see her again. She smiled and said only, "We'll meet again, don't worry." As of that moment I could think of nothing but her. Every time I took the omnibus I hoped to see her. A week went by, and at last I saw her get on. She was more beautiful than ever. She came up to me with a strange look and asked me to get off with her at the next stop and follow her from a distance. And so we got off, and I followed behind her for a few city blocks at a distance of about twenty yards. She walked fast, without ever turning round to see if I was still there. We turned down a narrow, dirty street. She opened a door and disappeared inside. I went in too and followed her up a dark staircase. We entered a squalid room with a mattress tucked into a corner. She took my hands and pulled me close to her. She said we had to hurry. As she was pushing me down on to the mattress, she said she wanted to get down to business at once. Later, in retrospect, it would all seem like a trick to me. I didn't understand what she meant, but didn't say anything. I only wanted to live that moment and think of nothing else, and I saw it through to the end. Afterwards, we lay there in silence for a while, in each other's arms. That dirty, empty room seemed beautiful to me. At a certain point she sat up on the mattress and said, "My name is Maria Conchita Veleza, and I am Nicaraguan. A year after the American invasion I joined a clandestine movement for the liberation of my country, to get rid of that blowhard Diaz. We carried out many guerrilla actions, but after a few years Diaz's men, with the help of the Americans, were able to track us down, and my comrades started to disappear. The survivors managed to escape the country two years ago. I'm not alone here. There are many of us, and we're planning an armed revolt to topple the government and throw the Americans out. If Diaz's butchers find us, there will be nothing left of us. Not even our names on tombstones. You have to help us," she said in the end. She looked at me with fire in her eyes. She was a passionate woman, in love with liberty . . . Are you sure this isn't too boring?' asked Diotivede. Everyone said no by shaking his head. The doctor took off his glasses and started cleaning them with his napkin.

'Maria Conchita's eyes were full of anger. She said the United States had to be stopped, otherwise, using the excuse that they were bringing democracy to backward peoples, they would end up conquering all of Latin America and turn it into their rubbish dump. In recent years they'd staged armed interventions in Honduras, Cuba, Panama, Haiti and Costa Rica. They had to be stopped at all costs. The organisation she belonged to was one of many ant colonies working towards this great dream, and in Nicaragua a man called Sandino was paving the way for victory. If I understood the importance of freedom, I should help them, she said. Then she explained how. She said I had to take a very important envelope to Managua, give it to a certain man, and then return. She and her fellow group members couldn't do it because they were sought by the authorities, and they considered the postal service unsafe. I, on the other hand, was an Italian doctor who could travel there as a tourist, since I had no connection to Nicaraguan politics. I could do it quite easily, without being searched at customs upon entering. I didn't ask her what would be in that envelope, and I swear I felt great admiration for her, for doing what she did. But I obviously also felt that she'd gone to bed with me just to use me as a courrier. I didn't like feeling like a puppet, and a short while later I left without saying anything. Two days later I saw her again on the omnibus. "It's on for Friday," she said. And she told me the time and place. She got off at the next stop without turning round. And, as she had asked, I did not follow her. That Friday, I showed up on time for the appointment. I didn't even know why. There was a guy there waiting for me. He signalled to me to follow him at a distance, and a few blocks farther on he went through a door and disappeared. I followed him inside, and he led me into a dark room. I realised there were other people there, because I could hear them breathing. A hooded man then came forward in the darkness. He handed me two envelopes, one to be delivered, the other containing my instructions, which I was to memorise and then burn. A minute later I was back outside. I didn't understand why they had chosen me, of all people, but I didn't care. What I really wanted to know was whether or not she had taken me for a ride. There was only one way to find out: do what they asked of me and then return. I arranged matters at the hospital and departed. I'll sum up my journey to Nicaragua very briefly for you, since it has little to do with the story. At any rate, everything went smoothly. I didn't talk to anybody on the ship, stayed the whole time holed up in my cabin, crushing cockroaches and thinking of Maria Conchita. I sailed through customs without a hitch and reached Managua by train. It was night, and very hot. The railway station was garrisoned by US Marines; one saw them all over the place in town as well, on foot and in their lorries. There was a palpable tension in the air. My first night in the hotel I didn't sleep a wink. It seemed absurd for me to be in that city. In accordance with my instructions, I waited two days, and then on the third day went to the address I'd been given. I got there exactly on time. A short bloke in glasses opened the door for me and let me in. After an exchange of passwords I handed him the envelope and left without saying another word. Then I waited another week, as I'd been asked to do. I was supposed to act like a tourist, and so all I did was wander about the city and sweat like a hog. Every so often I would hear gunshots in the distance, but most people seemed not to notice. Then at last I returned to Italy. Some twenty days in all had passed. I went back to my job at the hospital. I didn't seek out the rebels because I knew it was useless. I just lived my life and waited. Weeks went by, but nobody came forward. I began to think I'd been tricked like a child. All I had left of her was that half-hour on a dirty mattress.'

Diotivede stopped and, without asking, took another cigarette from Bordelli, who lit it for him. The doctor took a sip and continued.

'One day, as I was going out, I found her right in front of me. Her eyes were puffy and had dark circles around them, as if she hadn't slept for days. Even so, she still seemed very beautiful to me. We stood there looking at each other. My heart was pounding in my ears. "I'm leaving early tomorrow morning, and I wanted to tell you," she said. "Don't leave," I said. She shook her head. "I must," she said. "But let me in for now." We went into my place and spent the night together, without saying a word. We fell asleep at dawn, exhausted. Later that morning I reached out across the bed, but she wasn't there. I called out her name, but she didn't reply. I remember thinking: I'll never see Maria Conchita again. I got out of bed and started rummaging about the flat. In the bathroom I found a note attached to the mirror. *We are not alone on this earth. MC.* I crumpled the paper and hurled it across the room.'

The doctor stopped and gestured for Bordelli to refill his glass again.

'A year later I received a letter from Maria Conchita, posted in Peru. The plan to overthrow Diaz had gone to the dogs. Her brothers and many of her comrades had been killed. She'd managed to escape from Nicaragua again and gone into hiding in Colombia, and then Peru. Things were going very badly, in short. Maria Conchita was disgusted with the world and weary of life. She'd wept with rage when the Marines intervened in Guatemala just a few weeks before. Nothing had changed, she said, and nothing would ever change. Money and power were the only law on earth. She ended by saying she would like to see me again. That's exactly how she put it: "I would like to see you again." It seemed almost like a pat phrase, but it still got me excited. Then, right below it, Maria Conchita suggested we meet the following month in Lima. She even gave the date and time of day, and the name of the square. She would wait for me for half an hour, after which she would leave. She laid it all out in precise detail, like some sort of meeting between two revolutionaries. "If you don't come," she concluded, "at least think of me now and then." The whole thing still seemed so absurd to me, I felt like laughing. Nothing about it made any sense. A letter, an appointment on the other side of the globe. It was just too silly.'

Diotivede allowed himself another pause to take a sip. Ennio couldn't hold himself back.

'So what did you do? Did you go to Peru?' he said, staring at him. Diotivede turned towards Botta and kept looking at him for quite some time, as if telling the story only to him.

'Yes, I went to Peru. I took ship a week later and was in Lima on the appointed day. The rendezvous was at noon in a plaza in the centre of town. I got there an hour early. The plaza was huge and had a garden in the middle, and there were a great many people walking about. We would have to look hard to find each other. As I was quite early, I started walking around without straying too far. At ten minutes to twelve, I was back in the square. I started walking back and forth, looking for Maria Conchita. I must have gone round the plaza ten times, sweating and cursing all the women who looked like her from a distance. I took my watch out of my breast pocket and looked at the time: a quarter past twelve. I felt like a fool. I'd crossed the ocean to see a woman I barely knew. She wasn't going to come. By this point I was convinced of it. Still I kept searching the crowd for her face. But by one o'clock she still hadn't shown up. I was feeling worse and worse, and after searching for another half an hour I realised there was no longer any point in waiting. I would return home, she would never write to me again, and I would never again have any news of her. I wouldn't even know if she was alive or dead. I dropped down on to a bench, thinking that it had already been almost two months since I'd received her letter. Maybe she hadn't come because something had happened to her . . . Maybe she'd been arrested and was being tortured, or perhaps she was already dead. Or maybe she'd simply changed her mind. I would never know. I needed a strong drink. I slipped into a sort of bar and ordered a tequila. When I looked up, above the bottles behind the bar there was a clock that said two forty-five. I looked at my watch, and it said one forty-five. I called the barman over and gestured at his clock. "It's broken," I said, tapping my watch with one finger. "It's an hour fast." I said it all in Italian, but he understood anyway. And he smiled at me. "*No, señor,*" he said, "*ese reloj funciona perfecta-mente, es el suyo que anda mal.*" I almost got angry; it was *his* that didn't work. The man repeated what he'd just said to me, this time without a smile. But by then I no longer needed convincing; I'd understood everything. When getting off the boat I'd adjusted my watch to the local time, but I'd made a mistake. I'd been thinking of Nicaragua, whereas I was in Lima, Peru. In a different time zone, one hour ahead. Maybe she actually *had* come at noon, waited half an hour, and left. Maybe.'

Ennio was holding his glass tightly in his fist, as if wanting to break it.

'And so? Did you ever see her again?' he asked.

'No.'

Bordelli looked at his watch: half past three. Dante had just left, an hour later than the others. The inspector looked out the window. A fine, freezing snow was falling. He lay down in bed and turned out the light. Contrary to habit, he'd only pulled the shutters to, and the glow of a street lamp filtered through. He lay there for a spell with his eyes open, watching the shadows on the wall. He'd eaten and drunk a lot, but felt light. He lit his last cigarette, this one the hand-rolled kind, and smoked it slowly, watching the lighted end burn red in the semi-darkness. He thought about Maria Conchita, trying to imagine her, young and beautiful, hungry for freedom. Who knew whether she was still alive or lying dreamless underground.

He snuffed out the butt and got comfortable, and as usual started travelling through his memories. The moments before falling asleep were always peopled by long-departed images. The last one that passed through his mind was his mother's face at the moment she'd heard Mussolini's voice on the radio cry: '*War!*'

25 December

He woke up the following morning in a pleasant state of numbness, the taste of apples still in his mouth from the Calvados. Yawning, he thought distractedly of Odoardo with the scissors in his hand . . . And at that moment he heard a clatter of dishes. Slipping his trousers on, he went to investigate. There, in the sun-drenched kitchen, was Ennio washing up, fresh as a rose. He'd already made a good deal of progress.

'Coffee, Inspector?' The pot was already waiting on the stove.

'What time is it, anyway?' Bordelli asked, running a hand over his eyes.

'Almost eleven. And the sun is out, despite the Christian Democrats.'

The sky was blue and cloudless. Ennio dried his hands and lit the flame under the espresso pot.

Bordelli sat down, elbows on the table. He felt extremely lazy. 'My dear Ennio, I really didn't know you could cook like that . . . I'm speechless.'

'Next time I can make you a Turkish dinner, or even a Portuguese one.'

'Have you been in jail in those places too?'

'I did two years in Erzurum and one in Coimbra, for smuggling.'

'I'm beginning to be convinced that jail is good for you, Botta.'

'I've always had a passion for cooking, Inspector. Sometimes I feel more like a cook than a thief.'

'Have you ever been arrested in Romania?'

'No, though I had a close call once.'

'Too bad,' said Bordelli.

'Thanks, Inspector.'

'I only meant that I'm curious about Romanian cookery.'

'Nobody's going to lock up Botta ever again, Inspector. I've made myself a promise.'

'No more crime?'

'I didn't say that. But I'm getting on in years and have to start being more savvy when I work.'

'Makes perfect sense to me.'

Ennio put the litle cups on the table and dropped into the chair in front of Bordelli. They carried on talking about jails, cooking and women. There weren't many other subjects left to discuss.

It was already past noon when the inspector went to shave and get dressed. Botta started washing the last pots, singing a tune of Celantano's to himself. Before going out, Bordelli poked his head round the kitchen door.

'Ciao, Ennio, thanks again for everything.'

'Have a good day, Inspector. When you want to organise another dinner, just give me a holler.'

'I'll call you soon,' said Bordelli. He went out and got into the Beetle. With the bright sun shining, he felt like going for a nice little drive along some country roads. He decided to go as far as Impruneta again, by way of the Bagnolo road. Maybe if he asked around again in town he could find out if there were any old houses for sale that fitted his needs . . . and didn't cost too much.

After the rain and sleet of the previous days, it was nice to see such a clear blue sky. It was Christmas Day, and there weren't many people out. At that hour they were all at table. He wasn't even hungry. He drove slowly across the city, thinking of the stories he'd heard the previous evening . . . Fabiani's wife, the little Jewish girl, Maria Conchita. He felt the need for a cigarette and, holding the steering wheel still with his knees, he managed to light one.

He drove past the Certosa and after Villa Bottai, instead of proceeding straight for Tavernuzze, he took the Quintole road up the hill. Then he stopped almost at once, in front of the enormous gate of a villa. He'd had an idea. Leaving the motor running, he tried to unravel the fraying fabric on a sleeve of his raincoat and at last managed to extract a thread some three inches long. Then he drove off again. He rolled along slowly, and a little over a mile down the road, he turned onto Odoardo's unpaved driveway. As he neared the house he noticed the Vespa parked under the loggia. He left his car on the threshing floor, and before turning off the engine, revved it twice to make himself heard. He looked at the windows, but nobody appeared. Perhaps the boy had stayed up late and was still asleep. Bordelli got out of the car and went round the house to the back. He was in no hurry. He stopped and gazed for a few moments at the olive grove and the hills covered with woods and vineyards. The still-wet countryside glimmered like ice, but the sun was almost strong enough to warm oneself by. He went back towards the house and looked through a grille-covered window. Inside he saw a big earthenware jug with a wooden lid. It must be olive oil, he thought. He would have loved to make his own oil, with his own olives. But while waiting to make the big move, he could at least do as his father had done . . . He could go and buy a few gallons of good oil from a peasant. He could hardly stand the industrial crap he bought in town any more. He leaned his shoulder against the corner of the house. The bricks were warm. Breathing deep the cold country air, he decided not to light another cigarette. Then he heard a window open over his head. Looking up, he saw the hostile face of Odoardo Beltempo pop out.

'Hello, Odoardo. I've come to wish you a happy Christmas.'

'What do you want this time?'

'I was just driving around and ended up here. Could I come inside for a minute?'

'I'm about to go out.'

'Then I'll wait for you down here.'

Odoardo stayed there for a moment, staring at him, eyes burning with anger, then closed the window with a thud. Bordelli made for the threshing floor. While waiting, he started studying the carcass of the old Ardea for the umpteenth time. It had white sidewalled tyres on rusted wheel rims.

Some minutes later he heard a door slam and turned round. Odoardo was coming towards him, looking rather fed up. He stopped a few yards away, hands in his pockets.

'Don't you think you're taking this a little too far, Inspector?'

'Good morning.'

'Don't you think you're taking this a little too far?' Odoardo repeated.

'In what sense?' asked Bordelli.

'Why did you come?'

'It wasn't premeditated. My horse brought me here.'

'Your horse must be pretty bizarre.'

'That's quite possible. Going anywhere interesting?'

Odoardo stood there without moving, hands thrust deep into his pockets.

'Wherever I feel like going.'

'Into town?'

'Why do you keep asking me all these questions?' the boy asked.

Bordelli gave a hint of a smile, then turned to look at the distant hills covered with vineyards and olive groves. 'I just love this sun. I never saw a Christmas like this in all my life . . .'

'As usual you've got nothing to say to me, Inspector.'

Bordelli pulled out a cigarette, stuck it between his lips without lighting it, and looked the lad in the eye.

'You know what I think, Odoardo?'

'What?'

'That we shouldn't try to be what we are not. And you know why?'

'You tell me.'

'Because we might become dangerous. Have you ever thought about it?'

'No.'

'Try it some time.'

'I'll think about it all night,' Odoardo said. Then he turned and started walking towards the loggia. Bordelli followed him, walking slowly, fumbling with the thread that hung from the sleeve of his raincoat.

'Where'd you go to primary school, Odoardo?' he asked distractedly.

The boy turned and shot him a malevolent glance. 'Was that your important question, Inspector?'

'I must admit I sometimes ask questions without knowing why.'

'That's very interesting. Why don't you continue your little game with someone else?' Odoardo asked, putting on his gloves.

'Going to see your girlfriend?' Bordelli asked.

'Wrong. I have to go and kill a loan shark and I'm running late.'

'You see? I was right. Deep down, the subject does interest you,' the inspector said.

'It's all I ever think about,' said Odoardo, buttoning up his overcoat. Bordelli could still feel a hint of a smile on his lips. He liked this intelligent, stubborn kid.

'Tell me something, Odoardo. If it was you who killed Badalamenti . . . don't worry, I'm just saying this as an example . . . If it was you who killed a man as despicable as that, how would you feel now? Guilty or innocent? I'm just curious.'

'You've already asked me that.'

'Yes, but you didn't give me an answer.'

Odoardo remained impassive.

'I'm not very good at these things,' he said, opening the scooter's fuel injector.

'It doesn't seem like such a hard question to me,' the inspector said, all the while pretending he was trying to tear away the thread hanging from his sleeve.

'You never told me how many Nazis you killed, either,' said Odoardo.

'You shouldn't confuse matters. That was war.'

They stood there for a moment in silence. The birds cried loudly. They sounded as if they were being tortured.

'You know something, Odoardo? I've known killers who were convinced they had acted properly . . . and at times I've almost caught myself agreeing with them. I'm not joking. But if everyone acted that way, we'd be in a pretty nasty pickle, don't you think?'

'I'm already late, Inspector. If you have nothing serious to tell me, I'd like to go.'

'Absolutely, be my guest . . . Oh, but could you do me a little favour first?'

'What?' said Odoardo, sighing.

Bordelli raised the sleeve of his trench coat and took the thread between his fingers. 'Could you help me cut this? It keeps rubbing my wrist, and it always feels like a spider,' he said, smiling.

'I haven't got any scissors.'

'I saw some shears here somewhere,' said Bordelli, going under the loggia.

Odoardo walked round the Vespa and went to get the shears. He went up to the inspector with a sullen expression. 'Here,' he said, handing him the shears.

'Did I ever tell you how Badalamenti was killed?'

'Let's be quick, please.'

'Could you cut it for me? Otherwise I'll have to take off my coat and waste even more of your time.'

Odoardo practically snatched the shears out of his hand.

'Give me your sleeve,' he said, trying to remain calm. The inspector held out his arm.

'Try to cut it at the bottom, otherwise it'll just start fraying again.'

'Please don't move,' said Odoardo. And he grabbed the thread with his right hand and cut it with the shears in his left. Bordelli felt a shudder run down the back of his neck, but feigned a placid smile.

'There,' said Odoardo, tossing the shears on to a wicker chair.

'Thanks ever so much. Now I'll let you go and see your girlfriend.'

'I hope this is the last time I ever see you, Inspector,' the youth said, getting on his scooter.

'Do you ever think about time, Odoardo? Don't you think it's quite a mystery?' said Bordelli.

'I don't think a policeman should try to be a philosopher. He might become dangerous,' said Odoardo.

'I entirely agree,' said the inspector.

Odoardo started up the Vespa, turned it towards the courtyard, and stopped in front of Bordelli.

'Why don't you speak clearly, Inspector? It would all be so much simpler,' he said, letting the motor idle.

Bordelli rested his hand on the Vespa's headlight in a friendly gesture. 'You're lucky to live in a place like this, Odoardo. I have to say I envy you . . . But did you really not know Totuccio Badalamenti?' he asked point blank, looking the youth in the eye. He saw him tremble slightly, lips contracted.

'What kind of game is this, Inspector?' Odoardo asked.

'I'm not sure it's a game,' said Bordelli, putting his hand on the boy's arm. Odoardo put the scooter in gear and the Vespa leapt forward.

'You should have the clutch adjusted,' said the inspector.

'Thanks for the advice.'

'You know what, Odoardo? I have a theory all my own about killers . . . But I'll tell you about it next time, otherwise you'll be late . . .'

Odoardo moved his elbow slightly, just enough to release it from Bordelli's hand.

'Goodbye, Inspector,' he said. Popping the clutch, he left in a flash, followed by the usual cloud of oily smoke. Bordelli felt like staying a little longer to enjoy the beautiful day. He slowly circled the house again, to the back, and started walking around, gazing at the countryside glistening in the sun. He liked just standing there, admiring the spectacle, he liked the sound of the chickens scratching about in the coop, pecking the ground. He wondered whether this was a sign of old age. He even liked to hear the birds screaming. Sitting down on the bottom of an upended demijohn, he lit the cigarette he had between his lips. And he smoked it slowly, savouring it, eyes on the horizon, listening distractedly to the chickens scratch about . . .

After Christmas lunch with his aunts, uncles and cousins, Pietrino rang Sonia. Since it was a holiday, the call cost less and they could purr all they wanted without worrying about running up the bill. He still told her nothing about the whole suicide case, mostly because he didn't feel like hearing her tell him that a convalescing policeman should stay at home reading by the fire. She started saying silly things in her beautiful Sicilian accent and the raspy voice she used at times, which never failed to shake Piras to his foundations. Especially now, after they hadn't seen each other for quite some time.

The relatives went out to visit some friends on the other side of town, waving goodbye to Pietrino as they left. They would return late that afternoon, and everyone would eat together again.

After half an hour of talking, Piras kissed Sonia goodbye and went back to the kitchen. His mother was preparing more pastries and humming.

'What song is that?' Pietrino asked.

'I don't know what it's called . . . How's Francesca doing?'

'Francesca who?'

'Your girlfriend.'

'Ah . . . yes, she's fine,' said Pietrino. He sat in the armchair by the fire and started reading Maigret. After some twenty pages, he set the book down, listening to the fire, and dozed off.

Around four o'clock Pina and Giovanni knocked at the door, carrying a tray full of amaretti and *papassinos*. With them were also Giovanni's cousin and his wife, who'd come from Solarussa. He was short and stocky, she short and slender, thin as an anchovy. When they stood one beside the other, he looked as if he could snap her in two like a sprig of rosemary. Pina set the tray down on the table, as Maria put another pot of coffee on the fire. A few minutes later Gavino came in from the field, to which he'd fled right after eating. In winter the days were short and he needed to make the most of every hour of light, even on Christmas Day.

Maria poured the coffee into little cups. The wind was blowing outside, and every so often the chimney howled. They chatted of this and that, and after a while Gavino started talking about the war. Pietrino had heard those stories many times over, but whenever his father spoke about that period, people listened. His tales had more than their share of blood, and the power of lived experience.

Gavino was telling for the thousandth time the story of the night when they saw a column of Tigers pass along a country road . . . The sinister tanks were moving at a leisurely pace, about fifty yards apart. Covering their faces with mud, Commander Bordelli and his comrades had taken up positions in the ditches at the side of the road . . .

'Open the sweet wine,' he said to his wife. Maria uncorked a bottle and filled the glasses, and Gavino resumed his tale.

Pietrino felt good, sunk deep into the armchair and warmed by the fire, his father's story swirling about in his sleepy head, the sound of the fire consuming the wood in the background. The sun was setting, the room slowly darkening. After a while the only remaining light came from the red flames reflecting on the faces of those present. Maria stood up to turn on the light.

'Don't bother, Mamma,' said Piras. 'There's the fire.'

'I'm not sure everybody likes it, Nino,' his mother said, finger on the light switch. The others said it wasn't a problem, and Maria sat back down. Gavino finished his story, and everyone sat in silence for a few minutes.

'Pina, why don't you tell us something about Benigno?' Piras asked, wanting to hear another story. Pina nodded.

'Where was Benigno during the war?' Piras asked.

'He was in the Piedmont. He went through some terrible times there,' Pina said with a sad smile. But one could see she was happy to talk a little about her unlucky cousin.

'Forget that awful story,' Giovanni said, waving dismissively. Apparently he'd heard it too many times.

'Let her speak,' said Maria. Gavino also wanted to hear it.

'It's rather long . . .' said Pina, looking at her husband as if asking his permission.

'Let's hear it,' said Pietrino, curling up in the armchair.

Giovanni resigned himself and refilled his glass. Pina started talking, staring into the fire.

'When the king got rid of Mussolini, Benigno was a soldier in the Piedmont, at a base in Asti. Nobody knew what to do. Many of them actually thought the war was over. Nino wasn't even twenty years old, and all he knew how to do was to tend sheep . . .'

Piras closed his eyes and listened to Pina's story, translating her dialect into Italian, and her details into historic moments . . .

Marshal Badoglio announced the signing of the armistice on the radio, and by the following day the military commands ceased receiving orders. The country seemed left to its own devices. Nobody had any idea what might happen next. Word spread that the king had left for Brindisi together with Badoglio to welcome the Allies, who had already landed in Sicily some time before. Others said that *those two* had simply taken to their heels. Benigno didn't understand a thing about any of this. He sensed only that everything was up in the air and waited to see what his fellow servicemen would do. Then news came that Rome had been occupied by Hitler's troops, and a few days later Mussolini was freed by the Nazis. The Duce's voice returned to the radio waves and wearily announced the constitution of the Italian Social Republic. In barracks across the land, soldiers took off their uniforms and left, officers included. Benigno did the same. He threw away his uniform and started walking. He'd grasped just one thing in all this: that it was best to hide. He slept for three nights in an abandoned warehouse outside Asti. On the fourth day he started walking again, and after a few hours he stopped at the empty stable of a large villa along a road leading out of the city. The villa was about fifty yards away and must have been inhabited, because he saw smoke rising above the roof. To avoid being discovered by the owners, he would go out at sunrise and return after sunset. During the day, Benigno roamed the countryside, eating sour apples and knocking on the doors of peasants' houses asking for bread. He had no idea what was happening in the rest of Italy. At times he would ask the peasants, but nobody felt like taking the time to answer. One evening, when he returned to his stall, he found a bundle wrapped in paper. Inside was a piece of bread and a strip of lard. Someone had discovered that a stranger was secretly sleeping in the stable, and with that gesture had proved to be a friend. Perhaps it was even the villa's owners, but there was no way of knowing. The following morning Benigno went out shortly after daybreak as usual. When he returned that evening, he found bread and lard in the stall again. And there was even a cigarette. The bread was very dark but delicious. He fell asleep with a full belly after smoking the cigarette down to the end and burning his fingers. At dawn he jolted awake to the rumble of engines approaching. It sounded like lorries. He heard them stop in front of the villa. Spying through a crack, he saw some black-clad military men jumping out of the trucks in the fog. There must have been fifteen of them, all armed with machine guns and moving brusquely about. Farther ahead there was also a very fine black car with mud spattered along its sides. Two men began to thrust their shoulders into the villa's front door while three others started walking briskly towards the stable. Benigno felt his heart sink. There were no windows to escape through, and so he went and hid himself in a pile of straw. But the soldiers found him almost immediately. They wore shiny boots and had death's heads sewn on to their uniforms. They started kicking him at first, then dragged him out, screaming curses in his ears. When they were in front of the villa, they left him on the ground, and he stayed down, thinking that his life was about to end. The house's inhabitants were already lined up on the lawn: two women who looked like sisters, an elderly man, a young boy, and two little girls with jet-black hair. In the all-enveloping fog, it looked like a scene from hell. At that point the car door opened, and a man of about thirty stepped out, dressed in a very smart uniform. He came forward calmly, as if entering the opera house. He had a short whip in his hand, and as he walked he swatted it lightly against his thigh.

'My, my, look what we have here . . .' he said, examining the prisoners. He made a gesture with his head, and a handful of his men went back inside the villa.

'As if it weren't enough that you're Jews, I see you've also taken to hiding deserters,' he said calmly, looking at the woman and the old man.

'They didn't know,' Benigno ventured to say.

The demon turned towards him. 'What was that, cur?'

'I was sleeping in the stall in secret, they didn't know anything,' Benigno repeated, then put his head back down.

The man walked slowly towards him and stopped beside him. 'Apparently you're one of those curs that still has the courage to speak,' he said.

Benigno raised his head to look at him, and at once the whip struck him across the mouth. He fell face down into the mud, feeling blood pour over his tongue. Those who had gone into the house came back out in a flurry and gathered round the leader like chicks.

'We didn't find anything, sir, but there are marks on the walls where there used to be paintings,' said one of them, stiff as a tree trunk.

'Well, well,' the commander said, smiling. He dug in his heels and had a look around. Taking a deep breath, he took a gold cigarette case out of his pocket, opened it, took a cigarette, tapped it two or three times against the case, and put it between his lips. Before he had even begun to put the gold case back into his pocket, a lighted match appeared before him, held by a devoted soldier of his. He inhaled deeply, blew the smoke upwards, then lightly shook his head, as if something didn't seem right to him. Unlike the others, he didn't betray the slightest haste in any of his gestures. It was as though it were up to him to decide how quickly time should pass. Walking slowly, he approached the prisoners again. The boy looked at him with hollow eyes as though unable to grasp what was happening. The man stopped in front of the two little girls and tapped the ash from his cigarette. Then he moved on and stopped in front of the women.

'If you don't tell me what I want to know in ten seconds, I shall do the following: I shall order one of my men to take one of those lovely little girls, tie her to the back of the car with a rope and go for a drive through the mountains,' he said calmly.

The women fell to their knees, and with their eyes popping out of their heads said in unison that everything was hidden in the cellar, behind a brick wall.

'Get up,' the commander said, walking away. 'I don't like worms that crawl along the ground.'

The Fascists had already gone to the lorries to fetch pickaxes, and four of them went back into the house. There was a sound of hammering for a few minutes, and then one of them came out, half covered in dust.

'It's all there, sir.'

'Four of you stay here; everybody else, to the cellar,' said the commander.

'Yes, sir!'

In short order they removed a treasury of paintings and jewels from the cache and loaded their booty on to one of the lorries. They made the prisoners board the other lorry, and then the convoy left. The half-hour that followed was terrible. The Fascists raped the two women and beat up the men in front of the screaming children. Then the vehicles stopped along a mountain road in the middle of a wood. They made everyone get out and started walking through the trees. The captain led the way, whistling a march.

'Where are you taking us?' one of the women whispered, but nobody replied. The silence was worse than screams. The soldiers, on the other hand, seemed calm. They stopped in a clearing and made the prisoners stand in a line, with Benigno at one end and the old man at the other. The three children were in the middle, clinging to the women's legs. The Fascists took about ten steps back and raised the barrels of their machine guns.

'Shouldn't we have them dig a pit?' asked one of them.

'In a week's time, even their bones will be gone,' said another. 'It's full of wild boar around here.'

Benigno didn't believe such a thing could actually happen. He was wrong.

'Fire!' said the commander, and the Fascists started shooting. It was over very quickly. The children's bodies were thrown backwards by the force of the bullets. The others fell like empty sacks. Then silence returned. The air smelled of gunpowder. Benigno felt his shoulder burning, but he was alive. He lay still, with his eyes half open, the better to pretend he was dead. He'd fallen back with his face towards the Fascists and saw everything. One of them pulled out some cigarettes and passed them round to the others.

Somebody moaned. One of the women was still alive. The captain went up to her and gestured brusquely for a pistol. One of the soldiers ran and put one in his hand. The captain released the safety catch and shot the woman in the head. He did the same with the old man and then the children. After shooting them all he arrived at Benigno and pointed the gun at his head as indifferently as if looking at his fingernails to see whether they were dirty. Benigno saw his face through his half-closed eyelashes . . . He saw the round, all-powerful eyes looking at him with indifference. But by this point he was playing dead in earnest and not moving. Indeed, he remembered thinking: Let's hope he doesn't see a vein pulsing. Half a second later, the captain pulled the trigger and the pistol clicked. The others were some ten yards away, chatting. The captain fired again, and again the pistol clicked. And all at once it started raining, big fat drops that made a great deal of noise when they hit the trees and the ground. There was a clap of thunder, and a second later the floodgates opened.

'Bloody hell!' the Fascists yelled, covering their heads with their jackets. The commander stayed back for another second, looking at the deserter's body, then put the pistol in his pocket and ran off with the others. A few minutes later Benigno heard the lorries and cars drive away. As he raised his head, a sob rose up in his throat. He was alive. Still alive. He got on his knees, kissing the rain as it fell on his face, and started crying like a child. The bullet that should have killed him had remained inside the barrel. It was God who had done it. It was He who held it back . . . And then He sent the rain, the rain which crashed down like a waterfall, washing away the smell of his fear. His shoulder burned, but he had no other wounds. It all seemed so absurd to him. Before him lay the other bodies, pelted by the rain and bleeding, heads smashed in by that last bullet. The two little girls looked like rag dolls fished out of the sea. It was a scene so chilling, it didn't seem real. Benigno stood up but had trouble remaining on his feet. He wished he could bury those bodies, but he had no tools and couldn't move his injured shoulder without feeling great pain. He made the sign of the cross in the air, as he'd always seen the village priest do, then said 'Amen' three or four times and staggered away from that hell. He took meagre refuge under a large tree and uncovered the wounded shoulder. There were two holes in his flesh. The bullets had passed through him without stopping. The blood kept flowing out, washed away at once by the rainwater. Putting his shirt back on, he went towards a more densely wooded area. He didn't even know where he was. A few hours later he reached a secluded farmstead surrounded by abandoned fields, and collapsed on the ground. Some peasants attended to his wounds and let him stay in the stall for a fortnight or so, then gave him some bread and pancetta and asked him please to leave. They were afraid of the Nazis and the Black Brigades. They'd heard tell of some terrible things, they said, wide eyed. Benigno understood, thanked them and went on his way.

Up in the hills, deserters had formed armed bands and were roaming the countryside like him, in search of food. Benigno spent a few months with one such group, sharing what little food they could get from the local peasants. They numbered nineteen, and the oldest among them was under twenty-five. During the winter they hid out in an abandoned stable. It snowed a great deal, and they suffered in the cold but felt protected. For several months they ate only chestnuts and the few wild animals they'd managed to catch with rudimentary traps.

In late March they set out again. When passing through one mountain village they learned that in the Langhe, some partisan armies had formed to fight the Fascists. Nearly all of his group decided to join them, Benigno included. He hadn't quite understood what he was going to do, but it seemed like the right thing. And so the volunteers marched off, walking from sunset to sunrise and hiding wherever they could during the day. One evening, as night was falling, they were set upon by some trigger-happy Black Brigades along the banks of a stream. Three or four of Benigno's comrades fell into the water at once, while the others scattered in every direction through the woods. Benigno himself ran for at least half an hour without looking back. When he finally stopped, he was alone again. His face was scratched and bloodied by the branches he'd run through, but he was still alive, again. He even managed to survive the great round-up of November '44, hiding in an old tomb in a mountain cemetery. When the weather began to improve, he joined a band of partisan fighters as a cook and stayed with them until April of '45. Then in May he set sail at last for Sardinia.

For many years he continued to have nightmares about the day of the firing squad. He would see the round hole of the pistol's barrel again, the indifferent eyes staring at him, and instead of clicking, the gun would fire . . .

'When he used to sleep here with us I would hear him cry out in the night,' said Pina, her wrinkled face lit up red by the flames. Piras looked asleep, but he'd listened carefully to the whole story and was turning something over in his head.

'I didn't know that story,' said Gavino.

'I know it by heart,' Giovanni said, sleepy eyed.

'Poor Benigno,' Maria whispered.

'He always said that every new day was a gift for him . . . but then . . .' Pina said, trying to smile. Someone filled the glasses again. Giovanni relit his Tuscan cigar, tossed the match into the fire, and all at once started telling the story of a horrible vendetta that had taken place some twenty years earlier at Bauladu. Piras was unable to listen, however. He kept thinking of Benigno pretending to be dead, and tried to imagine himself in his place . . . He saw the Fascist commander approach, saw his eyes, saw the gun barrel and heard it go . . . click . . . click . . . click . . . click . . .

Rosa finished rolling the 'cigarette', licking the paper to seal it. She lit it, took two drags and passed it to Bordelli. It was already their second, but that evening neither of them felt like laughing. The Endrigo record ended, and the gramophone's arm returned to its cradle. Rosa was having one of her rare evenings of melancholy. She'd spent Christmas Eve with her girlfriends. She'd got too drunk and vomited. But it had been a pleasant evening, as was only fitting for the baby Jesus's birthday. At midnight they'd all sat in silence, listening to the church bells ringing, and then they'd put on some music and started dancing . . .

Now, however, she felt a little depressed. This often happened after a good party. As she watched the blinking lights on the Christmas tree and smoked that stuff, some memories came back to her, and she started telling stories, almost as if talking to herself. Having apparently understood the general mood, Gideon jumped into Rosa's lap and started sucking her woollen sweater as if it were his mother's teats. Bordelli lay on the sofa with eyes closed, listening . . . In his mind Rosa's words turned into images as sharp as a movie's . . .

Rosa was born in the countryside near Florence, in a small outlying ward of Tavarnelle. When she was six or seven she used to play with other peasant children who lived in the area.

There were five of them, two girls and three boys. They used to spend every afternoon together, year round, happily excluded from the compulsory education of the Fascist government. They had boundless territory to explore and sometimes didn't come home until after dark.

Other times they would stop in front of Andrea's house, which stood on an embankment supported by a dry retaining wall and looked out over the surrounding countryside. The vineyard descended in terraces down to a drainage trench they called 'the fallen waters'. Opposite them rose a big hill entirely covered with a dense, dark pine forest; and here and there the pointed black tips of cypresses stuck out above the boughs of needles. Everyone called the hill the Witches' Mount. One afternoon Andrea told them that there was a creature called the Monster of the Three Goats, half man, half beast, who roamed the pine wood at night and killed everyone he came across. Nobody believed him. It was a tale a little too tall to swallow. But Andrea swore it was all true, crossing his fingers over his lips and kissing them to prove it. And all at once they saw an old woman, thin as a rail, walking along the grassy path below the embankment. She was wearing a black scarf over her head, her bright white hair sticking out everywhere and reflecting almost blue in the light. She was coming towards them.

'She's a witch,' said Rosa, biting her lips.

'Hush! She'll hear you.'

The old woman continued walking, head down, as if she hadn't seen anyone. When she was directly below the embankment, she looked up and said: 'Ciao, Andrea, don't be such a stranger.' And she kept on going. Everybody turned and looked at Andrea, but he bit his lips and said he'd never seen her before in his life. They all called him a liar, saying he was just playing games, then they all got up and went down below to follow the old woman. They ran down the path and, rounding the bend, came to a halt. The woman was nowhere to be seen. They looked around. The spot where they stood afforded an open view of the entire valley and some hundred yards down the path . . . But there was no sign of the crone anywhere. And yet only a few seconds had passed. Splitting up into two groups, they started running in different directions. Three of them descended the slope, jumping from terrace to terrace, while the other two continued down the path. They ran hard, hoping to catch the old woman up and prove to themselves that what they were thinking was wrong. But the crone had vanished. When they regrouped, they all started walking home in silence, repeatedly looking back. They decided to find out who that old woman was. The following day they asked around whether anyone knew an old woman with white hair, as thin as a bean-pole, but nobody knew anything. In the end they resigned themselves to the fact that their fears were right . . . The old crone was a witch.

'If I close my eyes I can still see her,' Rosa said, leaning her head back on the sofa. The cat had stopped sucking her sweater and was asleep without a worry in his head . . .

'I agree that she was a witch,' Bordelli said without opening his eyes.

'I feel a little sad . . .' said Rosa.

'Why?'

'I don't know . . . I wish I could become a little girl again and start all over.'

'And what would you do?'

'Something else,' she said, stroking Gideon's belly. They sat in silence. All they could hear was the purring cat, who lay on his back on Rosa's legs.

'Are you asleep?' she asked softly. Bordelli didn't answer. He was drifting off, making no effort to prevent it. A few minutes later he was snoring.

26 December

Piras woke up very early. He ate a slice of bread with fig jam, drank a cup of coffee, stuffed a few *papassinos* into his pockets, went outside and started walking. The sky was clear, and although the sun hadn't yet risen, he could see rather well. He took the road to Seneghe and got busy with his crutches. A light fog hung over the woods. He breathed deeply, enjoying the feeling of the cold air in his lungs. He felt so restless he was jumping out of his skin. At last he had in hand a plausible explanation for what had happened to Benigno, and he wanted to try to sort it all out.

Pintus might well have been one of those Fascists in Asti, maybe even the commander. Two women, an old man, three small children and a deserter, slaughtered like dogs so as not to leave any living witnesses to the pillaging of the villa. Who knew how many other similar outrages had taken place. But unlike the other victims, Benigno had survived, and twenty years later he'd recognised one of his killers by accident when negotiating the sale of a plot of land. It made perfect sense. But perhaps it was better to try to reconstruct each stage carefully, to see whether the story held together.

The sun was rising over the horizon, dispersing the last few wisps of fog. Hopping along on his crutches, Piras began to see the first houses of Seneghe in the distance. He'd already gone two miles without realising it, head full of speculations about Benigno's death. He kept imagining the whole story from beginning to end on the basis of his hypotheses, then, upon reaching the end, he would start over again from the beginning, making new observations and adding new details.

So, Benigno sees Pintus and recognises him. He has no doubt about it: Pintus is one of the Fascists from Asti . . . And so he drops everything and walks out. Pintus realises he's been discovered, quits Musillo's office at once and starts tailing Benigno, already thinking about what he must do. It's dark outside by now, and without being seen, he follows him all the way home. Waiting for the right moment, he hides his car or Rumi motorcycle in the dark driveway or at a spot not visible from the road, then goes into Benigno's house and kills him with a shot to the temple . . . But in that case he must already have on him an unregistered, and therefore illegal, pistol, which would be careless in those times of heavy police presence on the island. No, if Pintus really was one of those Fascists, he couldn't take such a risk. So it must have gone like this: Pintus follows Benigno home, then tampers with the Ape to prevent him leaving. From the various talks he's had with the lawyer over the past few weeks, he's learned that Benigno lives alone in a house with no telephone. Thus Pintus has all the time he needs to go home and fetch the right gun. Then he returns, enters Benigno's house and kills him with a shot to the temple. He uses an old pistol from the last war, the kind of weapon anyone might have in his house. Pintus knows that such a pistol wouldn't draw much attention from the *carabinieri*, not even at such a time of runaway banditry on the island. After the war many soldiers brought their standard-issue firearms home with them and ignored the 1945 orders to turn them in. There were still thousands of pistols stashed away in cellars and attics, and nobody in the country-side bothered to report them. After killing Benigno, then, Pintus puts the gun in his hand, raises it up to the temple, then lets it fall back down. And so we have the suicide of a shepherd and former half-partisan who wanted to sell a plot of land fit for building . . .

It was all conjecture, but it had its own logic, thought Piras. For the moment he couldn't think of any other possible scenarios, and so he tried to work with this one. But where was the empty shell? It really seemed like one of those movie plots where a murder remains covered up for decades, suspended in a limbo that human judgement cannot penetrate, and then at a certain point everything comes to the surface, destroying in an instant the entire edifice of falsehoods that had seemed as if it would stand for ever.

Piras pressed effortlessly forward on his crutches, continually turning his hypotheses over in his head. If it really had happened the way he imagined, Pintus could be an assumed name . . . Even though all the man's papers appeared to be in order. But his past went back no farther than 1945, when he moved to Oristano. Whatever Pintus had been before that date had disappeared in the flames that consumed the Records Office of Custoza Sommacampagna in the Veneto . . . Unless, of course, the engineer had purposely stated that he came from that municipality precisely because he knew that their archives no longer existed. Maybe it was even Pintus himself who had set fire to the town hall . . .

Slow down, Nino, you're going too fast, he said to himself. When he reached the church of Seneghe, he did an about-face and started to head back home. He picked up his pace, panting heavily and sweating lightly under his clothes. His legs seemed to have an energy they didn't have even the day before, and so he tried to lean less heavily on the crutches. He realised his legs could manage almost entirely on their own, without help and almost without pain, and at once he felt his face heat up.

'Damn,' he muttered. Without stopping, he tossed one crutch in the air ahead of him and watched it skid down the road. He'd been imagining this scene for a long time. Then he bent down to pick it up. He realised he ought not to push things too far just yet, and he put it under his arm again. But he also felt that he would very soon be able to manage without those wooden sticks. He was almost as excited as his first night in bed with Sonia. For the first time in all these difficult months since the shooting, he felt the strength returning to his legs.

He chewed up the road as if it were nothing, as heated up as a child playing football.

Remembering the biscuits he had in his pocket, he stopped to eat them, sitting on a cement kerbstone. Pina's *papassinos* were the best in town, though his mother's were a close second.

By the time he returned home, it was past nine. His parents had already gone outside a while before. He picked up the phone to call Sonia in Palermo, then realised she might still be sleeping and decided against it. Imagining her lying in bed, her blonde hair enveloping her face, he smiled. He went and sat in front of the fire. He tried to read but was unable to follow the words. Putting the book down, he closed his eyes. Once again he reviewed in his mind the story of Benigno's murder from start to finish, trying to reconstruct the narrative in all its tiniest details. He had only two solid facts on which to base his conjectures. Benigno's reaction upon seeing Pintus, and the shell that had vanished. Everything else he had added himself. They might of course be nothing more than the fantasies of a convalescing policeman, but if he tied them all together they seemed to form a logical whole, like those puzzles in the *Settimana Enigmistica* where by connecting the numbered dots one obtained a coherent image.

At ten o'clock he went into the entrance hall and phoned Pintus. He told him he'd got a first reply from Benigno Staffa's heir and wanted to make an appointment.

Pintus was icier than usual. His tone of voice seemed to indicate that he was less convinced by the whole deal than before. 'If the heir hasn't accepted my offer, there's no point in you coming all this way to see me,' he said.

'Actually I'd rather not discuss this over the phone, Mr Pintus. And since I have to go to Oristano tomorrow anyway, I thought I might as well drop in on you for a few minutes,' said Piras.

'I can only see you at half past one. Is that all right?'
'Perfect.'

'But I can tell you right now that I won't have much time for you, Mr Piras.'

'I'll just take a few minutes of your time, sir, don't worry.'

'And please be punctual,' said Pintus, hanging up.

Piras stood there staring at the picture of Santa Bonacatu on the wall without actually seeing it. He still had no idea what he would say to Pintus. He had to find a way to make him talk about the war without arousing his suspicion. If the engineer really was one of the Fascists from Asti and really did kill Benigno . . . well, it was best not to let him know that he was investigating him. The whole affair could take a dangerous turn. But Piras felt he had no choice. If Pintus really had buried his past by changing his name, then the only way to unmask him was . . . was what?

The inspector picked up his matches, but then the telephone rang. It was the commissioner.

'Could you come up to my office for a minute, please?'

'I'll be right there.'

Bordelli dropped the unlit cigarette on to his desk and stood up with a sigh. He had a lot of things on his mind, and the last thing he felt like doing was talking to Inzipone. After falling asleep on Rosa's couch, he'd woken up around nine, relaxed and with a pleasant taste in his mouth. He had to admit that those hand-rolled 'cigarettes' were better than the state-issued variety. Rosa, however, still hadn't given him his Christmas present, and he was very curious to know what it was. He sauntered lazily upstairs, knocked on the commissioner's door and went in without waiting.

'Hello, Bordelli, have a nice Christmas?' asked Inzipone, looking as if he'd gained a little weight.

'Fine, and yourself?'

'Fine, thanks.'

'I didn't expect to see you here on St Stephen's,' Bordelli said, half smiling.

'I came in just to talk to you, actually . . . But tell me first, how's Baragli doing?' asked Inzipone.

'His time's almost up.'

'How sad . . .' he said.

'What did you want to tell me?' Bordelli asked, hoping to get things over with quickly.

'Well, I was wondering if there were any new developments in the case of that fellow's murder . . . what was his name?'

'Badalamenti.'

'Ah yes, Badalamenti.'

'Nothing serious yet,' said Bordelli.

The commissioner shook his head. 'Actually I wanted to see you about something else, Inspector. We've been having some trouble round Santo Spirito, and I was wondering . . .'

'Another round-up?' Bordelli asked.

The commissioner held up a hand to prevent any misunderstanding. 'No round-ups. It's just that . . . for the past few weeks, there's been a man going around beating people up in that neighbourhood.'

'Yes, I've heard mention of it myself.'

'So . . . why don't you go there and have a look around?'

'What exactly do you want me to do?' asked Bordelli.

'Just find out who this person is, and make him stop, obviously.'

'Could I ask you two questions, sir?'

'Go right ahead.'

'Why are you asking *me* to do this? And why are you so interested in something so silly?' the inspector asked.

Inzipone threw his hands up and forced a smile.

'I'm asking you because you know the neighbourhood well, that's all . . . And on the thirtieth President Saragat will be coming here. You knew that, didn't you? An official visit, but apparently he wants to tour the historic districts, the old quarters, and I really shouldn't want anything untoward to happen . . . You know what I mean? It would be quite unfortunate. The newspapers always make a big deal of these things and never miss a chance to embarrass us . . . You know this yourself.'

Bordelli put a cigarette between his lips.

'Message received,' he said.

'I'll look forward to hearing from you soon, Bordelli.'

'I'll go tomorrow,' said the inspector.

Inzipone patted his head several times with the palm of his hand, a tic that appeared whenever he grew nervous.

'I mean it, Bordelli. How do you think we'll look if something unpleasant happens right in front of the president? We're here to maintain order, aren't we? Then we should prove it.'

'I'll let you know as soon as I can,' the inspector said, heading for the door. His hand was already on the doorknob when the commissioner stood up.

'Ah, Bordelli, I almost forgot . . . I want you to have De Bono brought in before Thursday . . . You never know.'

'All right.'

Bordelli said goodbye with a wave of the hand and went out.

De Bono was an elderly anarchist with no teeth. A sorry sight. Fate had it that he was also called Emilio, like the Fascist bigwig and general.[39] Until a few years ago, whenever some high state functionary came to town, De Bono would be in the front row, waiting with a bag of rotten eggs in his hand. It was said that he always kept a great many eggs at home and would let them rot for just such occasions. Wending his way through the crowds, he would get as close as possible to his target, scream 'Long live anarchy!' and hurl his projectiles. He seldom missed. The few weeks he would spend in jail as a result served no purpose. In the end the police decided to not to arrest him any more for what he did, but for what he might do. They would go and get him at home the day before the dignitary in question was to arrive and then release him the day after the event. He would be held as a guest of the Murate prison, in a room with a cooker and a television set.

They termed the procedure a 'preventive measure'. De Bono made a scene every time, kicking and screaming and threatening to have the Union of Fighting Anarchists, of which he was the supreme leader, declare war on the state. The policemen only laughed at him.

'Oooh, we're so afraid!' they would say.

'Well, if you're not afraid, then why are you arresting me? Eh? Why the fuck are you arresting me, you bastards!'

Still laughing, the policemen would grab his arms and lift him off the ground. 'Calm down, De Bono, and let us do our job. We don't want any trouble.'

And he would start screaming that the rotten eggs were just the beginning, and that the attack on the Master State was imminent, the Power of Capital would soon be overthrown by Anarchist Fury and so on, all the way to his cell.

Walking down the corridor, Bordelli ran into a couple of colleagues and nodded in greeting. Everyone seemed to have gained weight, but it might just have been his impression. A door flew open, and out came Rabozzi. He was always in a hurry and carried as many weapons as a soldier on patrol. It was anybody's guess why an animal like Rabozzi had joined the police force. It surely wasn't only so he could drive a souped-up Maserati.

'Ciao, Bordelli, we're going on a raid,' he said, walking fast towards the exit. Two or three squad cars could already be heard revving their engines outside.

'During the Christmas holiday?' Bordelli asked.

'That's the best time!'

'Break a leg.'

'Thanks!' yelled Rabozzi, already at the end of the corridor.

Mugnai poked his head in, wearing a face like a boiled fish. He muttered something imcomprehensible to Bordelli.

'Come inside, I can't hear you,' he said.

Mugnai closed the door behind him and came towards the desk.

'There's a young lady here to see you, sir,' he said, raising his eyebrows.

'Why are you making that face?'

'Well, sir . . . she's a right pretty thing . . .'

'Does that worry you?' asked Bordelli, figuring it was Marisa.

'No, not at all, sir . . . But it's not every day you see a girl like that,' said Mugnai.

'Show her in,' Bordelli said, ending the discussion

'Straight away, sir.'

Mugnai went to open the door and told the girl she could come in. Marisa entered wearing a serious expression. She seemed a little intimidated. She was wearing a smart red over-coat cinched in at the waist.

'Good morning, Inspector,' she said.

'Good morning . . . You can go now, Mugnai,' said Bordelli, seeing that the officer was still standing in the doorway, watery eyes sizing up the girl. Mugnai vanished, closing the door behind him.

'Please sit down,' said Bordelli.

'I'll only stay a minute.'

'Then please sit down for a minute.'

Marisa eased herself into the chair, pulling her coat more tightly around her. Looking into her sullen face and dark, luminous eyes, Bordelli felt a sort of thrill and tried to appear nonchalant. It was hopeless; the girl reminded him of Milena . . . And, like her, she had something special about her. Sooner or later she would prob-ably use her beauty to make some money, which would likely spoil everything. Badalamenti was merely the first wolf she'd encountered along her path, perhaps not even the worst.

'I just wanted to tell you . . . that . . .'

'That what?' Bordelli asked, sitting up in his chair. Marisa seemed about to reveal something important.

'My brother didn't kill anyone,' she said.

'You've already told me that several times.'

'But you don't believe me.'

'I believe that you're convinced of what you say.'

'But you don't believe it's true . . .' she said. Every so often she forced a little smile, but it never lasted.

'If the police went only on what people told them, there would be a lot of innocent people in jail,' Bordelli said.

'But my brother . . . Don't pay any attention to his playacting. He likes to act tough, but he's very gentle.'

'You've already told me that, too, and I haven't forgotten it.'

Bordelli was beginning to think that the girl had not come to tell him these things, but for some other reason. But he couldn't imagine what. Or perhaps he was wrong, and she was just a naïve girl who wanted to defend her brother.

'He went only once . . . to see that guy,' Marisa continued.

'Does your brother know you're here?'

'No. He would only get angry if he did.'

Bordelli sighed and stood up, circled the desk, the girl's eyes following him. He stopped right in front of her.

'Signorina Marisa, forgive me for asking, but did you really come here to say these things to me?' he asked, trying to be gentle.

Marisa also stood up. 'I live right near by,' she said defensively, blushing.

'That's not what I meant.'

'I came to tell you my brother had nothing to do with this case,' she said, looking away.

'Do you know who did it?'

'Of course not,' said Marisa. Then her face suddenly changed, and her eyes lit up. She took a deep breath and folded her arms over her chest. Her gaze darted about the room and finally came to rest on the window.

'I don't know why I came,' she said in the tone of someone who was thinking the opposite of what she was saying. Then she turned back to the inspector and stared at him as if trying to frighten him . . . except that she was blushing and had a deep furrow in her brow. She continued to look at Bordelli without saying anything, breathing slowly as if trying to pluck up courage.

'Go back home and don't worry about anything,' the inspector said, knowing he'd said the most banal thing in the world. Meanwhile he was thinking that it wouldn't be so bad if the girl stayed a few minutes longer, either.

'I always feel so worried about everything,' she said, squeezing her arms more tightly round her breasts.

'I'm sorry,' said Bordelli. Ah, what a fine statement, truly original. But then why should he be original? He certainly wasn't there to impress a woman. There weren't any women in the room.

'I lied to you,' said Marisa, taut as a slingshot's band.

'About Raffaele?' asked Bordelli, feeling his mouth go dry. 'No.'

'About what, then?'

'I know why I came here,' she said, dropping her arms to her sides. The second that followed was one of the longest in Bordelli's life. His soul split in two. One half said: come on, old fool, give her a pat on the bottom and send her home to play with her dolls. The other half saw a fully fledged woman before him . . .

'I think you'd better go home,' said a third voice coming out of Bordelli's mouth.

'Don't you want to know why?' asked Marisa, looking like someone about to say something irreparable.

'No, I don't want to know,' said Bordelli. He went to the door and opened it.

'Are you throwing me out?' asked Marisa, more and more self-assured. The inspector's nervousness gave her courage.

'I didn't mean it that way,' he said.

'Then say what you meant.'

'I invite you please to leave,' said Bordelli, not moving from the open doorway. Marisa stared at him for a few more seconds, then left the room without turning round. Bordelli stood there listening to her heels clicking nervously down the corridor, then closed the door and sat back down. The office was as hot as hell itself, and he was sweating. He lit a cigarette and took a deep drag. Had it all been in his mind, or had he seen things clearly? He didn't want to know. But his pride was bleeding with satisfaction. He couldn't help it. He was about to go into the bathroom and look at himself in the mirror, but he immediately felt ridiculous and remained seated. Poor old fool. Maybe he wouldn't let her speak because he was afraid she might say something contrary to what he feared . . . Oh, a fine line of reasoning, that! Who knew what Fabiani might make of it! Still sweating, he unbuttoned his shirt. He would never know what Marisa was about to say. But he hoped he never saw her again.

The sky was a clean, deep blue. Still recovering from his boxing match with the goddess of beauty, Bordelli, wanting to go for a walk, went out of the station with a single cigarette in his pocket. Leaving the packet in the office was one of his latest brilliant ideas. The air was cold but tolerable.

Crossing Viale Lavagnini, he slipped into the Trattoria da Cesare, which didn't close for Boxing Day. The dining room was full with a wedding party. Bordelli greeted Cesare and the waiters and went into Totò's kitchen.

'You're just the man I was waiting for, Inspector,' said the cook, filling a glass. 'Have a taste of this wine.'

'It's got a nice colour.'

'Some relatives also brought me peppers . . . the real thing . . . would you like some?'

'Sure, why not?'

Bordelli took a sip of wine. It had an odd flavour but wasn't bad at all. Totò returned to the hob to move a couple of frying pans and stir the pasta. Then he lightly toasted two slices of bread, put them on a platter, poured a little bit of olive oil on them and solemnly laid a long green pepper on each.

'Now keep that wine within reach, Inspector. This stuff's worse than fire for you Northerners . . . Whereas back home even the babies eat it, and it does them a world of good.'

Bordelli took a first bite and a sort of fiery blaze immediately enveloped his tongue. He was about to spit it all out but then thought that if, in the south, even babies ate the stuff, he certainly didn't want to seem like a sissy, and so he kept on chewing. Totò fidgeted before him, awaiting a comment. After a sip of wine, Bordelli was finally able to speak.

'It's good, but I'll have to get used to it,' he babbled hoarsely.

Totò laughed heartily. 'Wha'd I say? You Northerners have weak mouths.'

The inspector took another bite of the toast. He wanted to get through the ordeal so that Totò wouldn't have the last word, and to test his own courage. Little by little, however, he started to enjoy it, as a pleasant aroma filled his nasal passages. Even the wine seemed to taste better, and he poured himself another glass.

'So, Inspector, have you found the good man who put the shark on ice?'

'Not yet, Totò.'

'If you ask me, you'll never find him . . .'

'Is that a prophecy or a wish?'

'Both, Inspector, both,' Totò said seriously.

Bordelli wanted to enjoy his lunch without any talk of loan sharks and tried to change the subject.

'So, Totò, what do you make of the Christian Democrats' latest opening to the left?' he asked.

'And what do you make of the Communist Party's opening to the right?'

'Interesting question,' said Bordelli.

And thus, chatting of this and that, he finished his wild boar and drank half a bottle of wine. When the coffee arrived, he lit the cigarette he'd brought with him in his pocket. It was all wrinkled and crooked, but it was all he had. He straightened it out and lit it.

They drank their coffees, talking about Fanfani and Nenni, Moro and Berlinguer, and even poor Togliatti, who had died far from home. Then they moved on to grappa and Mussolini, the war, and the Americans in Sicily. Totò said that in his home town the mural painting of Il Duce's face was still on the wall of the town hall. Nobody had ever removed it, and the old folks still said: 'Now there was a man!' An old uncle of his who had once shaken Mussolini's hand still kissed his palm from time to time. 'These fingers once touched il Duce,' he would say with tears in his eyes.

'The doctors keep telling me I'm going to get better, but they never look me in the eye when they say it. They treat me like a child . . .'

'Forget about the doctors, Oreste, and concentrate on the nurses.'

'I try, Inspector, but they always get away.' Baragli smiled, slowly tracing the gesture of trying to catch something in his hand. His fingers were skeletal and his fingernails black. The only time Bordelli had ever seen hands like that was during the war, but they belonged to corpses.

'A game of cards, Oreste?' Bordelli asked.

'I feel too tired, Inspector.'

'Do you need anything? Are you thirsty?'

'No, thanks. What can you tell me about that murder case? Any new developments?'

'Yes . . .'

'What?' Oreste asked impatiently.

'That boy who lives in the country, Odoardo . . . he's left-handed.'

'I knew it,' said Baragli, thrilled. He tried to pull himself up in bed but couldn't manage. The inspector helped him sit up, then adjusted the pillow behind his back.

'Is that better?'

'Thanks, Inspector . . . Are you really sure he's left-handed?'

'I came up with an excuse to make him use some scissors, and he held them in his left hand.'

'Still feel like a game of *briscola*?' asked Baragli, livening up. Bordelli took the cards from the drawer and they started playing. The sergeant was very weak and moved very slowly, but also seemed distracted by some worry. He took for ever to throw down his first card.

'What's wrong, Oreste?'

'I'm still thinking about that boy, Inspector.'

'You've caught the bug from me.'

'But I know it's not right to administer justice all by oneself . . .'

'I know what you mean, Oreste.'

They looked each other in the eye for a moment, but said nothing.

'Sometimes it's hard to judge,' the sergeant said.

'I think about it often myself.'

'That boy . . . I don't like the thought of him going to jail,' Baragli said.

'Have you already found him guilty?' Bordelli asked.

'You're right, I'm going too fast . . . Or maybe those who are about to die see things that others don't see,' said Baragli, half smiling. He threw down a card.

'Oreste! That's downright cruel of you.'

'Your turn, Inspector. I get the feeling I'm going to win this round.'

After supper Piras went out and headed for Ettore's house. He wanted to tell him and Angelo that *City Lights* was playing on the telly that evening. He knew the two had never seen it before. But he also wanted to ask Ettore again for the keys to the Fiat, hoping he wouldn't make a fuss.

He knocked on the Cannas' front door, and Vanda, Ettore's mother, opened up. She was as skinny as a rake and, without knowing, moved with a certain elegance.

'Come in, Nino, there's a war going on here,' she said. From one of the back rooms came the sound of Delia, Ettore's little sister, crying.

'She doesn't want to have her injection,' Vanda said with irritation.

'I know how she feels,' said Piras, and he followed the woman into Delia's room. They were all there. Dr Virdis was there too, with a syringe in his hand and a patient look on his face. Piras exchanged greetings with all present. The little girl was crying and hiding under the covers. She wouldn't hear of having her bottom poked with a needle. She was screaming that she would die if they touched her. She was lying, of course, but beautiful. Barely five years old, her little face promised good things to come. Her father Michele was trying to persuade her that if she would let them do that one little thing, which lasted only a second, he would give her a beautiful gift. He drew near to the bed, but Delia curled up and fled under the covers again.

'It hurts! It hurts!' she screamed through her tears. Michele threw up his hands and looked at Dr Virdis.

'Michele, the doctor hasn't got all night,' Vanda said to her husband. Michele ran a hand through his hair. He seemed the most upset of them all. A hale and hearty man like him, powerless against a little girl's will. He was in love with his daughter, and she knew it and took advantage of it.

'When something must be done, it must be done,' Vanda said severely.

Ettore looked on in amusement. It really wasn't such a big deal. Dr Virdis sighed and put the cap back on the syringe.

'But is it really so necessary?' Michele asked. He couldn't stand to hear his little girl whimpering any longer. He looked around at everyone in search of support, but nobody took his side. He went up to the child.

'Delia, look at Daddy. I'm going to get an injection now, too, and you'll see, it won't hurt at all.'

'No, I don't want it! The last time it hurt!' she carried on.

Michele turned towards the doctor. 'Isn't there another solution? Something she could swallow?' he said. Virdis sighed and shook his head. Michele turned to the child again.

'I promise that if you let him give you the injection, I'll buy you a present this big . . . I'll buy you a bicycle!'

The little girl stopped crying for a moment, as if considering the offer, then curled back up into a ball.

'It hurts! I don't want it!' she said.

'But you'd like a bicycle, wouldn't you?' Michele said wearily.

Then Dr Virdis took Michele by the arm and led him out of the room.

'Stay here and don't move. Everyone else, too. Out of the room,' he said.

Delia poked her head out from under the covers and watched the whole scene without saying anything. They all left the room and Virdis shut the door and turned the key.

'What the hell is he doing?' Michele asked, round eyed.

'Let him do as he sees fit,' his wife said, grabbing his elbow. The girl had stopped crying. No sound at all came from the room. Michele put his ear to the door.

'You can't hear a thing,' he whispered. He listened for a few more seconds, then started rattling the door handle.

'Doctor, please open the door,' he said. First calmly, then with increasing irritation. Virdis didn't answer, and Delia wasn't crying. Michele looked at the others one by one with a worried expression on his face. He jiggled the door handle again several times, then slammed his hand against the door.

'You're not a doctor, you're a butcher!' he yelled.

'Don't say that!' said Vanda, pulling his hair.

'Ow!' Michele cried. And at that moment the door opened. Delia was lying on top of the covers, looking serene. Virdis already had his medical bag in his hand.

'The butcher is done,' he said with a cold smile, walking between them and towards the door, followed by Vanda, who begged his pardon and said her husband was an animal. Michele went over to the girl and asked her whether it had hurt. Ettore waited to hear the front door close, then burst out laughing.

'What's so funny?' his mother asked, coming towards him.

'Nothing,' said Ettore. Vanda walked past him and into her daughter's room.

'Tonight they're showing *City Lights* on the telly . . . It's probably already started,' said Piras, looking at his watch.

'I'm going over to Nino's to see the movie,' Ettore said, heading down the hallway.

'Goodbye. Ciao, Delia,' said Piras, poking his head into the girl's room. Delia looked at him without saying anything.

'Shall I bring a bottle?' Ettore asked as they headed for the door.

'No, there's no need,' said Piras.

Out on the street, they went to get Angelo, who lived right next door. When they all got to Piras's house, the film had already started.

'Shhh,' said Maria.

The boys found themselves some chairs and sat down, trying not to make noise. The Setzus were also there, as well as a neighbour's young son. There was a ritual silence around the television set. All the lights were off, and the glow of the picture tube reflected off their faces. Every so often someone got up to refill his glass. The Christmas log of olive wood was still burning slowly in the fireplace, lightly smoking and filling the air with a pleasant scent.

When the film ended, the Setzus and the little boy went home, and Gavino got up and changed to Channel 2 to see what else was on.

'I'm going over to Angelo's house,' said Pietrino, and the three lads all got up and went out on to the street. It was cold and the sky was full of stars.

'Get a whiff of that air . . .' said Angelo. 'In Campidano they can only dream of such air.' He never missed an opportunity to point out the difference between life on the plain and life in the hills. He was like everyone else in town, convinced that everything was better in Bonarcado than down there: the wine, the honey, the land, the cheese, the women, the water, the bread . . . Even the eggs were better when laid by the chickens of Bonarcado. Not to mention that during the hot months the plain was blanketed with mosquitoes. Ettore agreed with Angelo, saying that, though he was forced to work down there, he would never choose to live there. Piras ribbed them about it, saying they talked like a couple of old codgers, but deep down he actually agreed with them.

'Ettore . . . I have to ask you to lend me the Five hundred again,' he said, vapour rising from his mouth.

'What the fuck!' said Ettore.

'It's important.'

'Can't you call Bernardo's taxi service?'

'Do you know much that would cost? Come on, don't be a jerk.'

'You're going to bring it back all dented.'

'Hey, speak for yourself. *I* know how to drive . . .' said Piras.

'What, you saying I don't?'

'Hell, Tore . . . I wouldn't be asking if it wasn't important.' Ettore give an irritated smile.

'Well, this time you have to put in some petrol for me,' he said.

'What a skinflint,' Angelo commented, chuckling.

'I'll even top it up . . .' said Piras. 'Gimme the keys.'

Ettore pulled out the keys, let them dangle from one finger for a few seconds, then put them in Nino's pocket.

'When'll you bring it back?'

'As soon as I'm done,' said Piras.

'You're not really going to fill it up for him, are you?' asked Angelo.

One night in '43, Bordelli and four of his comrades were forced to take refuge in an abandoned barn near the German lines. They entered through an unhinged door, just before sunset, and found a surprise inside. A living calf. They looked at it in silence, as if they had a Greek goddess before them. They were all hungry, famished in fact, and had seen no meat for months. There was a problem, however. They couldn't shoot the calf because the Nazis were rather close by and might start firing mortar their way. But neither did they want to wait to bring the animal back to camp with them the following morning. They had to kill it right then and there without making any noise, perhaps with a knife. But nobody could make up his mind. The sun had set completely, and they could hardly see any longer inside the stall. Luckily the only window gave on to the side facing the Allied lines, so they could use their torches without fear.

'But if we slit his throat, Captain, he might start lowing like the devil,' said Tonino, who knew about these things.

'And the bombs'll start raining down on us,' Moroni added.

Bordelli thought it over for a minute, then pulled out his *iron fist*, a tool he had created for himself from the propellor of a downed English aeroplane. It must have been made of aluminium or something similar. Light and durable. He'd worked on it during his free moments, during the long waits when nothing was happening. It had holes for the fingers and spikes over the knuckles. It was a deadly weapon. He had used it only once, on a Nazi's face, and the result was not a pretty sight. When he slipped it over his hands, the others started ribbing him.

'Hey, it's Dick Fulmine!'[40]

'What are you going to do, Captain?'

'You'll just comb his hair and he'll get pissed off . . .'

'Get out of the way,' said Bordelli.

By this point it had become a dare between him and the others. He took careful aim, cocked his arm, and struck the animal forcefully between the eyes. The animal collapsed at once, without so much as a cry, as if all four of its legs had been cut from under it.

'Holy shit!' said Gennaro.

'Thanks for the encouragement, guys,' said Bordelli, putting away his artificial 'fist'. His comrades slapped him repeatedly on the back and immediately got to work with their knives. The blood poured out in buckets, flooding the brick floor and sticking under their shoes. They cut little strips of meat and roasted them directly over the flame of a portable gas burner. It was as tough as leather and smelled burnt, but they ate it with gusto, tearing it with their teeth. Then they finished cutting the calf up into bits, and the following morning brought the rest of the meat into camp, carrying it in a number of firewood baskets they'd found in the barn. The poor animal hadn't had much luck, but they thanked it with all their hearts. They filled themselves with meat for two or three days, to the point of nausea. Their only regret was that they couldn't keep eating it for the rest of the year.

With that story in his head, he was almost asleep, thoughts already blending with dreams . . . when all at once he opened his eyes. What the hell! He sat up and turned on the light. He stared at the wall for nearly a minute, eyes fixed and mouth half open. He'd remembered something: the strands of hair that De Marchi had found in Badalamenti's flat. Shit! He got out of bed, grabbed his cigarettes and went into the kitchen in his underpants. Pouring himself a glass of wine, he sat down at the table. His head was still filled with images of the calf collapsing to the ground, blood running down the draining furrows in the floor. He lit a cigarette and started thinking about that hair . . . Who knew why he hadn't thought of it sooner. He wasn't ageing gracefully. Perhaps it really was time to retire.

27 December

When he turned down Via di Quintole, it wasn't yet midday. A ray of sunlight managed to pierce the clouds and light up the wet hillsides, but was quickly swallowed back up a few seconds later. Along the roadside a few narrow strips of snow still remained. If Odoardo wasn't at home, he would wait for him. There was no danger the inspector might feel bored in so beautiful a place. Other dense, black clouds loomed in the western sky.

He got to Le Rose and turned onto Odoardo's driveway. As he approached the farmstead he saw the Vespa parked under the loggia. Leaving the Beetle on the threshing floor, he got out and knocked on the door.

'Coming!' he heard Odoardo cry out. A moment later the lad came out, coat buttoned up to his neck, and slammed the door brusquely behind him.

'What is it this time?' he asked.

'I need a strand of hair from you,' Bordelli asked bluntly.

'A what?'

'A strand of hair,' Bordelli said again, serious. There was no longer any point in playacting.

'Am I supposed to laugh?' Odoardo asked.

'I don't think so.'

'A strand of hair . . .'

'That's right. One or more.'

Odoardo stared at him as if looking at a two-headed dog. Then he angrily tore out a clump of hair from above his ear and held it in the air, in front of the inspector's face.

'Will that be enough, or do you want my whole scalp?' he asked.

Bordelli opened his wallet, took out a small piece of paper folded in two, and opened it.

'Please put it in here,' he said.

Odoardo dropped the hair on to the paper. The inspector folded it up and put it back in his wallet.

'Thanks,' he said.

'What's it for?' the boy asked with a slight quaver in his voice.

'To help me understand some things I don't yet understand,' Bordelli said, putting the wallet back into his pocket.

'You're always so clear, Inspector. You should be a politician.'

'I'll be back to see you soon, Odoardo, probably for the last time.'

'To bring me a present for Epiphany?' the youth said with a malicious smile. He seemed to have recovered his sangfroid. Bordelli no longer felt like joking.

'Good day,' he said. He shook his hand and went back to his car. While manoeuvring, he noticed Odoardo still standing under the loggia, hands in his pockets and a serious expression on his face. Neither bothered to gesture goodbye. When he reached the end of the lane, Bordelli turned on to the road to Quintole. He dug around in his pockets for the sole cigarette he'd brought with him but was unable to find it. The sky was swelling with clouds, and it didn't look like a passing thing.

Attilia had been by. His office smelled clean, and the floors were still damp. The inspector left the window open and sat down with his raincoat still on. There were two telexes on his desk; one from the Ministry of Education, the other from Verona Central Police. The list from the Order of Engineers had two people who went by the name of Agostino Pintus:

Giovanni Agostino Pintus, born at Cagliari on 6 February 1896, graduated at Milan in October 1921 with a score of 110 cum laude. Residing in Milan, etc., etc.

Agostino Maria Pintus, born at Tresnuraghes on 16 April 1939, graduated at Bologna in May 1964 with a score of 110 cum laude. Residing in Bologna, etc., etc.

The Pintus they were interested in couldn't have been either of these two. One was too old and the other too young. The telex from Verona said:

Pursuant to your request concerning said Agostino Pintus, from research conducted. Archives of parish of Custoza di Sommacampagna, no result. Interrogation of Custoza inhabitants: nobody recalls anyone with surname Pintus. End message.

Grabbing the packet he'd left on the desk, he realised it was empty. He rifled through all the drawers and at last found a crumpled half-cigarette. He carefully straightened it out and lit it. It was his first of the day, and it was already almost half past noon. He was making progress. He inhaled deeply and blew the smoke towards the ceiling. Cold air came in through the window, but he didn't feel like getting up to close it. He took out his wallet, extracted the paper with Odoardo's hair inside and, without opening it, set it down on the desk. He looked for an envelope, found one, made sure it was empty and clean, then slipped the hair inside it and stapled it shut. He picked up the in-house telephone.

'Hello, Mugnai, please send me Tapinassi straight away.'

The cigarette tasted like pencil shavings, and he crushed it in the ashtray. He leaned back in his chair, letting it rock back and forth.

Tapinassi knocked, came in and went straight to the window to close it.

'Don't you feel cold, Inspector?'

'Please take this at once to De Marchi,' Bordelli said, ignoring the question and handing him the envelope.

'All right, sir.'

367

Tapinassi realised it was urgent and left at once. Bordelli rang Mugnai again and asked him please to go and buy some cigarettes for him. While waiting he searched his drawers again for another, but came away disappointed. Mugnai'll be along soon, he thought. He really felt like smoking. Maybe going without cigarettes all morning was too much. One was supposed to do it more gradually.

He phoned De Marchi to tell him Tapinassi was on his way with an envelope containing hair that he should compare with the samples found in Totuccio Badalamenti's flat.

'How long are you going to make me wait?' Bordelli asked.

'I'm right in the middle of some things, Inspector. If I abandon them halfway it'll be a disaster.'

'When do you think you can do it?'

'I'll have a look at it as soon as I can.'

'When you've got the results, forget the typewriter and call me at once.'

'Very well, Inspector,' said De Marchi.

Bordelli hung up and, as Mugnai still hadn't returned, he went out to look for him and ran into him in the hallway. He paid him what he owed and thanked him for the cigarettes. Climbing the stairs, he opened the packet and lit one. By the time he returned to his office he'd already smoked half of it. He had to calm down. De Marchi would have the results of the hair test soon enough. There was no point in letting his thoughts run away with him. Everything would go as it must. He sat down and tried not to think about the case. He cast a glance out the window. The sky was black, and the light looked like sunset. He remembered he had to go to Santo Spirito to look into that rubbish the commissioner was so worried about. What a pain in the arse. It was the last thing he felt like doing.

Half an hour later, a telex just received from Cagliari was brought in.

Based on research conducted at the Records Office of the municipality of Armungia concerning the names in question:

*Pietro Pintus, born Armungia (Cagliari province) on 12 July
1882 and Maria Giuseppina Gajas born Armungia (Cagliari
province) on 6 November 1887; we inform that at present
neither of the names in question appears in the above-
mentioned Municipal Archive. We further also point out that:
1) the Records Archives of the above-mentioned municipality
are incomplete prior to 1947; 2) the parochial registers have
deteriorated due to poor conservation; 3) no persons in town
recall anyone bearing the name in question. It must however
be added that such a result in this specific case is of no certain
value, given the sometimes extreme reserve typical of the people
of this region. End message.*

It was as though the engineer had left only a trail of scorched
earth behind him. The whole thing was beginning to appear
rather strange indeed. Bordelli rang Piras, but he wasn't at
home. His mother said Nino had left the house before eleven,
having gone on a drive to Oristano in Ettore's new Fiat 500,
and wasn't back yet . . . She then added that Nino hadn't
eaten a thing at breakfast, aside from two amaretti and a coffee,
and that much earlier that morning he had walked nearly all
the way to Milis, which was too bad because he was so thin
and the doctor said he should eat more . . . To say nothing of
the fact that he'd made some mysterious phone calls in the
past few days . . .

'Do you know Nino's girlfriend, Captain?' she asked out of
the blue.

'I didn't know he had one,' Bordelli lied, quick to catch on.

'Well, he does,' said Maria.

'He hasn't told me anything about it.'

'Her name's Francesca, but that was all I was able to find
out.'

'I'm afraid I can't be of any help,' he said. 'I'm sorry . . .
What's the weather like over there?' he asked, to change the
subject.

'It's sunny, but there's frost at night,' said Maria.

'Here it's about to rain.'

'Oooh, excuse me, Captain . . . I have to check the chicken,' said Maria.

'Is one of your chickens not feeling well?'

'I mean the one in the pot. I'm making broth.'

'Goodbye, Signora Maria, please give my best to Gavino.'

'Goodbye. I'll tell Nino you called, as soon as he gets home.'

They hung up. Bordelli lit another cigarette, took one puff, and set it down in the ashtray. In the lamplight the rising smoke looked oily and very white. He wondered how Piras had got his mother to believe that Sonia's name was Francesca.

He felt hungry and went out on foot, headed for Totò's kitchen. As he walked he started imagining the telex he wanted to send to every single police department in Italy, requesting an urgent, thorough search for *Agostino Pintus, born at Custoza di Sommacampagna (Verona province), 16 July 1912, son of Pietro Pintus, born at Armungia, etc., etc . . .*

It wasn't yet one o'clock and Piras was already in Oristano. He was still half an hour early for his appointment with Pintus. He parked at the start of Via Ricovero and went into a bar to drink a *chinotto*.[41] He felt a little nervous. To avoid letting the time go to waste, he went for a walk in the neighbourhood. The centre of town was busy with traffic, mostly Fiats and motor scooters. Walking past the Portixedda tower, he reached the bottom of Via La Marmora and started wandering the streets in front of the Duomo. Schools were closed, and there were a great many people walking about, especially mothers with small children, and thus it was better for him, with his crutches, to cede the pavement to them and walk in the street. Shop windows were decked out with festoons and coloured lights, and the pastry shops were already full of Epiphany stockings and sweet coal.

He glanced at his watch and walked slowly back towards the car. At twenty past one he got back inside, drove the entire length of Via Ricovero and turned down Via Marconi. He pulled up in front of the engineer's small villa. The dogs were already tied up and started to bark. The Alfa Romeo and Fiat 1100 were parked on the lawn, and the Rumi was there as well. He rang the doorbell. Pintus appeared in the doorway and slowly came forward to open the gate. They walked together into the house and sat down on the facing sofas, one in front of the other. Outside, the dogs kept on barking. Everything seemed the same as the previous time.

'So, what is it, Piras? I haven't got much time,' said Pintus.

'I'll get straight to the point . . .'

'Please.'

'The heirs have accepted your offer.'

'Good,' said Pintus, looking serious.

'Aren't you going to offer me a drink in celebration?' Piras asked, smiling. Pintus didn't move for a few seconds, then smiled in response.

'All right,' he said. He got up and went to get some wine and two glasses. He passed one to Piras and then sat back down.

'Where and when can we meet for the contract of agreement?' Pintus asked, practical as usual.

'Well, we have to wait for the rights of succession to be formalised,' said Piras.

'A signed, notarised statement is also fine with me. I can make the fifty per cent down payment straight away. The deed must be drawn up within six months, and succession procedures never last more than four,' said Pintus, apparently quite sure of himself.

'You know something? I bet you're more or less my father's age,' Piras said in a friendly tone.

'I was born in 1912.'

'My father's from '13. He was in the navy, but after 8 September he came ashore to join the San Marco regiment.'

'Pavolini was very proud of them,' Pintus said gravely.

'Probably not of my father. He was in Badoglio's San Marco,' said Piras, taking a sip of wine.

'There was some confusion at that time, as I'm sure your father would concur,' said Pintus.

'My father says that, all of a sudden, everything became clear to him, and the only Italy he wanted was an Italy without Fascists and Nazis . . . Or, as he puts it, "without those shit-eating Nazis and pants-shitting Fascists",' Piras said with a chuckle. He wanted to provoke the man into reacting.

'You're still just a kid. You can't possibly understand these things,' said Pintus, cold but calm.

'Sometimes you can get a better picture of things from a distance.'

'I really don't know what you're getting at,' said Pintus, raising his eyebrows as if it didn't really matter to him. He suddenly seemed in less of a hurry.

'Oh, I'm not getting at anything . . .' said Piras, pretending to be amused. 'I just find it rather fascinating to have a real, flesh-and-blood Fascist in front of me, for the first time.'

'I think you've misunderstood me. I was never a Fascist,' Pintus said with a cold smile.

'Ah, I'm sorry, I beg your pardon,' Piras said, raising his hands.

'No problem.'

'Anyway, I didn't mean there was anything wrong with it. People do a lot of silly things when they're young.'

'I completely agree,' said Pintus.

'And what did you do during the war? Don't tell me you were in the navy too?'

'No, I was in Switzerland. I went over the border to avoid the war,' Pintus said serenely.

'Did you come back after the armistice?'

'No.'

'And what did you do in Switzerland?' Piras asked.

'Do you always ask so many questions?'

'I'm sorry, I really do talk too much sometimes . . . But we've just made a wonderful deal! There's no harm in having a polite little chat, is there?'

'No harm at all,' said Pintus.

'I really am sorry, though, perhaps I was indiscreet and reawakened some painful memories for you.'

'No, it's nothing like that, don't worry. I simply stayed in Switzerland until the war was over. I took no part in any of it,' said Pintus, stretching his legs as if to relax. He crossed his ankles and then his arms. Piras distractedly looked down at the engineer's heavy shoes . . . and felt a wave of heat envelop his head. He'd just seen something that might settle the whole affair, and he couldn't quite believe it yet.

'Let's get back to business,' he said, looking up at Pintus. He was making a great effort to remain calm, but it was hard to disguise the thrill of being dealt the equivalent of a royal flush. He had no idea whether or not his excitement was visible.

'Let's set a date to meet again soon,' said Pintus, sitting up. Apparently he hadn't noticed anything.

'Shall we make it at Musillo's law office?' asked Piras, heart racing.

'It's all the same to me.'

'When would be best for you?'

'Any time at all is fine with me,' Pintus replied in a serious tone.

'Will you still be at home if I ring you in about two hours?'

'I have to go out around half past four.'

'Then I should manage all right. Thank you, sir. I'll be going now,' said Piras, standing up and grabbing his crutches.

Pintus showed him out. 'If I'm not here later, you can reach me tomorrow morning between seven and eight. After that I'll be at the construction site,' he said, accompanying him to the door.

Walking down the hallway, Piras felt quite tense . . . Perhaps Pintus really was the Fascist from Asti and had managed to deal Benigno the *coup de grâce* twenty years later . . . Maybe he realised he was under suspicion and was preparing at any moment to attack him and stab him to death . . . and then feed him to the dogs . . . But nothing happened. They went out of the house without a word. The dogs barked wildly as they crossed the garden, their chains clinking audibly as they pulled on them. Pintus waited for Piras to go out through the gate, then closed it behind him. As he walked towards the little Fiat, Piras turned round and saw Pintus releasing the dogs.

After having a bite to eat in Totò's kitchen, the inspector went back to the office and dropped into his chair. He wanted to write out the telex message and then get a few minutes' rest before going to Santo Spirito to look into the trouble there. What a bore. The first thing he had to do was drop in on Bolla, who always knew everything that was going on in that part of town.

He rang Mugnai and asked him please to go and fetch a coffee for him. He lit a cigarette, only his third of the day. He wanted to smoke it in peace, to enjoy it in full. That would help him to hold out longer before the next one. This was another theory he was trying to prove. He was about to start writing that blessed telex when the internal line rang. It was Rinaldi.

'Piras rang you twice, Inspector,' he said.

'I'll call him back at once.'

'He said he'd call you back, sir, because he's not at home.'

'All right,' said Bordelli, pleased to be able to postpone the bother of Santo Spirito for a precise reason. He continued smoking slowly. A few minutes later Mugnai knocked.

'Your coffee, sir.'

'Thank you . . . Did you get one for yourself as well?'

'You didn't tell me to, sir.'

'I don't need to tell you every time, Mugnai, it's understood.'

'Thank you, Inspector. I'll go and get it straight away . . . Did you see the letter?'

'What letter?'

'I put it right there on your desk,' said Mugnai, searching with his eyes.

'Are you sure?' asked Bordelli, moving some papers that had collected over the course of the day.

'Of course I'm sure,' said Mugnai. Bordelli keep searching, but found nothing. Then he heard a dull sound. Mugnai had slapped himself on the forehead and was now digging with his fingers into the pocket of his uniform.

'I'm afraid I'm a blockhead, sir,' he said.

'You've still got it in your pocket . . .'

'I really ought to see a doctor, sir. I was convinced I'd put it on your desk,' said Mugnai, handing him the envelope.

'There are worse things in life,' Bordelli said, smiling.

'I promise it won't happen again, sir,' said Mugnai, and after giving a military salute he went on his way. Bordelli put out the cigarette butt and distractedly opened the envelope. There was a postcard inside. *Panorama of Montevideo*. He felt a tingling in his arms and turned it over.

Happy Christmas. I think of you now and then. How about you? M.

Under these words was a lipstick imprint of a pair of lips. Bordelli closed his eyes and was back in Milena's arms. He could almost smell her scent. He sniffed the card instinctively, thinking that she had put her fingers and mouth on it. But he smelled only cardboard. He looked for the return address on the envelope, but luckily there wasn't one . . . Otherwise he would have been tempted to reply. Closing his eyes again, he tried to free himself from feelings he didn't even want to name. But it was easier to do so with eyes open . . . Why had Milena sent him that postcard? Couldn't she simply leave him in peace? She'd gone away. He'd tried to stop her, but she'd gone just the same. It was water under the bridge. Old news. Its only possible purpose was to make him bleed a little more. He had to erase the girl from his memory . . . He had no desire for an adventure like Diotivede's with Maria Conchita.

He put the postcard in his bottom drawer and closed it.

375

Then he changed his mind. There was no harm in the postcard; it only showed a view of Montevideo. He took it and slipped it inside the frame of a Dürer print he was very fond of, hanging under a photo of the president. He had to convince himself that Milena was just a pleasant memory . . . One that would fade like all the rest. That was the way things went. He'd even managed to forget Teresa, who'd probably been the most important of them all . . . A lot of time had gone by . . . Teresa, who'd left all of sudden, saying she didn't want anything more to do with policemen . . . Teresa with her mischievous smile and black hair like Milena's . . . Young, beautiful Milena, eyes full of fire . . . Milena who was now on another continent, never to return . . . Milena who . . .

The telephone rang, startling him.

'Yes?'

'It's me, Inspector.'

'Piras. Where are you?' He could hear a din of voices and dishes in the background.

'I'm in Oristano, near the police station. I'm calling from a bar.'

'I can hear.'

'I went to see Pintus again, and something strange happened . . . If what I think I saw is true, Lady Luck is still kissing me on the lips.'

'Tell me about it.'

'You're not going to believe it, Inspector.'

'Get to the point, Piras,' said Bordelli, looking for his cigarettes.

'We were sitting across from each other and talking, when Pintus stretched his legs and then crossed them, putting one foot on top of the other . . . He was wearing hiking boots, the kind with deep rubber treads on the soles. And you know what I saw?'

'Come on, Piras . . .'

'An empty bullet shell.'

'Cut the crap, Piras.'

'I told you it was a big deal, Inspector.'

'Holy shit.'

'It was stuck inside one of the rubber treads,' said Piras.

'Yeah, I got that already, Piras,' said Bordelli, holding the telephone with his chin so he could light another cigarette.

'Sorry, sir, I'm just a little excited,' said the Sardinian.

'Are you absolutely certain it was a shell from a pistol?'

'I saw it,' said Piras, his voice a little shaky.

'Let's keep our fingers crossed.'

'And I think I know why Benigno was so surprised to see Pintus again . . . But I'll tell you about that later. Right now I've got ants in my pants.'

'All right, then.'

'I would, however, like you to phone the central police here . . . just to tell them they should take me seriously,' said Piras.

'Call me back in five minutes,' said Bordelli, hanging up. He dialled the number for Oristano police and asked for Chief Inspector Stella, whom he'd met some years before, at an official gathering. He told him about Piras and the investigation he was conducting, about the mysterious Pintus who had no past and the missing bullet shell that Piras might have found under Pintus's shoe. He asked for help. Stella was quite well disposed and told him he would follow the case personally. Bordelli thanked him and hung up.

While waiting for Piras to call back, he started pacing about the room. He began thinking about Milena again, but then the telephone rang.

'It's all set, Piras. Inspector Stella's waiting for you,' Bordelli said.

'Thanks, Inspector. I'll keep you posted.'

'I didn't have time to mention it before, Piras, but I've received answers to my telexes. Verona and Cagliari turned up nothing at all. And the ministry has also got back to me. Our engineer is not on the official register.'

'I'll bet Pintus isn't his real name. I'll bet one of my balls it isn't.'

'Why not both?'

'Well, you never know.'

'Break a leg, Piras.'

'I already have. I'll call back soon.'

They hung up and Bordelli crushed his cigarette in the ashtray. Unable to sit still, he started pacing about the room again, hands in his pockets, thinking about Piras's investigation. Even assuming that the shell really was in the guy's shoe, who knew whether it was actually the one fired from the pistol found in Benigno's hand? And if not . . . well, the suicide would almost certainly remain a mystery.

He glanced at his watch and ran a hand over his face. He'd run out of excuses. It was time to go to Santo Spirito.

He got into the Beetle but didn't drive off straight away. He sat there awhile with his eyes half closed, head resting against the seat. Deep in his ears he heard a sort of background sound of surf. Maybe he was just tired. He started up the car and drove off, an unlit cigarette between his teeth. If he thought of Piras he felt a strong desire to light it. And now he had to concern himself with this idiotic problem at Santo Spirito . . . The postcard from Milena was the last thing he needed . . . A truly memorable day.

He waved at Mugnai as he left the courtyard. The sky was purple and the air smelled of imminent rain. The St Stephen's day sun hadn't lasted. He crossed the Arno and parked the Beetle in Via Maggio. As soon as he got out it started drizzling and he quickened his pace. He turned down Via Sguazza, and halfway down the narrow street he pushed on an unlocked front door and went inside. Feeling his way through a dark corridor full of spiderwebs, he reached the end and knocked on a low door. He heard some stirring inside, then an alarmed voice.

'Who is it?'

'Police.'

'I haven't done anything. I haven't even gone outside for the last month.'

'Open up, Bolla, it's me, Bordelli.'

The door opened barely an inch, and an eye appeared in the crack. Then it opened all the way. Bolla had changed. He had less hair, and his misshapen nose stuck out even farther under the hollow, ringed eyes. As always, his cheeks were ravaged by pimples.

'Inspector! What, you trying to give me a heart attack?' he said, still shaken. He wasn't old, but he wore all his years on his face, as if they'd been etched with a chisel.

'Can I come in for a minute?'

'You're always welcome, Inspector.'

Bolla stood aside and let Bordelli into his lair. A table, a bed and one old wardrobe. A black cobweb fluttered over the bathroom door, and a dim bulb hung from the ceiling but wasn't enough to illuminate the corners of the room. It was like being in a prison cell. Bolla opened a drawer and took out a tin box with biscuits inside.

'Like a snack?' he asked

'No thanks, no need to bother. How are things, Bolla?'

'Could be worse, Inspector, a lot worse,' said Bolla, putting the tin of biscuits on the table. Bordelli sniffed the air.

'Am I mistaken, or do I smell grappa?' he asked.

'I always keep a bottle ready just for you, Inspector.'

'Be careful, Bolla. One of these days you're going to blow yourself up along with the rest of this dump.'

'I don't make it here . . . I've got a little hut in the country with my cousin.'

'Careful or you'll burn your fingers off,' said Bordelli.

Bolla stuck a hand inside the tin and searched for an unbroken biscuit. 'I have to eat, Inspector,' he said glumly.

'How much do you get for a bottle?' asked Bordelli, taking out his wallet.

'Normally I sell it for two thousand, but for you, I'll make it fifteen hundred.'

Bordelli put two thousand-lira notes in his hand.

'That'll do. Are you sure I won't get poisoned?'

Bolla took offence. He said he knew perfectly well how to make grappa, and that he threw out *all* the head and *all* the tail, not like some arseholes.

'I either do things right, or I don't do them at all, Inspector.'

'Come on, Bolla, I was joking.'

Bolla reached under the bed and pulled out a clear-glass Bordeaux-style bottle with a cork in it, and put it on the table.

'What brings you to the neighbourhood, Inspector? A man like you doesn't usually come to this hole by chance,' he said.

'I wanted to ask you something . . .'

'What?' asked Bolla, nostrils flaring as if he were expecting some unpleasant news.

Bordelli took a roundabout approach. 'Apparently some things have been happening around here lately.'

'What the hell are you talking about, Inspector? What kind of things?'

'I'm talking about somebody who's going around bashing people in the face. Don't tell me you don't know about it.'

'Ah, that guy!'

'Maybe you know who he is . . . and maybe I know, too.'

'What, you trying to make me snitch or something?'

'Come on . . .'

'Is that why you bought the grappa from me?'

'Listen, Bolla, I haven't got all day for this . . . Do you know who it is or don't you?'

Bolla thought it over for a minute, then cracked a biscuit with his teeth.

'You know Gino's bar?' he asked, chewing.

'You mean the one in Via delle Caldaie?'

'That's the one. Go and have a coffee there. They make it really good, the way you like it.'

'Thanks, Bolla.'

'For what? All I told you's where they make good coffee.'

'I'll buy you one that you can drink later.'

Bolla smiled, face full of wrinkles.

'You're too good to me, Inspector.'

Bordelli grabbed the bottle of grappa and headed for the door, followed by the bootlegger.

'Take care of yourself, Bolla. And watch that you don't blow yourself up. I mean it.'

"Bye, Inspector.'

Bordelli stepped out into the rain and went and put the grappa bottle in the car. Then he set out on foot for Gino's bar. Every so often he had to jump down from the pavement to avoid the cascades of water raining down from the broken gutters above. The porphyry of the streets shone like porcelain. He crossed Piazza Santo Spirito and entered Via delle Caldaie. There weren't many people about, only a few hurried silhouettes with their collars turned up, covering their faces. An old man on a bicycle rode past, wrapped in a plastic sheet. He had a cigarette inside his mouth the wrong way round and was blowing smoke out through his nose the way war prisoners used to do when sneaking a smoke.

It started pouring. Bordelli ran to the end of the street and ducked into Gino's bar, dripping wet. The floor was sprinkled with dirty sawdust. Gino, the initial proprietor of the place, had died in '48 in a brawl, but his name had remained. The bar was empty. There was only a fat guy seated at a small table in front of the counter. He was playing solitaire. He barely looked up at the intruder, then dropped a card on the table and resumed playing. He held his round head down between his shoulders and didn't look disposed to conversation. Some scratchy-sounding music poured out from a small radio. Approaching the bar, Bordelli recognised a song by Celentano but couldn't remember the title.

'Could I please have a coffee?' he asked.

The man played another card, undisturbed, then dropped the deck and stood up. He was hardly any taller than when seated and had an enormous paunch. He went huffing behind the bar, pressed the coffee into the filter, inserted this into the machine, and placed a little cup under the spout. Then he turned and stared at Bordelli without saying a word, his oily face split in two by a broad sneer. Bordelli stared back at him. He thought he recognised those eyes, and the curl to the lip also rang a bell. It must have been an old scar. The coffee was ready. The barman took the cup, put a saucer under it, and slid them across the bar.

'Hello, Inspector,' he said.

The moment he heard that deep, gravelly voice, Bordelli realised who the man was.

'Amedeo! What the hell are you doing here?'

'If even you couldn't recognise me, I must be in pretty bad shape.'

Bordelli looked at him some more. In that swollen state he really was unrecognisable. And the inspector hadn't seen him for a very long time.

'You've just gained a little weight,' he said.

'It's prison, Inspector. When I'm inside, all I do is eat.'

'The exact opposite of Botta.'

'That guy, if it's not *canard à l'orange* he won't touch it,' said Amedeo. Wiping his hands on his apron, he came out from behind the bar.

Bordelli put a cigarette between his lips. 'When did you get out?'

'Two weeks ago,' said Amedeo, sitting back down at the card table.

The inspector drew near. 'So you were out for Christmas,' he said, lighting his cigarette.

'Some Christmas, all alone like a dog.'

'And what are you doing now? Do you work here?'

'Just doing a favour for a friend on holiday.'

'How much time did they give him?'

'Three months.'

'And what'll you do afterwards?' asked Bordelli, sitting down in front of him.

Amedeo threw down a card. 'I've got all kinds of ideas, Inspector.'

'Got any that won't put you back in jail?'

'Do I have to answer that, Inspector?' Amedeo pinched his lower lip, trying to decide which card to play next. They both remained silent for a few moments. It was still pouring outside. Amedeo played cards, the inspector smoked and watched the rain drip down the dirty windowpanes. There was a clap of thunder and the lights flickered for a second or two.

'Know anything about some rowdy bloke making trouble in the neighbourhood?' Bordelli asked offhandedly.

'There are a lot of people like that around here, Inspector.'

'I'm talking about someone who just recently came out of the woodwork.'

'How recently?'

'A fortnight or so . . . Didn't you say you got out a couple of weeks ago yourself? What a coincidence . . .'

'So what?'

'What are you doing, Amedeo? Playing neighbourhood bully again?' asked Bordelli, crushing his cigarette in the ashtray.

Amedeo threw down another card. 'I haven't done anything, Inspector. Just gone and taken back what was rightfully mine. In this den of thieves, the minute you turn your back they take everything, including the mattresses.'

'So you're the hooligan, in other words.'

'What the hell am I supposed to do, Inspector? I won't be played for a fool, I can tell you that.'

'Can't you be a little gentler?'

'Wha'd I do? A couple o' black eyes, a couple o' bruises? I ain't killed anybody, for Chrissakes . . .'

'You never know what'll happen when you punch somebody.'

'No, no, I know how to punch, don't you worry . . . And did you know that one prick went around saying they'd given me twenty years?'

'Just tell me one thing, Amedeo. Have you finished, or are there still a few people left to take care of?'

The ex-convict raised a hand.

'I'm done,' he said.

Bordelli sighed. 'Why don't you settle down, Amedeo? I say it for your own good. You're no longer a kid.'

'That's easy for you to say, Inspector. You've got a job,' said Amedeo.

'You're probably right.'

'Not probably. I *am* right.'

'I'll let you get back to your game,' said Bordelli. He took out his wallet and extracted five thousand lire.

'I ain't got change,' said Amedeo.

'Then keep it,' said Bordelli, laying the notes down on the table. Amedeo's oily face turned red, his eyes tiny and wicked. He squashed the deck in his hand, bending the cards.

'I don't take charity from nobody. I earn my money my own way, and the coffee's on me.'

'As you wish. But I wanted to pay for one for Bolla, too.'

'That one's on me too.'

Bordelli put away the money. Amedeo calmed down and resumed playing. The driving rain pelted the window. A lightning bolt flashed very close by, and the thunderclap that immediately followed made the glasses behind the bar tinkle. The lights went out all over the neighbourhood. A second later, the fluorescent lamps in the bar flickered back on. Bordelli stood up to leave.

'Thanks for the coffee,' he said. Amedeo folded his hands over his head.

'Inspector, you're a cop, and that's okay, nobody's perfect. But to me you're a friend.'

'Don't go spreading it around, or I'll get sacked,' said Bordelli. Amedeo smiled mischievously.

'I still haven't forgotten about the transistor radios, Inspector. If not for you, I'd 'a been fucked.'

'Never mind, Amedeo. That was another age.'

'Not for me, Inspector. For me, nothing's changed,' said the jailbird.

'Take care of yourself, Amedeo.'

'Aren't you going to wait till the bleedin' rain stops?'

'I'm parked just round the corner,' said Bordelli, who was anxious to get back to the office.

'Well, take that newspaper to cover your head.'

'Thanks,' said Bordelli, grabbing the copy of *La Nazione* that lay on the bar. The rain was still coming down hard.

''Bye, Inspector.'

'See you again soon.'

Bordelli went out the door and into the rain, newspaper over his head. The street was flooded, and the passing cars splashed water on to the pavements. He quickened his pace, thinking he had rid himself of the bad habit of never carrying an umbrella. When he got into the Beetle, he dried his face with his handkerchief. He could feel the water running down his back.

Upon receiving Piras, Chief Inspector Stella had listened patiently to his story of the strange suicide of Benigno Staffa. Piras omitted nothing, not even the near brush with death at the hands of the Fascists in Asti. He wanted Stella to know exactly how he had come to suspect Pintus.

Stella sent for a Sergeant Marras, and together the three took stock of the situation. They immediately checked to see whether Agostino had a firearms licence and found out that he did, having registered a 1915 Beretta 7.65. On the basis of this information, Inspector Stella made up his mind. They would detain Pintus on suspicion of premeditated murder and search his home. But the ballistics test had to be conducted extremely fast, otherwise they risked detaining an innocent man or letting a guilty one go before the assistant prosecutor had time to justify the arrest. They had exactly forty-eight hours from the moment of his capture. The news must not reach the newspapers before the eventual official arrest, and if the bullet shell proved not to be the right one, it was best if the news never made it out of the lab at all. Any mistake in this regard could unleash quite a storm. It was risky, but the evidence against Pintus was rather specific and justified trying.

Piras left Central Police in the company of Sergeant Marras, five officers and four young Blue Berets, the special unit created the year before by former partisan fighter Castellani to combat banditry. Three squad cars and two unmarked cars followed behind Ettore's little Fiat.

Piras was nervous. When the convoy was near the end of Via Sardegna, he wondered for a second whether he might be wrong, whether he might have simply imagined seeing that shell . . . Or perhaps he'd seen something else, a pebble, a dry twig, a bolt. He felt a drop of sweat roll down behind his ear.

The cars stopped one block away from Pintus's house. To minimise risk, they wanted to take him by surprise. If Pintus really did kill Benigno, he was almost certainly one of those Fascists from Asti and was therefore accustomed to killing. When he realised he'd been discovered he might become dangerous.

The policemen closed the street at both ends to prevent anyone from passing. The four Blue Berets, Piras and Sergeant Marras walked towards the house. When they reached Pintus's garden, the Blue Berets and the sergeant crouched down and advanced unseen, hidden by the low wall. Piras continued walking normally until he reached the entrance gate, and everyone else stopped a couple of yards away. It was cold outside. The dogs were barking and batting their paws against the gate. Pintus's cars and motor scooter were parked on the lawn.

Piras rang the bell. A few seconds later Pintus appeared in the doorway, saw Piras, put on an overcoat and came forward without first tying up the dogs. *He knows everything*, thought Piras . . . *And now the old Fascist is going to pull out his gun and start firing*.

'Hello, Mr Pintus,' he said, smiling. He cast a glance at Pintus's feet. The boots were gone, replaced by slippers.

'Weren't you supposed to ring me?' the engineer asked before he'd even reached the gate. He looked very serious and irritated.

'I talked to the heir over the phone, and since I was already in town, I decided to drop by,' said Piras, shrugging.

Pintus reached the gate, and the dogs calmed down a little.

'Can we arrange a meeting soon?' asked the engineer.

'Tomorrow morning at ten, if you're in agreement.'

'It's fine with me. Shall we make it here?'

'As you wish.'

'Then I'll expect you tomorrow at ten,' said Pintus, and after gesturing goodbye, he turned and walked back towards the house, followed by the dogs. Piras cast a worried glance at his colleagues. He had to think of something quickly.

'You didn't let me finish,' he shouted to Pintus, still searching for an excuse.

The engineer turned round. 'What is it, Piras?'

'The heir is ready to sell . . . but on one condition.'

'And what's that?'

'It's nothing, really, certainly nothing for you to worry about, but it's sort of complicated to explain . . . Could I perhaps come in for just a minute? That way I could tell you in detail and we can smooth out this little bump in a jiffy . . .'

Pintus paused a moment, thinking it over, hands in his pockets, then called the dogs over and chained them up.

'Get ready,' Piras whispered to the policemen positioned behind the wall.

Pintus came back, walking slowly, and opened the gate.

'If I don't like this condition,' he said, 'I'll call the whole thing off.'

'It's nothing unpleasant, Mr Pintus, I assure you,' Piras said, smiling. Then he made a hand signal and the policemen leapt out, ran into the garden and threw Pintus to the ground, immobilising him. Two officers pointed their machine guns at him. Pintus didn't react, but let himself be taken, not moving a muscle, not breathing a word. The dogs were in a frenzy, hurling themselves towards their master and jerking so hard on their chains that their legs flailed in the air.

They searched Pintus's person. Under his arm was a holster with an old Beretta 7.65 Glisenti with a full clip and loaded. It must have been his registered weapon. The engineer remained silent. He stared at Piras with disdain and sorrow, as one looks at a traitor. Marras came over to Piras and whispered in his ear, so that Pintus wouldn't hear.

'What about the shell?' he asked.

'He took his boots off,' Piras whispered.

The sergeant nodded and gestured at the Blue Berets, who stood Pintus on his feet, handcuffed him and took him away.

'Let's hope for the best,' Piras muttered, worried.

'What did you say?' asked Marras. The dogs were making a great deal of noise.

'Nothing, let's go inside.'

Marras took out his pistol and released the safety. They walked past the dogs, which were barking wildly. If the chains broke, their only recourse would be to shoot. They went into the house and closed the door.

'A proper pain in the arse, those dogs,' said the sergeant, putting his gun back in its holster.

They looked for Pintus's bedroom at once and found the boots beside the bed. Was it the right foot or the left? Pintus dropped his crutches on the floor, picked up both shoes together and turned them over.

'Hell, yes, it's there,' he said. He'd seen correctly. It was a 7.65-calibre shell. He sat down on the bed and tried to pull it out with his fingers, but it wouldn't budge.

'They'll take it out at the lab,' he said, passing the boot to Marras. He still couldn't believe he had been so lucky as to see that shell. It was half rusted and almost the same colour as the sole. Now all that remained was to prove that it matched . . . But of course it'll match, thought Piras, to set his mind at rest. Where else could it have come from? The shell had remained wedged inside those treads for over a week; it had clung to that shoe with all its might, just so Benigno could rest in peace . . . It was the one. It *had* to be the one.

Marras looked round the door and called one of the officers over. He handed him the boot with the shell and told him to take it at once to the forensic laboratory for a ballistics test. The officer ran off, got into a squad car and drove away with tyres screeching.

Piras and Marras were left alone in the house to conduct the search. They split up and started circulating through the different rooms. The house was big and furnished almost entirely with expensive modern furniture. The radiators were boiling, and it felt quite hot.

Piras entered a room with a desk with iron legs and a writing surface of red Formica. One wall was covered with wooden shelves holding only a few books and a great many knick-knacks. It looked like a sort of study. Piras circled behind the desk, sat down and opened the top drawer. Rummaging through some papers, he found an old, yellowed photograph on thick cardboard. In the oval centre was a naked baby boy of a few months, laughing, belly down on a pillow. On the back, in faded ink, was written: *Ruggero, 1913*. He put it back and continued searching. When he opened the bottom drawer, he noticed a cigar box with a black ribbon around it. He took it out and opened it. Inside was only a wrinkled envelope covered with small brown stains. It was a letter.

Republican Fascist Party

Salò, 12 September 1944 xxi

Most excellent comrade Ruggero Frigolin,

It is my supreme honour to inform you that, by the express personal wishes of His Excellency Party Secretary Alessandro Pavolini, as of this moment you are appointed Second Commandant of the Luigi Viale Brigade of Asti.

His Excellency has also taken it upon himself to convey to you once again his vast admiration for your indispensable assistance, from the early stages, in the creation and organisation of the glorious corps of the Black Brigades.

Shameful acts of treason by the King and Marshal

Badoglio have rendered our task of carrying Italy to the loftiest summits of civilisation absolutely crucial.

His Excellency Cavaliere Benito Mussolini shall know how to lead us all towards our Glorious Destiny as victors. We will crush the Allied invaders like useless worms, and the one True God shall strike fear into the hearts of the enemies of our Republic in every corner of the Planet.

We know one word alone, and that word is: Victory!
Viva il Duce!

Forever yours,
Italo Mazzadoca

It was signed with a flourish.

Piras touched his face and noticed he was sweating. But it wasn't only because of the radiators. If what he was thinking was true, there was no more mystery. He put the letter in his pocket and got up to look at the books. There weren't many. They took up only one shelf. A pair of Bibles, a number of engineering books, a few old classics, and several small paperbacks. He propped his crutches against the wall and started opening the books one by one to see whether anything was hidden between the pages. But he found nothing.

Continuing his tour of the house, he went into the kitchen. It was big and had a huge refrigerator and modern furnishings. Feeling hungry, Piras opened the fridge instinctively. He would have gladly eaten a sandwich, but at that moment he heard Marras call him and left the kitchen.

'I'm over here,' said Marras, popping out of a doorway.

'What's going on?' asked Piras, approaching.

'Come and see what I've found.'

Piras followed the sergeant into a small, windowless room and put his crutches in a corner. On the bottom shelf of an old armoire were two different nine-calibre Berettas, a Browning 7.65, and even a German Luger, the terrible nine-calibre pistol of the SS. They were all laid out on a thick piece of cloth, clean and well oiled, with their serial numbers legible. And there was no lack of ammunition. Some boxes dated back to the war, others looked much more recent.

'Shit . . .' muttered Piras, turning the Luger over in his hand. He'd never seen a real one, and it felt eerie. The very shape of the pistol gave one a clear sense of the spirit in which it had been created. It was aggressive, solid, inexorable. It looked almost like a miniature machine gun. He'd heard years ago that a single shot from the weapon could kill six people standing one in front of the other. Perhaps it was just a legend, but from the look of the gun, he was inclined to believe it.

'How about our engineer, eh?' he said.

'It's a small arsenal,' the sergeant said, biting his lips.

'Get a feel of this,' said Piras, passing him the Luger.

Marras started examining it carefully. Then he gripped it and pointed it at the wall. He looked through the sight. 'Who knows how many people this little demon has killed,' he muttered.

'Let's take everything away,' said Piras.

They wrapped the pistols up in newspaper and put them in two shoeboxes, along with the ammunition. Then they took another look inside the armoire. Hunting boots, old newspapers, a few tools.

'That should be enough for today,' said Piras, grabbing his crutches.

'Did you find anything else?' asked Marras.

'A letter. I'll show it to you later.'

They walked out of the storeroom and towards the door. After the morning's weariness, Piras could feel all the strength that had gathered in his legs over the prior months come back to him. He felt like running and jumping.

'What about those two fiends?' Marras asked. The dogs hadn't stopped barking for a second.

'We'll get the dogs' home to take care of them.'

It was still raining hard when Bordelli got to the police station. He walked into his office dripping water and laid his open trench coat down over the radiator. Then he went into the bathroom to dry himself off. Back in his office, while waiting to hear from Piras, he phoned Rosa to say hello. After a couple of rings, a woman whose voice he didn't recognise picked up.

'Yes, hello? With whom would you like to speak?' The accent and tone sounded like a poor imitation of a noblewoman.

'I'm sorry, I must have the wrong number,' said Bordelli.

'No, monkey, it's me!'

'Rosa! Why did you answer that way?'

'Did you really not recognise me?'

'It certainly didn't sound like you.'

'I was practising for the performance.'

'What performance?'

'My girlfriends and I are rehearsing a play.'

'A play?' asked Bordelli, somewhat surprised.

'I get it, you think us whores only know how to do one thing,' said Rosa, pretending to be offended. She loved to be won back. Bordelli tried to think of something nice to say, but nothing diplomatic came to mind.

'Are you doing something by Shakespeare?' he said at last.

Rosa relaxed a little. 'Go on, Shakespeare! It's something I wrote myself. It's fun and talks about some very deep things. I just know you'll love it.'

'When is the performance?' asked Bordelli, taking his time.

'Thursday, at my place. Only a select few are invited.'

'Such a wonderful idea could only have come from you . . .'

'Oh, it's nothing special,' Rosa said, laughing, embarrassed. She was very sensitive to flattery, and often reacted as though tickled. Now came the hard part, however.

'I'm sorry, Rosa, I'm looking at my diary . . . I can't make it on Thursday.'

'Oh, you're such a shit!'

'There's an important meeting here at headquarters . . .'

Silence.

'Sometimes these things go on all night,' Bordelli exaggerated, pretending to be disappointed.

'Ah, what a shame! What a terrible, terrible shame!'

'Hello? Rosa? Is that you?'

'Oh, I'm sorry, that was my character's voice again. I'm afraid I can't help myself,' she said, chuckling.

'It really is quite incredible. You're unrecognisable. Are you supposed to be a noblewoman?'

'Princess Doralice, mother of three daughters.'

'I like what I've heard so far.'

'But I was hoping you'd come, damn!'

'I'll come another time . . . Break a leg.'

'Oh, you really are too kind,' said Rosa as Princess Doralice.

'I'm sure you'll be great.'

'Come and see me some time, you rat. I still have to give you your Christmas present.'

'At last . . .'

'Lout!'

'It's just that I'm curious.'

Rosa fired a barrage of kisses into the receiver and hung up. All was silent again in the office. It was almost six. Bordelli went up one floor and knocked at Commissioner Inzipone's door to report to him on the problems at Santo Spirito. He wanted to get it over with quickly and didn't even bother to sit down.

'It's all taken care of,' he reassured the commissioner. 'The case is closed.'

'Did you find out who was doing it?'

'The guy wasn't bashing people at random, but for specific reasons. Now he no longer has those reasons, so there's no problem any more.'

'Can't you tell me any more?'

'There's nothing more to tell,' said Bordelli.

There was a knock at the door. The commissioner grunted and the door opened. A pale, uniformed officer came in and saluted his superior.

'Dr Pomella is here, sir,' he said.

'Give me five more minutes,' said Inzipone, holding up an

open hand. The officer turned and left, heels clacking, closing the door behind him.

'Thank you, Bordelli, that sets my mind at rest. Is everything arranged concerning De Bono?'

'I'm sending Canzano and Di Lello to get him tomorrow. The president's not coming till the thirtieth, yes?'

'Yes. I just wanted confirmation . . . What was it De Bono said last year? Rabozzi told me,' Inzipone said, chuckling. He was almost always serious, but certain things made him laugh in earnest. 'He yelled something like: "The Fighting Anarchists have planted bombs in the Parliament and the Vatican, and one word from me will blow them sky high!" The old crackpot . . .' the commissioner said, still laughing.

Bordelli put his hands in his pockets. He was not laughing.

'Did you know De Bono has only one lung?' he said.

The commissioner's laughter diminished to a smile. 'Only one lung?'

'The Fascists used to put him out in the square every morning and order him to give the Fascist salute to the Duce. And you know what he would do?'

'What?' Inzipone asked, serious now.

'He would burp. To hear it now, it may not sound like such a big deal, but I don't know how many people would have had the courage to do it. Obviously the Fascists didn't appreciate the joke, and they would club him on the back. Then they'd take him back to his cell and start all over again the next morning . . . And so he lost a lung.'

'I didn't know that. Poor old man, I'm so sorry.'

'He may look old, but he's the same age as you, give or take a few years,' said the inspector.

Inzipone sighed. 'What a terrible story . . .'

'Oh, there's worse,' said Bordelli, looking the commissioner in the eye. Everybody knew that Inzipone had been one of those "forced" to adhere to the Republic of Salò, even though he'd come out of it clean as a whistle.

'Still nothing on the murder of that . . . I can never

remember his name,' said the commissioner, glad to change the subject.

'We're working on it,' said the inspector.

'And how's our boy Piras?'

'He's fine,' said Bordelli. Then he waved and left the room without turning round. In the corridor was the fat Dr Pomella, slouching in an armchair, the bottoms of his trousers hiked up around mid-calf, exposing his black socks. The inspector nodded to him in greeting and continued on his way. Pomella was an errand boy for the Minister of the Interior, and Bordelli had never liked him.

Back in his office, he turned his trench coat over on the radiator, then flopped into his chair with a sigh. He felt a little tired. He decided to skip the cigarettes, and after a few minutes of hesitation, he rang De Marchi.

'What can I do for you, Inspector?'

'Sorry, but . . . have you by any chance finished yet?'

'I'd have called you myself, sir, as agreed.'

'Well, I thought I'd try.'

'I'll have a look at that hair very soon, Inspector. I had to finish some analyses for the prosecutor of Siena, it's taken a long time.'

'Listen . . . don't put anything in writing yet. This whole business is still only a hunch of mine. I'd rather check everything out first.'

'You've already told me that, sir.'

'Sorry. I'm a bit foggy today.'

'Happens to us all, sir.'

'Think you'll manage it by this evening?' Bordelli asked.

'Sounds like you're in a hurry, Inspector. I'll stay late tonight and have a look at that hair for you, I promise,' De Marchi said without a hint of annoyance.

'That's what I like to hear. If I'm not in the office you can find me at home.'

'Will do, Inspector.'

They said goodbye, and Bordelli stood up. He felt nervous.

He went over to the window and looked outside. Every so often a gust of wind caught the incessant drizzle in a swirl and blew it about, but the sky above was clearing. Bordelli would gladly have smoked two cigarettes one after the other, but the idea that abstinence multiplied his desire for nicotine bothered him. The chemical link between mind and body seemed like an occult power against which he should defend himself. A man's mind should be stronger than matter, he thought. Shit, what a brilliant idea. Very useful for trying to quit smoking.

The telephone rang. It was Piras, as expected. He was calling from a public phone.

'Let's hear it,' said Bordelli.

'It's all gone well so far, Inspector. We've arrested Pintus. He denies everything, but we're still waiting for the ballistic evidence.'

'Call me as soon as you get the results.'

'I've discovered something else as well.'

'Tell me everything without the guessing games, Piras.'

'I searched through some of Pintus's things and I believe I've discovered what his real name is. I found a letter written by a Fascist of the Salò government that was sent from the secretariat of the Party to a certain Ruggero Frigolin. He was named Second Commandant of the Asti Brigade . . .'

'That doesn't prove anything.'

'Wait, Inspector. I also found a photograph of a baby boy, with *Ruggero, 1913* written on the back. But here's the best part. Pina Setzu, the late Benigno's cousin, told a strange story about him the other day, a terrible experience Benigno had during the war . . .'

And Piras went on to recount the gist of Benigno's brush with death in 1943.

'And guess where it all took place,' he said when he'd finished.

'Near Asti.'

'Exactly. I'm sure he's the one, Inspector. Pintus and Frigolin are the same person.'

'It was awfully stupid of him to keep that letter,' said Bordelli.

'Maybe he'd hidden it together with everything he'd stolen and then fished it back out after things had calmed down.'

'Vanity plays nasty tricks sometimes.'

'It's him, Inspector, this time I'll bet both my balls.'

'In the meantime I'll have a search conducted in the Veneto and Piedmont for this Frigolin, and we'll see what turns up,' said the inspector.

Piras sighed into the receiver.

'How is it that certain people are still around, Inspector?'

'My dear Piras, after the war, for the sake of peace across the nation, between amnesties and pardons, the few gentlemen of Salò who had ended up in prison were released . . . And, in fact, many of them were kindly asked to resume their positions in the courts and police departments.'

'Even war criminals?'

'In the end, they all got off scot free. There were a few show trials for the big fish, just to look good in the public eye, but even they were set free after a while. The purge was just a dog-and-pony show, Piras. The authorities went much harder after the partisans who hadn't turned in their weapons . . .'

'Long live Italy, Inspector.'

'To her everlasting glory . . .'

Listening to the rain, Bordelli took a sheet of paper and started writing out the telex message he wanted to send to all the police departments of the Veneto and the Piedmont. Before he'd finished, he picked up the in-house phone to call Tapinassi, then put it back down. He'd suddenly had another idea . . . He could ring Pietro Agostinelli, a former naval companion of his nicknamed Carnera because of his size.[42] Admiral Agostinelli had entered the SIFAR at the time of its founding[43] in 1949, and now had an even more important post in the newly formed SID, constituted just over a month earlier. They phoned each other once in a blue moon, usually for work-related reasons, but navy men formed much closer bonds than did those in the other branches of the armed forces.

Bordelli glanced at his watch. Maybe Agostinelli was still in his office. The inspector looked up his number in the address book and rang the General Staff of the Navy in Rome. He squeezed his nose with finger and thumb to change his voice, and when someone picked up, he said: 'When the lion raises its tail, all other beasts leave the trail . . .'

'Who's speaking, please?' said a woman's voice.

Bordelli blushed and coughed as if clearing his throat. 'Good evening, this is Inspector Bordelli of Florence Police. I'd like to speak to Admiral Agostinelli, please.'

'Please hold. Thank you.'

There was a click and then silence. Half a minute later, there was another click.

'Franco! How are you, old boy?' said Agostinelli.

'I've just made an ass of myself with your secretary.'

'Oh, really?'

'I recited the rhyme of the San Marco Regiment . . . *Quando el leon alsa la coa . . .*'

'Good God, on your tongue it sounds like Portuguese,' said Agostinelli.

'How's it going, Carnera? I'll bet you have a flat arse by now, from all that sitting at a desk,' said Bordelli.

'Yes, but I get to play spy.'

'Then I have a riddle for you.'

'Let's hear it.'

'Got a pen and paper?'

'No, wait just a minute while I send someone to cut down a tree.'

'Are you so jolly because you get paid a lot to do nothing?'

'No, it's you who put me in this mood . . .'

'Write this name down: Ruggero Frigolin, almost certainly born in '13. He was probably a Second Commandant in the Black Brigades at Asti. That's all I've got.'

'What exactly do you want to know about him?' asked Agostinelli, now professional.

'Everything you can find out, and if you can manage to

get a photo of him, it can be your belated Christmas present to me.'

'Have you ordered other searches?'

'I was about to send a telex to all police departments in the Veneto and Piedmont.'

'Don't bother. I'll take care of everything myself,' said the admiral. 'It's better not to get too many things going at once.'

'Thanks, Pietro.'

'Now you owe me one.'

'Up the whale's arse, sailor.'[44]

They hung up. Bordelli crumpled the page with the telex message and tossed it into the wastepaper basket. Then he grabbed his cigarettes and went out. It had stopped raining. There were a lot of things hanging and he felt restless. The test for Odoardo's hair sample, the bullet shell . . . and he couldn't wait to forget about the bloody *Panorama of Montevideo*.

He thought he'd go and have a glass of wine at the Fuori Porta tavern, then remembered that it was closed on Mondays. And deep down he didn't really feel like drinking. It would make him feel like a feeble-minded old geezer trying to drink a woman off his mind.

He parked in Piazza Ferrucci and got out to stroll along the Lungarno, but after a few minutes it started raining again. Cold, fine drops. He got back into the Beetle and drove slowly round the Viali. There weren't many people about. At last he decided to drop in on Diotivede at Careggi, just to have a chat and kill a little time.

Poor Diotivede, he thought. Three more years and they would put him out to pasture. It was anybody's guess who would take his place. Perhaps an obnoxious young doctor full of himself, whom Bordelli would have to put up with for, well, not that long, really. Only five years . . . Shit, this hadn't ever occurred to him before. There were only five years left before he became a pensioner with a passion for gardening.

He tried to imagine Diotivede sitting in a public garden, crumbling stale bread for the pigeons and wearing big brown slippers. He couldn't picture it. Perhaps the old maniac really would set up a laboratory in his house so he could carry on studying bacteria in motion, and Bordelli would visit him every Sunday to bring him something rotten to squash between two slides for the microscope. A couple of old nitwits who couldn't make up their minds to get out of the way.

When he entered the laboratory, he found the doctor sitting in a corner, one arm propped on the test-tube counter, in what looked like a very uncomfortable pose. He was staring at the bare white feet of a corpse on the other side of the room, covered up to the head. Bordelli marvelled. He hardly ever saw Diotivede seated. Drawing near, he noticed that the doctor had a hand on his stomach and looked as if he was suffering.

'You feel okay, Diotivede?'

'Terrible, but it'll pass.'

'Is it Maria Conchita?'

Diotivede shook his head.

'I ate too many chestnuts.'

'My interpretation was much more poetic.'

'And a lot less painful, I assure you.'

'Anything I can do for you?'

The doctor gestured towards the corpse on the gurney.

'If you really want to help, you can cut that gentleman over there in two, so I can get a headstart,' he said.

'You don't say! I've been waiting all my life for this opportunity.'

'The knives are on the table over there.'

Bordelli stuck a cigarette between his lips and started puffing on it as if it were lit.

'You know, I just got a postcard from Uruguay . . . from a woman I liked very much,' he said.

'Oh really? And what did she say?'

'Nothing special. But she did write to me.'

'It's a start,' said the doctor, raising his eyebrows.

'I don't know why I told you that.'

'Don't worry, I can keep a secret.'

'Go ahead and mock me, but I really did like that girl a lot.'

'Eat some chestnuts and you'll get over it, I promise.'

'Thanks, you're a real friend.'

'If you've got nothing to do, why don't you come with me to say hello to Baragli?'

When Bordelli got home, he filled the bathtub. He wasn't hungry. He'd gone with Diotivede to see Baragli, and they'd stayed for a good half-hour. In spite of everything, the sergeant looked well. Or so it seemed.

He immersed himself up to his neck in the hot water and closed his eyes. He liked boiling himself in the tub, memory adrift . . . And from the tide of recollection surfaced a morning in '44 when he was looking out over a valley through binoculars and saw some large black birds circling round the same point. They were cawing then swooping low, gliding over the meadow. It wasn't hard to tell that they were feasting, and Bordelli decided to go and find out on what. He took two of his men and went down into the valley. They found the corpse of a smartly dressed English officer. He lay face down with his legs together and his face in the grass, one hand digging into the ground. His back was perforated by a high-calibre bullet. The birds had already started eating his ears, and they had to shoot to scatter them. Bordelli grabbed the officer's hand and turned him over. The man's disintegrating, blackened flesh oozed through his fingers like custard. He'd probably been dead for at least two weeks. Bordelli removed his ID tag and attached it to his belt. He would send it to British headquarters with the exact coordinates of the body's position. The stench of death had stuck to his hands for a very long time afterwards . . .

The burst of a firecracker woke him up. The water had turned cold, and he had to get out of the tub. Whenever his thoughts turned to the war, time started passing very fast. As he was getting dressed he wished he could have a quiet evening, without spending the whole time rehashing this or that or thinking about Milena. Things would turn out however they turned out, and the same was true for everything. As he was putting on his shoes, the telephone rang. It was De Marchi.

'I've just finished, Inspector.'

'And?' said Bordelli, holding his breath.

'The hair you gave me and the hair found in Badalamenti's flat belong to the same person.'

'Ah . . .' said the inspector.

'But I haven't written anything up yet, as you asked.'

'Good, thank you so much. Now go and get some rest.'

'Have a good evening, Inspector.'

Bordelli hung up and ran a hand over his face. *The hair you gave me and the hair found in Badalamenti's flat belong to the same person.* This was no small matter. He returned to the bedroom to finish getting dressed. If Odoardo had admitted having been in Badalamenti's flat at least once, then it might mean nothing. Shedding hair is not unusual. But Odoardo had lied, and clearly had his reasons for lying. Of course, he could have gone to Badalamenti's just to pay off his mother's IOUs or to try to get back the photographs and had lied only for fear of being considered a suspect . . .

Bordelli heaved a sigh. Aside from the hair that had betrayed him, there wasn't any hard evidence against Odoardo. All the same, from the very start, he'd had the distinct feeling that the lad was lying to him. Whereas Raffaele had always given him the opposite impression: a difficult, instinctual young man, even a bit of a blowhard, but as transparent as glass in sunlight.

He had to go back to see Odoardo. It would almost certainly be the last chapter of an unamusing novel. Perhaps he would go back the following morning. Perhaps. He no longer was in such a hurry. Before going out, he remembered the ballistics test and rang Piras.

'I tried calling a little while ago, Inspector, but your line was busy,' said the Sardinian.

'Any news?'

'The arrest has been upheld. The shell under Pintus's shoe was fired from the same gun that killed Benigno Staffa.'

'That sounds a lot like something someone told me just a minute ago.'

'What's that, Inspector?'

'Nothing. I'll tell you when you get back. I wanted to let you know I called up an old friend with the Secret Service and gave him all the information on Frigolin. We'll see if anything turns up . . .'

'Pintus has changed his story. Now he says he went to see Benigno to try and persuade him to sell that land, and he found the door open, went inside, found him dead, and ran away because he didn't want any trouble.'

'With a good lawyer, he might even get off,' said Bordelli.

'Pintus is the Fascist Frigolin, Inspector, I'm sure of it. You should have seen his face when I provoked him . . .'

'Being sure doesn't help, Piras. You need proof.'

'If that son of a bitch wriggles out of this, Benigno will turn in his grave.'

'Talk to Stella. Send a photograph of Pintus express to the RAI and ask them to broadcast it on the evening news. Maybe somebody'll recognise him as Frigolin and we can nail him for war crimes.'

'Shit, Inspector, I hadn't even thought of that.'

'It would have come to you tonight, Piras.'

'Can you imagine, Inspector? All Frigolin had to do was look once at the sole of his shoe, and he would have got off scot free.'

'As far as that goes, he would have got off scot free if nobody had shot you in the legs.'

'I suppose I have to admit that every cloud has a silver lining . . . Be sure to watch the news on Thursday,' said Piras.

'You're very optimistic.'

'No, I'm Sardinian. Goodnight, Inspector, I'm going to go and read a little Maigret.'

'Give him my best.'

They hung up. Bordelli went into the kitchen to make a cheese sandwich and drink a glass of wine. By the time he left the house it was already half past nine. The rain had stopped, but the sky was still choked with clouds. On the other side of the street the little boys sat on the kerb in the dim light of a street lamp. They were lighting firecrackers. As soon as they saw Bordelli, they all got up and ran towards him.

'Have you arrested the killer?' asked Mimmo.

'Not yet.'

'There's only four days left. You're not gonna break your promise, are you?'

'I never break a promise,' said Bordelli, walking towards his car.

'If you don't get us a new football we're gonna ring your doorbell every single day,' said Rabbit-teeth.

Bordelli got into the Beetle and rolled down the window. 'Actually I think you'd better all get ready to wash my car.'

The little boys giggled with delight. They waited for the inspector to set off, then hurled firecrackers after his car before retreating to their territory.

Bordelli crossed the bridge and turned down Via Tornabuoni. There was some traffic, and at moments the cars ground almost to a halt. Despite the cold, there was a good deal of bustle, and more than a few foreigners. The shop windows were already full of Epiphany stockings and sweet coal. Every so often one heard firecrackers popping. He crossed the centre of town and came out on the Viali. Holding the steering wheel with his knees, he lit a cigarette. He only wanted to take a few drags, he told himself, and then he would throw it out. He drove through Piazza delle Cure, and when he got to the end of Via Maffei, he still had the fag in his mouth. Turning left, he arrived at the Mugnone and parked the car. He got out and started walking down Via Boccaccio. He wanted to have a quiet stroll undisturbed. Dogs barked in the dark gardens of an immense villa. He continued down the dark road with his hands in his pockets. The asphalt was still wet, and there was nobody about. He could see the bluish light of televisions filtering through a number of windows. At that hour there must have been a film on. Here and there he heard dogs growling behind locked gates.

He was almost at San Domenico. On the ground floor of an ancient building that gave on to the street was a lighted window through which came some highly rhythmical music. Bordelli went up to it to look through the bars. Behind a thin curtain was a large, smoke-filled room with some thirty or more young men and women dancing and shaking their heads. Those not dancing had drinks in their hands. A lot of bare legs and childish faces. A blonde in a miniskirt jumped up and down as if suffering from tarantism, hair tossed about in the air. He could never jump around like that, he would feel too embarrassed . . . even in the privacy of his home, with nobody watching. He felt a twinge of envy for those kids' light-heartedness and continued spying on them. When at last he pried himself away from the window, he could think only of his own youth spent under the watchful eye of Mussolini. He returned towards Le Cure. When he got back in the car, it was almost eleven. He started it up and drove off. He didn't know what to do, and he didn't feel the least bit hungry. There was a present waiting for him at Rosa's, but at that hour her friends would still be there, rehearsing the play. He didn't feel like being with other people. He would go to Rosa's the following day before supper time, when she was alone. He was curious to see his present. She always got him very unusual things. When he'd turned fifty, she'd given him a beautiful stone, scaly and shiny.

'It grows like a rose in the desert,' she'd said, laughing, lips red with lipstick. 'Even the desert has its flowers, as you can see.'

It was a beautiful stone, and he'd put it in the kitchen, using it now and then to crush walnuts. He drove on slowly, headed nowhere in particular. Maybe he could take a spin up to Fiesole, turn towards Montebeni and then come back down by way of Settignano. Or he could take the Chiantigiana and just roll along nice and slow all the way to Siena if he felt like it. The third possibility was to go home and watch the late-night news broadcast.

28 December

He woke up early that morning, left home without shaving and went straight to the office. The previous evening he'd fallen asleep in front of the telly almost at once and woken up a while later in front of a blizzard of static on the screen.

He sent Mugnai to fetch him some coffee and then got some bureaucratic stuff out of the way. He had to pay a call on Odoardo, there was no getting round it. And he would do it one of these days, just not today.

Behind him he could *feel* the presence of that postcard. It was just a view of Montevideo, but it had a hold on the back of his neck. At a certain point he got up and threw it into a drawer. Adieu, Milena, he thought. Then Marisa came to mind, the little girl who already looked like a woman. He felt he needed to clear things up a bit, but it wasn't easy and so he put it all off till a more propitious moment.

Around eleven o'clock, a phone call came through from the General Staff of the Navy. A young woman's voice told him that Admiral Agostinelli was on the line.

'Don't tell me you've already found something,' said Bordelli.

'Not just something . . . we've found out everything there was to find out, just as you asked.'

'In less than a day?'

'We're not the police, you know,' the admiral said.

'*You* are starting to frighten me.'

'In a little bit I'll have an official telex sent your way, but I wanted to give you advance notice personally.'

'I'm all ears,' said Bordelli.

'I quote: ". . . Ruggero Frigolin, born 18 July 1913, at

Martellago, Verona province, where his parents resided. The Frigolin family moved to the city of Milan on 21 May 1922. His father died in Africa in April 1943, shortly before the capitulation. His mother is still alive and a patient at a hospice on the outskirts of Milan, suffering from a degenerative disease that has left her non compos mentis. With the creation of the Operazione Nazionale Balilla[45] in 1926, Ruggero Frigolin joined the association of the Avanguardisti di Milano. In 1928, he became a member of the Avanguardisti Moschettieri; in 1930 became a Giovane Fascista, and in 1934 entered the Fasci di Combattimento of the National Fascist Party. He attended the Istituto Superiore Agrario in Milan for one year with lacklustre results. On the other hand, within the ONB, and later in the Fascist Party itself, he distinguished himself with his tenacity and ability to command and was appointed to a variety of positions of increasing importance. These qualities soon won the admiration of Alessandro Pavolini, who wanted him at his side for the constitution and organisation of the Black Brigades. In September of the same year, Pavolini again recommended him to Mussolini for the post of Second Commandant of the Luigi Viale Brigade of Asti, which Frigolin was promptly granted. He immediately became known in the region for his cold ferocity, which earned him the nicknames of 'Lucifer' and 'the Kappler of Venice'. He surrounded himself with personally hand-picked men and carried out bloody actions that never left any witnesses behind, not even women or children. He devoted himself with vicious intensity to hunting down Jews, arresting whole families who were later deported to Poland, and saw personally to the confiscation of their possessions. He actively participated in the preparation and execution of the Langhe round-up alongside his Nazi colleagues. His name came up in many of the war-crimes trials of Salò officials, but he was never personally indicted. Ruggero Frigolin officially died on 4 April 1945. His dead body was found in a stable near Mondovì with its face disfigured by machine-gun fire. It was identified by the documents found in the corpse's pocket.

Many believed that this death had been staged and that Frigolin managed to escape under a false name, but there is no proof of this. Ruggero Frigolin did not like to be photographed and indeed there are no extant photos of him . . ." He was a true gentleman, in short,' Agostinelli concluded.

'He may still be. He may be alive, you know.'

'Why are you looking for him?'

'I want to invite him to dinner at Epiphany.'

'Then don't overcook the steak. He's the kind that likes it blood rare.'

'How the hell do you office moles always manage to know everything about everybody?'

'Our motto is: never throw anything away. You never know when you may need it. Our archives are the envy of the CIA itself.'

'God knows what my file looks like.'

'Rest assured we know everything: how many women you've slept with, what books you read, how many times you threw up as a baby and all the rest.'

'Too bad there's not a single photo of Frigolin available. That would have made things a lot easier.'

'Have the man's mug broadcast on TV and maybe someone will—'

'That's already been arranged.'

'So you gumshoes aren't really as feeble-minded as they say.'

'We even know how to drive cars, as far as that goes.'

'You don't mean to tell me why you're looking for this revenant?' Agostinelli asked.

'A few days ago, in Sardinia, a man killed himself with an automatic pistol, but the shell was never found . . .' Bordelli went on to recount in a few words the whole story of Benigno.

'He's good, this Sardinian. Think he might want to change jobs?'

'Piras is mine,' said Bordelli.

'Ah, then never mind.'

'If our suspicions are right, this Frigolin has been living in

Oristano under a false name since '46, even though his papers are authentic.'

'He may have obtained them himself, using real municipal records. It happened a lot during that period.'

'He left nothing but scorched earth behind him . . .'

'Those who were best prepared had already started arranging their escape in '44, when it became clear how it was all going to end,' said Agostinelli.

'The guy's been living undisturbed for twenty years, mixing concrete and money . . . I hardly think that's right.'

'I'll try again and see if I can't find a photograph,' said Agostinelli.

'If you don't succeed I'll start to think that none of you does a bleeding thing all day in your cushy offices,' Bordelli said, laughing.

'Even if there's only one copy of something in all the world, we'll find it, rest assured.'

'Call me at any hour of the day or night, even at home.'

'Sorry to ask, but isn't it enough for Frigolin to be convicted for premeditated murder?' asked the admiral.

'Well, yes and no, but that's not the point. What worries me most is that if through some legal quibble this Frigolin manages to slip out of jail for even a minute, we'll never find him again.'

'You can be sure of that. I'll get moving straight away.'

'Thanks, Carnera, really.'

'Thanks, Beast.'

Bordelli hung up. It was true, one of his nicknames during the war had been 'Beast'. He'd forgotten. Lighting a cigarette, he rang Piras at once to tell him about Ruggero Frigolin's accomplishments under the Republic of Salò.

Shortly before five o'clock the hospital rang him. Sergeant Baragli was unwell and wanted to talk to him. Bordelli put on his trench coat and went out.

He got to Careggi in only a few minutes. Driving through the hospital gate, he parked in front of the ward. As he climbed the stairs, he thought of all the people he'd seen die. The list was long and included his father and mother. And he would see more, until the day when he too joined their number. Turning down the corridor, he imagined Rosa at his funeral, a black veil over her face and Gideon in her arms. A mysterious blonde weeping in silence amidst the deceased's relatives and his law-enforcement colleagues, immobile as her spiked heels sank into the ground . . .

Baragli was in a pitiful state. He lay motionless with his eyes closed, face like a mask made of wax. His wife and son were sitting beside the bed and watching him in silence. As soon as she saw Bordelli, the wife took him by the arm and led him out of the room. In the hallway she burst into tears and pulled out her handkerchief. The inspector embraced her and awkwardly patted her head. He didn't know what to say. The son also came out, and they shook hands.

'If you're going to stay a little while, Inspector, I'd like to take my mother out to eat something.'

'I don't want to eat,' she said, sobbing.

'Mamma, please, you have to eat. What's the use of acting this way?'

Bordelli took one of the woman's hands in his. It was as cold as if it had just been taken out of a refrigerator.

'Your son is right, signora. You can even take your time. I'll stay until you return,' he said.

The son put an arm round his mother's shoulders and led her away. The inspector watched them walk down the corridor, then went back in and sat down beside Baragli's bed. The sergeant was asleep. Every so often his lips moved, as if he was dreaming. Bordelli took the cards out of the drawer and started playing solitaire on the bed. After a few minutes of this, he looked up. Baragli was awake and watching him.

'Ciao, Oreste.'

Baragli took a breath and moved his lips, but only a whisper came out of his mouth. The inspector brought his chair closer.

'What was that?'

'I have a beautiful family,' Baragli said in a faint voice.

'They've gone out for a bite to eat. They'll be back soon.'

'I'm afraid I've reached the end, Inspector.'

'Don't be silly, Oreste.'

The sergeant gave a sort of smile and said nothing. His eyes were sunken and ringed with black. The few hairs on his head were tousled, like a newborn's. The brunette nurse came in to administer a shot. The syringe was completely full.

'How's our policeman today?' she said, trying to be cheerful, but it was clear she didn't really feel like joking.

'Not very well,' said Baragli, half closing his eyes. The slightest movement cost him great effort. He wasn't even able to pull down his pyjama bottoms, and Bordelli gave the woman a hand. The sergeant's bum was swollen with needle pricks.

'Had any more bad dreams, Sergeant?' the nurse asked as she administered the injection.

'Yes,' said Baragli.

'What did you dream?"

'I was running through a field . . .'

'Now, how do you think that makes me feel? Don't you like me any more?' the woman asked, withdrawing the needle. Baragli tried to smile, and with great effort raised a hand to the nurse. She took it in hers and squeezed it.

'You are an angel,' said Baragli.

'My husband would not agree.' She laughed, laying the sergeant's hand down gently on the sheet. Then she took leave of the two men, walking away with her empty syringe.

'Inspector. Haven't you got anything to tell me about that boy?'

Baragli was exhausted, but his eyes burned with curiosity.

'Don't overtax yourself, Oreste.'

'Please, tell me about that boy . . .'

'De Marchi compared the hair samples,' Bordelli said, sighing.

'A match?'

'Yes.'

'I knew it,' Baragli muttered.

'Not so fast. We still don't know for certain whether he did it,' said the inspector.

'I knew it,' Baragli repeated.

Almost without realising, Bordelli shuffled the cards and dealt them for a game of *briscola*.

'Shall we play?' he asked.

'I don't think I can, Inspector.'

'Just one game.'

'When are you going back to see that boy?'

'There's no hurry,' said Bordelli.

Baragli closed his eyes and remained silent. He seemed to have suddenly fallen asleep. The inspector reshuffled the cards and started another round of solitaire. All at once someone grabbed his wrist. Baragli was pulling him towards him with all the feeble strength he had left.

'Oreste, are you all right?'

'I wanted to tell you something, Inspector.'

'Tell me.'

Bordelli brought his face near. Baragli's eyes were blazing, and staring at him. What life remained in him lay entirely in his pupils.

'A policeman must do his duty to the best of his ability, Inspector. But above anything else, he must be . . . *fair*,' he said. And his eyes added what he wouldn't put into words. Bordelli smiled nervously. He suddenly felt a strong desire to smoke.

He rang the buzzer and climbed the stairs, and when he got to the top, he found Rosa's door ajar. A voice rang out from within, and Bordelli recognised it at once. It was Princess Doralice, mother of three girls. He found her in the sitting room, all covered with silvery veils and a great big hat. She was standing in the middle of the room, repeating the same lines in a variety of tones, addressing them to the cat, who was sleeping quietly on the couch.

'*How could you do such a thing! My own daughter, a murderess!*'

'*How could you do such a thing! My own daughter, a murderess!*'

'*How could you do such a thing! My own daughter, a murderess!*
. . . Well, which one do you like best?' Rosa asked in the end, breaking the spell.

'The second,' said Bordelli, choosing at random.

Rosa tried another dozen times, then came towards him, moving the way she thought princesses moved.

'What do you think?' she said. She gave him a hug and a kiss on the ear.

'Touching . . . Is it the last scene?' the inspector asked.

'What makes you think that?'

'The tragic tone.'

Rosa gave a sly smile.

'Wrong! It may seem like the finale, but it's the *coup de théâtre* . . . Would you like me to tell you the story?'

'Of course,' said Bordelli, knowing that any other answer would have been taken as an insult.

'A nip of cognac?'

'If I must . . .'

'Sit down over there and get comfortable,' she said, excited. She pushed him down on to the sofa and took his shoes off. Then she filled two small glasses with cognac.

'What shall we drink to, monkey?' she asked, raising her glass.

'To Princess Rosa?'

'And to 1966 . . . I want it to be a marvellous year.'

They clinked glasses, looking each other straight in the eye, and took a sip.

'Now let me tell you the story of Doralice,' she said, setting her glass down on the table. Bordelli lit a cigarette, determined not to miss a word. Rosa stood up and clapped her hands, as if to open the performance.

'This story takes place in the past, centuries ago, in a great castle surrounded by cypresses at the top of a hill. Princess

Doralice, who's me, has three delightful daughters, Amelia, Camilla and Rinuccia, all very sensitive and sweet, all as beautiful as their mother, who's me. Rinuccia is the youngest and prettiest of all . . .'

Bordelli couldn't stop fidgeting. There was a spot on his spine that hurt. Perhaps a draught had chilled him. However he tried to settle, he felt a pinch in a vertebra halfway down his back.

'. . . all was going smoothly, when one day Rinuccia meets a man, Adalberto, and falls head over heels in love with him. And this is where things go awry, because Rinuccia doesn't know that Adalberto is her cousin, a distant cousin on the side of an aunt who was the second wife of her mother's brother, that is, *my* brother, and who Rinuccia had never seen before. In the meantime, Doralice's son-in-law, Otello, that is, *my* son-in-law, the one married to Amelia, my eldest daughter, falls in love with my second daughter, Camilla, who is, however, already engaged to Manlio, who is cheating on her with a peasant girl, the natural daugher of Gaspare, my second husband . . . Did I mention that Doralice is twice widowed?'

'I don't think so,' said Bordelli, feeling a mild headache begin to set in. Rosa was pacing back and forth on the rug, still moving like a princess.

'There's also a great-uncle, by the name of Giulio, a gloomy, wicked man who wants to marry me, even though, in fact, my second husband was the nephew of an in-law of his . . . But everything gets complicated when we learn that Romualdo is on his way there – he's my first husband's brother, and a distant relation of Ettore . . . Have I mentioned Ettore yet?'

'Of course,' Bordelli lied. Gideon raised his head and exchanged what seemed like a glance of tacit understanding with him, then went right back to sleep. He wasn't required to follow the plot of the story . . .

The whole thing grew even more complicated, with fourth cousins and illegitimate children, rival lovers and trysts so contorted that even a police inspector couldn't make head or tail of them. It was anybody's guess where Rosa had dug all this up. Bordelli felt numb and decided to stop trying to keep up. He simply stared at Rosa and occasionally nodded, but his mind was elsewhere. He was thinking of Odoardo, of the scissors stuck in Badalamenti's neck, of mortar fire, of Nazis rolling about on the ground . . . The important thing was to grasp the end of the story, rouse himself in time, and say something meaningful. He only hoped Rosa wouldn't ask him anything specific about the plot.

'. . . and so I run off to the castle like a bat out of hell and when I enter the dining hall I find Amelia, my eldest daughter, with a knife in her hand . . . dripping blood . . . and a dead body at her feet . . . Amelia has just killed Odoardo, stabbing him thirty times in the heart . . .'

Hearing the name Odoardo, the inspector suddenly snapped out of his reverie. He wasn't sure he had heard right.

'This is the scene I was rehearsing when you came in . . . *How could you do such a thing? My own daughter, a murderess!* And then I despair and fall to the floor, weeping, because I am convinced I'm the mother of a ruthless killer who has committed murder out of envy. But then I discover the truth, which is that Amelia killed Odoardo to achieve justice, because he was driving Zia Bettina's daughter to suicide so he could get his hands on her inheritance. And so I embrace Amelia, still crying, but now they are tears of joy, and it all ends well . . . What do you think?'

Bordelli scratched his head and started searching for his cigarettes.

'What about Amelia? Does she end up in jail?'

'Why should she? She certainly didn't kill Odoardo out of wickedness. She did it out of the goodness of her heart.'

'Ah, I see . . .'

'So, what do you think?'

'I think it's good. Really good, I must say.'

'Really?'

'Absolutely . . . A nice little intrigue. I'm just sorry I can't come to see it.'

Rosa blushed with delight. It was easy to make her happy.

'Do you like my hat? I made it myself, with a panettone box.'

Under the veils one could read the name *Motta*.

'Beautiful . . . Aaaah!' said Bordelli.

'What's wrong?'

'One of my vertebrae hurts. Perhaps a storm is on the way.'

'I guess you need a Bertelli plaster like the old folks.'

'Aaaah . . .'

'You're always so tense . . . Want one of my little cigarettes?'

'Not today, thanks.'

'Then I'll make you some herbal tea with honey.'

'With honey?'

'Leave it to me,' Rosa said with a maternal expression and then left the room.

Bordelli tried to relax. He looked out at the rooftops with their chimney-pots and antennas. Rosa was bustling about in the kitchen, rushing from cooker to sink in her spiked heels. Moments later she returned with a steaming cup and a plate of teacakes. Bordelli sat up and took a sip of tisane. Rosa was watching to see whether he liked it.

'That's good. What's in it?' Bordelli asked.

'Lemon balm, marigold, passion-flower, corn poppy and hawthorn . . . all mixed together.'

'Excellent.'

'Soon you'll feel all your muscles relaxing.'

'I can already feel it, I swear.'

Bordelli finished the tisane and stood up, back still sore. His headache had also intensified, but it certainly wasn't the fault of Mamma Rosa's herbal tea.

'I'm going to go,' he said, moving his neck to feel where it hurt most.

'Why don't you stay? My girlfriends are coming in a little while for a rehearsal.'

'I can't. I'm expected at headquarters,' Bordelli lied.

'Oh, rot . . .' said Rosa. Then she dashed into her bedroom and returned with her hands behind her back.

'Surprise!' she said, bringing one hand forward, a golden ribbon dangling between her fingers. Bordelli gave her a kiss on the cheek. He was about to unwrap the present when she snatched it back out of his hands and put it in his jacket pocket.

'Open it later,' she said.

'Whatever you say.'

The cat was still asleep, and on his way out Bordelli stroked his head. Gideon moved his tail but didn't open his eyes.

'Don't overtax yourself,' Bordelli said to the cat.

'All he ever thinks about is eating, and chasing girls,' said Rosa.

'I think he's discovered the meaning of life,' said Bordelli, heading for the door. In the doorway he kissed Rosa's hands, which she loved, then started down the stairs with the distinct feeling that his headache was getting worse.

'Will I see you before 1966?' Rosa called down the stairwell.

'I can't promise.'

'If I throw a party, will you come?'

'I can't promise.'

'You're such a shit!' she said, blowing him kisses. Bordelli reached the bottom of the stairs and then ran into Princess Doralice's daughters, all dressed in veils, in the entranceway. They made a big fuss over him and covered him up to the ears with lipstick.

'Ciao, Inspector, you coming to see us on Thursday?'

'Unfortunately I can't, I have to work.'

'Oh, bollocks!' said one of them. Even in their present get-up, they still hadn't lost any of their whorish manners. The one called Cristiana got her hair all tangled up in the letterboxes and let out a stream of rapid-fire obscenities. Then they raised their swishing skirts all together and ran up the stairs, laughing and calling each other tarts and sluts at every step. It would have been interesting to see how Rosa was going to persuade them to pipe down and rehearse . . .

The sky was black and laden with clouds, but it still wasn't raining. Bordelli opened Rosa's present while driving, steadying the steering wheel with his knees. He read the note and smiled: *To the handsomest monkey in the kingdom, from your Rosita.* The square little box contained a great deal of pink cotton, at the bottom of which was a tiny heart made of jade. It was smooth and sparkly. He pulled over to the side of the road and hung Rosa's heart from the little chain he wore round his neck.

After dessert, he poured a drop of grappa into his glass and lit a cigarette. His headache had subsided a little. During the entire meal Totò had done nothing but talk about violent crimes from his home town in the south . . . Hands chopped off, tongues chopped off, goat-tied corpses, dead bodies with rocks in their mouths . . . all the while turning juicy, dripping steaks over on the grill.

The inspector downed his grappa and got up to leave, patting the cook on the shoulder by way of goodbye. He walked out of the still-full trattoria and got in the Beetle. It was barely nine o'clock. He didn't feel like going home. Putting an unlit cigarette between his lips, he let the car take him where it would. When he found himself driving through Piazza Alberti, he suddenly had an idea. He parked in Via Gioberti and ducked into the first bar he encountered. The shelves inside were full of panettoni. Sitting at two small round tables were four motionless codgers, staring at their empty glasses and cigar butts. Over their heads was a television blaring at high volume. It looked like a film. Near them were some children playing pinball. The telephone was just inside the entrance, in one of the quieter spots. Bordelli bought a token and phoned the home of Fontana the barrister. A woman answered, probably the governess.

'Casa Fontana,' she said.

'Good evening, I'd like to speak with Signor Guido please,' the inspector said, covering the speaker with his hand.

'Who's calling?'

'This is Inspector Bordelli.'

'Please wait while I call him.'

'Thank you.'

He could hear a television in the background, broadcasting the same film as in the bar. A good minute passed, then he heard some footsteps approaching the telephone.

'Hello?' the young man said in a low voice.

'Hello, Guido . . .'

'Yes?'

'I'm calling because I'd like to have another little chat with you and Raffaele.'

'Oh,' said Guido, not the least bit surprised.

'Is Raffaele there with you now?'

'No.'

'Will he be coming later?'

'No.'

'You won't be seeing each other tonight?'

'Yes.'

'Yes in what sense?'

'We will be seeing each other.'

'Where?'

'Not here.'

'Guido, please, try to speak in complete, comprehensible sentences . . . This is starting to sound like an interrogation.'

'I thought it was.'

'Don't be silly . . . So you'll be meeting Raffaele somewhere else tonight, if I've understood correctly?'

'We're playing music,' said Guido. Prising a few consecutive words out of him was an achievement.

'Ah, I see, and where?' Bordelli asked.

'Via de' Bardi.'

'Then I'll meet you there. Number?'

'Thirty-two.'

'What's the name on the buzzer?'

'No name.'

'How will I recognise it?'

'There's just the number.'

'What time will you be there?'

'Ten.'

'Wait for me before you start playing, otherwise you won't hear me.'

'All right,' said Guido.

When Bordelli hung up he felt tired, as if he'd just done some heavy lifting. Talking to Guido was thoroughly exhausting. He went over to the counter and asked for a coffee. He drank it slowly, watching one of the elderly men in the mirror. The old codger was asleep in a sitting position, hands on his legs. He had a small head, a sallow face furrowed with wrinkles and two oval leather patches on the elbows of his jacket. Not even the noise of the pinball machine could rouse him from his slumber. The barman glanced lazily at him several times while rinsing cups.

It was almost half past nine. The inspector left the bar and got back in his car. He drove slowly, smoking a cigarette. He felt strange, as if he were on his way to a party where he didn't know anybody. Then there was the fact that he really hadn't been straight with the lad. There was no need to talk to Raffaele or Guido. For the moment there was no longer any need to talk to anyone . . . except Odoardo, that is. Whereas he'd gone and made up that story. Perhaps it was only out of curiosity, to see the two youths one more time from up close.

There was still half an hour to go before his unlikely appointment, and luckily it hadn't started raining yet. He crossed the Arno and left the Beetle in Via dei Renai. He went through Porta San Miniato on foot and started climbing the staircase that led to Viale Galileo. There were no street lamps, and he could barely see. The last stairs were the steepest, and he reached the top out of breath. Crossing the Viale he went all the way up to the basilica of San Miniato, which to him was the most beautiful church in Florence. The façade of white and black marble was decorated with fine inlay and geometric figures reminiscent of oriental textiles. At the top, in the place of the cross, was an eagle whose talons clutched a roll of fabric, symbol of l'Arte dell Lana, the wool guild of medieval Florence . . . Even back then, money was more powerful than faith.

He stood there looking at the thousand-year-old church with the monumental cemetery of the Porte Sante around it. He knew some of his great-grandparents were buried in there, but he'd never managed to find them. One day he would have to go and calmly search the graves and family chapels, and read the inscriptions one by one. Once, when he was about six or seven, one of his relatives had taken him for a stroll through the tombs, and they'd shown him the grave of the man who had written 'Pinocchio'. He hadn't gone walking in a cemetery for a very long time. Some years back, he used to do it rather often, just to relax. He knew all the ones around Florence, from Pratolino to Gli Allori. He'd even gone a couple of times to the American cemetery at Falciani and walked for hours through those thousands and thousands of white crosses lined up like rows of vines.

Glancing at his watch, he saw that it was already ten o'clock. As he headed back down the same dark staircase, he noticed two shadows at the bottom coming towards him. A man and a woman. When they got closer, he heard them speaking German and stiffened instinctively. The language still made him shudder, there was nothing he could do about it. When the couple walked past him he looked at the man's face. He must have been over forty. Bordelli realised he could easily be one of those Nazis who'd fled Florence in August '44 when the Allies entered the city, and had now returned with his wife to see the bridges he'd blown up before leaving. Or maybe not. Maybe he was just a former Wehrmacht soldier who'd come to visit the city of Michelangelo and Leonardo.

Reaching the bottom of the staircase he told himself that the war had ended over twenty years ago, and he had to stop looking at the world through its prism. He turned to the left after Porta San Miniato. Via San Nicolò was dark as usual. When he reached the end and turned down Via de' Bardi, a freezing drizzle started to fall. A bit farther on, he spotted Guido's BSA and Raffaele's Solex in the distance, parked along the pavement.

He walked past number 30 and, a few paces on, found himself in front of number 34. There was no number 32. Maybe Guido had taken the piss out of him. He turned round to have a better look, and between two majestic front doors he noticed a camouflaged door in the façade. There was only one buzzer, as Guido had said, enclosed in a carved marble setting. The doorbell was more precious than the door.

He listened hard but couldn't hear any music. He tried pushing the buzzer, but heard no ringing within. He pressed again. It was quite cold outside. He stuck a cigarette between his lips but didn't light it. He had a ticklish feeling in his stomach, like a child afraid to be caught doing something forbidden. Who knew whether those two had even heard the doorbell. He was about to ring again when the door opened. Guido invited him inside. The dark entranceway smelled of damp plaster and septic fumes. Behind the door were two staircases, one ascending, the other descending. Guido took the down staircase, with Bordelli following behind. It was a rather long, stone stairway. Some soft recorded music came from below, a sad sort of lament accompanied by a guitar. The inspector would have liked to ask who the singer was, but he refrained. He didn't feel like being treated like an old fogey again.

They entered a large basement room with brick vaults, illuminated by a pair of light bulbs with red plastic shades. Raffaele was sitting on a mattress, changing the strings on a black electric guitar. Seeing the inspector come in, he put the guitar down and got up to greet him. The air smelled of stale smoke and you could practically sink your teeth into the humidity.

'I hope you'll leave us a little time to play,' Raffaele said, shaking his hand.

Bordelli smiled and looked around.

'So this is your lair,' he said, glancing at the record player on the floor and two amplifiers as big as refrigerators.

'Call it whatever you like,' said Raffaele.

Guido sat down on the mattress and resumed the operation of changing the guitar strings.

'Are there only two of you?' Bordelli asked.

'We're looking for others.'

'Do you play stuff you can twist to?' the inspector asked, choosing at random a modern term that seemed appropriate. Raffaele and Guido exchanged an amused glance.

'The twist is for snot-nosed mummy's boys,' said Raffaele.

'What kind of music do you play?'

'Satanic stuff . . . we climb walls and drink the blood of virgins,' said Raffaele.

'I guess you don't like giving straight answers either,' said Bordelli.

It felt like an encounter between two tribes that had never met before. The sad music kept playing on the gramophone, and it wasn't at all bad. It entered one's ears and stayed there.

'I only try to avoid saying things you wouldn't understand,' said Raffaele, thumbs hooked into the pockets of his jeans. Guido watched the scene in silence, all the while fiddling with the guitar.

'It used to be old people who said that sort of thing to children,' said Bordelli.

'They still do, I assure you . . . but our ears have changed.'

'Grown longer and hairy?'

'We don't need your rules any more,' Raffaele said with a serious face.

'You always speak in the plural,' Bordelli observed, pulling out a cigarette.

'Perhaps it's because all dinosaurs look alike to me,' Raffaele said, shrugging his shoulders.

Hearing this, Bordelli began to understand a little better what it was he felt when dealing with these youths, Odoardo included. He didn't feel attacked so much as ignored. In their eyes he wasn't a man, but a category. And yet just a few days before with Rosa, he'd smoked some of the same stuff they smoked . . .

The disc ended and Guido reached out to put another on. Bordelli lit his cigarette. A song began playing, but again it was completely unfamiliar to him.

'I wonder where it is you're all running to,' he said, addressing them in the plural.

'As far as we can get from Methuselahs like you – from your suits and ties and straight and narrow paths we're supposed to follow without any questions . . . We've had it with all that crap,' said Raffaele, pleased with his speech. Guido in his corner approved with a grunt.

'What's a Methuselah? You called me that another time, too,' said Bordelli.

'He's an old man in the Bible.'

'Ah, thank you,' said the inspector.

'It's not your fault. You just happen to be an endangered species,' Raffaele said quietly.

'I wouldn't be so sure.'

Raffaele shook his head.

'Why did you come here, Inspector?'

'I wanted to ask you a question.'

'Go right ahead.'

'I want you to tell me . . . how many times, and from what telephone or telephones, you called Badalamenti,' Bordelli improvised.

'What do you need to know that for?'

'Never mind about that.'

'I rang him only once, together with my sister, from a bar in Piazza della Libertà,' said Raffaele. Bordelli still called the square Piazza Cavour, but he was careful not to reveal this, lest he appear even older.

'All right, then, there's nothing else,' he said.

Guido had finished stringing the guitar and looked at him as if expecting to be asked a question.

'We want to play,' said Raffaele, but the tone meant more or less *Get the hell out of here.*

'Where can I put this out?' asked Bordelli, holding his cigarette butt in the air.

'Just throw it on the floor,' said Raffaele.

The inspector dropped the butt on to the flagstones and

crushed it with the tip of his shoe. Then he gestured goodbye and went out, happy to leave that catacomb.

A fine freezing rain was falling, and the cold penetrated the skin. Bordelli walked quickly to the car, staying close to the buildings. When he finally got into the Beetle, his hair was dripping wet, and he tried to dry it as best he could with his handkerchief. His headache was making itself felt again, and at moments it was as though he had a nail stuck in each temple. Perhaps it meant that the weather was about to get even worse. He looked up at the sky. It was a uniform grey. If the temperature dropped another couple of degrees, it might snow in earnest this time. He started up the car and drove off. He felt a little muddled, maybe even sad. An old melancholic, wandering through the night alone. He crossed the Arno and instinctively turned right. He took Via Lungo l'Affrico and continued straight all the way to Salviatino. Then he turned down Viale Righi, drove past Piazza Edison and continued down Viale Volta. That was where he wanted to go. He wanted to see the house he was born in, the mysterious garden where, as a child, he had waged battle against the fiercest monsters . . .

While driving past he slowed down as usual and looked at the ground-floor windows. They were all dark. He would have liked to see at least one of them lit up, just so he could imagine that his mother was still waiting for him behind the curtains, praying before her makeshift altar of holy images and candles. As he drove away he felt like an old fool again, and as he entered Piazza delle Cure he saw his father again, with that old sea-dog's face of his . . . Whenever the old man got angry, his mother used to tell him to calm down, because mature men were not supposed to carry on that way. And Dad would always reply with the same thing: 'What are you saying? Even your precious Jesus got pissed off once!' And Mamma would start screaming that Florentines remembered the Gospel only when it was convenient for them, and they would start bickering about the Church and related matters . . .

But enough memories, old fart, or you're liable to start crying and loosening your dentures . . .

He still felt strange. He thought again of Raffaele's and Guido's lair and had the sensation that he'd just returned from a faraway city. He needed to recover his bearings. To distract himself and not think about anything. He felt like drinking with a friend and making light conversation, but he was too tired. He drove over the railway lines and turned up Viale Don Minzoni . . . When he wasn't careful, he still called it Viale Principessa Clotilde, which was what oldies called it. He instinctively looked up at the windows of the Montigiani flat. They were lit up. He imagined Marisa holed up in her bedroom, talking with a girlfriend on the phone as her parents dozed off in front of Mike Bongiorno on the telly. He shook his head and stepped on the accelerator. All those kids seemed to belong to another race – a strong race destined to survive. They moved through the world, as light as young colts and as heavy as donkeys laden with burdens . . .

Go home, old man, put on your longjohns and woollen nightcap and cover up. You're fifty-five years old. Prehistoric. A *Methuselah*.

29 December

After spending the whole day at the office, the inspector left the station without a hint of appetite but a strong desire to go and see a movie. Rosa absolutely could not join him, since she was still busy rehearsing Doralice. The première was the following evening.

Bordelli parked the Beetle in Via Pacinotti, next to the Cinema Aurora. It was starting to rain. The cinema's sign was made of neon tubes. One letter had burnt out and the others flickered as if about to blow, but they'd been doing that for years now.

That evening they were showing a Western, *For a Few Dollars More*. He'd already seen a couple of Sergio Leone's films and found them amusing. He bought a ticket and went into the dark theatre. The newsreel was still playing, showing a feature on the latest Paris fashions. The models wore extremely short skirts and their legs did wonders for the eyes. Clouds of smoke and comments on the fashion models rose up from the seats.

The film began. The protagonist was a tough guy with a remarkable face. Rosa would certainly have liked him. Bordelli succeeded in not smoking for most of the film, but when the final duel started, he found himself with a cigarette between his lips. They were all shooting their guns like madmen, and the bad guys were dropping like flies. Finally, the last remaining heavy fell to the ground, and the hero rode away alone on his horse, accompanied by music to fit the occasion.

When Bordelli left the cinema, it was drizzling outside. With a shudder, he headed off at a fast pace towards his car. He felt hungry. He got in the car, turned on the heat, and drove off.

As sequences of images from the film ran through his head, Odoardo's face kept appearing. He would pay a call on him soon, but had to find the right moment.

When passing in front of Cesare's trattoria, he slowed down nearly to a stop and glanced inside. Although it was already half past ten, there were still a lot of people. He parked the Beetle between two trees and slipped into Totò's kitchen, hungry as a wolf. The cook greeted him with a glass of wine. After a succession of dishes, they arrived at last at the grappa.

By the time the inspector crawled out of that dangerous place with Totò at his side, it was almost three o'clock in the morning. The restaurant had closed a good while earlier. They had both drunk a great deal during their supper and, as usual, had talked about many things. Totò had not spared him the customary blood-curdling stories of his ancestral lands, and Bordelli had suddenly found himself drunk. As he was downing his umpteenth glass of grappa, he'd heard an alarm go off in his head. One more sip and he wouldn't be able to drive home.

Totò pulled down the rolling metal gate and after a few failed attempts managed to stick the key in the hole. His little eyes were bloodshot and he could barely stand up, and he laughed at every idiotic comment he made. He wanted to drive home in his souped-up Fiat 600, but Bordelli wouldn't hear of it and forced him to get into the Beetle. The German engine whirred quietly, at minimum speed, as they glided down the deserted streets. It was still drizzling, the gleaming festoons reflecting off the wet asphalt. Totò's laughter resounded inside the car as he carried on with silly remarks that he alone found funny. A few long minutes later, the inspector dropped him off in Via Pisana and waited to see him go inside before driving off towards San Frediano, trying very hard to bring the road into focus.

Once at home, he undressed and collapsed in bed. The room was spinning round with all its furniture. He closed his eyes and was asleep in minutes.

30 December

At 7 a.m. his alarm clock woke him up unceremoniously. He turned it off and stood up, staggering, went into the bathroom, stuck his head in the sink and ran cold water over it. Then he sat down in the kitchen and, one cup after another, ended up drinking a whole pot of coffee. He thought of Odoardo, of course, and immediately felt like smoking. Unable to resist, he lit a cigarette. Odoardo was the one. He did it . . . He killed Badalamenti. The inspector was increasingly convinced of it. But the realisation gave him no satisfaction. He sat a while longer, ruminating, then got up and went into the bathroom to take a hot shower.

The day passed slowly, and at no point was Bordelli able to get in the right mood to go and have his little chat with Odoardo. He kept on putting it off, even if he didn't quite know why.

The national news programme that evening broadcast the photograph of Agostino Pintus, as Piras had promised. All they could do now was wait, hoping that someone would recognise him. His comrades from Salò certainly wouldn't talk, and nobody he'd paid a visit to was still on this earth . . . But perhaps there was someone who might remember him just the same. One had to hope for a little luck, following Piras's example. And secondarily, as they liked to say in the courts, there was always the charge of premeditated murder. There were some serious obstacles between Mr Frigolin and freedom, Bordelli thought . . . Even though, if the guy walked, it wouldn't be the first time someone of his ilk had got away with murder.

He rang Rosa to wish her a final 'break a leg' before the performance. Tonight was opening night.

430

'So you really can't come?'

'No, Rosa, I'm so sorry . . .'

'Oh, come on! What could be so important?'

'I have to go to . . . There's going to be a big meeting with people from the ministry . . .'

'At night?'

'When they come from Rome they always arrive late, you have no idea what a ball-ache it is . . . and these things usually last late into the night,' said Bordelli.

'Oh, go on . . .'

'Really, sometimes till three, four o'clock . . . You'll see.'

'Poor monkey . . .' said Rosa, touched. She'd swallowed it whole.

'Break a leg,' said Bordelli.

'Thanks.'

Rosa blew her usual barrage of kisses and hung up. Bordelli felt a little guilty, but the thought of going to Rosa's and finding the place full of people made him feel strange. For him, going to Rosa's was . . . well . . . how would you call it . . .

He lit a cigarette and went back to the television. The National channel was showing some sort of serial drama, so he switched to Channel 2 and started watching a Donald Duck cartoon. He thought of the president's arrival that morning from Rome. Saragat had met the mayor at Palazzo Vecchio, done a tour of the city, and then returned home . . .

'I really have to go and see Odoardo,' he muttered to himself. Tomorrow. He would go tomorrow. Or maybe the day after tomorrow.

31 December

Round mid-morning Diotivede went into the cellar of his home. He hadn't set foot in it for years. He measured the room in paces, then stood and reflected for a few minutes. Perhaps Bordelli was right. Perhaps someone who'd been cutting corpses open his whole life couldn't suddenly just stop. He went back upstairs and picked up the telephone.

'Hello, Bordelli. This morning I went down to my cellar.'

'You have a cellar? With wine in it?'

'It's full of rubbish, actually . . . But I could imagine a nice laboratory in it.'

'Ah, I see. And I could bring you the corpses, if you like.'

'You Igor, me Frankenstein?'

'I'm sure your monster would be a lot nicer.'

'Well, for starters, I would create a woman,' said the doctor.

'You know what? I myself think of moving to the country to live the peasant life.'

'I can't picture you doing that.'

'I may just do it anyway.'

They chatted awhile of this and other things, taking their time. Diotivede seemed rather argumentative. He couldn't resign himself to the life of the retiree lounging about all day with nothing to do. Bordelli was thinking that five years would go by quickly, and if he wanted to retire to the hills, he'd better get moving.

'What are you going to do tonight, Diotivede?'

'Put wax plugs in my ears,' said the doctor.

They said goodbye. Bordelli had a leisurely shave and went out. There was a postcard in his letterbox. He turned it over

432

slowly, fearing it might be from Milena. But it wasn't. It was from Paris. The image was of a vineyard in Montmartre.

Dear Bordelli,
We are born to suffer. All people do here is eat a great deal and drink even more, and you need a pitchfork to keep the women at bay . . . In short, a crashing bore! Lucky you who get to work all day.
Yours, the Baron

What a shit, he thought, smiling. Either he had posted it the minute he'd got off the train, or the Italian postal system had made tremendous progress. Bordelli put the card back in the letterbox and went out into the street. The sky was brimming with clouds in motion, but the sirocco warmed the air. He got into his car and drove off. He would gladly have lit a cigarette but tried to resist. His melancholy practically stuck to his skin. At Porta Romana he turned on to Via Senese, drove past Galluzzo, and after the Certosa took the road that led to Le Rose. By now the Beetle knew the way and drove itself.

He turned on to Odoardo's unpaved driveway. His desire to smoke grew by the minute. He parked in the usual spot and got out. The Vespa wasn't there, but that was all right. He'd almost grown fond of the place. As usual, he circled round to the back of the house. The expanse of olive trees had the colour of certain lakes. Farther on, the black tips of cypresses jutted above the broad boughs of pine forest. He walked away from the farmstead and sat down on the wooden flatbed of an old cart. All that peace made him want to smoke a cigarette, and at last he lit one. He smoked slowly, looking out at the horizon. The sky was full of sinewy clouds, and the warm wind blew in waves through the olive trees, sounding like rough seas . . . That wind brought to mind a morning many years before . . . It was April, and he was walking along a secondary road with Gavino Piras. Bordelli was always happy to go out on patrol with him. They spoke little, sometimes not a single word. There was a strong wind blowing that morning. Bordelli liked the feel of it against his face. The spring was entering his blood and head with force. All at once they heard the sound of motors on the wind. They barely managed to get off the road and jump into a ditch in time. A second later, round the bend appeared a Wehrmacht motor convoy. It was endless. It passed so close to their heads that they could hear people speaking German. In the last lorries the men were singing in chorus a now famous song about worthless Italian traitors. Piras started squirming and sweating rage. He couldn't stand to hear Germans singing, especially that song, and he removed the magazine from his machine gun to prevent himself from opening fire. When the final lorry disappeared over the horizon, Gavino climbed out of the ditch. His eyes were very dark and full of malice. He walked calmly over to the nearest tree, dropped his machine gun on the ground and attacked the trunk with his fists. It sounded like someone chopping wood; it made the same noise. The final blows were quite fierce and left the bark stained with blood. When he stopped, he was out of breath. He picked up the machine gun and magazines from the ground, then lit a cigarette. His knuckles were bleeding, his face full of bitterness. Bordelli saw all of Italy in that face. A Duce with delusions of grandeur had brought the Nazis *into our house*: that was what hurt the most, the thing that could not be forgiven.

A few months later Gavino lost an arm. And he was the luckiest one. As they were removing a mine from its hole, the other two went flying through the air. The Germans had invented a new hair-trigger safety catch attached under the mine, a hellish thread that lit the fuse when broken.

Bordelli had last seen Gavino Piras in June 1945, in a train station mobbed with people walking in every direction. A throng of silent figures: wounded soldiers, hollow-eyed women, barefooted children, families of old people with their lives inside their suitcases. And instead of voices, one heard the sound of thousands of footsteps. Piras was taking the train to Civitavecchia, where he would take ship for Olbia. He was wearing a military jacket with an empty sleeve and stared at the railway carriages as if looking out over the plain of Campidano. Bordelli didn't quite know how to say goodbye to him. They weren't in the habit of talking much, and in the end he gave him a slap on the back.

'Good luck, Gavino,' he'd said. He couldn't think of anything else. Gavino had headed off to his train, empty sleeve dangling at his side.

The cigarette was finished, and Bordelli already wanted to smoke another. He put one in his mouth but didn't light it. The midday bells were ringing. A lightning bolt flashed on the horizon, and a few seconds later he heard a muffled sound of thunder. More flashes followed at once, one after another, and a long drum roll of thunder rang out. A storm was approaching. The warm wind was bringing an almost summer-like storm.

He heard a hen clucking after laying an egg. Putting the cigarette back into the packet, he got up and went into the chicken coop. He found the egg atop some straw in the shed. Taking it in his hand, he felt its warmth. He made two holes in the shell with the car keys and sucked hard, swallowing the white first. Just as the yolk was descending, he heard Odoardo's Vespa pull up in the forecourt. He went back to the loggia with the egg still in his hand, smiling.

'I stole an egg of yours,' he said.

Odoardo took off his gloves and goggles. He looked very tired, even drunk. It was as if he remained on his feet thanks only to an invisible hand holding him up by the hair.

'The hens were my mother's,' he said. His breath smelled of vomit.

'It's been ages since I drank a just-laid egg,' said Bordelli. He finished the yolk and left the empty egg in his hand.

Odoardo pulled a crumpled cigarette from his pocket and stuck it in his mouth. 'Just throw it on the ground . . .' he said, slurring his words. 'Got a match?'

The inspector tossed the shell on to the tall grass, then lit a match before the boy's wasted face.

'Tell me something, Odoardo. If you were me, what would you do?'

'I'm not you.'

'A man has been killed. He was a loan shark, a despicable man, someone who ruined people's lives, who threatened the weak, blackmailed them, and maybe even killed them sometimes. At some point I find out that the killer is a twenty-year-old kid who works for an architect and raises chickens . . . If you were me, what would you do?'

'And what would you do if you were me? I have a headache and would really like to sleep, but I've got a police inspector standing in front of me wanting to make small talk and stealing my eggs.'

Bordelli smiled.

'If I were you, I'd invite the inspector into the house, make some coffee, and tell him everything.'

'Let's talk right here,' said Odoardo, eyes feverish.

'All right.'

'As luck would have it, I wanted to tell you a story myself. I heard it last night from a poor half-drunken bastard.' Odoardo went and sat down in a wicker chair. He shivered and then hunched his back. He gestured for Bordelli to sit down in another chair, whose wicker bottom was partly staved in.

'Please sit down, Inspector. It's not a long story, but it's not very short, either. Are you sure you want to hear it?'

Bordelli lit a cigarette and sat down beside Odoardo. The youth was staring at a braid of garlic hanging from a rafter.

'See that garlic? My mother braided it herself. She's gone, but the garlic is still there. I can touch with my own hands something my mother touched . . . But that's not what I wanted to say . . . My story's about something else . . .'

'I'm all ears,' said Bordelli.

Lightning flashed in the distance, followed by muffled rumbles of thunder. The wind began to pick up, but it still wasn't raining. Odoardo seemed stuck. He rested his hands on his knees and kept looking at his dirty fingernails.

'It's a long story and a short story, I don't know if you know what I mean.'

'I'm in no hurry,' said Bordelli.

'Between one glass and the next, that drunkard started telling me his mother was beautiful, she was good, she loved him very much, all the usual bullshit people say about their mothers. They lived together, and everything was going nicely, without any problems. But one fine day his mother got run over by a car, a Lancia Flaminia that hit her at the edge of a country road and never even stopped. She didn't die immediately, but spent a few days in agony. Her son stayed by her side, holding her hand. His mother couldn't talk. Every so often she would open her eyes, but she didn't even recognise him. Then she died. And there you have it. End of story. As you see, it doesn't take long to tell, but the guy told me that it's actually a long story, a very long story. It lasts a lifetime.'

An acidic burp escaped him involuntarily, and he grimaced. He was pale and trembling slightly.

'And do you know what the guy's father was called?' he asked.

'Let me guess . . . Was he called Ciro?' said Bordelli.

'Well done, Inspector. But you may not know that there are people going around saying that it's not true . . . that that ring is a lie, and he was born in a brothel and his father was one of the many Americans passing through to drain his balls.'

'The world is full of liars.'

'And drunks who talk rubbish . . .'

'Tell me something, Odoardo. The guy who told you that terrible story, what made him feel worse, the fact that his mother died, or the fact that his mother . . .'

'Was a whore?'

'Yes.'

'I didn't think to ask him. What do you think?'

'I think the kid shouldn't worry himself too much over the slander of a loan shark.'

437

'That what I told him, too,' said Odoardo, throwing his cigarette butt on the ground.

'And what did he say?'

'Nothing. He just said there were some photographs around . . .'

'Has he ever seen them?'

'He can't. A police inspector keeps them locked in a drawer.'

Odoardo was scowling. He kept sighing repeatedly, as if gasping for air, and biting his nails till they bled. Bordelli looked at his bloodshot eyes and felt terribly sorry for him. The thunderclaps were growing near, and the first drops of rain started to fall.

'You know what you should have asked this friend of yours, Odoardo?'

'He's not my friend . . .'

'You should have asked him how a ring can end up in a loan shark's stomach.'

'I did ask him.'

'And what did he say?'

'He told me the whole story. He'd already given a fair amount of money to the guy, basically everything he had, because he wanted his mother to rest in peace and without debts. Then one day he went to see the loan shark and brought the ring with him, to try to persuade him to let him at least see the photos of his mother . . . Because he didn't want to believe that story about the brothel. That ring was important to him. It was a cherished memento, a gift from his father to his mother. He wanted to leave it with the man as collateral while he looked for the rest of the money, but only on the condition that he let him see those photos immediately. The shark took the ring in his hand and looked at it up close and started laughing. He started telling him that it was all bollocks, that this Ciro didn't exist, that the ring had been made by a poor mother who didn't want her son to know what she used to be: a whore for the Americans. Then he told him that the only thing he should think about was finding a way to pay the debt down to the last lira, and that only then, and only if he felt kind, he *might* give him the photos. My "friend" swallowed that bitter pill and said that of course he would pay it all in full, but if he couldn't see the photos now, he wanted the ring back. The shark shook his head and said he would keep it as a guarantee. My "friend" said no, he wanted to leave with his mother's ring in his pocket. But the guy wouldn't listen. And so my friend started protesting. He was determined to get that memento back, even by force, but the moment he reached out with his hand, the shark swallowed the ring and said that if he didn't get the hell out of there immediately, things might take a bad turn . . .'

'And then?'

'And then they started bullfighting. But only the last part, where the torero sticks the sword into the bull's back, and the bull collapses in the dirt . . . You know what I'm talking about? It's a very sad sight.'

Odoardo sneered with disdain. He was paler than ever. He lit another cigarette and took a deep drag. The rain was coming down harder and harder. Bordelli's legs felt numb, and so he stood up and started walking about under the loggia. Glancing at the braid of garlic, he wondered distractedly how long it would have lasted in Totò's kitchen.

'Feel like a coffee?' he asked, turning towards the lad.

'Even two, but it's too much effort to go and make it.'

'I'll make it myself,' said Bordelli.

Odoardo ran his hands over his face, as if to wipe away his weariness, then stood up from the chair with an effort and leaned against the wall. He searched his pockets a long time for the keys, and at last he found them. On the third try, he got the key in the hole and opened the door. They climbed the stairs in silence. Odoardo pointed the inspector to the kitchen and then went and lay down on the couch, in front of the cold fireplace. Bordelli had a little trouble finding things, but he was in no hurry. He liked the silence. Calmly and slowly, he got the espresso pot ready. He found two little cups and set them on the table. While waiting for the water to boil, he went and looked out the window. It was pouring, the thunder growing still louder and more frequent. He stayed there for a spell, watching the raindrops pound the Beetle, thinking about what was happening in that house. Hearing the coffee bubble up, he went and turned off the flame. He put some sugar into the two cups, poured the coffee over it, and went over to Odoardo. The boy seemed to be sleeping, but then he opened his eyes and sat up. He looked unwell. The inspector set the coffee down on the table and put another cigarette in his mouth.

'Shall we make a fire?' he asked.

'Do whatever you like.'

A lightning bolt struck very close to the house, the thunder shaking the windows. Bordelli went and knelt down in front of the fireplace. He rolled up a few pages of newspaper, put some wood on top, and set fire to it all. He watched the flames envelop the logs, which were very dry and started burning at once. Then he went and sat down in an armchair in front of the boy.

'And how's your friend from last night feeling now? Satisfied?' he asked.

Odoardo stared at the steaming little cup.

'Are you talking about his conscience and stuff like that?'

'More or less.'

'The loan shark had led him to understand that his mother's death had not been an accident, and he laughed in his face.'

'Why would he have killed her?'

'The poor woman was exasperated and had threatened to report him to the police.'

'She should have.'

'It's water under the bridge. My friend has other worries . . . He feels like he has a mouse gnawing at his head.'

'The photographs?'

'He only wants to know whether certain things are true, or rubbish.'

Odoardo looked devastated. It must have been rather unpleasant to learn all those things from a delicate soul like

Badalamenti. The fire started crackling loudly, the flames beginning to rise. Bordelli finished his coffee and set his cup down on the table.

'Tell your friend I can tell him what the truth is,' he said.

Odoardo raised his head and looked him in the eye.

'You can tell me,' he said, 'and I'll pass it on to him.'

Bordelli pretended to think it over for a minute, then leaned back in the armchair.

'Those famous photos were shot in Birkenau,' he said.

'What's that?'

'A Nazi concentration camp in Poland.'

Odoardo's upper body lurched, as if struck with a club.

The inspector continued his lie. 'Your friend's mother was of Jewish extraction. She didn't want her son to know of the humiliations she'd suffered in that camp. She was afraid he'd grow up with too much anger inside. The photos show some horrifying scenes.'

'What do they show?'

'If your friend ever saw them, he would understand why his mother wanted to keep them from falling into his hands. By some strange inner mechanism, some survivors of the camps feel ashamed, and your friend's mother was an extreme case of this, to the point of letting herself be blackmailed by an extortionist. The only remaining mystery is how those photographs ended up in the hands of someone like Badalamenti . . . But you can't always know everything in life,' the inspector concluded.

Odoardo seemed paralysed for several minutes. Then he got up and went over to the window to enjoy the storm. He kept his hands planted firmly in his pockets.

'And what can you tell me about Ciro?' he asked.

'Ciro? . . . Well, he was your friend's father.'

'And how do you know that?'

'I did some research. It's easy for us policemen.'

'Is Ciro alive?'

'He died right after the war.'

'How did he die?'

Bordelli made up the first lie that came to mind.

'Typhoid fever,' he said.

Odoardo remained immobile and said nothing. The only sounds came from the fire and the rain falling hard outside. Every so often there was a pop in the fireplace, and an ember came flying out. The thunder was beginning to die down, but it was still raining buckets. At last Odoardo turned his head towards the fire, and Bordelli saw him smile for the very first time. It was not a happy smile.

'Thank you, Inspector. For me, at least, that's enough. I really don't give a fuck about any of the rest,' he said. Then he turned to look outside again.

'You haven't drunk your coffee,' said Bordelli.

The youth was staring avidly at the rain-battered landscape.

'The game is over, Inspector. Now you can go back to being a policeman.'

'What do you mean?' said Bordelli.

'You know perfectly well what I mean.'

Bordelli got up and went over to him, stopping behind him.

'For a game to be over, all the players have to be in agreement,' he said.

Odoardo turned to look at him. He had dark circles round his eyes. 'What are you trying to tell me?'

'Stop playing dumb. You already know,' said Bordelli.

'But I don't understand why.'

'Because it's the last day of the year.'

'Ah . . .' said the lad, and he turned to face the window again.

'There's one question I can't answer. Why, when your friend realised I was about to discover the truth, didn't he run away?'

'Because he doesn't give a shit about going to jail, he only wanted to know the truth about his mother.'

'Well, now he knows everything. Next time you see him, give him my regards.'

'What about those photographs?'

'They'll just rot inside a file in the court archives,' Bordelli lied. He planned to burn them, along with the promissory notes.

'Will you be back, Inspector?'

'I don't think so,' said Bordelli. He took out the ring the non-existent Ciro had given to Rosaria and dropped it on the table.

'Don't forget to give this to your friend,' he said.

Odoardo turned around for a second, to look at the ring.

'Thanks,' he said, then turned round again.

Bordelli headed for the stairs, lighting his umpteeth cigarette. It wasn't yet two o'clock, and he'd already lost count of how many he'd smoked. He would have an easier time of it the next day. As he descended the stairs, he felt light, as if relieved of a burden. He went out, closing the door behind him. It was raining cats and dogs. The Beetle was almost hidden by the curtain of water. He pulled his trench coat tightly around him and, paying no mind to the rain, walked out from under the loggia and towards the car.

Just before supper, Piras told his mother he was going out for a minute, and headed for the door without his crutches.

'Nino! You're walking!' his mother said, hand over her mouth.

'I used to walk before, too, Mamma.'

'Are you sure it's not dangerous?' Maria asked, running up behind him.

'I'm taking it slowly, don't worry.'

'Where are you going at this hour?'

'To say hello to Pina and Giovanni.'

'Ask them if they want to come and watch the television later.'

'All right.'

'And don't be late for supper. You know your father gets upset,' said Maria.

'Where is he?'

'In the shed.'

'I'll be right back,' said Piras. He went out of the house and walked slowly towards the Setzus' front door. It was the first time he'd gone outside without crutches. He'd been wanting all afternoon to tell Pina what had happened, and in the end he'd made up his mind. She still knew nothing about it, Giovanni likewise. Pintus had appeared in the local newspaper, but they didn't know how to read, and talk of the arrest hadn't yet reached their ears. It was bound to happen sooner or later, but Piras wanted Pina to start the new year thinking that Benigno was in heaven, enjoying the view in the company of angels.

'Ciao, Pina.'

'Nino, you're cured! Come in.'

They went into the kitchen. Giovanni was there, too, sitting in his chair.

'You've chucked your sticks,' he said.

A pot of polenta hung from a chain over the fire. Pina took a bottle of wine and filled three glasses.

'Would you like a biscuit, Nino?' she asked.

'No thanks, Pina. Mamma asked if you want to come and watch television later.'

'What's showing?' Giovanni asked.

'There's Mina at ten o'clock, then they're going to replay the best things of the year . . . It's supposed to last until past midnight.'

'All right,' said Pina.

'Actually I came here because . . . I have something to tell you,' said Piras.

'What?' asked Pina, alarmed. It was as if she already understood.

'Don't get upset . . . I just wanted you to know before the new year . . .' said Piras, at a loss for words.

'About Benigno?' asked Pina.

'Maybe . . . He didn't kill himself . . .'

'I knew it,' said Pina, crossing herself.

'So what happened, then?' asked Giovanni, who didn't quite understand.

'He was murdered,' said Piras.

'By who?' asked Pina, squeezing her glass.

'Almost certainly by the Fascist who was about to shoot him in '43.'

'*Santa Bonacatu!*' Pina cried, crossing herself again.

Piras briefly told them everything that had happened. Pina and Giovanni listened to him dumbfounded.

'. . . and they broadcast Pintus's photo on the TV news, but so far nobody has called in. I'm convinced he's the one. There are too many coincidences. But since there aren't any photographs of that Fascist, nobody can prove it,' Piras said in conclusion.

'Benigno once drew us a picture of him,' Pina said, frowning.

'Where?' asked Piras.

'Right here. He was here with us, and he drew us a picture of him. Remember, Giovanni?'

'Yes . . . Wha'd you do with it?' asked Giovanni.

'I put it away somewhere 'cause I didn't want to see it. It scared me,' said Pina, eyes wet with tears. Piras stood up.

'So you've still got it?' he asked.

'Maybe,' said Pina.

'Well, please try to find it.'

Pina wiped her face and went off in search of the drawing. Piras stayed in the kitchen with Giovanni. The fire was consuming a big olive branch. It would take a long time to reduce it to ash, but it would succeed in the end. Pina returned a few minutes later, holding a page torn from a notebook. She handed it to Piras as if it were burning.

'That's him,' said Piras.

'Jesus Christ,' said Pina, crossing herself again.

'Though I have my doubts whether a drawing like this would hold up in court,' said Piras, perplexed. All the same, he folded up the drawing and put it in his pocket.

'I have to go home to eat, or Dad'll get upset,' he said. Pina walked him to the door, put her hands on his shoulders, pulled him down to her level and kissed him on the forehead.

'I told you Nino wouldn't go to hell,' she whispered.

Piras gave a hint of a smile and left. When he got home, Gavino was already sitting at the table. The evening news report had begun some time before.

'What smells so good?' asked Piras. The aroma suggested rabbit and potatoes.

'Why are you never here when we sit down to eat?' asked Gavino.

'Don't start . . .' Maria said to her husband. She put the pan on the table and started filling their plates. Rabbit and potatoes. When *Carosello* began, all three of them started watching. When Calimero appeared, Maria stopped eating and watched the skit to the very end. It was her favourite. Pietrino liked the animated puppet of *Lagostina* best . . . Gavino, for his part, was waiting for the women, who were always beautiful on TV.

When *Carosello* ended, President Saragat appeared and gave his year-end speech to the nation . . . Unemployment, Vietnam, European unity, disarmament, NATO . . . High rate of production, wider distribution of wealth . . . The twentieth anniversary of the end of the war in Europe . . .

'And to every one of you and your families, I wish peace and prosperity and the brightest of futures.'

After supper the Setzus arrived, and they all sat down to watch Disney cartoons. Pina's eyes were wet, but she seemed more serene. Her Benigno was in heaven. Around ten o'clock Ettore and Angelo also showed up to watch Mina. Then the Faddas arrived with their little girl. Then the Congius. Soon the Piras kitchen was completely full. Everyone wanted to watch the montage of the best skits of 1965. Now and then some dancing girls came on, and Gavino watched with eyes a-glitter. Maria noticed, but that night she didn't care.

Piras was thinking that it would have been nice to spend the evening with Sonia, at her place, in Florence, alone, over a candlelit dinner with a good bottle of wine . . . He was planning to call her just after midnight to tell her he would start the new year without crutches . . . and then he would tell her: '*Saludi e trigu e in culu a s'aremigu.*'[46]

Bordelli lay in bed, slowly smoking a cigarette. It was still drizzling outside. He hadn't even bothered to undress. The room was in total darkness. On his way home he'd remembered to buy a leather football for the little boys. He'd won the bet, but had decided to lose it. He thought that in the end, the person most guilty of the murder of Badalamenti was Judge Ginzillo, who had denied him the search warrant he'd asked for many months before. If the usurer had been arrested, nobody would have killed him, and therefore there would have been no murderer . . . He was well aware that this reasoning didn't hold water in the eyes of the law, but he didn't care. He blew the smoke out of his mouth and imagined it rising to the ceiling. His head began to fill with the usual images of the past . . . his mother, his father, a few women, the war, the dead. He wished he could empty his mind and sleep.

It must have been almost midnight. He began to hear the first fireworks. But Bordelli didn't feel like celebrating. Baragli had suddenly died early that evening, around seven o'clock. He hadn't made it to the new year. His wife and son had seen him alive at lunchtime and found him dead that evening. The funeral was set for the following day.

A difficult question arose in the inspector's mind: what the hell do we live for? He had no answer, but didn't feel too anxious about it. Perhaps the explanation would arrive all by itself one day, or else it would never come at all. He remembered the time he'd asked Semmai the same question in '44, with the Germans within spitting distance. It was night, with the moon casting a ghostly light over the fields. Semmai was a Sicilian with fiery eyes as black as pitch. He'd looked at Bordelli and smiled, then turned towards the valley.

'I have no idea what the fuck we live for, Commander, but I like living.'

Easy as crushing a fly. It was anybody's guess how Diotivede or Rosa might answer the question, or the newspaper vendor on the corner, a poor old man with the face of someone who has just been dealt a slap for no reason at all . . .

He just couldn't relax . . . He couldn't stop thinking about the past two weeks. Meeting all those young people had been interesting, but also rather distressing. In their presence he'd felt awkward and superfluous, unfit for the world round the corner. But his biggest fear was that of becoming an old man full of regrets. Perhaps that was why he'd let Odoardo go. So he wouldn't have to remember sending someone like him to jail. Baragli's words came back to him: 'Above anything else, a policeman must be fair'. He'd said it with his eyes full of fire, the final flame before dying.

The inspector put out his cigarette and turned on to his side. He would have liked to fall asleep, but outside, pandemonium broke out. It sounded like a bombing raid; 1966 had just begun.

Acknowledgements

For the third time I would like to thank my father, in the hope that he can read the stories of Inspector Bordelli up there and let me know what he thinks ... even if only in a dream, or through a *Hamlet*-esque ghost. I am constantly reminded that he has never read a word of mine. Not because I hadn't started to write yet when he was still alive, but simply because *his son* never gave him anything to read. At first owing to a residual rancour from a confused and not yet revisited past, then out of excessive modesty. These memories are a little sad for me... but clearly it could have been worse. I could have not made peace with my father before he died. Luckily, however, I did, and was able to accompany him to his burial place with a fondness not too darkened by shadows.

For the third time I thank Véronique Seguin for having come up with the name of Commissario Bordelli . . . who has become a sort of neighbour to me.

Thanks also to Franco Di Francescantonio, because Inspector Bordelli was born at his place, a pleasant flat he had kindly lent me use of for three months.

I also thank:

my editor Daniela De Rosa, for her infinite patience;

Adele Urtis, Delia Silvia Dessì, Diana Bettoni Dessì, Emanuela Minnai, Francu Pilloni, Leonardo Dessì, and Ruggero Sanna for their indispensable information on Sardinia, which, together with old personal memories, made it possible for me to stay at home;

Marco Vichi

Adele Urtis, Francesco Asso, Leonardo Gori and Maurizio Matrone for having read this novel in its early stages and given me suggestions and opinions that helped to make it better;

Francesca Vichi and Enzo Lucchetti for their expert medical advice, which protects me from blunders;

Silvio Bozzi (police forensics) and Maurizio Matrone (writer and police officer) for having served me magnificently as 'police informers' in reverse;

Francesco Badalamenti for having graciously 'lent' me his surname for a character like the loan shark.

I also thank, in alphabetical order:

Alessia Conte
Antonio Leotti
Aquila, a 'living encyclopedia'
of rock
Cesare Rinaldi
Duccio Viligiardi
Elia Cossu
Gabriele Ametrano
Giancarlo Cannas
Giancarlo De Cataldo
Giampaolo Vichi
Giampiero Vichi
Gianfranco Caruso
Giovanna di Lello
Giuseppe di Cara
Jordi Curbet
Leonardo Russo

Lucia Montigiani
Lucina Balboni
Marco Colli
Marco Rosi and family
Monica Barbafiera
Neri Torrigiani
Orla della Bandabardò
Paola Cannas
Piera Biagi
Piergiorgio di Cara
Piero Pelù
Pietro Mansueto
Pietro Ottobrini
Rossella Pisanu
Seba Pezzani
Sonia Salvagnini
Véronique Seguin

for all the indispensable information they provided me with, or for having aided me in my search for information.

NOTES

by Stephen Sartarelli

1 – Italian card game.

2 – Sardinians consider the diminutive *Sardegnolo* an insult.

3 – The conical megaliths of central Sardinia, which have come to symbolise the island and its people.

4 – Mina is Anna Maria Quaini (née Mazzini), born 1940, a much-beloved Italian pop singer, one of the first Italian women to adopt rock and roll among her various styles.

5 – Literally, 'black cabbage', a dark red, leafy cabbage similar to kale.

6 – In 1959 Socialist MP Lina Merlin passed the law that bears her name, outlawing organised prostitution, including brothels, while keeping prostitution – that is, the exchange of sexual services for money – technically legal. The upshot was to drive most prostitutes into the streets.

7 – Rosa is singing the opening verse of Rita Pavone's 1963 hit 'Il ballo del mattone' ('The Slow Dance'). The lines translate respectively as: 'Don't be jealous if I dance the rock with others; / Don't be jealous if I dance the twist with others; / With you, with you, my love, my life, I only dance the slow dance, the slow, slow dance.'

8 – i.e. *dans les yeux*, written phonetically according to a typical Italian mispronunciation.

9 – In Italy the Christmas/New Year's holiday lasts until the day after Epiphany (6 January, the twelfth day of 'Christmas').

10 – A Sardinian grappa.

11 – Graziano Mesina (born 1942), former Sardinian bandit

and proponent of Sardinian independence, famous, among other things, for his numerous prison escapes.

12 – Sardinian for 'goodbye'.

13 – Raffaele Attilio Amedeo Schipa (1888–1965), known as Tito, a world-renowned tenor.

14 – Sardinian expression meaning roughly 'What a pain in the arse'.

15 – An Italian card game where one calls out '*scopa*' when the hand allows the player to collect the cards on the table.

16 – Vernaccia is a sweet white Sardinian wine produced in the Oristano region and drunk both as an aperitif and a dessert wine. It is not to be confused with the Tuscan Vernaccia di San Gimignano, a dry white wine.

17 – At the time of the story's action, divorce was not yet legal in Italy.

18 – A spicy, walnut-flavoured liqueur.

19 – Domenico Modugno (1928–94) was a popular Sicilian-Italian singer, best known for his international hit song 'Volare'. '*Vitti 'na crozza*' is Sicilian for 'I once saw a head'.

20 – Translation: 'I don't want the curly-haired woman, no . . .'

21 – 'Beltempo' means 'good weather'.

22 – Another Sardinian way of saying 'goodbye', one that expresses the wish that things will be better (*mellus*) the next time.

23 – Wild boar stew.

24 – Abarth is an Italian racing car manufacturer that in the 1960s and '70s used to sell trademarked tuning kits for increasing road performance in Fiats.

25 – This was the Fascist 'battle cry', invented during the First World War by the poet Gabriele d'Annunzio, who claimed it was once the battle cry of the ancient Greeks. Mussolini later adopted it as a vocal equivalent to the Fascist salute.

26 – April 26 1945 was the date of a partisan insurrection at

Padua against the Nazi-puppet Salò Republic. It left over five hundred Germans and Italian Fascists dead, as well as 224 partisans.

27 – Carlino is referring to the famous 'amnesty' granted in June 1946 by popular communist leader and anti-Fascist Palmiro Togliatti (1893–1964) to those guilty of political and common crimes, including conspiracy to commit murder. Togliatti was Minister of 'Grazia e Giustizia' ('Pardons and Justice') in the post-war government.

28 – A famous Italian cyclist.

29 – Epiphany marks the end of the Christmas/New Year's holiday season in Italy and, in imitation of the Gospel Epiphany, involves another round of gift-giving, including the children's custom of hanging stockings to be filled by *la Befana*, the 'good witch', who goes around rewarding good children with sweets and presents and 'punishing' the naughty with lumps of 'coal', normally a sugary black sweet made to look like coal. The witch's name *Befana* is actually a simple linguistic corruption of the Italian *Epifania*.

30 – *Carosello* was a half-hour-long programme of adverts, comic skits and cartoons that used to follow the evening news on national television.

31 – *Fegatelli* are chicken livers.

32 – An immensely popular Italian weekly periodical of puzzles such as rebuses, acrostics, crossword puzzles, riddles, etc. Created in 1932, it is also published in a number of other European countries.

33 – A powder which, when added to water or other liquids, makes them fizzy.

34 – In proper French, *Pâté de foie gras, vols-au-vent de fruits de mer, soupe à l'oignon, dinde aux marrons.*

35 – *Charlotte au chocolat.*

36 – *Repubblichini* are those Italians, in this case soldiers, who worked for the Republic of Salò, the pro-Nazi puppet government set up by the Germans in the northern Italian

town of Salò not long after the armistice of 3 September 1943, which followed the fall of Mussolini's original Fascist regime.

37 – In Italian, a *botta* is a blow or an explosion.

38 – A Sardinian lemon biscuit.

39 – Emilio de Bono (1866–1944), an important Italian general in the First World War and later a member of the Fascist Grand Council, among other things.

40 – An Italian comic-book character created in 1938 by Vincenzo Baggioli and Carlo Cossio, Dick Fulmine is an Italian-American plainclothes police detective from Chicago.

41 – A soft drink flavoured with the bitter orange variety called *chinotto* in Italy.

42 – Primo Carnera (1906–1967), a famous Italian boxer who was world heavyweight champion in 1933/34 and known for his tremendous size.

43 – The SIFAR (Servizio Informazioni Forze Armate) was a military intelligence agency that was formed after the war and folded into the SISMI (Servizio per le Informazioni e la Sicurezza Militare) in 1965, in particular the subdivision called the SID (Servizio Informazioni Difesa).

44 – A 'naval' form of the expression *in bocca al lupo* ('into the wolf's mouth'), used to wish someone good luck without jinxing them by saying so (like the English 'break a leg').

45 – The parascholastic and paramilitary Fascist Youth organisation founded by the party in 1926.

46 – A Sardinian greeting that means 'Greetings and plenty [*trigu* means 'grain'], and up the devil's arse [literally 'the enemy']'.

The fourth Inspector Bordelli mystery and winner of the Scerbanenco, Rieti, Camaiore and Azzeccagarbugli awards for Italian crime

Florence, October 1966. The rain is never-ending. When a young boy vanishes on his way home from school the police fear the worst, and Inspector Bordelli begins an increasingly desperate investigation.

Then the flood hits. During the night of 4th November the swollen River Arno, already lapping at the arches of the Ponte Vecchio, breaks its banks and overwhelms the city. Streets become rushing torrents, the force of the water sweeping away cars, trees, doors, shutters and anything else in its wake.

In the aftermath of this unimaginable tragedy the mystery of the child's disappearance seems destined to go unsolved. But obstinate as ever, Bordelli is not prepared to give up.

Coming out in hardback and ebook in February 2013

HODDER &
STOUGHTON

Do you wish this wasn't the end?

Join us at www.hodder.co.uk, or follow us on
Twitter @hodderbooks to be a part of our community
of people who love the very best in books and reading.

Whether you want to discover more about a book
or an author, watch trailers and interviews, have the
chance to win early limited editions, or simply browse
our expert readers' selection of the very best books,
we think you'll find what you're looking for.

And if you don't,
that's the place to tell us what's missing.

We love what we do, and we'd love you to be part of it.

www.hodder.co.uk

@hodderbooks

HodderBooks

HodderBooks.com